THE PLUS-ONE LIST

Also available by Amy Ewing

Novels

The Irish Goodbye

The Lone City Series

The Jewel

The White Rose

The Black Key

The House of the Stone

Garnet's Story

Lucien's Story

The Cerulean Series

The Cerulean

The Alcazar

THE PLUS-ONE LIST

A Novel

AMY EWING

alcove
press

Books should be disposed of and recycled according to local requirements. All paper materials used are FSC compliant.

This is a work of fiction. All of the names, characters, organizations, places, and events portrayed in this novel are either products of the author's imagination or are used fictitiously. Any resemblance to real or actual events, locales, or persons, living or dead, is entirely coincidental.

Published in the United States by Alcove Press, an imprint of The Quick Brown Fox & Company LLC.

Alcove Press and its logo are trademarks of The Quick Brown Fox & Company LLC.

Library of Congress Catalog-in-Publication data available upon request.

ISBN (hardcover): 979-8-89242-534-6
ISBN (paperback): 979-8-89242-535-3
ISBN (ebook): 979-8-89242-536-0

Cover design by Sarah Horgan

Printed in the United States.

www.alcovepress.com

Alcove Press
34 West 27th St., 10th Floor
New York, NY 10001

First Edition: October 2026

The authorized representative in the EU for product safety and compliance is eucomply OÜPärnu mnt 139b-14, 11317 Tallinn, Estonia, hello@eucompliancepartner.com, +33757690241

10 9 8 7 6 5 4 3 2 1

For Pep
amor de mi vida

And for Pippin
the first senior rescue to touch my heart

1
Eloise

I push open the door of Uptown Veterinary Hospital and step outside into the cold January air.

The sky is covered with granite-gray clouds, so stony and dead they look like they could flatten the skyscrapers. It's January 2nd. A new year. It's supposed to be a day of new beginnings.

Instead, it's an ending.

It's seven blocks to my apartment, and each one feels like an eternity. Walton Doggins's food will still be in its place in the cupboard. His toys will be on the couch where I left them. Bony fingers curl around my heart, squeezing it with every agonizing beat. I clutch the small carrier at my side—a purse, really, with a space cut out so Walton could stick his head through. I think of all the times I took him to Central Park in this bag, after he got too sick to go on walks.

When I reach my building, Hector is standing outside in his doorman's cap and long black coat, smoking. He freezes when he sees me, then his gaze travels to the empty bag. His face falls.

"Oh no," he says.

I nod.

"Why do you do this so many times, mija?"

I shrug. How can I explain that someone needs to care for the sick and elderly dogs that no one else wants? And someone needs to be there to hold their paw, so they won't be alone when they pass. I never know the right words. There are a lot of things I don't know how to say. So I don't say anything.

Hector opens the door for me, and I step into the lobby. The fake Christmas tree is still up, lights twinkling. The reception desk is polished marble, and a pair of leather couches sits in the corner opposite, beneath some weird abstract painting that probably cost a fortune. If I hadn't inherited a rent-controlled apartment on Central Park West from my Uncle Lenny (who'd inherited it from my grandfather), I'd never be able to afford to live here. And if my best friend, Rachel, hadn't told me to create Silver Snoot Rescue and then used her influence on social media to get donations, I wouldn't be able to care for so many old dogs. My side hustle, making specialty dog treats for an online pet bakery, *Treats Gourmand*, isn't enough to cover all the vet bills.

I trudge past reception to the elevator and check my phone. I haven't heard from Rachel in a couple of days. She's been out of the country with her boyfriend, Diego, ringing in the New Year someplace warm and sunny in Mexico, where Diego is from.

I should tell her about Walton—she would want to know. But I think she might be on a plane back to the city right now.

I push the button, and the elevator doors open, taking me nine flights up to my floor. I step off into a hall with dark green carpeting and gold Art Deco-style lights on the walls. I can hear Miriam in 9A talking to her cats. Miriam is the only neighbor I know, and the only reason I know anyone else's name in this building. I watch her cats for her when she goes to visit her mother in Utica. She's extremely nosy and extremely talkative, which is great for someone like me who hates having to keep up a conversation, but also difficult because I never know how to get her to stop.

I pass 9B and the faint strains of a viola weave their way through the heavy wooden door. That's where Mr. Bloom lives. He used to play in the New York Philharmonic—or that's what Miriam says. But he got sick, and now he only plays at home. Mr. Bloom hates socializing as much as I do. Whenever I see him out in the park, when I'm with the Pack, we pretend we don't know each other.

I hear the baby crying and a toddler screaming in 9C. 9D I've never seen but the air outside his apartment always smells like marijuana. 9E I nicknamed Soul Cycle—a lesbian power couple who are in offensively good shape. I always see them in matching, expensive workout gear when I'm taking the dogs out. 9F is Madame Boularès, a French widow who dresses in black and listens to a lot of Édith Piaf and Jacques Brel. I can hear the chorus of "La Vie en Rose" as I pass.

And then me. 9G.

The bag hanging from my shoulder feels heavy in its emptiness. My hand shakes as I slip the key into the lock. I hate this part. Coming home without one of them. My throat pinches as I turn the latch and open the door.

The sounds of Mozart waft down the long hall from the living room. The Colonel loves Mozart.

I put the bag down, take off my boots, and hang Walton's leash on its peg. I have seven pegs in total, though only four dogs.

Three. I have three dogs now.

I pass the kitchen on my left and start down the hall to the living room, where the Pack is. The moment my feet creak on the hardwood floor, I hear the thump that signifies Charleston has become aware of my presence. The next thing I see is a roly-poly black pug with a graying chest and muzzle coming at me as fast as his chubby little legs can carry him. Charleston is mostly blind, but his nose is as sharp as a puppy's. He barrels directly into my legs, and I drop down to stroke his ears, soft as silk. Charleston sniffs at me, then sniffs around expectantly. My chest aches. He's looking for Walton.

"No buddy," I say quietly. "He's not coming back. Let's change your diaper."

Hazelnut is just waking up from her snooze on the large dog bed in the living room when I enter. Hazelnut is an eleven-year-old long-haired dachshund and the queen of the house. She kept getting returned by her adopters. "Mean," people called her. But they were wrong—she's not bossy, just particular. She likes things how she likes them.

Her soft, caramel-colored coat gleams in the cold light coming in through the windows. My corner apartment is huge, especially by New York standards. When I lived here with Uncle Lenny, everything was so sterile and bland. Ikea couch, basic coffee table, bookshelves full of dusty leather-bound tomes. Uncle Lenny was a lawyer.

Now, the furniture is all vintage and mismatched, the books are dog-eared romances and mysteries, and every surface is covered with plants. There's a spider plant in a smiley face mug, two enormous dracaenas, a creeping fig, some peace lilies, a couple of flamingo flowers, a Boston fern, and all matter of succulents that line my windowsills, or sit in large ceramic pots along the walls, on side tables, or tucked on the bookshelves. Nothing toxic, of course.

I pick up Hazelnut and nuzzle into her softness. She starts to lick my face rapidly. I hadn't realized I'd started crying again.

A low moan brings my attention to the Colonel, sprawled out on the plaid blanket that covers one side of my 1970s rust-colored couch. He's a German shepherd, my newest adoptee with only eight months in the Pack, and the youngest at nine years old. The Colonel is diabetic but the sweetest old man you'll ever meet.

"Hey Colonel," I say, carrying Hazelnut over to sit beside him. Charleston follows but misses the mark and trots past us into the wall before righting himself and finding his way back to my feet. I give a watery chuckle.

I take a moment just to be with the Pack. To smell the Colonel's dog breath, to listen to the snorts of Charleston, to feel the skin on my cheek begin to chap thanks to Hazelnut's excessive grooming. I feel the absence of Walton, the space he's left behind. But I also feel his presence, the energy that remains from him. Like I can still feel Ginger Doggers and Summer and Lucky Lou.

I love them all so much, and I miss them all so much, and I love all the ones I haven't even met yet, and, somehow, I miss them too.

Rachel once asked me if I'd ever thought about loving a human that way. A human man in a romantic way, she clarified before I could tell her I love *her* that way. I laughed, and it must have been a different kind of laugh because she looked a little worried. I told her I didn't need a human man in my life. I've got plenty of four-legged males to look after.

Dating also requires two things I'm no good at. 1. Meeting new people. 2. Talking.

Rachel knows my diagnosis better than anyone—well, besides my therapist. I can recite it by rote at this point. Generalized anxiety disorder, likely stemming from a combination of early childhood trauma due to the sudden death of my parents at age two, plus differences in my brain chemistry and function. Symptoms: persistent worrying, overthinking, perceiving situations as threats even when they aren't, fear of making the wrong decision . . . blah blah blah. So, yeah. Even taking a daily SSRI and using the breathing exercises my therapist has taught me, I'm still a mess when it comes to interacting with people. From my limited experience, men aren't all that crazy about hanging out with someone who can't go to Sunday brunch without having a panic attack.

Besides, Rachel is the only soulmate I need. We've known each other since we were in first grade—I was the weird kid with the dead parents, and Rachel was the weird kid in foster care. Things like father–daughter dances or making family trees in art class didn't apply to us. My family tree had one little Lenny leaf on it. Rachel used to pretend she was related to a whole bunch of famous people—Marilyn Monroe, Denzel Washington, Lin-Manuel Miranda.

Even when she moved to a new foster family in a different district during high school, we stayed close. Rachel outshines everyone in every room she walks into. She's gorgeous—slender yet curvy with light brown skin and thick dark hair, her lips always painted a bright scarlet, her wardrobe meticulously curated. The polar opposite of me: Short. Wild brown curls. Small features. Hesitant smile. No makeup. Partial to overalls and nineties band tees.

We're going to grow old together and live in adjoining rooms at some old folks' home in Yonkers and learn how to play Mah Jong. And there will be dogs. There will always be dogs.

As I'm getting up to change Charleston's diaper, my phone starts to ring. More tears fill my eyes as I see Rachel's name and contact photo appear on the screen. I used a selfie of us having a picnic in Central Park, Rachel holding up a bottle of Prosecco and making a funny face, her tongue sticking out and her eyes crossed.

I take a deep breath before answering, preparing myself to break the news, but before I even get out a hello, she cuts me off.

"EL!" she shouts, so loud I have to hold the phone away from my ear. "Eloise Madigan Whitechapel, do I have NEWS for YOU!"

Rachel does this sometimes when she gets excited, emphasizing certain words in a way that makes them feel like cymbals crashing together.

A sudden shiver of trepidation runs up my spine, though I can't say why.

"Okay," I say, my voice barely a whisper. When Rachel gets loud, I get soft.

"Diego and I are ENGAGED!" This is followed by a series of shrieks and squeals and maybe some other words, but the world has muted around me. I feel an out of body sensation, like I'm floating above this scene, like the hands holding my phone are no longer my own.

Engaged? I knew it was kind of serious with Diego—this has certainly been her longest relationship to date. And Rachel and I are in our thirties now. I guess getting engaged is a normal thing for people our age to do.

But she's my Rachel. She's my best friend who I can call in the middle of the night if I'm spiraling, or who knows she can only drag me out for margaritas on Mondays when El Taco Loco isn't crowded, or who purchased specific Halloween outfits for all my dogs and then threw a party for them at my apartment with only the two of us because she knows how anxious parties make me.

She's *my* soulmate.

Not Diego's.

But . . . now she *is* Diego's. She'll be his wife. Wives are more important than friends. I'll be second, forever now.

"El?" Rachel says, quieter this time, like she's finally hearing my silence. The way she always does. She always hears what I don't say.

For the second time today, my heart breaks in two.

But this is Rachel, and I won't ever ruin her happiness, even if it feels like it threatens my own. So I hitch a smile on my face and take a breath.

"Congratulations!"

2
Agustín

Five Months Later

I am not supposed to be here.

I try to keep my leg from bouncing as the man sitting across the desk from me adjusts his glasses, his eyes fixed on his laptop screen and the article I wrote.

A series of fortunate yet unfortunate events has led me to this moment—somehow, after only five months of living in New York, I've landed in the sleek, professional offices of *The New Yorker*.

The window behind Neil Rasmussen, senior editor, lets in the bright May sunlight, the Hudson River sparkling as it curves around the lower tip of Manhattan and stretches north. This is the first really warm day I've experienced since moving here in January. I thought March was supposed to be when spring started, but it turns out the weather stays pretty cold all through April. My mom was so worried I would freeze to death in my tiny apartment in Bushwick that she sent me a care package with assorted gloves, mittens, scarves, and one extremely wooly hat complete with a giant pompom. In Mexico City, where I'm from, it never drops below six degrees. That's Celsius. I really don't understand the resistance to Celsius here. Same goes for the metric system.

But it turned out I loved the cold! I loved the snow, and the gray skies, and the wind that chapped my skin, and the slush that formed in huge puddles around streetcorners. I love everything about New York. It's the place I've dreamed of living ever since my abuelo moved here when I was just a little kid to help support our family.

A man who, as I've recently discovered, was not the person I'd thought he was.

My jaw clenches, and I swallow down the anger that threatens to rise in the back of my throat like bile. Anger is not a comfortable emotion for me. I'm a pretty positive person—my mom always teased that I should be in El Club de los Optimistas, an NGO in Mexico back in the nineties.

But I idolized Abuelo. He was my damn hero. I grew up hearing all the stories from my mom and my tías about how he would help those in the neighborhood, always quietly without fanfare—buying groceries for the single mom down the street, enrolling a pair of rebellious teens in a volunteer program, hosting a huge party on Nochebuena for all our neighbors that would last into the early hours of Christmas morning. To me, he was larger than life.

I was only five when he moved to New York City—another sacrifice, another sign of his greatness. Leaving his family to provide us all a better life. Working as a janitor to send money home. He could never afford to come back and visit, but he always called on our birthdays. I've held the few tangible memories I had of him close, clutching them tightly. I can still smell the scent of his pipe tobacco and hear his deep laugh and feel the scratch of his whiskers when he would wrap me in one of his warm hugs. He was a man who embodied everything good in this world. Or so I thought.

Neil looks up from my article and leans back in his ergonomic chair. I have to press my foot against the floor to keep my leg steady.

"So," he says. "Your grandfather was El Rasca?"

I nod. If someone had mentioned El Rasca to me five months ago, I'd have no clue what they were talking about. I'd only just unpacked my bags on the 2nd of January when my older sister, Lupe, called me. Manuel, Lupe's husband, accidentally served Abuelita ponche con pikete—spiked punch—on New Year's Eve. Suddenly, she started talking about Abuelo, and dropped a truth bomb that detonated the holiday mood.

Abuelo had a secret second family in the US. A wife and a son.

"And you're saying," Neil says, steepling his fingers together and fixing me with a sharp gaze, "that he had a second family back in Mexico the whole time he was working as an activist here in the city?"

My jaw clenches again. Neil is making it sound like *we* were the secret second family, when it's the other way around.

But! I'm not about to insult the man who holds my dreams in the palm of his hand. What's the English expression? Don't look a gift horse in the face?

"Yes," I say. When I first got the call from Lupe, it felt like earthquake sirens going off, the foundation of my being beginning to crumble. Abuelo was a man of legend in my house. I was named after him. And he was a liar and a cheater.

So I did what any good journalist would do. I started digging. I dug, and I dug, and I found out there were more lies. Abuelo wasn't even working as a damn janitor at all. He was an activist, a well-known figure in New York City, fighting for the rights of immigrants and the Latino community. They called him El Rascacielos—the Skyscraper. Probably because he was short. Latinos do nicknames like that.

Lupe is pissed at me for uncovering the truth about him. But I'm a journalist, and uncovering the truth is my literal job description. No matter how painful it might be personally.

"He took his second wife's name to hide his true identity. He lied to my grandmother—to my family. And yet, he did good for the community here in New York. I think his story fits with the series you're doing."

My boss at *The Brooklyn Daily News* is friends with a fact-checker here who told him *The New Yorker* was planning a series of features on important figures in recent New York history, calling it *The Voices of the City.* They were also looking for "diverse viewpoints," and broadened their submission rules exclusively for the series. Writing for *The New Yorker* has been a dream of mine since I decided to go into journalism, and this is my one shot.

Neil glances at his laptop. "You've done thorough research."

I nod.

"You've got a great sense of humor," he adds. "And your voice certainly fits with our publication. Your English is very good."

My English is damn near perfect. Now let's hope I don't accidentally misgender him.

"Thank you," I say.

"Yes, your résumé is very impressive," Neil says. "*Reforma, El País, El Universal* . . . And now you work for *The Brooklyn Daily News*?"

I nod. "Antonio Lopez sponsored my visa." Antonio has lived in New York for twenty years but he's from Mexico City, like me. I met him through my cousin, Nacha, who is dating Antonio's nephew. Even in cities as big as New York or CDMX, you can always find someone who knows someone you're related to.

"Don't you worry about tarnishing El Rasca—sorry, your grandfather's legacy?"

I purse my lips. "I think the truth matters more than a legacy."

It wouldn't be professional to say I'm *hoping* to tarnish his legacy. That exposing Abuelo's lies feels like the only way I can exact any justice for my family. Even though Abuelo has been dead for eleven years, the sense of betrayal I feel is acute, like a fresh cut from a razor blade. There's a special kind of pain that comes with learning your childhood hero wasn't who you thought he was.

I love my family more than anything else in this world. I thought we were good, all of us, to the core. So yeah, Abuelo's "legacy" isn't something I'm interested in protecting.

I've been working on this article in my spare time and on weekends, in between covering things like the new recycling rules in Park Slope, or something called the Polar Bear Plunge in Coney Island, which sounded intriguing but turned out to be a bunch of white people jumping into the ocean at subzero temperatures. I do not think I will ever understand that.

"I really like the intersection of the personal and the political. The activist and the man. El Rasca was a force in this city. This is exactly what we're looking for. But what about the family, the . . ." He skims his fingers over the trackpad of his laptop. "The Cuevas family?"

My skin prickles at the name. "Fernanda Cuevas died of cancer five years ago. She and my abuelo had one son—Ricardo Cuevas. I've been trying to contact him."

"Well, we'd need a quote from him in order to run this," Neil says, leaning back in his chair again. "To cover our bases." A seagull swoops past the window and out toward New Jersey. I have to press my palm to my knee to keep my leg still.

I've been trying to talk with Ricardo for over a month. He works for a huge Mexican media company called Grupo Real. All my emails have bounced back, and I can't get through on his direct line because apparently all the receptionists have been highly trained in evasive tactics like they're working for the pinche Centro Nacional de Inteligencia.

But if Neil says I need a quote from Ricardo, then I'll get a quote from Ricardo.

"Of course," I say. "No problem."

"Okay," Neil says, closing his laptop with a click. "The series is running for a year, starting in June. We can pencil your article in for publication in early January. Which means I'd need the final draft by mid-November for edits."

"Not a problem," I reply immediately. I feel a faint buzzing sensation in my chest.

Neil stands and shakes my hand.

"Welcome to *The New Yorker*," he says.

I step into the late afternoon sunlight and have to suppress the urge to fling my arms out and spin around, like that nun in the movie with the Nazis.

The sun glints off the glass windows of the surrounding skyscrapers and the wind off the water is crisp and cool. I weave my way through a group of tourists taking photos of the 9/11 Memorial and take out my phone. I have a text from Lupe on our family thread with a video of one of my nieces' figure skating lessons, one from Antonio asking how the interview went, and another from my younger sister, Carolina.

Dude, you think Lupe's trying to live out her childhood Disney on Ice dreams?

I chuckle. Caro and I are really close.

With three aunts, six cousins (all primas), two sisters, and four nieces, my family is about 95 percent female. And it's great! I love women. In a respectful, noncreepy way. There's no machismo in the Martinez family. My dad is probably the most mild-mannered, open-minded person I know. Caro calls him an accidental feminist. When she came out to my parents as bisexual, my mom immediately started making tacos campechanos—my mom's reaction to any big emotion is cooking—and my dad just nodded, gave her a hug, and put on a Juan Gabriel record.

I text Antonio the good news, thanking him for helping me get the interview, then duck into an empty ATM vestibule to get to work. Surely some receptionist at Grupo Real will at least let me through to his company voicemail.

I'm not sure exactly what I should say to him though. *Hi, I'm your nephew. Your father cheated on my abuela with your mom. Surprise!*

Don't think Hallmark sells cards for that.

I dial the number, and a woman I'm sure I haven't spoken to before says in polite Spanish, "Grupo Real, how can I direct your call?"

"Hi," I say. "I'm trying to get in touch with Ricardo Cuevas."

"I'm sorry, Mr. Cuevas isn't here."

"Can I leave a message?"

"What is this in regard to, sir?"

It's like they think I'm trying to steal state secrets. I've tried being upfront about being a journalist, told them I was a relative, and pretended to have a delivery that needed his confirmation. All with no luck. Maybe the receptionists at Grupo Real *should* work at the CNI.

"I used to work with his father," I say, attempting yet another tactic. "Before he died," I add, for sympathy. "And I've got some of his things I thought Ricardo might want to have. I know they were very close."

I have no idea if they were close, but I'm hoping this woman doesn't either.

"Oh," she says. "That's so kind of you." She hesitates then adds, "But Mr. Cuevas is working in the Beijing offices at the moment."

Beijing! Dammit. At least I'm getting somewhere with this receptionist though.

"Ah," I say, "that must be why I can't get through. Tell me, is there an address I could send his things to?"

"I can't give you an address," she says.

"No, of course not," I say. "How silly of me for asking." Then I give a big sigh. "It's just some personal correspondence from his father that I think he'd like to have."

"Well," she says slowly, "Mr. Cuevas will be at the wedding in October. Mr. Alvarez has invited many people in the company to attend. Mr. Cuevas is in the marketing department, and I know they're all going."

Jorge Alvarez is the CEO of Grupo Real. I did some light background. He's already married—though I haven't checked anything personal on him in a while. Maybe he got divorced?

"The wedding, of course," I say. "Thank you so much."

"Have a good day," she chirps and hangs up.

I immediately Google *Alvarez wedding Grupo Real.* The first article that pops up is from a couple of months ago, in the society pages of *Quién*.

Diego Alvarez to wed in splashy affair in Mexico City

The photo is of a good-looking Chilango dude with his arm around a beautiful Latina woman. There's no date for the wedding, just the general month of October. Which would technically give me enough time to meet Neil's deadline of mid-November. But I bet this wedding is going to have incredibly tight security, so there's no way I'll be able to sneak in or pretend to be a guest in order to talk to Ricardo.

I head back out onto the street, my mind churning. The only way I can get a quote from Ricardo is if I get an actual invite to this wedding. My heart sinks. I may as well be asking for a trip to the moon.

No, I think the moon would be easier.

3
Agustín

I'm still lost in thought as I head to the subway.

I love the New York subway system. Yes, sometimes it stinks, and it's crowded, and unreliable on weekends, and there's usually someone asking you for money or urinating on the platform, but there's this sense of community on the train. We're all in this together. Even though no one ever looks at each other and when someone starts shouting about Jesus, everybody just pretends it's not happening. I love the sense of time travel the subway gives you—going underground and emerging in a totally different part of the city. There's a feeling of endless movement, of connectivity, of neighborhoods sprouting up like mushrooms. The subway is the connective tissue of New York, its nervous system, pulsing with energy and electricity.

I get off at Borough Hall and head toward the small cocktail bar on Henry Street that my friend Eva has apparently been dying to try. Nicolas and Eva Garcia are brother and sister—they live in Bushwick (like me) and they're Chilangos from Mexico City (like me). That's about where our similarities end. I met them at a local dive bar in our neighborhood back in February, and we started hanging out. I could never tell what they did for a living, and then I realized: nothing. They do nothing. Their father runs a huge real estate company in CDMX, and they've been living in New York for three years, just throwing parties and going on vacations and generally existing, as far as I can tell.

Apparently, this is a thing in Bushwick: kids from rich families living in a scruffier neighborhood and pretending they are "of the common man."

My scalp prickles as it occurs to me that they are exactly the kind of people who would run in Diego Alvarez's circle.

The cocktail bar is on a corner, with big windows revealing circular booths inside. I catch sight of my reflection as I enter—my thick black hair can most charitably be described as "unruly" and the wind off the water back in FiDi did not do me any favors. I run my fingers through it and pull open the door. It's five thirty, so there are only a handful of other patrons inside. Nico and Eva sit in one of the booths facing the windows, and Eva leaps up to greet me.

"Oh my god, look at you!" she cries in Spanish, kissing my cheek. "Qué guapo." She runs her fingers along my blue button-down shirt, which is, to be fair, the nicest one I own. I'm generally a tee and hoodie type of guy.

"Qué tal, wey," Nicolas says, getting up to give me his usual quick, two-pat bro hug.

"How was the interview?" Eva gushes, as Nico waves the waitress over.

"Good," I say, switching to English to order a negroni, then back to Spanish. "They're giving me a chance."

"No mames!" Eva gasps. Eva is always gasping. She's one of the most excitable people I've ever met. She styles herself a bit like Amy Winehouse, with big hair and cat-eye makeup and red lips.

"That's great, bro," Nico says, sipping his old-fashioned. Nico, in contrast to Eva, always looks like he just rolled out of bed and threw on whatever clothes were within reach.

"So what did they say? When can I buy my copy? This is so cool," Eva says breathlessly. "*The New Yorker*!"

I shift on the faux leather, and it creaks. All Eva and Nico really know about the article is that it's about an activist from Mexico. They had no idea who El Rasca was when I mentioned his name. Besides, they aren't the sort of immigrants Abuelo was fighting on behalf of. I don't begrudge them their money; they just don't get what it's like for people like me.

"I still have some work left to do," I tell her. "Actually, I could use your help."

Eva sits up, her dark eyes sparkling.

"Any chance you guys know a Diego Alvarez? His father runs Grupo R—"

Eva shrieks so loud I jump.

"Know him?" she says, then starts laughing. Even Nico gives a chuckle as he downs the rest of his drink. "Obviously! Nico used to play golf with Diego at Club de Golf Chapultepec. Our mom has lunch with his mom all the time at Hoyo 20."

"Yeah, he has a killer backswing," Nico grumbles.

My pulse trips in my veins. Surely I can't get this lucky twice in one day. "Seriously?"

"He got engaged to some gringa a few months ago," Nico says lazily.

"Rachel Lazcari," Eva pipes up. "Her Insta is fire. Their wedding is going to be insane. I can't wait. It's all anyone is talking about back home."

"So you two are going?" I ask. Eva nods eagerly. I lean forward. "Is there any chance you could get me an invitation?"

Nico looks confused and Eva frowns. "Why?" she asks.

"I need to talk to someone at the wedding," I admit. "One of the other guests. This person is the last piece of the puzzle I need to complete the article, and I'm having a hard time getting in touch with him."

Eva's face crinkles with pity. "Oh, Agustín," she says, patting my hand as the waitress comes over with my drink. "There's no way. This wedding is, like, the event of the year. Of the decade. Of the century! Jorge Alvarez is loaded." She enunciates each syllable, then plucks an olive from her martini glass and chews. "He's even bought out most of the Four Seasons for the guests. They're, like, gonna close down Centro."

"They're not closing down Centro," Nico says, rolling his eyes. Centro Histórico is the historic center of Mexico City, full of museums and iconic buildings.

"Okay, but you know how protective Señor Alvarez is about privacy."

"You don't even know the wedding will be in Centro," Nico points out.

Eva purses her lips. "True. The invitation is just a QR code to RSVP. No location or even an exact date yet, because they're keeping things so locked down for security. I heard Diego Luna and Gael García Bernal are going to be there. And there's a rumor Luis Miguel might sing."

Holy shit, if Jorge Alvarez can get El Sol de México to perform at his son's wedding, then he's got more influence than I thought.

"Eva, no fucking way Luis Miguel is singing at the wedding, that's just Abril de la Fuente making shit up as usual," Nico says. "But yeah, there will definitely be celebrities."

I take a drink of my negroni, its bitterness coating my mouth. There's no chance I could talk my way into an event this high profile.

"Wait!" Eva gasps. "I could put you on the list of más-unos!"

"A plus-one list?" I ask, frowning. I've never heard of anything like that. Maybe it's a rich-person thing.

"It's just for close family and friends," Eva says, taking out her phone, its jewel-encrusted case flashing in the sunlight. "You know, people in our circles." Yup, definitely a rich-person thing. "Everyone needs a más-uno at weddings. No exceptions."

Nico chuckles. "Remember that time I brought Maria-Victoria Ramirez to Tía Jimena's wedding, and she drank so much mezcal she threw up on the sound system?"

Eva slaps him on the shoulder. "Yes, I do, and you know what? You and the rest of your friends could do with making a list of your own, so shit like that doesn't happen again. Men," she mutters, rolling her eyes and typing frantically. "Anyway, we share names of potential dates on the list, so that if any woman needs one, they know they have a trusted recommendation. You cannot attend a wedding without a date. It's mandatory. And can you think of anything more embarrassing than going to a wedding *alone*?" She shudders delicately.

"Eva," I beg. "Please, can you put me on that list?"

"Claro," she says, playfully nudging my arm. "But I can't promise anything. The engagement was only announced in January and everything is moving at lighting speed. Everyone I know who's going already has a plus-one. Nico, you know anyone available?"

"Sorry, bro," he says to me.

Eva scrolls down her phone and then cocks her head, looking at me.

"What?" I ask.

"Just thinking how I'll describe you," she says.

"Describe me?"

"Every man on the list comes with details. Bits of personal info. So the woman can pick the right match."

I do not love the sound of that. I can't imagine what details Eva is going to put down about me.

She types something out quickly. "I'm sending this out to my contacts now as *Updated Más Unos*. And . . . sent!" She beams at me, then her smile falters. "It's a long shot, though."

Long shots are my specialty. Moving to New York? Long shot. Getting a meeting at *The New Yorker*? Longer shot. This wedding invite may be my longest shot yet.

But I'm an optimist. Pon chonguitos, there's someone, somewhere out there who still needs a date to this wedding.

4
Eloise

"El, you need a date to the wedding."

I choke on my complimentary champagne as Rachel throws back the curtain of the private dressing room at Atelier Unveiled and steps out into the little circular show area.

"What?" I cough and put my glass down, temporarily blinded by the thousands of crystals sewn into the bodice of the wedding gown my best friend is currently strapped into. "No!"

"No to the dress or no to the date?" Rachel asks.

"Both," I say, as she turns to examine her reflection in the large mirrors.

"Yeah, this feels like a Swarovski store threw up on me," she says, frowning. "And god, it's tight. Okay, next."

She disappears behind the curtain to try on another option. This is the seventh dress shop we've visited in the months since her engagement. Rachel's deep-seated pickiness is going to result in her wearing a burlap sack down the aisle. Honestly, she'd probably look amazing in burlap and start a new trend.

Ever since her call back in January with the news, I have been determined to stay positive. Or at least, to not let Rachel sense the spiraling panic that's been slowly tightening within me. The fear that I'll lose her. That things will change. That she won't be my Rachel anymore.

But I've looked at flower arrangements and bridesmaid dresses and hairstyles and makeup options—Rachel has that covered, seeing as she's about to open her own line of cosmetics. She's a well-established influencer on social media, and her makeup tutorials have gained her a massive following. I've done all the things a best friend is supposed to do, and I've even managed to smile through most of it.

A date, though, is a bridge too far. And Rachel should know that.

I've never had real a boyfriend. I dated, kind of, back in college. I've hooked up, had sex, ticked off those experiences. But real intimacy is just not in the cards for someone like me, and guys don't like to wait around, or so I've discovered.

She sweeps the curtain aside and steps back out. This dress isn't as bad as the last one—strapless, skintight, with a fishtail skirt. It hugs Rachel's incredible figure, and her light brown skin complements the ivory fabric.

"Better," I say. "But I don't know if it's you."

While part of me has been tempted on more than one occasion to tell her just say yes to the damn dress already so I don't have to keep going to all these appointments, I could never do that. I know how important this is to her. I understand Rachel's perfectionist tendencies the way she understands my anxiety.

She angles one hand on her hip, and chews on her lower lip. "Yeah," she agrees. "I don't know, maybe strapless isn't the way to go for this. Diego's family is, like, mega conservative. He keeps telling me that whatever I want is fine, but I'm like, honey, I worked in the Hamptons for a summer. These kinds of people do not know the meaning of 'fine.' There is no fine. I need to . . . I don't know . . . fit."

You fit with me, I want to say.

"You fit wherever you are," I say aloud. "Because you're Rachel. If his family doesn't see that, they're idiots."

She turns her gaze on me, a smile blooming across her face. Rachel has the best smile. It makes you feel like you've just eaten a lemon drop—sunny and tart and sweet all at once. She shuffles over, the skirt so tight she can barely move her legs, and plops down next to me.

"You know you're my best friend ever, right?"

"Right," I say.

"And you know I need you with me for this, because no one else gets me the way you do, right?"

I feel a pinch of pride.

"Right," I say again.

"I know this is a lot for you," she says. "Even though you're like the first maid of honor in the history of weddings with approximately zero responsibilities."

I grin. Rachel knows that planning a bachelorette party or a bridal shower is simply not within my capabilities. Coordinating with people I *don't know*? Not a chance. I can't send an email without rereading it twelve times and then having a mild panic attack afterward. Rachel's other friends are loud, and cool, and fun, and the opposite of me.

"But I was wondering if you could take on just one teeny tiny responsibility . . ." she says hesitantly.

My pulse kicks up, and I feel the beads of sweat start to form under my arms. Rachel chuckles.

"It's not scary, it's a good thing," she promises. She can always tell when my anxiety revs up. She purses her lips. "Okay, maybe it's a little scary."

"Not helping," I say.

She squeezes my hand. "Will you say a few words at the reception? Not like, a whole big, long speech or anything but . . ."

Her voice trails off, and I feel like the bottom has dropped out of my stomach. All the blood drains from my face, and my heart rate accelerates as the Worry Wheel goes into overdrive.

After years of therapy, I've learned to visualize my anxiety as a wheel, like on Wheel of Fortune, except instead of $500 or *Mystery Vacation*, the little wheel slices say things like *This Interaction Will Haunt You Forever* or *Unbearable Shame* or *They're Probably Mad at You*. It's always the same pattern: something happens, my heart rate spikes, the sweat starts to form, and the Wheel click-click-clicks away, spinning faster and faster until it lands on a slice. Then the signals shoot to my brain, and the thoughts come, too fast—horrible thoughts popping up like whack-a-moles, making it hard to breathe.

When I can picture it as a wheel, I can try to slow it down. I've tried to put good slices on the Worry Wheel, to counteract the bad ones. *Dogs*, for example. *Rachel*, for another.

But this request sets the Worry Wheel flying and of course it lands on *I Will Be Bad at This and Ruin Everything.* Because I will be so bad at this. And ruin everything.

She wants me to *speak in front of people*? At the wedding?

With everyone looking at me? There will be like five hundred people there.

What if I say the wrong thing? What if I don't say anything at all, and my brain stops working, and there's an endless excruciating silence before I melt into a puddle of shame?

What if I *ruin Rachel's wedding*?

My throat has closed up so that only a thin wisp of air can reach my lungs. My scalp pulses. I'm fully sweating under my arms now. My fuzzy pink cardigan feels too constricting.

"Eloise," Rachel says calmly, squeezing my hand, and suddenly I can breathe again. I look into my best friend's warm face, feel her hand in mine, and bring myself back into my body. "Please. I need you. George and Mina will be there, but it's not the same. They're not *you*." George and Mina were Rachel's foster parents when she was in high school. "You're my ride or die. You're my rock."

And I know that I have to say yes. Of course I will say yes. Because this is Rachel. She's my rock, too.

"Yes," I squeak.

"Ahhhhhh!" Rachel cries and throws her arms around me. She's the only person who can hug me like this, and I feel her laughter against my chest, and then I'm laughing too, because Rachel's happiness is infectious.

"Oh my god, thank you, El, thank you," she says, releasing me. She bounces up and down on the couch gleefully.

"Is it really that exciting?" I ask, bemused.

"Oh, the fact that you just agreed to stand up in front of hundreds of people to support me? Yes, that's exciting. And before you freak out, literally two sentences is fine. You do not need to make a long speech."

My stomach twists. The wedding is already taking me away from the Pack for a week—the longest I've ever been away from home in my life. I've been trying to figure out what to do about dog sitting. With the Colonel's shots and Charleston's diaper and Hazel's attitude, they're quite the special needs bunch. Rachel keeps saying I'll love Mexico City, but I'm not so sure. I don't believe there's a place on earth better than New York.

"But," she says, "you still need a date."

My muscles freeze. "No," I say. "Rachel, come on. A date? With who? I don't know any men. I don't date!"

"That's a whole other conversation you know I would love to get into," she says, standing. "Let me get out of this dress, I feel like I'm a sausage in a casing." Her high pony swings back and forth as she scurries behind the curtain and closes it. "Listen," she calls out as I down the rest of my flute of champagne. "This isn't me being pushy for no reason, I swear. This is an Alvarez family thing."

I don't know much about Diego's family except that they're very wealthy, run a media company in Mexico, and Diego works at their offices here.

"What do you mean, a family thing?" I ask warily.

"So, there's this whole story Diego told me. About a curse."

I raise an eyebrow. "A curse."

"Yes, and I can picture that face you're making, and I know it sounds insane BUT." Rachel pokes her head through one side of the curtain. "I think it might be real."

I slip out of my cardigan, my body temperature still too high from my almost-panic attack, and fold my arms over my chest. "Okay . . ."

She grins and disappears back behind the curtain. "So," she continues, "his family is, like, crazy superstitious. And most of the superstitions are whatever, like don't walk under a ladder or broken mirrors causing bad luck. But, this one time, like forty years ago, Diego's Tío Abuelo Alberto—"

"What's a tío abuelo?" I ask.

"It's his great uncle," Rachel explains. Rachel is Latina, but she doesn't speak Spanish. Well, she's been learning since she started dating Diego. But she was raised by a white foster family, then a Black foster family. "Anyway, Tío Abuelo Alberto didn't bring a date to this one family wedding. And as a result, he never married, *and* he had bad luck in love for the rest of his life." That feels less like a curse and more like a very judgmental family getting up in Tío Abuelo Alberto's business. "*And*," Rachel adds, "the couple whose wedding it was ended up divorcing only two years later!"

She pokes her head through the curtain again. "I cannot get divorced, El. I can't be cursed. I don't want to be the one who breaks tradition. I love Diego so much. I know it sounds nuts, but what if? What if it's real? And if you don't bring a date to the wedding, and I lose the love of my life, and his family hates me forever and . . ."

Her brow pulls together, her voice trailing off. She sounds like me at the height of a Worry Wheel episode.

"They're so rigid about this, El," she says.

"Can't I . . . just bring a friend or something?" I ask desperately.

Rachel cocks an eyebrow. "Sure. Which friend would you like to invite? I'm taken, unfortunately."

Dammit. She's got a point. I slump back against the couch. "What do you want me to do?" I ask quietly. "I can't conjure up a man out of thin air. You know me. You think I can just hop on Tinder and find a wedding date?"

Rachel bites her lower lip. "Let me ask Diego if he knows anyone."

She disappears back behind the curtain, which is good, because I can't hide my expression as my mouth puckers in distaste. I don't want Diego to set me up with someone. That sounds worse than Tinder.

It's not that I'm against dating. I would love to be normal and go on dates and do the whole "find my person" thing. I used to dream about having a boyfriend and getting married one day, back when I was a teenager. But it's just not that easy with GAD. I'm too sweaty, and awkward, and I overthink everything. And now Rachel wants to pair me up with one of Diego's buddies? Someone who probably loves CrossFit and keto diets and listens to Joe Rogan? The Wheel starts to click away again but before I can really work myself up, Rachel dramatically throws open the curtain.

I gasp.

This dress is perfect. The bodice is meticulously crafted out of overlapping layers of lace, forming intricate patterns, with a high neck and cap sleeves that just cover her shoulders. The skirt falls in satiny waves to the floor, so that it billows around her. It's stunning. It's majestic and a little bit vintage and exquisitely Rachel.

"You like it?" she asks eagerly.

"I love it," I say.

She looks at herself in the mirror, and her hands fly to her cheeks. "El, I look so pretty!"

I laugh. "You're always pretty," I remind her. "But this is . . ."

"Yes?" Rachel asks, her eyes sparkling.

"Yes," I say emphatically.

"Eeep!" she squeals, as she turns this way and that, admiring the dress from every angle. "The fit is amazing. I don't even think it will need that much tailoring . . . oh, El! I'm getting *married*!"

I try to ignore the dip in my stomach at her words and beam at her instead, in a way that I hope looks enthusiastic. Just then, her phone pings with a text. She grabs it, and her eyes widen. Her mouth falls open. "Oh my god, Eloise. You are not going to believe this."

My stomach dips again, with trepidation this time. "What?"

"Diego came through." She holds up her phone.

On the screen, I see a document titled in Spanish.

"What's that?" I ask her.

Rachel looks triumphant. "The Plus-One List."

5
Eloise

"I can't believe they have an actual list," I say to Rachel as we head down the steps to the C train.

"Apparently, it's not just for his family," she explains. "Diego says it's something the women in his—I don't know, sphere, I guess?—use when they need wedding dates. But it comes in pretty handy when you're trying to avoid a curse."

A train arrives just as we reach the platform, and we hurry through the turnstile and onto the crowded car.

"Anyway, it's better than Tinder." Rachel winks at me as the doors close with the ever-familiar *beep-boop.*

"Tinder was never a valid option."

"Exactly. And this . . ." She grabs onto the pole as the train lurches forward, then pulls up the list on her phone again. "This is amazing. It's all in Spanish, though, so I'll need to translate it."

"It's more than just names?" I ask.

"Yeah, it's got brief descriptions of the guys. Let's see . . . 'alto, más alto, super alto.' Guess these ladies like tall men."

"I don't like tall men," I say. I'm five foot nothing. Tall men give me a crick in my neck just trying to make eye contact. But I find myself warming to the idea of the plus-one list. It's transactional. These men understand the rules. Whoever I choose will know he is here so that my friend doesn't supposedly curse her own wedding. Maybe I won't even have to talk to this person much. As long as they arrive with me, I've done my duty, right?

"Okay, no 'altos,'" Rachel says. "Oh my god, check this one out: Rodrigo Sarmiento. 'Músico.' So he's a musician. 'Humor negro, no es apropriado en todas las familias.'" She pops it in Google Translate. "It means 'dark humor, not appropriate for all families.'" She snorts.

"No," I say immediately. Dark humor and I don't mix.

"Yeah, that wouldn't work. What about Daniel Belmont? 'Bastante horny, pero muy buen bailarín.' I don't need Google for this one: Really horny, but a very good dancer." Rachel waggles her eyebrows at me.

"I'm not even going to entertain that," I say.

"Fair. How about Miguel Casco? 'MUY intenso, pintor, nunca en México.' Soooo . . . very intense, a painter, and never in Mexico."

"Why is he even on the list then?" I ask.

"Yeah, seriously. Also, you and intense do not mix."

I chuckle and have to admit, this is a little bit fun. The train stops at 86th Street and we get out, emerging onto the Upper West Side.

"Wait a minute," I say as we head toward my apartment. "Are all these guys in Mexico?"

I don't think I want to meet this person only *after* I land in a totally unfamiliar country, right before an event that, let's face it, I'm not exactly thrilled about. Not that I want to hang out with him for any length of time. But it's still over five months to the wedding. I can't handle five months of stressing about this.

"Good question," Rachel says. She switches to her WhatsApp and messages Diego. "He says he'll do some recon and highlight the ones who live in New York. Which means he's gonna ask his mom. I guess there are some guys that live in LA, as well as Buenos Aires and London."

"An international plus-one list," I mutter. Who are these people?

Rachel cheerfully greets Hector as we enter the lobby and take the elevator up to my apartment. As soon as we walk through the door, we hear the familiar stirring of the Colonel, then the tippy tap of Charleston's feet as he comes careening into view.

"Charleston, buddy, over here," Rachel says as he sails past her, skidding into the door. He pants up at her as she bends down to scratch his ears, then he plows into my legs, licking my jeans, his tongue making little scratching sounds.

I head into the kitchen to preheat the oven—I've got an order of sweet potato peanut butter dog bones to make for *Treats Gourmand.* I pull the family-size jar of peanut butter out of the cabinet and grab some sweet potatoes, wrapping them in foil. I hear Rachel talking to the Pack in the living room. When the oven beeps, I set the potatoes to roast and set a timer.

Rachel is on the couch with the Colonel when I enter the living room. I plop down next to her and scoop up Charleston, sniffing his diaper. No pees or poops yet. I rub his ears as Hazelnut snores lightly from the giant dog bed.

"Diego sent the list back with highlights," Rachel says, showing me her phone. "I say we find a few options and then set up a meet and greet."

I cock an eyebrow. "A meet and greet?"

"Would you rather I call them dates?" she says.

"No," I say quickly, a flash of panic skittering over my ribs. "Fine, give me the list." I should be in charge of my own destiny. I know approximately zero Spanish, but I scroll the highlighted names and Rachel translates. Definite nos to Angel Ruiz ('medio famoso,' which causes Rachel to immediately Google him and find out he's a Sunday morning talk show anchor for Telemundo) and Juan Carlos Garcia (recently divorced, really into rock climbing).

We get to the end of the list, and I point at the last name. "What about this guy?" I ask.

Rachel squints. "Agustín Martinez. 'Bajito. Hoyuelos. Sencillo y trabajador.' So that means . . . short, but like in a cute way? Dimples, oooh like those. And lower class but a hard worker."

"Him," I say immediately. We end up choosing two other highlighted names: Luis Gonzalez (works in finance, has a cat) and José Miguel Suarez (pilot, always wears black).

"I'll set up the dates," Rachel says.

I grip her arm as the Wheel starts to spin, click-clicking away in my chest like a second, frantic heartbeat. "You are not sending me out there alone."

She gives me a gentle smile. "Obviously not. I'll be right there with you. Let's set them up so they all come to us—same place, same time, different days. Will that help?"

I nod, trying to calm my racing heart, but now I feel a thread of shame mixed with the panic. This shouldn't be so hard. I shouldn't need so many rules.

"What about Vin de Table, on 85th?" Rachel suggests, naming a nearby wine bar. "We love that place. It's close, it's quiet, and it's small."

If I think too much, I'm going to lose it, and I already promised Rachel.

"Okay," I say. "Let's do it."

6
Agustín

"So, you're actually getting published in *The New Yorker*?" Carolina asks. "Like, for real?"

I adjust my phone on the desk so I can better see her face on the screen. "Well, not if I can't get access to Ricardo. Then I'm screwed."

Caro sits back and tilts her head. We have the same thick black hair, but hers is cut short on the sides, with a thatch that curls across her forehead. She recently dyed it with streaks of electric blue. I think it looks great—Lupe nearly had a heart attack when she saw it.

"You'll find a way, big bro, don't stress it."

Caro has always believed in me fiercely.

"Thanks, hermana," I say, turning my attention to my laptop. "I wish I had your confidence."

I'm multitasking, typing away on my next article for *The Brooklyn Daily News*: a public interest story about a middle-aged woman who donated her kidney to her best friend of forty years. It was nice talking to them—they were quite a funny pair. Told me some great stories about Brooklyn in the eighties.

It's been two days since drinks with Nico and Eva and no word about a wedding date. Maybe Eva was right, and the plus-one list is going to be a strike. A strike out? I don't understand baseball.

"You aren't mad?" I ask Carolina.

"At you? No."

"Lupe won't talk to me."

"Lupe always has a stick up her butt about something."

"Aren't you mad at Abuelo?" I insist. Why do I feel like I'm the only member of my family having a normal reaction to this? My mom won't talk about it or let me talk to Abuelita at all. My dad pretends like he's suddenly got some pressing issue in his garden any time I bring it up, and Lupe acts like *I'm* the one who's betrayed the family.

"Mad at him for what? I hate to say it, Tín, but Abuelo ain't unique. Color me shocked—Mexican man moves to the US and starts a secret second family. It happens a lot, dude."

"So that makes it okay?" I demand. "That he lied? That he cheated on Abuelita?"

"No, but I don't know if you've noticed that Abue seems pretty okay with it? When she told us, it wasn't like she broke down crying."

I'm positive that's not true. Abuelita is strong, that's all. I'm sure she didn't want to show her heartbreak to her family. I wish my mom would let me talk to her. She and Lupe and my tías have all gone into protection mode, only passing along messages from me, never handing their phones to her when I call.

"There's no way Mom isn't pissed about this too," I say.

"Mom doesn't get pissed. She cooks. A lot. Which is great for me. I could eat her lasagna every day." Caro's septum piercing glints in the sunlight streaming through the high windows of her apartment in Colonia Juarez. "Don't worry about Lupe. She'll call you the minute she needs your help with the Minions."

That's what we call our nieces. Four girls, all under the age of twelve. Going to visit is like heading into a war zone. I always come armed with presents. Candy, crayons, stickers, whatever it takes.

I slump back in my chair. "It isn't just the cheating," I say quietly. "It isn't even the second family. You know *when* Abuelo became El Rasca? When his name first started appearing in the papers here? At the exact same fucking time we got evicted from the house in Coyoacán."

Caro shifts uneasily on her chair. We were just kids then, only ten and eight, but that memory is imprinted in our brains forever. We were forced to leave our home, the house I had grown up in, and squeeze into a tiny apartment. And why? Because the Mexican government made some backroom deal with a shady contractor. No one spoke up for my family, or the many others who were affected. No one gave a shit about us.

It's why I wanted to become a journalist in the first place. The only way to make change, to give power to the powerless and a voice to the voiceless, is to get loud. As journalists, we have to grab people by the shoulders and shake them and say Look! Look at what is happening.

Abuelo was fighting for people he didn't even know, while leaving his family to fend for themselves.

I swallow back my anger.

"Enough about Abuelo," I say, cracking my knuckles and leaning back in my chair. The cramped office on Court Street is pretty quiet—the rest of the small news team is out covering stories or getting their afternoon caffeine boost. "How are things going with the new job?"

"Ugh, fucking Alonso. He's a total control freak. Needs seven different versions of the same design. I wish he'd just let me do my thing. I know how to sew a fucking jumpsuit."

I grin. "This is just a steppingstone, remember. Next, you start your own company."

Caro works in fashion. She finally got a job working for a small clothing company with a store in Colonia Roma—the hipster area of CDMX.

"That's the plan. Can't have my big brother hogging all the spotlight."

"I don't like spotlights," I tell her.

"Sure. I'll remind you of that when you're winning your Pulitzer."

"Ha ha."

Suddenly, my phone buzzes and I see a text from an unfamiliar number.

"Hold on a second, Caro," I say, switching to my text messages.

> Hi Agustín. My name is Rachel Lazcari, I'm engaged to Diego Alvarez. My maid of honor needs a date to our wedding in October, and you were recommended as someone who might be available to be her plus-one. Are you able to meet this Sunday at six pm? Let me know and I can confirm a location. Thanks!

For a moment, I just stare at the text, almost confused. Then a huge smile breaks across my face, and I hurriedly type my reply with shaking fingers.

"Good news?" Caro asks.

I switch back to FaceTime and beam at her. "The best," I say.

7
Eloise

Rachel has successfully set up all three of my plus-one list dates: one Friday, one Saturday, and one Sunday.

But as six PM on Friday rolls around, the panic I've kept at bay starts to creep in. Even before I arrive at the little French wine bar, the Worry Wheel is spinning out of control.

What if I say the wrong thing and embarrass myself so thoroughly that I'm forced to walk into the Hudson, never to be seen again?

What if he makes a joke but I don't recognize it as a joke, and I don't laugh and then there's awkward silence, and I am haunted by it forever?

What if I actually *can't* get a plus-one, not even from a transactional list? What if all the dates reject me, and I ruin Rachel's wedding, and she gets divorced, and it's all my fault?

It's a beautiful spring day, but I'm already too hot, my pulse sprinting and beads of sweat forming on my hairline and dampening the curls that frame my forehead. I'm in an orange and yellow striped romper and my worn, trusty leather boots, with a butterfly clip pinning one side of my hair back to try and tame the curls. I didn't bother putting makeup on because I'll probably just sweat it off anyway.

"You look so cute!" Rachel says as she greets me, looking effortless in a gauzy white sundress.

When Luis Gonzalez (works in finance, has a cat) arrives, I can tell instantly that he wishes this date was with Rachel and not me. He's tall and excessively muscular, with dark, slicked back hair. It looks like he threads his eyebrows. He has a very large, very showy gold watch that keeps catching the sunlight and flashing directly into my eyes. He orders a whiskey, neat, and seems offended when the bartender tells him they only serve beer and wine.

Did he not look the place up before he got here? I do extensive research anytime I have to go somewhere new.

"So," he says to Rachel. "You're marrying Diego Alvarez."

His eyes seem to constantly drift to her chest. I clench my teeth and instantly decide I do not like this person.

"Yes," Rachel says. "And this is Eloise, my best friend and my maid of honor."

He juts his chin in my direction. "Hey."

My pulse pounds at the base of my throat.

I take a breath.

This is it, Eloise. You can do this. Just . . . say hello.

But the word feels stuck to the roof of my mouth. The sides of the room blur. Why is he looking at me like that? Why can't he look somewhere else for a second? His gaze drags down the length of my body but not in the creepy way he was looking at Rachel just now. His eyes drip with disdain. Like I'm not good enough. Like I should never have deigned to interrupt his whiskey-neat-gold-watch evening with my curly-haired-romperness.

I try to imagine arriving at Rachel's wedding with this man. Sitting at the same table as him at the reception. Every cell in my body repels the idea. I glance at Rachel, aware of how wide my eyes are.

Just say hello, Eloise. Come on. Don't be weird!

But my lips feel like they've been glued shut.

"Does she, like, talk?" Luis asks Rachel, chuckling.

OhmyfuckinggodIhatethisman. Shame prickles over my scalp and down my back. I hate the tears that well in my eyes. Yes, she talks. Yes, she can hear you. She doesn't *want* to talk. She just wants to be back home with her dogs.

Rachel's nostrils flare. "She talks," she says, standing up. "Just not to dickheads like you. Come on, El." She grabs my hand, and I stumble out the door behind her.

"We didn't pay," I squeak as she heads down West 85th toward the park.

"Fuck that asshole," she says. "He can pay."

My limbs are shaking, and I feel lightheaded. "I'm sorry," I croak.

"Don't you dare be sorry," Rachel says, whirling around, her eyes flashing. "He's the one who should be sorry. Did you see the way he was staring at my boobs? No, you are *not* going to the wedding with a creep like that. I'd rather be cursed."

The following evening, we're back at Vin de Table at six PM to meet José Miguel Suarez (pilot, only wears black). This time I'm slightly better prepared. It's one of those blazingly hot days in May where you really feel summer coming on, and the windows to the little wine bar are thrown open, tables set up outside with red wicker chairs. Rachel is already seated at one of them, along with a man who is, unsurprisingly, dressed all in black. Rachel smiles and waves when she sees me. My skin feels tight on my bones, but I force my lips to curve upward.

"Eloise, this is José Miguel," she says. He stands and shakes my hand.

"Hi," I say, because I'll be damned if I don't say *something* this time at least.

"Nice to meet you," he says. He's thin and wiry, with light brown hair and a very long nose.

I sit beside him as the drinks Rachel ordered for us arrive.

"So," she says to José Miguel. "I hear you're a pilot."

"I am," he says. "I work for AeroMéxico. I'm based here and in Mexico City."

They launch into a conversation about Mexico City, which Rachel has visited a lot with Diego, and I happily sip my Chardonnay and watch a group of yoga moms sitting on the steps of a brownstone across the street, sharing a bottle of rosé and laughing about something. It looks very freeing, all of them so comfortable being in a group. Groups stress me out. Talking with a group of people feels like participating in a giant game of Double Dutch, where everyone competes to be the skipper, but there are no clear rules, and I never know when to tag in.

"El?"

I glance up to see Rachel staring at me.

"Mm?" I say.

"José Miguel asked what you do for a living."

I meet his gaze for only a moment before looking away. I was happier when I was being ignored. "Nothing," I mumble, which, oh my god what am I saying, I have a *job*.

He frowns. "What do you do all day then?"

"She didn't mean nothing," Rachel says. "Eloise works freelance."

I nod, my gaze flitting to him and then back to the yoga moms. I shift in my chair.

"Oh," he says. "Freelance what?"

"Treats," I say. Nope, that didn't come out right. "Baking," I add. My face starts to heat up, and I feel the prickles of heat race across my hairline. "For dogs," I say, making everything worse.

"Eloise bakes specialty dog treats for an online company," Rachel explains. "*Treats Gourmand.* She's really good, her treats are hands down the most popular on the site."

She makes it seem so easy, putting the right words in the right order.

"Oh," he says again, then turns the conversation back to Rachel.

Blissfully, the interaction only lasts about forty-five minutes. Now I can spend the rest of the evening working on a batch of bacon maple biscuits and reading Agatha Christie.

Rachel comes back to the apartment with me to say hi to the Pack. As we step out of the elevator, I hear the faint strains of Mr. Bloom playing Bach. Uncle Lenny was a big fan of classical music, so I can usually recognize Mr. Bloom's pieces.

"That went well, right?" Rachel says.

I shrug. Did it? I guess I actually said words this time. Someone get me a medal.

But I can't picture attending the wedding with José Miguel any more than with Luis. The plus-one list was much more fun when it was just names on a screen.

A door opens down the hall, and Soul Cycle struts out of their apartment, dressed in matching lululemon. I wonder if they're going to meet the yoga moms for rosé on the stoop. I don't know their names, even though we've been neighbors for years. One is short and blond and muscular, the other a strikingly attractive, willowy Indian woman. Both have their hair in high ponytails. My muscles tense, and I avoid eye contact as they walk past. Rachel gives a faint, "Hey." She's seen them around of course.

We've all seen each other around, but I'm happier when we pretend we're strangers. Like Mr. Bloom and I do. He gets it. That's the best part about New York—everyone's a stranger, even when they live in the same building as you. I wouldn't even know anyone's name at all on this floor if it weren't for Miriam.

We step inside my apartment. Charleston is in the kitchen having a drink of water. Hazelnut is chewing on her SpongeBob squeaky toy while the Colonel watches, having managed to temporarily reclaim the giant dog bed. I sidestep Charleston to open the fridge and grab a package of bacon.

As I turn on the oven to preheat and line a baking sheet with parchment paper, Rachel's phone pings. She looks at it and frowns. "So . . . it's a no from José Miguel."

"Oh." I feel an odd mix of rejection and relief. "Why?"

"No real reason," Rachel says airily as Charleston wanders over and starts licking her shoe.

"Is it the fact I couldn't look at him or the fact that I can't speak in complete sentences," I say flatly.

"You *can* speak in complete sentences," Rachel points out. "You just did."

I sigh and lean back against the kitchen counter.

"There's still one date left," she says.

"You really think it's going to be any different?" I ask bleakly.

She comes over to lean beside me and nudges me with her shoulder. "You never know."

I glance at her, and can't even come up with a snarky comment, because I see the hope in her eyes, tinged with desperation. Of all the people Rachel could fall for, it had to be someone with the most bizarre family superstition.

The next day is cool and overcast. I slip into a pair of jeans and a green tank top, throwing on a cardigan with big crochet daisies stitched on it. I have to make an effort this time. For Rachel. So I spritz some of the curl reactivator spray she insisted on buying me into my hair and put mascara on. I stare at my reflection in the mirror. A pair of pale green eyes stares back at me. My eyes are probably the only thing I like about my appearance.

"Bye, guys," I say to the Pack. "Be good."

Charleston is chewing on one of his front paws. Hazel ignores me. I give the Colonel a scratch behind the ear and he licks my hand.

I'm waiting for the elevator, listening to the faint strains of Brahms coming from 9B, when Miriam pokes her head out of her door.

"Where are you off to?" she says. She's wearing scrubs, her tight black curls puffing out in a halo around her open, friendly face. Miriam used to be a nurse at Mount Sinai, but now she runs her own business, as a home aide. Her husband made a small fortune running some big shipping company—they moved into the building when I was just out of college. He died a few years ago, though. As she takes me in, her eyes narrow. "Are you wearing makeup?"

"Going out to meet Rachel," I say. I definitely do not want to tell Miriam about the plus-one list. She'd have way too many questions and be way too excited about it.

The elevator doors open and I step inside just as my phone rings.

Rachel.

"El, I'm so sorry," she says. "I can't make it tonight"

My heart plummets like a stone. "What?"

"There's been an issue with one of the eyeshadows, and I have to go to Jersey to sort things out. But you can do this! I believe in you. I'm sending a text to you and Agustín so you guys will have each other's numbers, just in case."

What? No! That's even worse. I don't want him to have my number.

But before I can say anything, I lose the signal. When I reach the lobby, my phone buzzes.

Rachel: Hi Eloise and Agustín! Now you have each other's numbers 😊

I walk stiffly past Hector, who gives me a jovial wave. I try to smile back, but my mouth feels like it's made of glass, so brittle it could crack.

I try to come up with excuses to bail on this date the entire walk to the wine bar. Food poisoning. Sprained ankle. Unexpected relative popping into town for a visit. Abducted by aliens. But I know, deep down, that I can't cancel. I have to try.

The Worry Wheel starts clicking as I push open the glass front door. About half the tables are full, people sipping Bordeaux and snacking on cheese plates. A man sits at the bar with his back to me. He's wearing a white button-down shirt and dark jeans; he turns just as I enter.

I feel a weird stutter in my chest, like my heart tripped on itself.

Then everything stops.

The man's face is broad and warm. His eyes are the color of dark brewed coffee, and his thick black hair is shaggy, falling to his jawline and curling at the ends in every direction. His olive skin almost seems to glow against his white shirt.

"Eloise?" he says.

Some part of my brain acknowledges that is Agustín Martinez.

Then he smiles, and his dimples make an appearance, dancing in his cheeks like they're winking at me. He has the widest smile I've ever seen. It reminds me of Rachel's, in a way. But where her smile is a lemon drop, Agustín's feels more like a mug of hot chocolate—rich and deliciously inviting, a smile you can sink into. It pulls up a little higher on the left side than the right.

He's not as short as I was expecting—maybe five foot eight or nine. He's not sculpted like Luis or wiry like José Miguel. He's somewhere in between.

His warm smile starts to fade, and I realize I'm just staring at him. My heartbeat, which a moment ago had felt suspended in time, kicks in at a frantic pace. The Wheel spins and spins and spins but doesn't land on anything. I feel a clenching in my throat and a tightness in my stomach, and it takes me a second to sort out what these sensations mean.

Oh shit. I'm *attracted* to this man.

No, no, no. This is worse than whiskey-neat-gold-watch.

Agustín is now looking concerned. "You are Eloise, yes?"

His accent is lilting, his voice as rich and warm as his smile. I don't know what to do. It's been years—feels like decades—since

I've been attracted to someone. In real life. I mean, obviously Pedro Pascal can get it. But that's imaginary. This is a flesh and blood human, and oh no, I do not like this at all. Sweat gathers at the nape of my neck. My knees have become puffs of air.

I am *so* grateful Rachel isn't here.

That snaps me out of it. No, I need Rachel here even more now. How do I get out of this situation? This is so much worse than I imagined.

Eloise, speak.

"Hi," I say in one breathless rush. "Yes. Eloise. Yes."

The hot chocolate smile is back. *Ohmygodthosedimples.*

"Agustín," he says, taking a few steps toward me and offering his hand. "Nice to meet you."

I glance down at his hand and know that I cannot touch him. Absolutely not. That would not be good. Shivers erupt in my belly just thinking about it. My brain flashes *Danger, Danger, Danger.*

Instead, I do the totally normal thing and ignore it, walking past him to sit on the bar stool. The Wheel has wedged itself between *Abject Humiliation* and a pie slice simply labeled *AHHHHHHH!*

It's been a while since *AHHHHHHH!* has registered on the Wheel.

But Agustín slides onto the next stool casually, like it doesn't matter that I was rude. I can feel the heat of his body, and I clench my hands into fists.

"Can I get you a drink?" he asks.

I point at his glass of red wine. Whatever it is, I'll drink it, I don't care. He flashes those dimples at the bartender. "Can we get another Côtes de Rhône?" he asks.

She pours one for me, and Agustín raises his glass. "Salud."

I lift my glass in a trembling hand, and we clink.

I am so completely fucked.

8
Agustín

Eloise Whitechapel is quite the puzzle.

She's clutching her wineglass like it's the last life preserver on the Titanic and refusing to make eye contact. She almost seems frightened of me. I haven't gone on many dates since I've moved here—maybe I'm doing something wrong.

"So," I say, after a few moments of silence. "How long have you lived in New York?"

I've found this to be a standard question—there are deep levels of pride in New Yorkers about the amount of time they've called the city home. A competitive nature to it. According to *Sex and the City*, it's ten years of living here before you can officially call yourself a New Yorker.

I can see Eloise's pulse fluttering beneath her jaw. Her skin is very pale, and there's a smattering of golden freckles across the bridge of her nose. Her chestnut hair is wildly curly, falling to just above her shoulders.

She swallows hard—I swear I can hear the muscles in her throat working. "I was born here," she says. Her voice is so quiet, I have to strain to hear her.

"Really?" I say, delighted. "I didn't think anyone was actually born here. Well, no, of course people are born here, but I haven't met a born-and-raised New Yorker yet. You're the first! I moved here in January. Very much a 'newbie,' as my friend Eva says."

Eloise nods, still not looking at me, her curls bouncing. I wait to see if she'll elaborate. Nope.

Well, Lupe always says I'm the gold medalist at wrangling conversations out of people. And I want Eloise to like me—I got the definite sense from Rachel that this is an interview, that I'm one of many candidates plucked from Eva's list of más-unos.

"I love New York," I say. "It's been my dream to live here ever since I was a kid. I'm from Mexico City. Have you ever been?"

Another quivering of curls as Eloise shakes her head. There's something at once fragile yet strong about her. The delicateness of her features, the softness of her pale skin, contrasts with the iron grip on her wineglass and the tense set of her shoulders.

"Oh, you'll love it. You're the maid of honor at the wedding, right? Eva's told me that it's in CDMX—sorry, that's what we call it, Ciudad de México—but no one knows the exact location because of security stuff." I chuckle. "My sister's wedding was in the backyard of a house in Coyoacán. That's an area of the city, kind of like Fort Greene. We got this local restaurant to supply the food—tacos and sopes and tortas. Mexico City has the best food anywhere in the world. Real Mexican food, not nachos or whatever. No offense."

She shrugs. Hm. I've found Americans really love to proclaim their devotion to nachos. I thought I'd get more reaction here. I see her glance at her phone, then her eyes dart up to me briefly. They're a startling shade of green—like sea glass, soft and clear. Then they widen in panic, and she looks at her phone again.

I take a sip of wine, stumped. She's wearing an oversize cardigan with big flowers on it, hiding her figure. Her jeans are tucked into a cool pair of worn leather boots that come just above her ankles. They look vintage. Caro would love them.

"I like your boots," I say.

That seems to surprise her. Her wide green gaze flies back to me. "They're old," she says.

I chuckle, glad I've coaxed a response out of her at last. "The best things in this world have history, don't you think?"

Her eyes dart to my mouth, then back to her phone. I'm definitely doing something wrong. She keeps looking at the time like she wants to leave. And I notice sweat dewing along her hairline. Maybe she's ill?

I lean forward and catch a faint whiff of something fresh and citrusy. "Are you feeling all right?" I ask her softly.

Her entire body goes rigid. Suddenly, without warning, she shouts, "Rachel was supposed to be here!"

Her voice is so loud it's shocking, after all the nods and whispers. A few of the patrons sitting at tables turn to look at her. Her face flushes bright pink. Eloise grabs her wineglass and, in a pretty impressive display, chugs the entire thing.

She puts the empty glass back on the bar and leaps off her stool. "I'm finished," she declares, then suddenly lets out an enormous burp. Her blush deepens to a rich scarlet that crawls down her neck and blooms across her collarbone. "Sorry," she gasps, covering her mouth. Then she turns on her heel and flees the wine bar, running off down the street and out of sight.

"Everything okay over here?" the bartender asks, coming over.

"Yeah, fine, thanks," I say, feeling anything but.

What just happened? What did I do wrong? Whatever it was, I've got to fix it.

I've got to get to that wedding.

9
Eloise

My legs are wooden beneath me as I stumble down the block toward the safety of my home.

I can't do this. I can't. He was . . . and I just . . . the Wheel spins frantically, tears pricking my eyes. When I reach the corner, my phone starts to buzz in my pocket, startling me so badly that I shriek and cause an elderly woman walking her cat in a stroller to give me a serious side-eye.

For a wild, panicked second, I fear it's going to be Agustín, calling to ask what in the hell is wrong with me. But then I see it's the number for Safe Haven Animal Shelter.

"Hello?" I say.

"Eloise, hi, it's Alexis at Safe Haven. How are you?"

Currently having a panic attack on 85th and Central Park West. "I'm fine, thanks," I lie.

"I'm so sorry for calling so late on a Sunday. And I know it's only been a few months since you lost Walton," she begins. My throat tightens automatically at his name. "But I have a dog who really needs a home, and I think you're the only option. He's a twelve-year-old chihuahua—we've named him Picante because he's, um, spicy."

That's code for aggressive.

"He was found as a stray in New Jersey," she continues. "He's very reactive with humans, but he's fine with other dogs. But no one will take him. We adopted him out this week, and he was just returned because the adopter couldn't handle him." It breaks my heart when dogs get returned. Of course, it's better for a dog to be in the right home, but still. "If he doesn't get adopted within the next couple days, I don't think we'll be able to keep him here. We're over capacity as it is."

Adding another dog to the Pack only months before I have to leave for the wedding isn't ideal. But if I don't take him, he could be sent to shelter after shelter. Or, more likely, he could be euthanized.

"Of course I'll take him," I say to Alexis.

"Oh thank god," she says, and I can hear the emotion in her voice. Alexis is a real advocate for senior dogs—it's one of the reasons we get along so well. "When can you pick him up?"

"I'll come right now," I say, my voice taking on a note of determination.

"You're amazing, you know that, right?"

I crack a small smile. I don't feel very amazing right now. I feel overwhelmed and sweaty.

"Thanks, Alexis. See you soon."

I get off the 6 train and emerge out into Lower Manhattan, trucks trundling down Canal, the streets lined with vendors selling knockoffs, the sounds of Mandarin mixing with English as the neighborhood blends toward Chinatown. I walk the block and a half to Safe Haven, on Centre Street.

The familiar smell of dog and cleaning solution greets me as I walk inside. I managed to shove Agustín Martinez and his hot chocolate smile into a box in the furthest recesses of my brain on the ride here. My stomach is still a little wriggly but it's not like I'll ever see or speak to him again. I will just squash all of these feelings and focus on what's important—a new Pack member.

Alexis is waiting behind the reception desk with a carrier.

"Eloise," she says with relief, smiling broadly. "Thank you so much. Picante here is going to be such a great addition to the Pack, I know it. He just needs stability and love."

From inside the carrier, I hear a tiny growl. I lean down and look through the thin bars. A small creature is huddled in the very back of the carrier.

"The vet has checked him out," she says. "Except for a slight heart murmur, he's fine. He really enjoys the company of other dogs. Like I said, it's just humans he doesn't seem to tolerate."

Same, little man. Same.

I sign the paperwork and pay the adoption fee. Then I call an Uber—no way I'm going to stress this little guy out on the subway. As the car trundles up toward my apartment, I talk to Picante in a calming tone, his little squeaks and yelps breaking my heart.

Hector looks up from his crossword as I enter the lobby.

"Evening." His eyes light on the carrier. "A new dog?"

I only nod and scurry past him to the elevator. When I reach my apartment, I walk into the living room, where Hazel is snoozing on her back in the giant dog bed, her stumpy little legs splayed up in the air. I bought that bed for the Colonel, but once Hazel saw it, she immediately claimed it as her own. The Colonel is curled up on the couch and Charleston is on the floor, licking the rug. All three lift their heads at my arrival.

"Guys, this is our new Pack member," I say. I'll have to think of a name for him. I never use the shelter names. They get a new life here, and a new life needs a fresh identity. "Let's make him feel welcome once he's had time to settle in. Okay?"

The Colonel looks at me with his wise, serious gaze and gives an approving snort. Hazelnut—I swear to god—rolls her eyes and goes back to sleep. Charleston is now licking the leg of the coffee table.

"Great," I say. I head into the decompression room, put the carrier down, and open its door. This room used to be Uncle Lenny's office. Now, it's been outfitted for new Pack members, a safe space for them to decompress and get used to their new home. It's got dog beds, water and food bowls, treats, toys, and blankets. I lay out a pee pad and then head to the bathroom to fill the empty water bowl.

"It's all right," I say gently when I return. "You can come out now."

A little snout, peppered with gray, appears at first. Slowly, the rest of Picante comes into view. His body is black, with a patch of white and tan on his chest. I'd guess he's about seven pounds. I'll have to make an appointment with Dr. Chaudry at Uptown Vet once he's acclimated.

"Welcome to your new home," I say. He snarls at me, baring his teeth, and I scoot back to give him space. Still growling, he trots over to the water bowl and drinks. When his eyes meet mine, they are cold and dark. He bares his teeth again.

"Okay, I'm leaving," I say. I keep the door ajar so he can come out if he wants to.

I sit on the couch with the Colonel, who stretches out across my lap so I can rub his belly. I take out my phone and see a missed text from Rachel.

Rachel: How did it go??? Updates please!!

A burst of shivers scatter across my skin. The box with my squashed feelings and Agustín's smile rattles in the back of my mind. I don't want to tell Rachel I failed her, not yet. So I give a tiny white lie instead.

Me: Got interrupted by Alexis at Safe Haven. I've got a new Pack member.

Rachel: What!!! Omg, pics please! What breed? Backstory? Scale of cuteness? No, that's silly, they're all 11/10.

I find myself smiling for the first time this evening.

Me: Chihuahua. Lots of trauma. Hates people.
Rachel: Just like you! A match made in heaven.
Me: He's in the decompression room now, I'll try and get a photo.

As I unearth myself from beneath the Colonel and head toward the decompression room, my phone buzzes again. I assume it's Rachel but when I see the text from an unfamiliar number, my stomach falls into my butt and the room starts to spin.

Holaaaaaaa, Eloise! It's Agustín. Just wanted to make sure you got home okay. I had a great evening. We should do it again sometime!

I start to panic. How did he get my number? Then I remember Rachel put us on that damn group thread. I read the text again, my pulse stuck in my throat.

We should do it again sometime. I stare at those six familiar words, my brain completely unable to comprehend them in that order. Was he somehow not on the same date that I was? Did he miss the fact that I couldn't speak, or shake his hand, or drink wine like a normal person?

This must be an accident. Or maybe he's fucking with me. There's no way anyone would ever want to see me again after that performance. I literally fled the premises.

I'll just ignore him, and he'll go away. I bet he'll wake up tomorrow relieved that I didn't respond.

Besides, I have a new Pack member to worry about.

10
Agustín

Me: Holaaaaa Eloise! It's Agustín. Again. Just checking in! Wanted to see if you'd like to meet up. I hear there's a free concert in Central Park this weekend. Lmk!

I hit send, feeling like an idiot. This is the third time I've texted her since our date last weekend, all with no response. I take a bite of my hot dog—the most heroically disgusting yet addictive New York street food—and turn my attention back to the neighborhood block party I'm covering for *The Brooklyn Daily News*. It's Memorial Day Weekend, which Eva and Nico have informed me is the unofficial start of summer in the city. Paulina, the photographer at *BDN*, is taking some shots of a few kids squealing as they run through the stream of water coming from a nearby fire hydrant. An enormous grill is set up, wisps of smoke and the scent of roasting meat wafting down the street toward a huge, inflatable bouncy house.

People sit on stoops of brownstones, sipping from red plastic cups, or line up to get burgers, hot dogs, and chicken from the middle-aged Black man holding court over the food with a pair of tongs, in a red apron that reads *King of the Grill.*

When I asked Nico what Memorial Day was about, he shrugged and said it was an excuse to go to the Hamptons. Eva invited me, but I've got to work. Covering this block party, for one. And trying to get another date with Eloise. For all I know, she's already chosen someone else from the plus-one list. I tried to search Eloise out on social media, to learn more about her, maybe get some clue as to what I might have done wrong on the date, but she has zero presence. And I mean zero. Fully off the grid.

My phone starts to ring with a FaceTime call. It's Lupe. I steel myself for another argument about Abuelo. But when I answer, it's my twelve-year-old niece Sofia's face that I see.

"Sofia!" I say.

"Hola, Tío Tín!" she says, smiling. "Cómo estás?"

"Bien, y tú?" I ask.

"Mom won't let me bring a friend to Mama Rosita's birthday party," she says, rolling her eyes. "Can you talk to her? She acts like I'm still a baby!"

"I don't know, Sof," I say. "Your mom isn't my biggest fan right now."

"Because you're writing that article about Bisabuelo?"

"Yeah," I say.

"That's dumb. I think you should write about it. Men get away with whatever they want. We need to hold them accountable. Fuck the patriarchy."

"Whoa!" I say. "Love the sentiment but watch the language, niña. Where did you learn that expression?"

She grins. "Tía Caro taught it to me."

Well, that tracks.

"Where are you?" she asks.

"It's a holiday in the US this weekend," I say. "I'm at a big street party. Like a barbecue. Mira."

I switch the view on my phone and show her the kids running around the fire hydrant.

"Cool," she says, as I switch back.

"Where are the rest of the Minions?" I ask.

Sofia giggles, and then I hear her calling to her sisters. Suddenly, the phone tilts and sways as three other faces squish next to Sofia: nine-year-old Veronica, and the six-year-old twins, Camila and Elena.

There are choruses of, "Tío Tín!" and Vero whines, "Stop shoving, Elena."

"Hola, Minions!" I say.

"Tío Tín, will you bring us presents from New York when you come back to visit?" Camila asks.

"Claro que si!" I say. "Are you girls being nice to your mom and dad?"

Vero huffs. She looks the most like Lupe, with her long nose and deep-set eyes. "Mom is making us wear matching outfits to Mama Rosita's birthday party."

That's what the Minions call Abuelita. My mom is Abuela to them, or Abu. My chest pinches at the thought of missing my abuelita's birthday this year. Birthdays are huge in my family. As are holidays. Any excuse to celebrate with family, really. And cook. I really miss my mom's cooking.

"Tío Tín is it true that New York is dangerous?" Elena asks shyly. "I heard Mamá talking about it to Abuela."

"No," I reassure her. "It's totally safe here."

To disprove my point, someone sets off firecrackers in the middle of the street. The girls start shrieking.

"It's okay!" I say. Oh god, the last thing I need is them telling Lupe about this. "It's just firecrackers. See?"

I show them the street.

"Bouncy house!" Camila shouts.

"Yeah, there's a big party here," I say. "Listen girls, I've got to get back to work. Besitos en tus frentes!"

"Besitos," they say.

Sofia's face fills the screen. "Don't worry, Tío," she says confidently. "Mamá will get over it. I think she just misses you. You always know how to make everyone feel better."

"Thanks, Sof," I say. "That means a lot."

"Don't give up," she says. "Y chingue a su madre El Patriarcado!"

Caro is really going to have to answer for that one.

I hang up and her words ring in my ear.

Don't give up. You always know how to make everyone feel better.

Maybe I've been looking at this plus-one list situation the wrong way. Eva doesn't know anything about Eloise, and I don't feel comfortable approaching Diego—that could backfire and neither Eva nor Nico has offered an introduction. But I have the bride's number. Rachel Lazcari.

I send her a quick text.

Me: Hi Rachel! This is Agustín Martinez—I met Eloise the other day. If I'm overstepping, I'll back off, but I enjoyed our date, and I'd like to see her again. Not sure if you had any advice. Thanks!

I sigh. That's the best I can do. Unless I want to blow up my credit card and book a flight to Beijing. I'm about to put my phone in my pocket when it buzzes with a new text. My pulse kicks up as I see it's from Rachel.

Rachel: Hey Agustín! Thanks for reaching out. I'm so pleased to hear you'd like to see her again. You probably noticed Eloise is a little shy.

My spirits lift. Shyness! That makes sense. Why didn't I think of that?

Me: I did! I've been reaching out for another date but she hasn't texted me back.

There's a pause. I see three dots appear, then vanish, then reappear.

Rachel: You've been texting her?
Me: Yes. I didn't want to be creepy, but I wanted to see her again. I just reached out again today, but no response yet.

Another pause. I get the feeling something significant is happening on Rachel's end. My journalistic instincts are buzzing.

Rachel: I haven't heard from her at all today. She's not answering any of my calls or texts. Which is very unusual. To be honest I'm a little worried.

My response is immediate and has nothing to do with going to the wedding.

Me: How can I help?
Rachel: Seriously? You want to help a woman you barely know?
Me: Of course.

Helping people is what I do.

There's a longer pause.

Rachel: Do you promise you're not an ax murderer?

I laugh.

Me: I promise. I get faint at the sight of blood. And I don't even know where I would find an ax in the city. You can ask Eva or Nico Garcia for my references—they know Diego. Eva put me on the plus-one list.

Though to be honest, I don't think Eva and Nico are that close with Diego.

Me: I know them from my neighborhood. We all live in Bushwick.

Rachel: Trust fund kids?

I chuckle.

Me: Correct. Not me, though.
Me: I mean, I have a job.
Me: And I live in a studio apartment with only one functioning sink.

My landlady is a very intimidating Ukrainian woman who seems to always be promising repairs that never materialize.

Rachel: Lol.

I feel hope bloom in my chest.

Rachel: Listen, I would NEVER normally do this but . . . would you be willing to go to her apartment and check on her? I'd go myself but I'm stuck in New Jersey. And there's no one else I can ask. I've even tried calling the doorman but no one is answering the phone.
Me: I'd be happy to! And I can share my location with you so you can track me if you'd like. So you'll know I've left after I've made sure Eloise is okay.
Rachel: That would be great, actually.

She sends me an address in Manhattan, on Central Park West. Which seems quite expensive. Eloise didn't strike me as a Nico/Eva type.

Me: I'll head over there now.

I send her my location info, setting it to share for three hours. Then I weave through the crowd to find Paulina.

"I've got to run," I tell her. "Family emergency."

11
Eloise

Not to be dramatic but . . . death has come for me.

In the form of food poisoning, I think. I'm never getting chicken vindaloo ever again.

Or maybe it's some horrible virus that's gripped me in its clutches and won't let go. Or maybe I've been poisoned, Agatha Christie style. Just when I think there's nothing left inside me to vomit, my stomach lurches, and all the progress I've made trying to get into bed is ruined as I have to crawl back to the bathroom. I've set up shop here, resting my cheek on a towel pulled down from the rack, my back pressed against the cool porcelain tub. My skin is clammy and prickles with fever. My throat is parched, my muscles ache, and there's a constant, dull pounding in my head.

The dogs are worried. Hazel is pacing back and forth between the bathroom and the living room. I think Charleston has pooped on the floor somewhere, but I can't leave the bathroom long enough to clean it. The Colonel has been sitting in the doorway watching me, his head on his paws, his deep brown eyes full of concern. Thank god I gave him his insulin this morning, before this thing really took hold.

I have no idea where Pip is—that's what I've renamed Picante, after the character from *Great Expectations*. My guess is he's in the decompression room, where he's been pretty much all week.

He's having a lot of trouble adapting. Not with the Pack—after the first day, Hazelnut immediately pushed her way into the room and asserted herself as the Boss. To my surprise and delight, Pip seems to enjoy being bossed around by her. She even lets him share the giant dog bed with her sometimes, on the handful of occasions he's come out into the living room. And Charleston and the Colonel are both so amenable, that Pip has fit right into the dynamic. Hazel rules the roost, and everyone else falls in line.

But he won't let me come near him, and he still spends most of his time in the decompression room. Every time I try to pet him, or put on a harness, or offer him a treat, he snarls and snaps at me, or runs and hides. He's even bitten my hand a couple times. I've been nipped by a scared or anxious dog before, but still. Usually after the first few days, the dog warms up to me. The rule of threes and all that: three days, three weeks, three months. But we're at week one and there's been no real change in his attitude toward me. It hurts that this poor animal was so betrayed by humans. I can't imagine what he's been through.

But you don't rescue seniors without having a high level of patience.

And I'm glad the Pack has taken to him and vice versa. That's the most important thing. But I want to get him out of the house and on walks, and I can't do that if he won't let me get near him.

So being on my deathbed right now is more inconvenient than usual.

I need water so badly. But I think I'll only throw it back up.

Tears prick my eyes. Haven't I suffered enough this week? I totally ruined any chance of finding a date for the wedding, I humiliated myself in front of Agustín, and the worst part is, he won't stop texting me! I just don't get it. Why does he keep asking me out? Is this some sort of prank? No one in their right mind would want a second date after the way I behaved.

No, the real worst part is, I *want* to say yes. Despite all my efforts to keep the Agustín Feelings Box closed, I think about him all the time. Those dimples. That hot-chocolate smile. The way he smelled when he leaned in close to me, warm and spicy, like cardamon and leather. He's lodged in my mind, fluttering in the pit of my stomach, a constant pulse next to my own.

I cannot see that man ever again because if I do it's going to become an *If You Give a Mouse a Cookie* type situation and that is the last thing I need. He doesn't know what he'd be getting into anyway. I'm a joke. A total mess. I have my dogs, and that's all I'm cut out for. Romance is one thousand percent off the table for me.

I feel another wave of nausea and scramble into a sitting position just in time to vomit again. I slump back onto the floor, my head throbbing, my skin burning, and wish I had someone to call for help. Miriam is clearly the best (and closest) option. But I can barely make it to my own bedroom, much less down the hall. I don't know where I left my phone, but Rachel is in Jersey all day, making sure everything is ready for the launch. I don't want to bother her.

I'll just die here quietly. I hear a whine as Hazelnut pushes past the Colonel. She licks some of the sweat off my face. I hate that the Pack is so stressed out. They should be going on their walk now. There's gonna be so much pee in this house.

The Colonel lifts his head, and the next second, I hear the doorbell ring. My heart lifts. Maybe it's Miriam, coming to gossip. I've never been so grateful for her nosiness.

I sit up and the bathroom spins. I take a few deep fortifying breaths. I try to stand, but I'm too dizzy, so I resort to crawling. I can do this. I crawl past the enormous poop Charleston left on the living room rug, and down the hall, past the kitchen. My arms are shaking as I reach the door just as the bell rings again.

I'm coming, Miriam.

I reach up and turn the knob, barely managing to crack the door open before slumping back against the wall, my head spinning, the nausea resurfacing.

"Oh my god," a voice says from above me. "Are you okay?"

Several things click together at once. This is not Miriam's voice. But it *is* a voice I recognize. A voice that has been haunting me for a week.

I look up into Agustín Martinez's wide, kind face, and for a moment I wonder if I'm hallucinating.

He pushes the door open and kneels down in front of me.

"Eloise? Eloise. Are you all right?"

He touches me gently, pressing the back of his hand against my forehead. So he's real.

I want to say something—*why are you here* and *how did you get my address* come to mind—but I'm pretty sure if I open my mouth, I'll throw up on him.

"You're burning up," he says.

I shake my head. *Go away!* I want to shout. But the movement makes my stomach lurch. I clap my hand over my mouth. It's like I can feel my skin turning green.

"Hold on," Agustín says, and then he disappears into my kitchen.

He's in my house. Oh my god, *he's in my house*! The Wheel just spins hopelessly, my anxiety nameless because there is no pie slice for this kind of situation. Not even *AHHHHHHH!* covers it. Then he's back with a trash can, lined with a fresh bag, and he hands it to me just in time for me to retch into it.

If only the earth would open up and swallow me whole. I can think of nothing more mortifying than this—plus there's no way my house doesn't smell like dog pee and poop. Agustín crouches down next to me again, seemingly unperturbed by the vomit. He touches my forehead again, and the feel of his hand leaves faint sparkles along my hairline.

"I'm going to help you to bed," he says. "You need rest. And medicine. Do you have anything? Pepto Bismol or Advil or . . ."

He snatches the trash can and puts it in front of me just as my stomach gives another lurch, and I vomit again. He has excellent reflexes. At least there's nothing much coming up anymore. But still.

I need Miriam. Miriam can help.

"I . . . need . . ." But that's as far as I can get without retching.

"Okay, I will help you up," he says. He glances down the hall. "Oh," he says, his face brightening. "You have dogs!"

I manage to turn my head and see the Colonel and Hazelnut watching him suspiciously. Just then, Charleston barrels down the hallway and runs right into Agustín's thigh. He chuckles and scratches his ear.

"Hey there," he says softly.

"Who . . . told . . ." I croak.

"Rachel sent me," he says.

Rachel did this? I feel a flash of betrayal but then it occurs to me that I haven't talked to her all day and that's extremely unusual for us. She was probably so worried.

"Up you go," Agustín says and before I can protest, he's slid one arm around my back, then another under my knees and suddenly, I'm airborne. He cradles me against his chest, his cardamom-leather scent surrounding me, and in any normal situation I would be panicking but right now it just feels so . . . good. Safe. I don't even have the energy to be ashamed that he's seeing me in a sweat-dampened Aimee Mann tee and terrycloth sleep shorts. I just want to close my eyes and live in his arms forever.

I feel a waft of cool air as Agustín nudges open the door to my bedroom with his foot. Then he lays me down on the bed, gently rolling me onto my side. He vanishes and reappears with the trash can in one hand and a glass of water in the other. He sets the can beneath me on the floor and the water on my nightstand.

"I didn't see anything in your medicine cabinet," he admits. "It looks like it's all for dogs."

Yeah. I tend to forget to buy things for my own needs. And I haven't been sick in ages. But Miriam has stuff.

"My neighbor . . ." I croak.

My lips feel cracked, my tongue swollen. I blink, my eyelids heavy. My bed has never felt so soft or so comfortable. I see Agustín's face, creased with concern next to mine. His coffee-colored eyes are like deep pools, the softest, warmest brown. I bet I smell terrible.

"Your neighbor can help?" he asks.

I manage a nod before my eyes close and I drift into unconsciousness.

12
Agustín

I'm really glad I texted Rachel.

Eloise has some kind of awful stomach virus, I'd guess. I've taken care of the Minions during all sorts of illnesses, so I've seen this type of thing before. I spring into action. First, I wet a hand towel with cool water and lay it over her forehead. I need to get her fever down, and some water into her.

I'll have to find this neighbor. I don't know if Eloise has any health conditions or allergies, but she needs medicine.

I send a text to Rachel that Eloise is very sick, but not to worry, I'm going to help. I ask her about medications or allergies and promise to keep her updated. Then I head out into the living room. Eloise's apartment is enormous. I wonder again how she affords it. The corner windows look out over Central Park, and the interior is beautifully designed, with an eclectic mix of furniture, lots of bookshelves, and plants everywhere. It feels almost like a mix between an eccentric aunt's parlor and a conservatory. There's a giant dog poop on the rug—I grab it with a piece of toilet paper and flush it, before laying a pee pad I found under the sink over the stain. There are a few puddles of pee, and I cover those with pads too. I'll clean more thoroughly when I've gotten Eloise taken care of. At least for now, none of the dogs will step in them.

I leave Eloise's apartment door on the latch and step out into the hall. She didn't specify which neighbor. I start with 9F. Old French music comes muted through the door, strains of "Non, je ne regrette rien." I knock. I hear a shuffling sound, then the door creaks open. A woman in her late sixties, with fantastically coiffed hair and red lipstick, peers up at me. She's elegantly dressed in a long-sleeved black blouse, a knee-length black skirt, and black heels.

"Can I help you?" she asks in a French accent.

"Hi, my name is Agustín Martinez, I'm a friend of Eloise's," I begin.

The woman wrinkles her nose. "Who?"

"Um, the woman who lives in 9G."

"Ah, ze girl with ze dogs."

"Yeah, that's her," I say. "She's really sick and said you could help."

"Me?" the woman says, her eyes widening in surprise. "I am not sure what I can do. Sick how, you mean?"

"Pretty much every way," I admit. "Fever, nausea, vomiting . . ."

The woman shudders delicately. "I do not need details, merci." She glances over my shoulder at Eloise's door. "She asks for my help? One moment please."

She shuts the door and then returns a few seconds later, handing me a small mason jar filled with teabags. "These are a special mix. I make them myself. They will settle the stomach."

"Oh," I say. Not exactly what I was looking for, but it's pretty cool that French Lady makes her own tea. Also, maybe I've got the wrong neighbor. "Well, thank you."

"Her name is Eloise, you say?"

"Yeah, that's right."

"You tell her Madame Boularès wishes her well."

"I'll do that," I say, as the door shuts in my face.

I try the next door, 9E. A sporty blonde with impressive biceps wearing yoga pants and a sports bra answers.

"Hi," I say. "My name is Agustín Martinez—"

"Sorry, not interested," she says, starting to close the door.

"Wait, no, I'm a friend of Eloise," I say.

She frowns. "Who?"

Does Eloise not know her neighbors? I've lived here only five months, and I can tell you everything about the people in my building. Though now that I think of it, maybe that's because I love asking questions.

"The girl with the dogs?" I say.

"Oh! That's her name?"

"Yes, and she's very ill, I think some kind of stomach bug, and I was wondering if you could help, or knew if she has any allergies or . . ." I trail off. I do not sound like a very close friend, asking these questions.

"Sanvi!" the woman shouts. "Do we still have those supplements for nausea?" She turns back to me. "I'm Kate, by the way. My wife and I sell our own line of supplements. Herbal Pride. Do you work out? We've got some great protein powders."

"Oh, um, no," I say as a tall Indian woman comes into view.

"This guy is the dog-girl's boyfriend," Kate says.

"No, I'm—"

"Oh my god, so cute! I've literally never seen her with anyone except that hot chick with the amazing hair." She hands me a bottle of supplements emblazoned with a rainbow label. "If her stomach is upset, these should help. Did Kate tell you about our line of protein—"

"Thank you so much!" I say, hurrying away before they can try to sell me anything else.

9D has the distinct scent of weed surrounding it. I knock, and even though I can hear the sounds of a video game coming from inside, no one answers. I move on to 9C.

The door opens and a middle-aged, Latina woman answers. "Can I help you?" she asks in heavily accented English.

"Hola," I say, switching to Spanish. "My friend Eloise lives down the hall and needs help with—"

"On moment please," the woman replies in Spanish. She's Colombian—I can tell from her accent—and she disappears into the apartment. I hear her talking to someone in the kitchen in English. Then a white woman with a brunette bob wearing a blue striped blouse and pearls comes to the door.

"Hi," she says. "Sorry, you must have the wrong apartment, I didn't order delivery."

I grimace and plow ahead. "My name is Agustín Martinez, I'm a friend of Eloise's from 9G."

"Oh, the girl with the dogs!" the woman cries. "Hi, I'm Gretchen." There's a wail from down the hall of, "Mommy, I want TV time!" Gretchen turns and shouts, "Begonia, I told you, finish your smoked salmon and then you can watch more *Bluey*!" I don't even know where to begin processing a sentence like that. Gretchen turns back to me. "Sorry, you were saying?"

"Eloise is very sick and—"

But just then, the Colombian woman appears with a baby in her arms.

"Oh, thank you, Paloma," Gretchen says. "Is it time for little Mansion's nappy-nap? Yes, it is. Yes, it is. Isn't that right, Mansion?" She kisses the baby on the forehead as he squirms in Paloma's arms. I wonder if I need to get my hearing checked or if Gretchen actually named her children Begonia and Mansion. "So, the girl with the dogs is sick? Paloma, can you get this gentleman some Tylenol? Or do we only have children's? I keep forgetting to put it on the grocery list. Baby brain," she says to me with an indulgent smile.

I do not want to burden Paloma with any more responsibilities as she wrangles a struggling Mansion.

"It's fine," I say, backing away. "Thank you!"

Gretchen closes the door just as the one next to hers, 9B, creaks open. A man in his seventies, with thinning gray hair, wearing a plaid shirt under a sweater vest, pokes his head out.

"You want Miriam," he says to me.

"Sorry?" I ask.

He jerks his head toward the door opposite him. "Miriam, in 9A. She's a nurse. She's the only one who really knows the girl with the dogs."

"Eloise," I correct him. He shrugs, then vanishes back into his apartment.

I knock on 9A.

"Coming!" a voice calls from inside, then the door is thrown open. A Black woman wearing pink scrubs and holding a mug of coffee eyes me up and down. "How can I help you, honey?"

"Do you know Eloise?" I ask, desperate.

She perks up. "Yes. Who are you?"

"I'm Agustín, I'm her friend," I say.

"Ha. No dice. Eloise has only one friend besides me."

"Rachel?"

Miriam raises an eyebrow. "Okay, maybe you are her friend." Then she snaps her fingers. "The mascara! It was for *you*!"

I have no idea what she's talking about. "Please," I say. "Eloise is very sick. She only has medicine for dogs. I got . . ." I hold up the jar of tea and the supplements by way of explanation. "But I think she needs real medicine, and I don't know if she has any allergies or—"

"Let me grab my bag," Miriam says, cutting me off. She vanishes and reappears with a small backpack. I follow her to Eloise's apartment, where the dogs seem happy to see her. "Where's the other one?" she asks me.

"What other one?"

"The new member of the Pack. I think it's a chihuahua. Haven't seen him yet."

I count a German shepherd, a dachshund, and a pug.

"Oh dear, Charleston doesn't have his diaper on," she tuts, as the pug plows into her. She glances at the scattering of pee pads on the floor. "This was his work, I assume?"

I didn't stop to ponder whose poop it was before I flushed it. Miriam disappears into Eloise's bedroom. I hear her talking to Eloise softly. I decide to take action and begin Operation Pee and Poop Cleanup. The shepherd and the dachshund have followed Mirian into the bedroom, while the pug licks the living room wall. I grab supplies from under the bathroom sink—Eloise has just about every type of cleaner, brush, and sponge anyone could need. There's one for rugs, with an attachment for cleaning. There's a spray for the hardwood floors, and some disinfectant. I grab a roll of paper towels from the kitchen and get to work on the rug first. The pug seems to realize his buddies have left him, and he trundles into Eloise's bedroom to join them, bumping into the doorframe on his way.

As I move on to the pee puddles, I hear the tippy tap of little feet and turn to see a black and tan chihuahua, shivering in the doorway of another room.

"Hola. You must be the new arrival," I say to him gently in Spanish.

He sniffs in my direction, and I hold out my hand.

"Está bien," I say. "I'm a friend."

He inches forward, still sniffing. I stay completely still, until his little black nose touches my knuckles. Then he skitters back a few steps. "Don't be scared," I tell him. I think he likes the sound of my voice, or maybe it's just the Spanish, but he walks forward when I talk. So I keep talking. "What a handsome little guy you are. Want a treat? I bet your mom has treats somewhere around here. Come on."

I get up and head to the kitchen. There's a white ceramic jar that says *Paws Off* in black lettering. I open it and hit the jackpot. There are treats in various shapes and sizes, and they all look fresh, like they're homemade, not stale ones from a store.

"Here you go," I say, breaking a biscuit that smells like maple syrup and bacon in half and leaning down to offer it to the dog. He creeps toward me, then grabs the treat and runs back down the hall and into the second room.

It's about half an hour later when Miriam comes out of Eloise's bedroom.

"Fever of one-oh-two, and poor thing can't keep anything down," Miriam says. "I gave her an IV to replenish her fluids, but Tylenol would help break the fever. Can't take that on an empty stomach though. You can stay and watch her, right? Make sure she eats something, get her to take the pills? I would stay but I've got to get to work."

"Oh, uh—" I hadn't thought much past the arriving here stage.

"Great," she says. "The Pack is easy to handle for the most part. Charleston is mostly blind and a bit deaf, so don't worry if he walks into the walls from time to time. He needs a diaper when he's inside though. She told me the Colonel already got his shot today, so you don't need to worry about that. Hazelnut is . . ." Miriam sighs and shakes her head. "That girl will do whatever she damn well pleases, and it's best you just go along with it. The leashes and harnesses are by the door, food's in the kitchen. If you see the chihuahua, don't worry about him, Eloise says he's a tough nut to crack." She suddenly scoops me up in an embrace. "I'm so glad she found someone. She's really special. Biggest heart of anyone I've ever met. Always takes the hard cases, dogs nobody else wants. No human has ever gotten past those walls she keeps up, though."

I find myself a little speechless. I am definitely never telling Miriam that Eloise and I met via a plus-one list.

"I'll be back this evening, if you need anything," she says. "I've left Tylenol and Pepto, but see if she has any broth or saltines. She's going to be hungry when she wakes up. Once she eats, she can take the meds. And keep changing that compress." She winks. "You're a smart cookie, aren't you?"

"I've got four nieces," I explain.

She laughs. It's a nice, big loud laugh that fills the space. "I like you," she says.

She bustles past me and out the door. I check my phone—still no word from Rachel. I text her to explain that the situation is under control, and Miriam the neighbor helped and that I'm staying longer to watch Eloise so don't be alarmed if my location still shows me at her apartment. I'm not about to leave Eloise on her own. I creep toward the open bedroom door. Eloise is sleeping peacefully on her side, her mouth slightly open, one curl sticking to her temple. Her fingers are clutched around a sheet that's tangled between her legs. I'm struck again by the delicateness of her—the slender curve of her wrist, the tiny arches of her feet.

I hear a whine, and the German shepherd pads over to me. He looks out the door and back up at me with wise, soulful eyes.

"Is it time for your walk?" I ask.

At the word *walk*, the shepherd barks and then the dachshund comes careening around from the other side of Eloise's bed, followed closely by the black pug. The dachshund jumps on my leg and paws at me, while the pug yips excitedly.

I can't help but smile—these dogs are quite a group of characters. I like them a lot.

"Okay, come on," I say, mirroring their enthusiasm.

I walk into the living room and down the hall, the dogs eagerly chasing my heels. There are leashes hung on name-tagged pegs by front door, attached to various sized harnesses. *Charleston, the Colonel,* and *Hazelnut*. There's another smaller harness for *Pip*. That must be the chihuahua. He's still hiding in the second room, and I think I have my hands full as is.

I've never walked three dogs before. But they've all lined up dutifully, like they know the drill. Well, except Charleston, who is facing the wrong direction.

I take the first harness labeled *Hazelnut* off the wall. "Let's go," I say to them.

13
Eloise

I have the most vividly disturbing dreams.

In one, Pip has grown to the size of a dragon, and he sprouts wings, and breathes fire at me when I try to put his leash on. In another, I'm walking down the aisle at Rachel's wedding, and everyone is whispering and pointing at me, and when I get to the altar, I realize I'm wearing a bathrobe and slippers, and the guests all start to laugh, louder and louder, and Rachel yells at me for ruining her wedding. The most vivid, though, and the most disturbing, are the dreams about Agustín. When he comes into my room and talks to me softly, or lays something cool against my forehead. Sometimes, those dreams come with the clicking of little doggy nails against the hardwood floors. They feel so real. But the blackness always pulls me back under.

When I finally peel my eyes open, I can tell from the pale light creeping in under my curtains that it's early morning. I don't remember closing the curtains last night. My skin is still clammy, but much cooler, and my head isn't throbbing so badly anymore. I notice a glass of water perched on my nightstand, and there's a trash can on the floor next to the bed.

Oh fuck. Those weren't dreams.

I remember now. Agustín carrying me into bed. The cool touch of his hand on my feverish skin. The shape of his arms around me. Oh no. No, no, no. This can't be happening. He cannot have seen me at my sticky, raggedy-T-shirt-wearing, vomiting-in-a-trash-can worst. Maybe it really was a hallucination brought on by the fever. Please, god, let me have been hallucinating.

But then I remember—Miriam came. She gave me an IV. There's Tylenol and Pepto on the nightstand. How did she know?

I slowly push myself up into a sitting position. No nausea, so that's good. I'm desperately thirsty. I grab the glass of water and take a swallow. Then another one. No need to push it. The trash can is empty, so someone must have swapped out the bag. Probably Miriam. Or maybe Rachel came to check on me. Another memory resurfaces—Rachel sent Agustín here. We are going to have *words* about that. How did it even happen, anyway? She knows how private I am. I don't like anyone in my space. My stomach lurches but not in the nauseous way.

I glance at my bedroom door. It's closed. Where's the Pack? I climb out of bed on trembling feet and pad out into the living room.

My knees lock and my heart leaps to my throat.

Agustín is here. On the couch.

Agustín is *still here.*

He's asleep, sprawled out in a heather gray T-shirt and jeans, his feet hanging off the edge of the couch, clad in socks with green and blue stars on them. The Colonel and Hazelnut are snoozing in the big dog bed. Charleston is nestled in the crook between Agustín's calves. He's wearing a diaper. Did Agustín put a diaper on my pug?

But that's not the most shocking thing I see.

Pip is sleeping peacefully in Agustín's arms, curled up in a little ball on his chest.

I feel another lurch, this one a confusing mix of jealousy, attraction, and exhaustion. Agustín's hair is messy and his shirt rumpled, his face relaxed in sleep, his dimples playing hide-and-seek. I try and fail not to trace the lines of his arms, smooth olive skin over subtle musculature. One broad hand curves around Pip's tiny body in a protective embrace.

Panic creeps up the back of my throat. He can't be here. I can't . . . I can't be seen like this. I'm overexposed, like a badly developed Polaroid. Like my bones are visible through my skin.

Rachel. I need Rachel. Where's my phone?

I tiptoe around, feeling like an intruder in my own house. This is why I don't have people over! This is *my* safe space, the one place I can be myself. And he's barged into it like a . . . a . . . a beautiful Mexican battering ram.

I finally find my phone perched behind the Boston fern on the coffee table. Slowly, I lean forward and stretch out my hand.

Pip's eyes flash open. Oh, shit.

He growls and lunges toward me, causing Agustín to wake up with a startled yelp as Charleston topples off the couch and rolls across the floor. Hazelnut immediately starts barking, which makes the Colonel start barking, just as Pip leaps onto the coffee table, knocks over the plant, jumps onto the floor, bites my foot, then scampers into the decompression room.

"Ow," I cry, though at least Pip didn't break the skin this time. Agustín blinks around at the noise.

"What . . . Eloise . . . hi! You're awake!" he says enthusiastically, his dimples popping as he smiles at me.

I am suddenly, deeply aware of the fact that I'm not wearing a bra.

"How are you feeling?" he asks, standing and trying to smooth down his hair, which only makes it more ruffled and infuriatingly adorable. "Can I get you anything?"

That's it. I've hit my limit.

"What are you *doing here*?" I shout, not caring if I'm being weird. "You aren't supposed to—this is my home, how did you—Rachel should never have . . ." I trail off, pressing the heels of my hands into my eyes. Stupid tears slip from under my lids. I don't know why I seem to cry at any and every emotion. "I'm tired and I'm hungry and I stink and I don't know you," I continue. "And I don't like people in my space and the Pack—" My head whips up as I remember what I just saw. "How did you do it?" I demand. "How did you get Pip to sleep on you like that? Tell me!"

I step forward, pointing a finger at him, my eyes wild, fully aware I must look like a crazy person. Agustín opens his mouth then closes it. He seems to consider for a moment.

"He likes Spanish," he says simply.

I blink. "Huh?"

"Pip. I think he likes hearing Spanish. It's . . . I don't know, it calms him. So I was talking to him a lot yesterday."

Charleston has started licking my leg. I glance down at him and my throat tightens. "Did you put him in a diaper?"

Agustín nods. "There was poop, you see. And pee. Miriam said he needs diapers. I found them in the bathroom. You are very good at organizing."

I force myself to repress the image of Agustín poking around under my bathroom sink, among my tampons and home waxing kit.

"I didn't know about the medicines, though," he admits. "Is one of the dogs, um, how do you say it . . . diabetic?"

"Yeah," I say, my anger quickly deflating. "The Colonel."

Agustín chuckles. It's a low, pleasant sound that resonates in my own chest. "I like their names. Can you explain me—sorry, explain *to* me how you came up with them?"

"The Colonel is a character from *101 Dalmatians*." The reason seems to fall out of my mouth on its own accord.

His warm eyes brighten and somehow his smile gets even wider. "Ah! *La Noche de las Narices Frias*!"

"Huh?"

"That's what it's called in Mexico. The Night of the Frozen Noses. My nieces love that movie."

All the fight goes out of me, and I feel myself sag. I'm too confused and tired to argue with him anymore.

"How about this," Agustín says quietly. "You take a shower, and I'll heat some broth and make tea. I got saltines too. Miriam's orders. And then, if you still want me to leave, I'll leave. Deal?"

I nod because honestly, broth sounds amazing. And I can feel the fever sweat still clinging to my skin and my mouth tastes awful. I really, really, *really* want a shower. And a minute alone.

Charleston follows me into the bathroom and curls up on the bathmat as I strip off my clothes and turn on the shower. It is very weird to be naked in my apartment with a man here. I can't remember the last time that happened. Probably not since college, which is its own depressing sort of thought. I push it away and step under the hot flow of water, determined to have the fastest shower in the history of ever. But once I let the steam relax my muscles, I find I don't want to get out. It feels achingly good. For one moment, my anxiety doesn't pulse in my ears or pound in my chest. I can pretend Agustín isn't here. Just the sound of water and Charleston's occasional snorts. When I finally pull back the curtain, I wrap a towel around me and step out of the tub, and Charleston goes back to licking my leg. He loves being in the bathroom when I shower. I wrap another towel around my hair and brush my teeth. Twice.

The Wheel starts spinning now that I've lost the soothing thrum of hot water. I stare at the back of the bathroom door, fingertips tingling, my skin tight. Agustín is out there.

I crack the door and peer out. I wait. I can hear him in the kitchen, the sound of the faucet turning on and off, of mugs clinking. He's humming some song I don't recognize. The sound sends prickles across my thighs. In a panicked flash, I dart across the hall into my bedroom and slam the door. I sink onto my bed, adrenaline making me dizzy. My heart has swollen to twice its normal size and careens against my ribcage. I really need some food. I get up and open my closet door, staring into it blankly. I have no idea what to wear, and my stomach is making horrible growling sounds. I rub my eyes and remind myself I'm not trying to impress Agustín. I'm trying to get him out of my house. I just need a bra.

I end up choosing a black tank top over a soft cotton sports bra and a pair of rainbow-patterned sweatpants. I'm still feeling weirdly hot and cold at the same time, though I can tell the fever is pretty much gone. I grab the bottle of Tylenol then creep out into the living room. I don't know why I'm still creeping around. He knows I'm here. He's literally making me tea. The Colonel gets to his feet and pads over to greet me. As soon as I sink my fingers into his soft, thick fur, I relax a fraction. He whines and licks my wrist.

"They were worried about you."

I jump. Agustín stands in the middle of the hall, a steaming mug of tea in each hand. He walks forward and sets them on the coffee table, on the funky vintage coasters I got on a trip upstate to Beacon with Rachel.

The man uses coasters.

"Madame Boularès gave me this tea," he says. "I haven't tried it yet. But it smells very good."

I rub my ear. "Sorry, did you say Madame Bou—like my neighbor? The French woman?"

He nods. "Please, sit," he says, gesturing to the couch. "Let me get you some crackers."

I don't love being told to sit in my own house, but my legs are still kind of shaky and the tea does smell really good. Agustín seems to have cleaned up the mess Pip made with the Boston fern. The Colonel jumps up next to me, leaning against my side as Hazel trots over. I think Charleston is still in the bathroom. Probably licking the floor.

I pick up Hazel and plop her on my other side—I do not want Agustín sitting next to me. Armed with two dogs, I grab the closest mug. It's one Rachel got for me, white with pink lettering that reads *May You Have the Confidence of a Mediocre White Man.* I take a small sip. It's *wonderful*—minty, and gingery, and slightly floral, orange blossom and a hint of lavender. Agustín comes back with the bowl of broth and a packet of saltines. My stomach growls so loud, Hazelnut side eyes me then huffs in disgust.

Agustín gives another resonant chuckle. "She has opinions, that one," he says. "You must be starving."

He grabs the other mug—with an illustration of a beagle giving two middle fingers with the words *Fetch This* under it—and plops down in Uncle Lenny's old armchair. It's one of the few things I kept of his after he died. He used to read the paper in it on uncomfortably silent Sunday mornings. It's an olive green, midcentury modern, with walnut legs and high wingbacks.

I nibble at a saltine and sip some broth. When I finish the cracker, I feel like a new woman.

Charleston wanders into the room and bumps into Agustín's leg. Agustín smiles. "Hola, gordito," he says. He seems perfectly at ease, drinking his tea and scratching Charleston under his chin. I watch him suspiciously over the top of my mug. I should tell him to leave now. He's done what he said he would.

Instead, I blurt out, "Why did you get tea from Madame Boularès?"

He seems delighted I've asked him a question. "You said a neighbor could help but you did not specify which one. So I went to all of them."

I blanch. "You talked to *all* my neighbors? What . . . what did you tell them?"

"I said I was your friend and that you were sick. I got tea and some supplements that, to be honest, I do not trust. But they're in the kitchen if you want them."

"From who?" I ask, bewildered.

"The sporty lesbian couple," he says.

"Soul Cycle gave you supplements?"

Agustín laughs. If his smile is like chocolate, his laugh is like a hot spring. Deep and clear and natural. "Is that what you call them? They call you the girl with the dogs."

"This is New York," I say. "No one knows anybody's name."

"You know Miriam," he points out.

"Yeah, well, Miriam is nosy."

"I like her," he says, his left dimple winking at me. "She cares about you very much."

I don't know what to say to that. My stomach squirms and I grab another saltine.

"You have a very nice home," he says, taking a sip of tea and looking around. "I love all of your plants."

Heat blooms in my chest. "Thank you."

"How long have you lived here?"

"Since I was two years old," I say.

He raises an eyebrow. "Really?"

I shrug and lean into the Colonel for support. Somehow, the more I talk to Agustín, the easier it gets. The words come in the right order. "I inherited it from my uncle. He raised me." I don't want to talk about my parents, or how they died, or any of the darkness of my early childhood. I hope Agustín doesn't ask. "And my uncle inherited it from my grandfather."

"Ah," Agustín says, nodding. "So it's . . . what is it called here, rent-controlled?"

I nod. I am fully aware that I hit the lottery in the housing department. But I lost big time in the family department, so I guess the universe evens things out.

Silence wraps around us, but it's not an uncomfortable one. Agustín seems completely relaxed. I don't understand it. I'm weird. I've been ignoring his texts all week. I vomited in front of him. I don't know why he's still here.

And I don't know why I haven't told him to leave yet.

I realize too that I don't know anything about him, except *short, dimples, lower class but hard worker.* The whole disastrous date is a blur in my mind. I remember he said he was from Mexico City. That's about it.

"How did you get on the plus-one list?" I ask.

He brushes a stray lock of unruly black hair out of his eyes. "Nicolas and Eva Garcia. Their family knows Diego's family. Eva put me on the list. Are you excited about the wedding?"

"No," I say automatically.

Then I clap my hand over my mouth.

14
Agustín

Somehow, this answer doesn't surprise me.

In the almost twenty-four hours I've spent in Eloise's apartment, I've noticed much about her. She's very private. She seems to love plants and dogs but not people. There are no family photos, only pictures of her and a woman I identify as Rachel, based on the wedding announcement photograph I'd seen in *Quién*. She has lots of books. Mysteries and romances seem to be her favorites, but there's some nonfiction and classics in there, as well as some books with titles like *How to Rewire an Anxious Brain*.

This is a woman who has taken in a diabetic dog, an incontinent dog, a dog who is (no offense to Hazelnut) a bit of an asshole, and a traumatized dog who bites her. I can see in the photos of her and Rachel that she adores her friend. I wonder what happened to her parents—why she was raised by her uncle, why she lives in this apartment but keeps no memories of him, or them. I sensed she did not want to talk about it when I asked about her home.

One thing I've come to learn, through talking with Miriam and texting with Rachel, is that Eloise is a very unique, very special person. The few people she lets in love her fiercely.

"I don't . . . I didn't . . ." She splutters, her face turning red, her chest heaving. Her legs tremble in her rainbow sweatpants. "You can't—didn't hear me say that."

"Of course not," I say easily. I think she does not want to be looked at when she's anxious like this, so I turn back to Charleston for a moment, who happily licks my hand. "You are the maid of honor, right?" I ask. "So, you will give a speech?"

She squeaks. I glance up at her, and she's shaking, both hands gripping her mug of tea, her lips pressed together into a thin line. I once again have the sense that there's strength lurking beneath her delicate surface. Of powerful emotions that scare her. Her sea-glass eyes are like literal windows—so clear, I can see the inner workings of her mind through them. Panic. Fear. Something deeper too. Some innate sense of predetermined failure.

"Listen," I say gently. "I can help you. I know what Mexican weddings are like. Well, I've never been to one this . . . glamorous, but I know what to expect in general. I'm very good with words—I'm a journalist. I can help you write your speech. I can tell you about all the traditions. And I'm Chilango—that's what someone from Mexico City is called. I can help you navigate the city. I know it inside and out. It's my home."

She stares at me almost helplessly for a moment. "Why?" she asks. "Why do you want to be my plus-one?"

I study her features, the high cheekbones, the little point of her chin, the hesitant curve of her lips. I feel like there must be a smile inside her so big and radiant that if she ever actually unleashed it, it could outshine the sun.

I wonder if I should just tell her the truth.

"My abuelita always says helping people is in my blood," I say. "You see . . ." I pause, trying to figure out the best way to explain about Abuelo and Ricardo and the article, but then Eloise puts down her mug on the table and straightens her shoulders. Oh boy. I can tell she's about to lay out the law. Or is it lay down the law? Ya valí madres.

"You can be my plus-one," she says. "On one condition."

"Anything," I say eagerly.

"This is a *business arrangement*," she says, stressing every syllable. "There is nothing romantic about this. It's not a date. It is a transaction. Because yeah, I could really use some help. As you've probably noticed, I'm not good in social situations. But I don't want you getting the wrong idea. I don't need any new people in my life, okay? Not friends, not boyfriends, no one. I'm good. You help me prepare for this . . ." She waves her hand, fluttering her fingers. "And then we're done. We go our separate ways after the wedding. Deal?"

"Deal," I say quickly. I should definitely tell her I've got my own reasons for wanting to go. But as I open my mouth to explain, she seems to sink in on herself, her shoulders wilting, her eyes turning impossibly sad.

"I'll probably ruin it for her," she mumbles.

I don't need to ask who *her* is. And I have a sudden instinct that this isn't the right time for my reasons—this isn't about me. She doesn't let anyone in, and I've just been given half a centimeter. Anything to upset the balance, and I'll get shut out for good.

"No, you won't," I say gently.

She sighs, and I feel a heaviness that belies her age—a deep weariness, like she's been carrying some ancient weight around for so long, she's forgotten what it's like to live without it. It's a weight that has soldered itself to her bones.

"I need to give the Colonel his shot," she says, yawning. "Then I need to sleep. No, shit, I need to walk the dogs."

"I'll walk the dogs," I say. "I've already done it a couple of times. Pip really likes being in the park."

Strong emotions spasm across her face—something like grief and shock mixed together. "You walked him?" she gasps. "You walked them all?"

"It was intimidating at first," I admit. "But they seem to know what they are doing. They have a routine."

She nods, dazed, then puts her mug down. "Yeah," she says. "They do. I . . ." Her voice trails off, then she rubs her temple. She glances toward the second room, where Pip is still hiding. "Okay," she says quietly.

Okay.

I grip the word like a token.

I can tell Eloise about Ricardo later.

For now, I'm officially her plus-one. And I have some dogs to walk.

"And how exactly does this prepare me for the wedding?" Eloise asks, standing outside the door to 9F with the jar of teabags clutched in one hand.

It's been a few days since her illness, and she's recovered nicely. Her alabaster skin has a healthy pink flush and her chestnut curls coil in thick tendrils around her face. As May has seeped into June, the days have gotten hotter. Today, I met her in the park with the Pack—I taught her a couple of words and phrases in Spanish, and Pip has been slightly less aggressive with her. At least, he lets her put his leash and harness on now. He was very happy to see me, something I can tell Eloise is half-delighted, half-irritated by.

We dropped the Pack off at her apartment and now, her training begins.

"You need to learn how to introduce yourself to people," I say. "Isn't that what your therapist has been telling you? To get out of your comfort zone? Practice talking to someone new?"

She explained to me a bit about her diagnosis, after we'd finalized our agreement. I did my own research on generalized anxiety disorder. I wanted to be as prepared as possible.

She narrows her eyes. "I'm starting to regret telling you all that."

"You *needed* to tell me all that. I can't help you unless I know you."

She rubs her nose obstinately, making the smattering of golden freckles dance. "Why do I need to practice introductions? Everyone's going to be speaking Spanish at the wedding anyway."

I cut her a look. "The people at this wedding are going to speak English."

She blanches. "All of them?"

I realize she may have been counting on no one understanding her. How odd that she'd find that comforting.

"All of them," I say. "Even the abuelitas. These are wealthy families from Mexican high society. Everyone speaks English."

She grimaces. I take a step back.

"Don't leave me," she says, panicked.

I hold up my hands. "I'm not going anywhere. Just giving you space."

"I don't want space. Can't I just leave the tea outside the door?"

"You're stalling."

She glowers at me. "Has anyone ever told you, you're very annoying?"

I smile beatifically. "My sister Lupe tells me that every day." Then I gesture at the door and mime knocking. Her glower deepens.

"I know how to knock on a door."

"Great."

We stare at each other. I can see the faint flutter of her pulse beneath her jaw, and a tiny bead of sweat forms on her temple.

"The French Lady wanted to help you, when I asked," I remind her. "She isn't going to be angry that you're returning the tea."

"That's not the problem," Eloise says tightly.

I cock my head. "What *is* the problem?"

Her jaw works furiously, and she shakes her head hard. "Why do you have to be so pushy? This isn't going to—there's nothing—look this was a bad idea. I don't—I think it's better if—"

Suddenly, the door opens, and Madame Boularès stands before us in all her bouffant-hair, scarlet-lipstick, black-heeled glory.

"Excuse me for interrupting," she says, "but must you two argue right on my doorstep?"

Eloise looks like she just swallowed a lemon. Her whole face puckers, and her eyes widen. She shoves the mason jar out in front of her, like it's a lit stick of dynamite. She squeaks out a word that might be "Tea," but it's hard to tell.

Madame Boularès' eyes brighten. "Ah! Ze girl with ze dogs."

Eloise nods vigorously, still holding the tea.

"Eloise, oui?"

Another nod. Her lips are pressed so tight together they've turned white.

"I don't remember your name," Madame Boularès says to me.

"Agustín," I say with a little wave.

"Agustín. Wonderful name. From the Latin, Augustinus, meaning venerable or majestic." She swipes the tea out of Eloise's hand. "Come in, come in."

Eloise shoots me a terrified look. I gently take her elbow and walk her across the threshold. She yanks her arm from my grip and follows me down the short hall to the living room. This apartment is the same layout as Eloise's but there aren't nearly as many plants—Madame Boularès seems to favor large oil paintings in gilt frames, and velvet covered couches. She's got a vintage record player and a record collection that would impress my father.

"Do you take milk or sugar in your coffee?" Madame Boularès calls from the kitchen.

"None for me, thank you," I say.

Eloise shakes her head.

She can't see you, I mouth.

She glares at me. *I don't want coffee,* she mouths back.

So tell her that, I suggest.

"Eloise?" Madame calls.

"No coffee," Eloise croaks out.

I smile encouragingly and give her a thumbs up as Madame comes back with a silver tray laden with cups and saucers and an ornate coffeepot. It seems Madame has decided we are getting coffee whether we want it or not.

"Eloise is a French name, you know," she explains as she sets the tray down and starts to pour. "Héloïse. Derived from the Old German name Helewidis, meaning healthy or wide."

"Wow," I say, giving Eloise a tiny nudge toward the couch to encourage her to sit. She keeps glancing toward the door. One more little nudge and she plops down on the sofa. "You know a lot about the stories of names."

"A hobby of mine," she says.

I perch beside Eloise as Madame hands me a cup.

"You have a very beautiful home," I say. "Eloise, doesn't Madame Boularès have a beautiful home?"

Madame Boularès hands Eloise her coffee. Eloise's hand is shaking so hard it's a wonder she doesn't spill it. She takes a sip, makes a face, then puts the cup down.

Madame Boularès watches her thoughtfully. "You are a very strange person," she says.

Eloise coughs and turns pink. I can feel the tension vibrating off her in waves. She's gripping her knees with her fingers, the tendons on her hands popping.

"My husband was a strange person too," Madame says, her eyes wandering to a side table where some kind of shrine is set up with lots of old photographs. It looks a bit like an ofrenda for Día de Muertos, except that there is no color, no papel picado or flowers, just lots of pictures of a man with a thick beard in various outfits—a military uniform, a bathing suit, a seventies style blazer. "He was in the French navy. A hero. He died at sea."

She takes a mournful sip of her coffee.

I look pointedly at Eloise, then at Madame Boularès. Eloise's expression is confused.

What? she mouths.

"I am sorry to hear that," I say to Madame.

Eloise's cheeks turn a darker shade of pink. Her jaw is a blade of tension, and her shoulders are bunched up nearly to her ears. I see her swallow hard, her throat bobbing. I suddenly worry she's stopped breathing.

"He was a remarkable man. A passionate man. We had the most fantastic sex life. You would not believe it."

Eloise shoots up from the sofa. "ThankyoufortheteaIneedtogo nowthankyou."

The words jumble together as she tries to step past me, trips on my foot, catches herself on a large metal sculpture of a cat beside the couch, spins around once, steadies herself, then runs down the hall and out the door.

Madame Boularès seems completely unfazed by this. "It was very nice to see you again," she says as I stand to leave. "Please do stop by sometime. I never have company."

"Sure," I say, privately thinking I'd rather not if it's going to involve stories about her and her dead husband's sex life. "Um, thank you for the coffee."

"De nada," she says with a small smile.

15
Eloise

Agustín finds me having a full-blown panic attack in the hall.

I'm on my knees on the thick green carpet, my forehead pressing against the wall, sparks flaring in my vision, my lungs unable to expand. Tears spill down my cheeks and the shame is so so so bad, the agony of it, the tightness in my chest, the faint ringing in my ears. I will *always* be like this. There's no helping me, there's no escape, there's no amount of practice that can fix me, there's no air, I can't find air, the Wheel spins and spins, so fast it hurts, my chest is on fire, and why do I have to be like this, why why why . . .

Count in five. My therapist's voice comes back to me, and I press my fingers against the wall one by one in a five count, thumb to pinkie.

Inhale one, two, three, four, five.

I hold it, my body quivering, my lungs aching.

Count out five. I press my fingertips to the wall again, and exhale to a five count. The throbbing in my head starts to fade. I do this two more times before I hear the door open. My ribs are sore and my lungs feel like they've been wrung out, but at least I can breathe again.

"Are you okay?" Agustín asks, sliding down the wall to sit beside me. I press my forehead harder against the wall. Touching something helps. That tension, the sense of being in contact with something strong and sturdy and immovable.

"I can't do this," I croak. I hope he can't hear me. I wish he couldn't see me. I wish I could just disappear.

"Of course you can," he says. "You just did."

My head whips up to meet his eyes. "That?" I choke. Does he really think *that* disaster was a success? I couldn't even take the most basic social cue of "tell an old widow you're sorry her husband died." I shake my head. "I'll never—can't talk in—"

Ugh, why are words so hard? How am I ever meant to make an actual speech in front of hundreds of wedding guests?

"Sure you will," Agustín says cheerfully. "You just need some practice."

Something in me snaps. I can't stand his upbeat attitude, or his dimpled smile, or his kind eyes. Not when I'm this pathetic broken thing curled up in a hallway having a panic attack after someone offered me a coffee. The words begin to pour out in a torrent, a flood unleashed.

"You don't know me at all," I snarl. "You don't know anything about me. This will never work! I'm not normal. I can't just talk to people like you can, okay? Stop acting like I can do this when I *can't*! Stop being so fucking positive! We're done. This is over. I never want to see you again. Just . . . just . . . GO!"

I shout the word, my withered lungs expelling it in one powerful whoosh, shocking both of us. I didn't know I had that kind of sound in me.

Agustín looks blank with surprise for a moment. Then he stands.

"Okay," he says mildly. He opens his mouth like he wants to say something else then stops himself. He offers his hand to help me, and I fold my arms across my chest and look away. Yes, I am giving him the toddler treatment. Very high road of me. But right now, all I feel is molten, aching shame. I just want him gone.

Agustín walks down the hall. I hear the ding of the elevator doors open and turn to see them close behind him. I let out a long exhale and lean my back against the wall, squeezing my eyes shut.

What am I doing? Tears seep beneath my lids. How can I face five hundred strangers when one little old French woman sends me spiraling?

"Psst."

The voice is so soft, at first I wonder if I imagined it.

"Psst."

I open my eyes and look down the hall. Mr. Bloom is poking his head out of the door to his apartment, his silvery hair catching in the Art Deco lights, a pair of bifocals hung around his neck. I blink.

"Mr. Bloom?" I say. We've never actually spoken before.

"Are you all right?" he asks.

"Huh?"

He gestures toward the elevator. "Was that young man bothering you?"

What an odd thing to ask. Why would Mr. Bloom care?

"No," I say. "He was trying to help me."

"With what?"

Mr. Bloom and I stare at each other from opposite ends of the hallway. It's easier to talk to someone when they aren't so close. I wonder if he feels the same.

"With being social," I admit.

Mr. Bloom snorts. "Overrated," he says.

A tiny smile cracks on my face. "Yeah," I agree.

We stare at each other for a moment longer. Then he clears his throat. "Well," he says. His face disappears, and I hear the click of the lock. I sigh and get to my feet, my legs achy and trembling.

Suddenly, the door opens again and his head pops back out into the hall. "I'm Harold, by the way," he says.

Then his door slams shut.

"So you agreed to let him be your plus-one last weekend, but now . . . he's not?"

It's Bath Night for the Pack, and the tub is full of soapy, sudsy water. I've got Charleston on deck as I finish washing Hazel, looking a bit like a drowned rat, her long elegant fur now plastered to her tiny sausage body. She glowers at me as I fill a measuring cup with water and pour it over her, rinsing her off and handing her to Rachel.

"No," I say, then "Gah!" as Hazel shakes out her fur, spraying us with water and looking extremely pleased with herself. Rachel wraps her in the towel as I pick up Charleston and plop him in the tub.

"All because the French lady across the hall overshared about her late husband and their sexy times?"

I shudder. The embarrassment at the memory makes my cheeks flame.

"It was a bad idea to go over there," I mumble.

"I think it was a great idea."

I shoot her a look.

"What?" she asks. "It's good to know the people who live around you. I'm impressed he got you there at all." She hesitates. "So . . . now you don't have a plus-one?"

I sigh. "No. I'm sorry, Rach." The truth is, Agustín has still been texting me. I've just been freezing him out. Again. It's been three days since I told him to get lost. I really don't understand him.

But there's also a tiny little part of me that's glad he hasn't stopped texting. That he hasn't just given up on me. It's like a sliver of sunlight that I can't quite dim. And that part scares me more than anything.

Rachel rubs the towel over Hazelnut's ears, earning a disgruntled look. "It was really nice of him to take care of you when you were sick."

"I still haven't forgiven you for giving him my address," I warn her, lathering shampoo into Charleston's fur. He pants approvingly and licks my wrist. Charleston loves bathtime.

"Yes, you have," Rachel says happily. "You can't stay mad at me. And I did the right thing—you needed help. I had literally no one else to call, and I was physically incapable of getting to you myself. And look how it turned out! He took care of the Pack. He brought Miriam over."

I hate that she's right.

"I think he's the perfect fit," Rachel says. "Way better than those other two guys from the plus-one list. You should call him and tell him you changed your mind."

I give her a look like she's sprouted three heads. She quickly backtracks.

"Not call, of course," she says. "Text. You should text him."

"No."

"What if we made it like a group thing? We could all three of us meet up and talk. I could help facilitate."

The last thing I need is Rachel seeing me around Agustín. I'm fairly certain she'll hear my pulse kick into a higher gear and know it's not just my usual anxiety. That it's something else.

And there it is. The crux of the matter. I understand attraction is a very normal thing for normal people. But I loathe it. Attraction sits so uncomfortably in body when I'm already uncomfortable. I have all these physical reactions to Agustín's presence: My mouth starts to water, my skin itches, my stomach clenches.

And the worst of it is, that little sliver of sunlight I keep trying to squash wants *more* of it. It's undermining me at every turn.

"He won't want to talk to me," I mumble, trying not to think of the text he sent just last night when he asked if we could talk. "I yelled at him."

Charleston starts to croon his happy bathtime song as I lather his chest, running my hands down his front legs to clean his paws.

"I think that's progress," Rachel says, holding Hazelnut in a death grip, determined to get her as dry as possible before releasing her. The Colonel waits patiently for his turn. He always goes last. "When was the last time you yelled at anybody?"

"I'm not sure we can count me being a dickhead as progress," I point out.

"Progress has many forms," Rachel says piously. She finally releases Hazelnut, who shakes out her fur one last time right in Rachel's direction, then trots out of the room. I hear her doing zoomies in the living room, her little feet pattering back and forth on the carpet.

I rinse Charleston off and Rachel grabs a clean towel. "Is Pip getting a bath?" she asks.

"No. He's in the decompression room," I say. I haven't told Rachel how good Agustín was with him. She's already got her pompoms out for Team Agustín, and I don't need to give her any more ammunition. I've talked to Pip in very bad Spanish, and he does respond to it—at least, I can finally get his harness on for walks now. But he still hides out most of the time.

"So . . . should we look at the plus-one list again?" Rachel asks. I don't need to be Poirot to detect the despondency mixed with panic in her voice. And I can't go on any more dates. This stupid curse is going to ruin both our lives.

Maybe Agustín and I could just arrive at the wedding independently. Yes! Good plan. No talking or contact until October. I can assuage Rachel's fears of being cursed, I can do my part as maid of honor, but until then, no more hot-chocolate smiles or kind eyes or dimples. Or luxurious thick black hair that my fingers ache to—no! None of that, thank you very much. Stomach, you can stop clenching now.

This is the perfect solution. I decide to ignore the fact that I'm still me, and there will still be five hundred guests at this wedding, and I will have to make a speech in front of them. I can deal with that later. But before I get a chance to tell Rachel my brilliant new plan, the doorbell rings.

We freeze, staring at each other.

"Is that him?" she asks excitedly, echoing my own thoughts but with a wholly different tone.

"It's probably Miriam," I say, my voice shaky. I hand Rachel a wet Charleston and stand on trembling legs. My pulse hammers in my temples as I walk down the hall to the front door. There's a war raging inside me. That stupid sliver of sunlight brightens, hoping it *is* him. That I get to see those warm coffee-brown eyes again, that I can be on the receiving end of one of those enormous smiles that lights up his whole face.

The other part of me is freaking out, the hot shame at how I behaved bubbling up like lava. The Wheel spins and spins and spins as I reach for the doorknob.

I've worked myself up into such a frantic state that I'm shocked when it's *not* Agustín on my doorstep.

It's the woman with the two little kids from 9C holding a blue Le Creuset casserole dish. She wears a pair of white capri slacks and a peach-colored sleeveless blouse, a string of pearls around her neck, her brunette bob curling perfectly at her jawline. My first thought is that she's at the wrong apartment.

"Hi," she says brightly. "Eloise, right?"

There goes that theory.

"Yes," I say before I can overthink my own name. I am Eloise. Eloise is me.

"I just wanted to stop by and give you this." She holds out the casserole dish, balanced on her palm.

"Why?" The word tumbles out of my mouth before I can stop it and the Wheel instantly jams on *This Interaction Will Haunt You Forever*. My heartbeat pounds at the base of my skull, mortification creeping over my scalp in sharp prickles.

"Your boyfriend came looking for medicine when you were sick, and I'm so sorry, I didn't have anything but Children's Tylenol, and Mansion was being fussy before his nap, and I wasn't much help. I'm Gretchen, by the way. Mansion and Begonia's mom."

She beams at me like those are sensible names to call your children. Or that I'd know her children's names at all.

Then my brain screeches to a halt at the word *boyfriend*. No, no, no. How can I explain this? I can't, I don't have the right words in the right order, and why is she even here? I didn't ask for a sympathy casserole! I feel the moment stretching out, the appropriate window of time in which I should respond expanding into longer and longer silence. It's getting awkward. Gretchen blinks at me, her smile faltering.

"Hi!" Rachel's voice come from behind me, saving me like she always does. "I'm Rachel, Eloise's friend."

Gretchen's smile brightens to a thousand watts, clearly relieved she's encountered someone who knows how to hold a conversation.

"I'm Gretchen," she says. "I live down the hall in 9C."

"That smells amazing," Rachel says, looking at the casserole dish. It really does smell good.

"It's my specialty," Gretchen says proudly. "Chicken Divan. My kids love it. Well, Begonia isn't eating anything ultra processed right now, but I thought something homey after being sick might be comforting. I'm really sorry I couldn't help—I was just telling Eloise, her boyfriend was so kind, coming by to see if we had any medicine."

My face feels hotter than the surface of the sun. I didn't tell Rachel about how Agustín went from neighbor to neighbor trying to find Miriam—just that he went and got her. I didn't tell her *why* we went to Madame Boularès' apartment the other day, just that he wanted to help me socialize.

I can feel Rachel's eyes boring into the side of my face. I stay extremely still, like she's a T-Rex, and if I don't move, she can't see me.

"Oh my god, that's *so* sweet of you," Rachel says, descending on Gretchen to sweep the casserole dish out of her hand. "Isn't Eloise's boyfriend just the nicest guy?"

At that, my head whips around to glare at her but now it's Rachel who's refusing to make eye contact.

"He is," Gretchen says eagerly. "Oh, I brought this too." She holds up a bottle of white wine, condensation dewing on its glass surface.

"Oooh El, it's a sauvignon blanc, our favorite," Rachel says, finally meeting my glare, her face alight with triumph. "Gretchen, come on in. Want to stay for a glass?"

No! Gretchen cannot come in. We cannot have a glass of anything. This is my space. Why is Rachel doing this?

"I'd love to!" Gretchen says. "If it's no bother."

It is so much bother. I am supremely bothered. But the two of them walk past me into the hall. "My word, your apartment is incredible, Eloise. Look at all these wonderful plants. Oh hello, who's this?"

A very wet Charleston has padded forward, his sharp nose detecting a new arrival.

"That's Charleston," Rachel says. Charleston sniffs her shoes as Gretchen coos.

"He's so cute," she says.

Then I watch in horror as Charleston wobbles around, lifts one leg, and lets out a stream of pee right on Gretchen's probably-definitely designer loafers.

"Oh!" she cries, as the Wheel spins frantically in my chest and jams on *AHHHHHHH!*

I leap into action, grabbing Charleston around his middle and hauling him away from her.

"I'm sorry–I'm sorry–I'm sorry," I stammer, the embarrassment a violent writhing thing, like a thousand bats have been released in my chest, all flapping wings and sharpened claws. I can't look Gretchen in the eyes. With shaking hands, I awkwardly tuck Charleston like a football under my arm, grab a roll of paper towels from the kitchen counter, and unspool it like a huge, Brawny ribbon, trying to mop up the pee as Charleston wriggles in my grasp. "I'm sorry–I'm sorry–I'm sorry," I gasp, trying to keep the tears at bay, wishing she had never come here with her stupid, delicious smelling casserole and her crisp cold bottle of my favorite wine, being all nice and neighborly, as if that's something I can handle.

Suddenly, she's crouched down next to me. "Oh sweetheart," she says, putting one hand gently on my shoulder, and I don't like strangers touching me, but something about the words and action combined are so . . . so . . . motherly. Such an unfamiliar sensation. It stops me in my tracks.

I meet her gaze. Her eyes are a very dark blue, almost navy.

"It's okay," she says slowly. "They're just shoes. I have two little kids—dog pee is nothing. Try getting vomit out of your hair at four in the morning on zero sleep." She stands and steps out of both her shoes. "I'll just leave these here by the door if that's all right. I'm sure my dry cleaner can sort them out tomorrow."

Just then, there's the pop of a cork and Rachel, who has watched this scene unfold with her usual discerning eyes, smiles at us broadly. "Wine?" she says.

16
Agustín

"Hey Agustín, it's Neil Rasmussen with *The New Yorker*. Just calling to check in about that interview with Ricardo Cuevas. If all is going well on your end, we can confirm you for edits in mid-November with the article published in our January issue. Talk soon."

I listen to the voicemail for the third time then stare at my computer screen, an old article in *El Diario*, New York City's oldest Spanish-language newspaper, staring back at me.

I haven't called Neil back yet. I'm not ready to accept defeat. But the truth is, I'm not going to make it to that wedding.

I rub my eyes and scroll the article. It's the first time Abuelo was mentioned in the press—a couple of Puerto Rican kids were wrongfully arrested, accused of assaulting a man on the 5 train. Abuelo went to the courthouse and a reporter asked him why he was there, if he was family. He gave an impassioned response about how we are all one big family and any injustice that happens against someone from the community is an injustice against all. He talked about the system working against the poor, the marginalized, the ones with no voice, no money, no influence. His words resonate because they are so similar to mine.

The date of the article haunts me. It's the day after we were forced to leave our home. I remember it so clearly, my mom with red-rimmed eyes, Lupe sobbing, Caro asking if we could take our garden with us—especially the fig tree. Dad tried to stay positive, telling us this was an adventure. Abuelita was silent but strong, iron faced as she left the home where she'd raised her children. Did she know then that Abuelo had betrayed her? When did she find out? How did she keep this from us? And why? Why protect him?

I glance at my phone. Still nothing from Eloise. It's been three days. I should just stop trying. Clearly, my invitation as her plus-one has been rescinded.

I turn back to my computer and open my own article.

October 12th was a Monday. All throughout Mexico City, kids were headed to school, adults were on their way to work, the buses ran their usual routes, the traffic on Insurgentes was as bad as ever. It was a normal day. But not for my family.

I pause and lean back in my chair, my gaze wandering over my studio apartment, cramped but clean. My tiny kitchen table also functions as a desk. And a counter. And sometimes an ironing board. I have a floor lamp with an orange shade that casts a warm glow over the room. A couple of button-down shirts are drying on a rack near the window that looks out over Troutman Street. I wonder if I should get some plants. I really liked all the plants in Eloise's apartment.

Why did I have to push her? My mom is always telling me I used to try and run before I could crawl. Always rushing to the next thing, always impatient. And now that impatience has cost me—Neil keeps making it painfully clear that no interview means no article. This article is more than just the pinnacle of my career. It's more than just exposing the truth. I need others to witness Abuelo's betrayal. I need people in this city to know that *we* were important too. My family mattered.

And there's another part of me that honestly is worried about Eloise. I've never met someone so consumed by fear. I don't know her well, but I feel this urge to . . . I don't know, protect her? No, that's not it.

I crack my knuckles and pull my laptop closer. I'm determined to fine tune the article, even if it never sees the light of day. I pull up the section about Fernanda, Ricardo's mother. Abuelo's second wife. Her family immigrated from Guadalajara in the fifties and she was born and raised in New York. She worked at a bakery for most of her life from what I can tell. I wonder if that's how they met. Abuelo stopping in for his morning coffee and maybe a pan dulce. Starting a conversation with the petite Mexican-American woman with dramatic eyebrows (I've seen a couple of photos of her). Abuelo charming her with his gift of gab. He was always telling stories, always animated, always making me and Lupe laugh when we were kids. Did he charm Fernanda with one of his wild tales? There's so much that research can't tell you. Tone and nuance are lost in black and white print, or census information, or public records.

I tweak one sentence, then stand and grab a beer from my fridge. I crack it open and look down at the street below. It's seven PM on a Saturday in June, so the sun is still out and the streets are bustling with people, a hundred stories carried in each one, a hundred threads weaving together to create the living, breathing tapestry that is New York City. I take a sip of Pacífico and wonder what Eloise is doing right now. I was so close—she was finally beginning to peek out of that shell. I don't know why that matters so much to me. The point is the invitation, right? She was the one who made it very clear this is a business arrangement and she never wanted to see me again after the wedding.

It just feels like she's existing on the edges of life, getting by on scraps. But life is a full, multicourse meal. She deserves to enjoy it.

And this wedding is going to be quite the meal, both figuratively and literally. I started following Rachel and Diego on social media. He doesn't post much but she's mega successful, with a huge following, and whenever she shares her wedding plans she gets tons of likes and comments. Which in turn boosts the makeup line she's launching this summer. She's very smart with her brand. I wonder how she and Eloise ever ended up as such close friends. They seem like polar opposite types of people.

Eva was right, there's absolutely no information on where the wedding will be held in Mexico City. I bet Eloise will love all the plants and flowers in Mexico. She'd love how green Colonia Roma is, how the tree roots bubble up through the concrete sidewalks with their pure force of nature. She would love the jacarandas that bloom in March, bursting in froths of brilliant purple, lining Paseo de la Reforma, the most beautiful avenue in Mexico City. I think there are a lot of things she would love about my city.

Suddenly, an idea occurs to me. A way to help Eloise and also maybe salvage my invite. I started too big; I shouldn't have jumped right into socializing. And if she's not going to talk to me, maybe I need to think outside the box. Use my other skills. Try a different approach.

Maybe I should be getting her *excited*—not about the wedding, but about Mexico City.

I take another swig of beer, my nerves buzzing, and sit back down at my laptop. I open Adobe InDesign and find the right template.

Then I get to work.

17
Eloise

"And I said to him, I said well Harrison, she's your daughter too, and if you don't start dealing with some of this s-h-i-t," Gretchen spells it out like Rachel and I might not be able to handle hearing a curse word, "then I'll tell everyone at the club that the '82 Margaux your mother served at Thanksgiving last year was really a 2012 Pomerol!"

I sense this is some kind of devastating insult only to be understood by the upper echelons of New York society. But Rachel and I nod like we totally get it, and Rachel says, "No way," while shooting me a private grin, and Gretchen says, "Right?" and the whole thing kind of makes me smile. Because I feel in on the joke, even if I don't quite understand it.

Our plates sit on the coffee table, scattered with Ritz cracker crumbs and stray bits of chicken and broccoli from the casserole. Our wineglasses are empty. Maybe it's because Rachel is here, or maybe it's the wine, but I haven't felt quite as awkward with Gretchen in my house as I thought I would when Rachel first invited her in.

I haven't said much, but no one seems to mind. And I wonder if it's more than Rachel or the wine. If, in the wake of all my interactions with Agustín, and the disastrous Madame Boularès incident, I'm slightly more prepared for human contact. Which means, to my chagrin, that Agustín might in fact be right on the money about practice before the wedding.

"Oh lord, look at the time," Gretchen says, checking her diamond-encrusted watch. "I've got to get back and let Paloma head home for the evening." She beams at us. "It was just lovely to get some girl time. And talk to adults." She chuckles. "We'll have to do this again!"

I don't know if I'm up for that yet, but I do manage another smile, so that's a win. Rachel, of course, agrees enthusiastically and gives Gretchen a hug on her way out. She closes the door and turns to me.

"Wow," she says.

"Yeah," I agree, assuming she means that Gretchen is kind of a trip.

"ELOISE!" Rachel shrieks, jumping up and down. "Look at you! The hostess with the mostest!"

I flush and pick up Hazel like she's my security blanket, holding her to my chest. "I didn't do anything."

"What are you talking about? You just hosted a total stranger in your apartment for one whole hour."

Was it only an hour? It felt like the entire night. I glance at the clock on the wall, and it's almost eight-thirty. I can still feel the adrenaline humming in my veins. Hazel struggles against me, displeased with my vice-like grip. Rachel grabs the plates from the coffee table and takes them into the kitchen. I sink down onto the sofa. Hazel wriggles out of my grasp and gives me an indignant huff as she jumps down to claim her rightful spot on the giant dog bed. The Colonel pads over and puts his head on my knee. He still needs his bath. Charleston is in the kitchen with Rachel.

"Don't let him lick all the plates!" I call to her.

There's a pause. "Okay," she calls back.

Charleston has definitely already licked all the plates. Rachel is such a pushover.

I stroke the Colonel's head and chew on my lip. I survived. I managed to sit and have a conversation with a stranger and not die. Well, "conversation" might be a stretch—I said, "Oh really" one time and then a few nods. But that's pretty big for me. And even though I feel that weird combo of itchy/jittery/exhausted, I haven't started spinning out over all the ways I embarrassed myself yet. I'm sure that will happen later tonight, probably around three AM, but still.

I have to admit that I made the wrong decision, telling Agustín to get lost. And showing up independently from him at the wedding isn't going to work either. I need more—I need the help he offered me when we made our deal.

I grab my phone off the table.

But then I see I already have a text from him. It came in only a couple of minutes ago. Usually his texts start with *Holaaaaaaaa* (always a long string of As), and then some stream of consciousness thoughts or questions. But this one is just an image.

I pause, frowning, then open the link.

My jaw drops.

It's a . . . newspaper?

THE AGUSTÍN DAILY, blares at me, along with today's date. Then there are articles.

See You in La Ciudad (de Mexico)! contains a list of relevant areas in Mexico City, along with a bit of history about each one.

Si, Acepto—an unofficial guide to Mexican weddings.

Holy Jacarandas! talks about the various plant life in Mexico, while *Did Someone Say Perritos?* details the best spots for dog watching.

My lips twitch when I see an article titled *Martinez Attempts to Ingratiate Himself Using Humor—Will It Work?* alongside an opinion piece called *The Clock Is Ticking: Can Agustín prove to Eloise that he's the perfect plus-one?*

I press my fingertips to my mouth in a poor attempt to hide the smile that's threatening to split my face clean in two. This is . . . this is . . . I don't have words. This might be the nicest thing anyone has ever done for me. It's simple and accessible and doesn't require talking. And it's not just about the wedding, either. I've kind of been ignoring the fact that I have to fly to a whole other country, that I have to exist someplace for a week without any of the comforts of my home. And not just my apartment—the familiar streets of my city as well.

Of course I start with the article about dogs. Apparently, there's a park called Parque México where local shelters will bring adoptable dogs out on Saturdays. A picture of a boxer mix with a vest that reads *Adóptame* makes my heart squeeze. I start to click on the other articles. There are photos of a huge boulevard, sort of like Park Avenue, but it's lined with jacaranda trees, blooming in rich clouds of purple. It's so beautiful it makes my chest ache. There's a section on food, and I'm instantly assaulted with delectable pictures: tacos piled with shredded meat and onion and cilantro, whole roast fish slathered in green sauce, and some kind of sandwich called torta de chilaquiles, oozing crema and chips and red sauce. Even though I just ate, my mouth starts to water.

"Whatcha looking at?"

I jump so hard I drop my phone as Rachel comes into the room, drying her hands on a dishtowel.

"Nothing," I say too quickly, scrambling to pick it up off the floor.

She narrows her eyes at me. I give a huff worthy of Hazel and hand over my phone. Rachel's eyes widen as she looks at the fake newspaper.

"He put all this together for you?" She blinks. "El, I've changed my mind. Don't just let him be your plus-one again. Marry this man."

I blanch as my stomach plummets all the way down to the lobby, making me dizzy. "What?" I yelp.

"Kidding!" she says. "But for real, this is like the nicest thing I've seen anyone do for someone they barely know."

"Yeah," I say, trying to quiet my racing pulse. "That's kind of what I was thinking too."

There's a long silence. I can feel Rachel's eagerness. The sliver of sunlight inside me rejoices, glowing a fraction brighter.

"So?" Rachel finally says, barely hiding the glint of excitement in her eyes.

I groan. "I'll ask him to be my plus-one. Again."

"Yay!" she squeals, tackling me with a hug. The Colonel decides to get in on the action, rearing up and landing on top of her with his front paws.

"Oof," I gasp.

"You're not going to regret this," Rachel says.

"I already do," I say, my voice muffled against her shoulder.

She laughs, and kisses the top of my head.

18
Agustín

I stand outside El Mercado Mexicano on 116th Street and check the time.

Maybe I should have offered to pick Eloise up from her place. I couldn't believe my luck when she texted me back so quickly last night. I'm officially her plus-one again. I'll call Neil tomorrow and confirm the interview is a go.

THE AGUSTÍN DAILY was more effective than I thought. It was also really fun to put together, deciding which pieces of my home would speak to her most strongly. I knew I had to put Parque México on there, for the dogs. And the jacarandas on Reforma, of course. It's a shame she's not coming in March when they bloom. There will still be plenty of green places for her to explore in October though.

The streets of East Harlem are bustling this afternoon, people coming home from church, abuelas doing their shopping, kids crowding around the woman selling raspados from a little cart. The sounds of my native language are everywhere. They call this area Spanish Harlem, though in the US, "Spanish" seems to be a blanket term. I don't think many people from Spain live in this neighborhood. It's all Latinos. Lots of Puerto Ricans. I also hear accents from Colombia, Guatemala, El Salvador . . . and Mexico, of course. There are big baskets of produce outside the market, with its weathered, faded awning in the colors of my country, green and white and red.

It felt right to take a step back from the socializing front and let Eloise focus on something a bit more fun: food. Mexico has the best food in the world. Yes, I may be biased, but it is also the truth. While I'm sure this wedding will have extravagances like caviar toasts or miniature beef Wellingtons, there's also no way it won't have some basics. Things that are quintessentially Mexican but that Eloise won't be familiar with.

Just then, I spot her down the street, scurrying past the man with a table set up selling agua frescas, huge plastic tubs filled with vibrantly colored juices, tamarindo and jamaica and pepino con limón. She darts around a cop and nearly runs into two teens on scooters. It's a perfect summer day, not too humid with a handful of fluffy clouds playing tag with the sun. Eloise wears those same vintage leather boots, and a pair of denim short overalls over a white tank top. Her curls are pinned back with clips shaped like butterflies and a pair of yellow-framed sunglasses hides her eyes. She's so focused on avoiding the crowds that she walks right past me.

"Eloise!" I call, and she jumps and whirls around. I smile and wave. Her cheeks turn pink as she hurries back toward me.

"Hi," she croaks, then clears her throat. "Hello. Hi."

"Hello," I say cheerfully. "You came!"

"Yeah," she says. I can tell her eyes are darting around behind her shades, assessing the social-interaction threat level of whatever my plan might be.

I sweep my hand out at the store behind me. "Today, I thought we'd cook."

She blanches. "Here?"

I chuckle. "No, at your apartment." I don't miss the relief that flickers across her face. "But we need supplies. Come on."

I lead her inside. The market is cramped and smells a little funny and the floors are a mismatched pattern of brown and beige tiles, but oh, all the familiar sights! Packets of dried chiles hang on the walls, there's a fridge full of quesos, Oaxaca and cotija, along with a large metal stand with all the Mexican snacks I grew up eating. I swipe a bag of Takis Fuego.

Eloise looks at them, intrigued. "I've seen those before," she says.

"Yeah, they sell them everywhere here," I say. Most bodegas will have them, and I've seen them in Duane Reade too.

"Are we cooking with them?"

"No, no, you don't want to eat these," I promise her.

She frowns. "But I like chips."

"Not these. Trust me."

The man behind the counter chuckles. "El de atrás paga," he says.

"What does that mean?" Eloise whispers.

I grimace. "Well . . . it means your butt is gonna poop fire," I explain.

Her eyes pop open wide. "Okay, no chips."

"But try these," I say, grabbing her a package of Gansitos. "They're chocolate covered cakes filled with strawberry jam and cream."

"Ooh," she says, examining the package with interest, and I know food was the right call. It's hard to be nervous around food.

I switch to Spanish and ask the man behind the counter for the ingredients I need. They've got chiltepin chiles, and I get a couple of jalapeños and a serrano as well. Not sure how much spice Eloise can handle, so best to cover all the bases. I get a bunch of limes, a cucumber, red onion, and cilantro, along with a bag of tostadas and a few ripe avocados. I brought my tortilla press with me in my backpack—a gift from my mother, who was very concerned there wouldn't be good tortillas in New York. And sopecitos require extra love and fresh tortillas. I get a bag of corn flour

(Maseca, obviously), a can of refried beans, a pound of chorizo, some queso fresco, lettuce, and white onion for toppings.

I'm hungry already.

"What are you making?" Eloise asks as the man bags everything up.

"Let me guess," he says to me in Spanish. "Sopes y aguachile?"

"Exacto," I reply. I turn to Eloise. "It's a surprise. And I'm not making it—*we* are making it."

Our next stop is a local fishmonger for some shrimp. The guy serving us is from CDMX; he and I chat about the city for a bit while Eloise hovers behind me like a shadow. She seems to be trying to take up as little space as possible, shrinking from one side of me to the other. Then we head to the 2/3 train. It's been nice to spend an afternoon speaking Spanish. Rejuvenating, like a brief spa day for my brain, where it doesn't have to be constantly translating.

We get off at 96th Street and head toward the park. The stately brownstones that front the tree-lined streets, with their sweeping stoops and large windows, feel like a world away from the rusted fire escapes and cramped storefronts of Harlem.

We walk a few blocks down Central Park West to Eloise's building. The Archer, it's called. All the buildings on this street have names, like they're more important than other buildings. There's a Latino dude in a cap standing outside smoking a cigarette. I saw him when I came here the first time.

"Hola," I say, giving him a cheerful wave.

"Qué tal," he replies, offering me his hand. "Hector."

"Agustín."

"Mucho gusto."

We shake.

"I didn't know Miss Whitechapel had a boyfriend," he says in Spanish, glancing at Eloise.

"Just friends," I reply.

"Oh," he says, frowning as if that makes just as little sense as her having a boyfriend.

Eloise gives him a tight nod without quite making eye contact, which seems to be her typical greeting for everyone. Hector opens the door for us, and we walk into the cool lobby with its sleek couches and modern art.

As soon as the elevator doors close behind us, I feel a strange tension fill the air. Eloise is still wearing her sunglasses, so I can't see her eyes, but she grips the bag of shrimp tightly, and the space between us hums. I shift my backpack, the straps digging into my shoulders. The tortilla press is like an anchor. But it will be worth it.

The elevator doors open with a ding, and the second we step out into the hall, Miriam throws open the door to her apartment.

"Hello again," she says to me, as an orange tabby cat weaves around her ankles.

"Hello," I say brightly.

"It's nice to see you," Miriam says, her eyes darting between me and Eloise, a sly smile on her lips.

"It's nice to see you too," I say. Eloise seems determined to stay out of this conversation. She's hugging the bag of shrimp to her chest now, like it's a talisman that can ward off evil.

"What are you all up to on this fine sunny Sunday?"

"I'm teaching Eloise how to cook some Mexican dishes, so she'll know what to expect at the wedding," I say.

Miriam's eyes bug. "I'm sorry the *what*?"

"Gotta go, talk to you later Miriam, bye!" Eloise says, grabbing my wrist, and suddenly I'm yanked forward as she walk-runs down the hall, dragging me along behind her.

"You know I won't let this go without an explanation, honey!" Miriam calls after us. "And you better be sharing some of that Mexican food!"

Eloise fumbles with the key, turns the lock, and we spill into her apartment.

"She doesn't know about the wedding?" I ask.

Eloise shakes her head. I see her lips part like she wants to say more, then she clamps her mouth shut as Charleston comes running down the hall, barreling into my leg. Eloise drops the shrimp on the counter and goes to the living room to greet the dogs. I decide to give her a moment to decompress. I set about unpacking the bags in the kitchen and searching for bowls and knives and some cutting boards.

"Time for your shot, Colonel," I hear her say. I set the tortilla press to one side and put the two Pacíficos I brought in the fridge. Her kitchen is long and narrow but with a lot of counter space, and a big window at the end that looks over the park. There's a blue and yellow tile backsplash and a drying rack next to the sink with some plates and wineglasses in it. Her kitchen is pretty intuitive, and I find all the items I need. She's also got some really nice equipment—a shiny KitchenAid mixer, a set of gleaming baking sheets, plus quite a few plastic molds in various shapes, like paw prints, dog bones, and fire hydrants. I think back to that biscuit I gave to Pip the first time I met him and wonder if Eloise made those herself.

I've set up two stations with knives and cutting boards, laying out the ingredients on the counter, when I hear the tiny clicking of nails and see Pip's little face peeking around the edge of the kitchen doorway.

"Hola, chiquito," I say, crouching down. He scurries over to me and licks my fingers. I scratch the back of his ears. "Sí, te extrañé mucho también. Pero por qué no hangeas con tu mamá?"

Pip makes a tiny yip. I grab a treat from the Paws Off jar—heart-shaped and smelling of peanut butter and strawberries—and feed it to him.

"You're part of a family now, amigo," I say in Spanish. "You've got a pack. You know it's okay to trust them, right?"

"Oh!" Eloise stops short as she sees Pip and me in the kitchen. Pip whirls around and growls at her. She takes a step back.

"I'm sorry buddy," she says. "I didn't mean to scare you."

Pip keeps growling as he skirts the edge of the kitchen, then flees down the hall. Eloise sighs and rubs her eyes.

"He'll come around," I say.

She nods morosely, as Charleston and the Colonel come to join us. I bet Hazelnut is snoozing in the big dog bed in the living room. Charleston has clearly been activated by the scent of food and the Colonel nudges my hand to say hello. I give him a pat.

"Let's start with the aguachile," I say. "So this is kind of like a ceviche. Have you had ceviche?"

"Yeah. Sure. Maybe. One time." Eloise puts her hands in her pockets, then seems to reconsider and folds her arms over her chest. It's like she doesn't know quite what to do with them. The Colonel leans his head against her thigh.

"Great. So the difference here is that in ceviche, you marinate the fish for a longer time in the lime juice and spices, but aguachile is super quick. Now, what's your spice tolerance? How much chile can you handle?"

Eloise bites her lip. "Medium?" she offers.

That means mild. "Perfect." No chiltepin, then, just the jalapeño and serrano. "First, we make the marinade."

I set her to work squeezing limes into a bowl while I slice the jalapeños and a bit of the serrano. Then she chops up some cilantro while I mince a bit of garlic.

"Now, try this," I say, taking a little spoonful of the mixture and offering it to her. She sniffs it tentatively then takes the spoon and tastes a tiny sip.

"Oh," she says, then gives a little cough.

"Too spicy?"

"No, it's . . ." She licks her lips and finishes the spoonful. "Wow. That's really good."

I beam. "Gracias. Now we cut up the shrimp and veggies. Which do you want?"

"Veggies," she says, so I hand her the cucumber and red onion.

"Thin slices," I tell her.

We work in companionable silence for a few minutes. Charleston plants himself directly between Eloise's feet, the perfect spot to swipe any falling food, and the Colonel lays down in the doorway and rests his head on his paws, watching us with soulful eyes.

"Can I ask you a question?" I say, putting some sliced shrimp in the bowl and grabbing a few more from the bag to lay them on my cutting board.

She stiffens. "Um . . . sure."

"When did you start adopting old dogs?"

Her shoulders relax, and I feel like I've asked the right thing—something safe, something she enjoys talking about.

"Right after college," she says. A small smile lights on her lips as she slices the cucumber into half-moons. "I'd been living here by myself for a while—it was a couple of years after my uncle died—and Rachel had been bugging me to get a pet. She wanted me to get a cat, since they're so easy to take care of." The smile widens a fraction. Slice-slice-slice. "Rachel's always looked out for me, and she was worrying about me being alone all the time. I like being alone. But I can't ever say no to Rachel."

Her eyes dart to me. "Case in point," she says, gesturing up and down with her knife. "Once Diego sent her that list, it was game over. Do you know about the curse?"

"Curse?" I ask, frowning.

"The wedding curse? Tío Abuelo Alberto?"

"I am unfamiliar with Tío Abuelo Alberto."

She tells me the story, and I can't help but laugh. "We Mexicans can be very superstitious," I say. "I bet Tío Abuelo Alberto was just, like, gay or something."

Eloise gasps. "Oh my god, yes! And didn't want his family butting into his business."

"Just let Tío Abuelo Alberto live his life," I add.

"For real," she agrees.

Our eyes meet, our smiles mirroring each other. Then she blinks and blushes, turning back to the cucumber. She accidentally-on-purpose drops a slice on the floor and Charleston happily gobbles it up.

"Anyway, Rachel took me down to Safe Haven Animal Shelter," Eloise continues. "It's one of the only shelters in the city that has animals on site. All the others have networks of people who foster the dogs in their homes, so you have to make appointments to meet them. Well, Rachel knows me well enough to know that was not going to work. Emailing strangers? Coordinating meet and greets? Going to their homes? Nope. No way."

She chuckles softly, sliding the cucumber into the bowl and picking up the onion. "We walked in, and Rachel was doing all the talking of course, really selling them on how I was the perfect candidate to adopt a pet—I lived alone, worked from home, all of that. And then, from under the reception desk, this little gray face peeked out." She pauses peeling the onion, and swallows, her eyes growing distant with the memory. "And I locked eyes with the tiniest, ugliest dog I'd ever seen. He had a wispy mohawk and one snaggletooth. His eyes were clouded with cataracts, and he had patches of fur missing. And I just melted right then and there."

Her voice goes so soft, I pause in my own slicing to listen. I can feel her memories bubbling to the surface, feel something private and tender that she never shares with anyone fighting its way toward the light.

"It was like I saw myself in him," she says, her voice barely a whisper. "This small, unwanted, broken thing." I stop breathing, certain if I make a sound, I'll shatter this moment. She blinks, and a crystalline tear lands on her cheek. The silence swells and billows around us. Is this really how she sees herself? My heart throbs a painful beat.

Eloise clears her throat and the noise seems to startle her back to the present. She sniffs and hurriedly wipes the tear away.

"I mean, he wasn't cute or fun or playful, he wasn't a puppy, and I didn't realize at the time how hard it is for seniors to get adopted," she says, suddenly very focused on slicing the onion, like she's determined not to make eye contact with me. Following her lead, I pick up another shrimp. "And I knew right away he was coming home with me. Alexis—she works at Safe Haven—was so excited when I asked about him. He'd been there for eight months and not one single inquiry. Eight whole months. No one wanted him." She shakes her head, making her curls quiver, her brow furrowing into a hard line. "That's no way to live. His name at the shelter was George but I named him Lucky Lou. Because it was the luckiest day of my life when I met him."

Her eyes turn glassy again, and she blinks quickly. "He lived for six more years. He was fourteen when I got him and twenty when he died. Chihuahuas can live for a long time." She sighs and glances toward the doorway. "Pip is the first chihuahua I've had since Lucky."

"How many dogs have you rescued?" I ask. I'm feeling a bit in awe of this woman. The pure energy of love inside her radiates out as she talks about this dog. I wonder how her small frame can contain it all.

Her face lights up. "Pip is my seventh senior rescue. First was Lucky Lou, and then Summer, she was a Maltese. She had the most beautiful silky white hair. And she was such a princess, she loved when I dressed her up in little outfits with bows on her ears. Not all dogs like to wear clothes, but Summer had a whole box of clothes just for her, and every morning she'd prance over to it—she definitely pranced, I can show you a video—and I would hold up different items, and she would sniff them and decide what she wanted to wear that day." Eloise chuckles softly. "Then I got Ginger Doggers. She was a terrier mix. She was so funny—she loved to listen to music. Specifically, eighties hair bands. I don't know why, but she just loved herself some Def Leppard. I can't listen to

'Pour Some Sugar on Me' without thinking of Ginger, her little butt swaying back and forth, giving her signature Ginger howl."

Then she does a full-on impression, making a little "Awooo" sound. Charleston instantly takes up the mantle with his own howl, then the Colonel joins in. Eloise makes these dogs come alive as she talks about them. Her face has become so animated. I think this might be the first time I've seen her truly relaxed.

I hear Hazel awooo from the living room, and I'm not about to be left out.

"Awoooo!" I howl and Charleston gives a happy bark.

Eloise laughs, and another tear trickles down her cheek, but she doesn't seem embarrassed. She smiles at me and the force of it knocks me breathless for a moment. The light that shines from those clear green eyes is brighter than the summer sun and warmer than waters of Holbox.

"Then I got Charleston—nobody wanted him because he's incontinent." I glance down at Charleston, in his diaper, happily licking the kitchen floor. "Then Walton Doggins. He was a Yorkie. He died in January."

"I'm so sorry," I say.

"It's part of the deal. The pact I make with them. To love them for as long as they have left."

"Still. That must be very hard, to know you will lose them."

"It's not about me," she says simply.

I take her words in. Let them sink to my bones. I can't imagine how she does it. I don't think I'd be able to.

"I got Hazelnut right after I got Walton," she says. "She kept getting returned. No one understood her." Eloise's nostrils flare, and she shakes her head, slicing the onion with extra vigor. "And then the Colonel—he's the largest breed I've ever had, but he's probably the sweetest dog I've ever met. Aren't you, bud?"

The Colonel raises his head and smiles, his tongue lolling out of his mouth.

"But any dog with a medical issue is a tough case for adoption," she says. "And then there's Pip," she adds. "My most recent rescue. And I . . ." Her voice trails off. "I don't really know what to do about Pip."

"I think you're doing a great job with him," I say.

She shakes her head with a sort of solemn finality, effectively ending the conversation, then dumps her sliced onion into the bowl. I add the rest of the shrimp.

"What's next?" she asks.

19
Eloise

"Next we make the sopesitos," Agustín says, holding up what looks like a metal torture device.

I'm feeling more comfortable than I would have ever thought possible given that there's a man in my kitchen, and it appears I'm going to be eating raw shrimp (I totally lied about the ceviche). But I love talking about my dogs, especially the ones who have passed. It makes them feel alive again. God, I want to listen to Def Leppard now. And maybe some Bon Jovi. Ginger really loved "Livin' on a Prayer."

I like this type of preparation for the wedding much more than coffee with Madame Boularès. At first, I was terrified—standing in my small kitchen with Agustín, his smoky, leather-cardamom scent surrounding me, his lean tan arms being all lean and tan and omg-right-there-next-to-me. But as I focused on the feel of a blade slicing through cucumber flesh, the scent of onion filling my nose, and talked about Lucky Lou and Ginger, and remembered that first trip to Safe Haven, I started to relax.

Talking to Agustín is almost like talking to Rachel. As long as I don't look at him. That's when things go wonky, what with all the mouth-watering and stomach-clenching, and my thoughts drifting to things that are definitely not allowed. Like how strong and confident his hands are as they wield the knife, how the muscles in his forearms ripple beneath his olive skin as he chops a jalapeño, how expressive his eyebrows are when they're furrowed in concentration. I love how one cocks slightly above the other when I say something that surprises him.

Oh my fucking god, I'm attracted to his *eyebrows*. I need help.

"What is that?" I ask, inspecting said torture device. Its metal is painted a deep blue, and it appears to be two circles linked by a hinge, with some longer piece of metal attached to it.

"This is a tortilla press," he says.

I can't help myself. "We're making tacos?" I ask excitedly. Yes, I am that basic white girl who loves me some tacos.

"No," Agustín says, and then he legit winks at me, which should be creepy but when he does it, it looks cool and makes my pulse splutter. "We are making sopes. I call them sopesitos, because in Mexico, we use the diminutive a lot—adding 'ito' or 'ita' to words to make them cuter."

"Oh," I say. I sound it out. "So-peh-see-tos."

"Perfecto!" Agustín says, dimples flashing. "Now, sopesito also means a small sope—it's not just an Agustín flair on the word. There might be little sopesitos at this wedding as appetizers since they are so traditional. My sister Lupe had them at her wedding. Even though Diego's family is estupidamente rico, no red-blooded Mexican can resist the call of the sope."

"Really?"

He purses his lips. "That was an exaggeration, but they are very good, I promise."

"What are they?" I ask.

"You'll see," he says. "Do you have a large skillet? Or a comal would be better."

"I've got a few skillets," I say, pulling them out from a cupboard. He sets the largest one on a burner and turns the heat on.

"First, we make the masa. That's the dough." He opens the huge bag of corn flour as I grab another bowl from the cupboard. He measures out the flour. "Then we add water. Just a bit at a time. I used to love watching my mom making masa for his sopes when I was a kid."

I frown. "You mean her sopes?"

Agustín shakes his head. "Pinche genders," he mutters. "Yes, sorry. Her sopes."

I watch as he adds a bit of water, mixing it into the flour with his fingers, then a little more, then more, until it's all blended together. He forms a smooth round ball.

"This is the consistency we want," he says, holding it out so I can touch it. "Not too wet and not too dry. Now we take this ball and make little balls. Let's make eight."

We work together, breaking off pieces of dough and rolling them between our palms until we have eight identical-sized balls on the counter.

"Bueno. So, for tacos, we would be pressing these flat-flat," he explains. "But for sopes, we want a thicker tortilla, because it acts like a little plate." He opens the press using the long metal handle-type thingy and there's two sheets of plastic inside. He lifts one sheet, puts one ball on the other, then tops it with the first sheet. "Now we press," he says, flashing me a smile that makes my heart stutter.

He presses the top metal disk down over the ball. When he lifts it and peels back the plastic sheet, there's a perfectly round, slightly thicker-than-normal tortilla resting in the center. He plants it on his palm, then carefully peels off the bottom plastic sheet.

"Do you have a big plate?" he asks. I get out a large serving platter from a bottom cupboard, one of those accumulated kitchen items of unknown origin—neither Lenny nor I ever did much entertaining. I run it under the sink and dry it off with a paper towel before placing it on the counter in front of the bowl with the aguachile. Agustín places the tortilla on the hot skillet.

"Now. I will keep pressing, and you cook the chorizo."

I grab the chorizo from the fridge and set another pan on the stove, heating it up with some olive oil then chop the meat and add it to the pan where it sizzles homily. Agustín methodically flips the tortilla in the pan until it puffs up slightly and both sides are browned. Then he puts it on the platter and adds another tortilla to the skillet.

"This is the hard part," he says. "We need to make a little rim around the edges of the tortillas, and it must be done while they are still hot. Like this. Ow," he mutters, as he crimps up the edges of the tortilla slowly. I try to help and realize that yeah, that sucker is super hot.

"There are tamaleras who are experts at this," he says. "Their fingers are so tough because they are used to making these."

He keeps pressing and cooking tortillas, and we both try to crimp them without too much damage to our fingertips. Once the chorizo is done crisping and put aside in a bowl and the refried beans are seasoned with some sort of sauce and another kind of chile, we chop up some white onion, then shred some of the lettuce and finely grate the cheese. I cut a little piece to try—it's cheese, so it's not like I'm *not* going to sample it—and find that it's slightly chewy and wonderfully light and salty.

Agustín claps his hands together. "Listo! Let's build our sopesitos."

He gives me a spoon and tells me to put a thin layer of beans on each one, then we add them in batches to the pan where the chorizo cooked. We make a little assembly line, topping the finished ones with some chorizo, then adding the tomato and onion mix, some shredded lettuce, and sprinkle them all with cheese.

The smells in my kitchen are so rich and spicy and wonderful, my stomach lets out a huge growl. Agustín laughs, but somehow, it never feels like he's laughing *at* me. Even when it's my stomach being growly.

"That is the noise we like to hear," he says, his smile so big it makes the corners of his eyes crinkle. He looks at the platter and whistles. "Can I take a picture very quickly to send to my mom?"

"Oh, yeah, sure," I say.

He snaps a few photos, then pockets his phone. "Where do we eat?"

There's a small breakfast bar in my living room, on the wall that joins to the kitchen, with two high stools. We set it up with bowls of aguachile, and plates with two sopes each. Agustín brings out two beers that he must have brought with him, and cracks open the bottles.

"Salud," he says.

"Cheers," I say.

We clink. The beer is light and refreshing, the bubbles tickling the back of my throat as I swallow. Now the real test. I'm not a raw seafood kind of gal, but that marinade was something else. I pick up my spoon and take a small bite of the aguachile.

The moment it hits my mouth, I feel transported. It's like that scene in Ratatouille when Remy tries to get his brother to appreciate flavor combinations. I can practically see all the different flavors springing to life in front of my eyes: there's the tart burst of lime juice, like green fireworks, mixed with the sizzling heat of the chiles, low flames flickering across my tongue. Then the meaty punch of the shrimp, contrasting with the cool, pale crunch of cucumber. The onion gives a much-needed zing, sparkles of red-purple, and then, at the very end, the floral, herby taste of the cilantro, elegant swirls that bring the whole dish together.

I'm dumbstruck. I feel for a moment like I'm somewhere else, somewhere far away from the skyscrapers of Manhattan and the honking of yellow cabs on the street below.

"You like it?" Agustín asks, and I can tell he's nervous.

I swallow. "I love it."

His dimples flash, and he runs a hand through his hair to smooth it, but it just flops right back over his brow. We're sitting very close together, I realize, our knees only a couple of inches apart.

"Try it with some tostada," he says, taking one of the crisp tortillas we bought at the store and breaking a piece off. I scoop up more of the aguachile, and it's just as delicious the second time, only now I get to eat it with the salty crunch of a tortilla.

"Good, right?" he says. His eyebrows pinch together hopefully, two dark slashes above encouraging brown eyes.

I flush and nod, then turn my attention to the sopes. "How do we eat these?" I ask.

"With your hands," he says. "But you can use a knife and fork too."

Tentatively, I pick up the little sope and take a bite. About half the toppings fall onto my plate but I don't care about that because holy fucking *wow* what is this magical culinary experience I am having on a random Sunday afternoon? The tortilla is still warm, and slightly chewy, the beans give off a gentle heat, combined with the meaty spice of the chorizo. Then there's the freshness of the raw veggies, the crisp lettuce, the mild bite of the white onion. And the salty tang of cheese to top it all off.

"Ummahgod," I mumbled through my mouthful.

Agustín laughs through his own bite. "Ssgoodyuh?"

"Ughsssogood."

I wash it down with a drink of the beer, and now I understand why he brought them. The cool refreshing drink pairs perfectly with the rich, spicy flavors.

"Wow," I say.

"Yeah?" he asks.

"Yeah. If this wedding was just about me eating the food, I would nail it. Ten out of ten."

Agustín laughs loudly at that and holds up his hand for a high five, which I obviously do not reciprocate because what if I miss, or what if I do it wrong, or what if I accidentally hit him in the face. But then he just high fives himself with his other hand and grins at me. I blush, grinning back, and for half a second, my eyes dip to his mouth, and I wonder what his lips would feel like on mine. Then a spasm of *Danger, Danger, Danger* rips through me and I yank my gaze away.

"Diez de diez," he says.

We both decide the sopes might be a little too messy to eat with our hands, so I grab us some forks and knives and napkins. We spend the next few minutes demolishing the food. I alternate between the sopes and the aguachile, delighting in the combination of flavors, hearty versus fresh. When we are both finished, we lean back in our stools, sipping our beers. I don't think I've ever felt this relaxed in my apartment with anyone besides Rachel.

The dogs have gathered around us while we eat, Charleston doing his best impression of a desolate starving orphan who hasn't eaten in days, the Colonel waiting patiently with hopeful eyes, Hazel pacing around the legs of our stools and glaring at us for not sharing anything yet. There are some chorizo crumbles and bit of tortilla and cheese on my plate. I hand out treats equally among my dogs, and Agustín gives Charleston some extra chorizo because Charleston bends all humans to his will when it comes to food.

There's a tiny squeak and I see Pip, emerging from the decompression room.

"Hey there," I say gently. There's one last bite of chorizo left on my plate, and I pick it up and hold it out as I walk very slowly over to him. He takes a step back but doesn't run from me. I crouch down, the meat in my outstretched hand. I don't move. Pip's nose twitches and his tongue flashes out. "It's okay," I say. "It's yours. Go on." I try to think of the Spanish phrases Agustín taught me. "Um . . . qué buen perro. Está bien."

I cringle at how terrible my accent is, but Pip creeps toward me, still sniffing. He snatches the chorizo from my hand, and I smile. "Qué buen perro," I say again. Pip swallows, licking his chops, and sniffs my fingers. Then he gives them a quick lick. It's the first time he's touched me without biting. Keeping extra still and my eyes on Pip, I say to Agustín, "Hey, could you get me some more chorizo?"

I hear the squeak of his stool and then his footsteps going into the kitchen. I don't want to break eye contact with Pip. "Qué buen perro," I say softly. He gives a little whine. A plate sets down next to me, with a handful of crumbles on it, and I pick up another piece and hold it out to him.

"Oh no you don't, cabrón," Agustín says, and I imagine he's keeping Charleston from attacking the plate. But I only have eyes for Pip. He eagerly takes another chunk of chorizo from my proffered hand. And this time, when I reach for more, he doesn't skitter at all.

When the plate is clean, Pip licks his lips again, looking satisfied. He sniffs my hand, gives my fingers a final lick with his long tongue, then lets out a huge yawn. He pads over to the dog bed and starts digging, like chihuahuas tend to do. Then he circles around a few times and curls up, closing his eyes.

I look up at Agustín in wonder. "Did you see that?" I whisper.

Agustín is holding Charleston on his lap, beaming. "I saw it."

Hazel looks indignant at the audacity of someone taking the bed she rightfully stole from the Colonel, but I grab her as she trots over to give Pip a piece of her mind. "Oh no you don't," I say, standing and tucking her in my arms. I feed her a bit of chorizo and she relents.

"Hey," Agustín says, standing and putting Charleston down now that it's safe. "Why don't we bring some sopes to Miriam?"

I narrow my eyes at him. "Is this some sneak attack way to get me to socialize?"

"No," he admits. "I just don't want to be on her bad side."

He makes a good point.

"Fine," I say. "But we're bringing Hazelnut. I don't trust her not to kick Pip to the curb once we leave."

20
Agustín

Miriam opens her door on the first knock.

"Took you two long enough," she says, ushering us inside. "I could smell your cooking from down the hall."

She nods at me approvingly and gives me a wink when Eloise's back is turned.

"Hey, Hazelnut, how's my little princess?" Miriam says, stroking Hazel's head while the little old dachshund soaks up the attention.

Miriam's apartment is wonderfully chaotic. It's open plan, with the kitchen spilling out into the living room. There's a bright yellow teapot on the stove, and a huge circular chair with an enormous purple cushion set in a wooden frame overflowing with decorative pillows by the large windows that look out over West 89th Street. A couch covered in about five different afghans sits against one wall, with a coffee table shaped like a tree trunk, and a series of mismatched, sparkly patterned poufs scattered around on the floor. An elaborate system of platforms covered in scratchy carpet are mounted on the wall behind the couch, zigzagging nearly up to the ceiling. The orange tabby we saw earlier is lounging on one of the platforms, and I see a calico tail peeking out from beneath a maroon and navy afghan.

Miriam has a pair of glasses perched in her tight black curls, and she wears light jeans, a Cornell T-shirt, and a pair of fluffy pink slippers.

I hand her the plate with two sopes on it. "They're messy," I say.

"All the best food is," Miriam says. "Go on, make yourselves at home. Checkers, Milhouse, say hello to our guests."

The orange tabby stretches out on the platform, showing us her claws, and I hear a hiss from beneath the afghan.

"Don't mind Milhouse, he's got no manners," Miriam says, grabbing a knife and fork from the kitchen and settling herself at the small dining table set up next to the kitchen. Eloise perches daintily on the edge of the couch, but I take the huge cushioned circle chair. It looks like a fun place to sit. My whole body sinks into it, buffeted by the pillows. I throw Eloise a thumbs up, which makes her mouth twitch.

"It's nice, right?" Miriam says, noticing my expression. "My husband gave me so much crap when I bought it, but he loved that chair in the end." She takes a bite of the sope, and her eyes pop. "Damn!"

Eloise and I exchange a smile, and something about it feels different—like there's a thread connecting us. Like we're really on the same team. "You like them?" I ask.

"Oh my lordy lord, I could eat these all day." She quickly dispatches the first sope, then wipes her mouth with her napkin and leans back in her chair. "Now, Eloise, you know I'm going to need some more information on whatever the heck is going on here." She points her fork at me.

We both look expectantly at Eloise. Her eyes bug wide, and she turns to me with a look that says, *You tell her.* I give the slightest shake of my head, *No.* Her eyebrows knit together. *Please.* I give her a nod. *You can do it.*

"As lovely as this little mime routine is, can we all start using actual words now?" Miriam says, starting on her second sope.

Eloise heaves a sigh so big, it could probably be heard all the way on the east side of the park. Her brows furrow together, her face taking on a look of determination.

"I needed a plus-one to Rachel's wedding because Diego's family thinks they're cursed, so I met Agustín off a list of plus-ones, and now he's making me talk to people and learn about Mexican food so I can be prepared for the wedding because I don't know how to talk to people, and I have to make a speech and honestly everything about this wedding feels awful and scary, and I don't want to do it but I have to because Rachel is my best friend and she needs me," Eloise says in a rush.

Miriam pauses midchew. I wonder if this is the most she's ever heard Eloise say before. It's certainly impressing me, and I've only known her for like a week. Slowly, Miriam finishes her bite and swallows.

"Well," she says. She folds up her napkin. "Hm," she adds, rubbing her chin. "Well," she says again. "Isn't this quite the turn of events."

Eloise is holding a struggling Hazelnut to her chest, while the other cat, Milhouse, peeks his head out to glare at the intruder. Eloise's lips are pressed in a tight line, like she's wishing she could swallow back the words she just blurted out.

Miriam turns her sharp gaze on me. "And what is your plan, then?"

"Well, we tried having coffee with a neighbor," I admit. Eloise lets out a sound that's half squeak half cough. "But Madame Boularès was a little . . . intense."

"Ha!" Miriam roars. "Did she start talking about how she and her husband had an amazing sex life?" She shudders. "That woman is one strange cookie, I'll tell you. But harmless. And lonely, I think. Stuck in the past." She finishes the sope. "How big is this wedding?"

"Big," I admit. "The Alvarez family is one of the wealthiest in Mexico City."

Miriam looks at Eloise. "Girl, you didn't tell me Rachel snagged a rich boy! She's gorgeous though, and funny, and smart as a whip, so I'm not surprised." She looks back at me. "Let me guess—three hundred guests?"

"More like five hundred," I say, which gets another squeak from Eloise.

"Oof."

Silence falls around us, broken only by Checkers, the tabby, scratching at the rug on her platform. Even Hazel has stopped squirming, as if she can sense Eloise needs stillness. I watch Eloise's jaw work, her throat bobbing as she swallows, then she takes a deep breath and says in a clear, plaintive voice, "Gretchen from 9C came over for dinner last night."

"What?" Miriam and I say in shocked unison. I think I'd be less surprised if one of the sparkly poufs came to life and did a tap dance in front of me.

Eloise shrugs and focuses very hard on stroking Hazel's ears. "She came over with wine and a casserole and had dinner with me and Rachel."

"I'll be," Miriam says.

"This is wonderful!" I say. "Was it fun?"

She frowns at me then purses her lips. "It . . . wasn't terrible."

Miriam beams with pride. "Look at you! Wedding schmedding, you can handle this no problem. Now let me think. I know there's more we can do to help."

Eloise seems to have hit her limit at the word "we." Or maybe it's the "more" that's scaring her. Either way, she shoots to her feet, her cheeks flushing with color. "I need to walk the Pack."

"Sure, sure," Miriam says agreeably. "If you two ever do any cooking again, though, you know where to find me."

21
Eloise

I practically shove Agustín out of my apartment as soon as he's packed up his things.

He offered to help me clean the kitchen, but I steadfastly refused.

I need a minute. I need several minutes. A whole bucket of minutes. Probably hours. Possibly days. My muscles are twitchy and sore, my heart thumps tiredly against my ribs, and my brain feels like it's on fire. So much talking. So much newness. I just want to snuggle in bed with the Pack and an iced tea and reread *Murder on the Orient Express.* I want to be a Victorian invalid and take to my room, refusing all visitors. I rinse off the knives and cutting boards, clean the skillets, put away the leftover aguachile, and stare at the two sopes that are left.

An idea springs to mind, an idea that sounds very much like it's being whispered into my brain by Agustín's voice. I swat it away, because Victorian invalid. Tea. Agatha Christie. Just let me *be.*

The voice whispers again.

I stand there debating for what feels like hours before I decide I may as well just do it, or else I'll be standing here until midnight.

I put the two sopes on a plate, leave my door on the latch, and creep down the hall, my sock feet making no sound on the plush green carpet, the Art Deco lights illuminating the walls. I hesitate halfway down and start back home, then stop and turn around. The indecision is killing me. But I look like an idiot just walking back and forth over the same patch of carpet and the more time I spend in the hall, the more chance someone comes out of the elevator or leaves their apartment. I take two more steps forward. I'm level with Weed Dude's door now. I pass it, then Soul Cycle, then Gretchen in 9C (I can hear Mansion wailing), then I hover for a moment. This is so stupid. I'm so stupid.

I run the remaining few steps to 9B, put the plate down on the ground, ring the doorbell, then flee back down the hall, like I'm some asshole kid playing ding-dong-ditch. I wait by my door, heart in my throat. Then I hear the click of a lock. Mr. Bloom's face pokes out. He looks down at the plate, frowns, and looks up. His eyes meet mine.

"I made them," I say.

He picks up the plate. Sniffs the food. Gives me a nod. Then shuts the door.

22
Agustín

What makes someone a hero? How do we reconcile those we idolized with the truth of their actions? In researching my grandfather's life, I learned so much more about him than the stories I'd been told throughout my childhood. And yet, there's still so much I don't know. I'm left with the burden of unanswered questions and the silence of the dead.

It's impossible not to wonder. Did he ever think about us, when he was standing at that podium on the steps of City Hall? Or when he put his son to bed at night—a son who was younger than his youngest grandchild? Did he feel shame? Or did he not care—perhaps he was able to simply wall up his past, his history, his family in Mexico and live his life in New York without a second thought about us.

I sit back and stare at my computer screen, wondering if I should cut that series of questions in the second paragraph.

Tinkering with the article has become a compulsion. There's nothing left to do on it until I get the interview. And I can't help thinking that there *is* someone who can give me answers—Ricardo would know more about Abuelo's life in New York than all the old footage or archival research in the world. Ricardo would know what kind of man Abuelo was here.

I can't deny that part of me resents Ricardo for that. I know I'm only supposed to get the interview so that Neil can say we've done our due diligence, and show readers that we've gotten an alternate viewpoint from someone else involved in El Rasca's life. But I can't help wondering if any of Abuelo's lies, the secrecy, the cheating . . . if any of it was passed on to his son. If Ricardo is some twisted, perverse version of my grandfather, inheriting all the bad parts. And I'll have to face that in real life, when I talk to him.

My phone buzzes on the table next to my computer.

Eloise: I think I have to cancel tonight.

I kind of guessed this text was coming. I glance at the clock on my stove. It's T-minus three hours until Rachel and Diego's engagement party. Apparently, it was supposed to be in the spring, but they had to move it because Rachel got busy with her makeup line, and Diego got sent to deal with some issue in the Buenos Aires office of Grupo Real. Eloise has been hoping they'd push the party back again—or more likely she was dreaming they'd just not have an engagement party at all. Eloise is a master at wishful thinking.

Me: You can't cancel.

Eloise: Rachel will understand. I think I'm coming down with something.

Even if I hadn't gotten to know Eloise so well over the past month, I'd still be suspicious of this excuse.

Me: 🙄

Eloise: Seriously. I think it's probably the flu. Or something even more contagious. The plague. Yeah. It could definitely be the plague.

Me: The plague.

Eloise: I hear it's making a comeback.

Me: I don't think we can put the plague in the same category as low-rise jeans.

There's a pause long enough to make me turn back to the article. I wonder if Ricardo looks at all like Abuelo. The thought makes my stomach squirm.

Eloise: There are approximately seven new cases of the bubonic plague in the US each year.

Me: Did you just Google that?

Eloise: No, it's totally common knowledge.

Eloise: Okay yes, I did. But seven cases! I could be one of seven cases.

Me: You can't miss Rachel's engagement party. She's your best friend. You're the maid of honor. I'll pick you up at six like we agreed.

I go to put my phone down, then type one last thing.

Me: I *might* have believed you if you said one of the dogs was sick.

Eloise: Oh crap, why didn't I think of that!

I chuckle and turn back to my laptop.

I arrive at Eloise's building at quarter to six.

I've found it's always best to be early, so that Eloise has time to acclimate to my presence. And I want to say hi to the dogs. Over the past four weeks, Pip has been coming out of his shell more and more every day. I know he likes it when I'm around. And Eloise does too. She won't admit it, but I know it's nice for her to have someone help out with their care, especially on days when she has to make a lot of orders for *Treats Gourmand*, the online pet bakery she's got a freelance agreement with. We'll all go to the park together, or sometimes I'll hang out with them if she has to take the Colonel to the vet or Hazel to the groomer.

So far, our wedding prep has consisted of mostly more cooking, some slideshows with facts and details about Mexico City, and a couple of movie nights. We watched *Roma*, which she loved—I think she enjoys learning about the history of the city, even though it can be very dark. I told her how the fighting in the film was real: the Tlatelcolo massacre, when the Mexican government murdered hundreds of protesting students and teachers. I decided against showing her *Amores Perros* because of the dogfighting. We watched *Spectre*, because the opening scene features James Bond running around Centro during Día de Muertos. Fun fact: There was never a parade like the one in that movie, but it was so popular that the tourism industry in Mexico City pressured the government to make one.

But tonight is our first real test: a social, wedding-related event. It's also the first time I'll be meeting Rachel—and Diego, though Eloise almost never talks about Diego. When I asked her once what she thought of him, she tensed and said "He's fine" before changing the subject.

I enter the lobby and give Hector a wave.

"Looking good, bro," he says to me in Spanish.

"Thanks, man." I'm wearing a light green, short-sleeved linen button down with checkered detailing along the hem of the sleeves and the breast pocket. The color reminded me of Eloise's eyes when I saw it in the store. I wait for the elevator and wonder if I should have brought something. Flowers? But then I think that might freak her out. She was very clear about the rules of this arrangement.

The doors open, and Gretchen steps out with her two kids and Paloma, the nanny, in tow.

"Agustín!" she says brightly. "Don't you look handsome. Begonia, say hi to Agustín."

The little girl with blonde pigtails looks up at me. "Hi," she says.

"Hi," I reply. "Hola," I say to Paloma, who nods and smiles at me, balancing Mansion on her hip.

"Going to see Eloise?" Gretchen asks.

I nod. "It's Rachel's engagement party tonight."

"Oh, that's right! Miriam was talking about it the other day."

Most of the ninth floor of the Archer has become enmeshed in Eloise's preparations for the wedding. Miriam has rallied the troops. Gretchen, Madame Boularès (who still brings up her dead husband a lot, but thankfully without any references to their bedroom activities), and Kate and Sanvi, the sporty couple from 9E, have all been offering advice and support to Eloise—often whether she wants it or not, which I think is even better preparation for when she's in Mexico because I can imagine that Diego's family might be a bit, er, assertive.

I haven't met Mr. Bloom, the violist in 9B, yet but Eloise tells me they've been exchanging small gifts, like food and books.

None of us ever see the guy in 9D. The Weed Dude, Eloise calls him. Even Miriam doesn't know his name.

"We're off to the Met," Gretchen says.

"The museum?" I ask.

She gives a tinkling laugh, diamonds glinting at her ears. "The opera. It's Begonia's first time seeing *La Traviata*. Have fun tonight!"

The four of them bustle out of the lobby and into the waiting black SUV. I get in the elevator and step off into the now-familiar hallway of the ninth floor. Miriam, ever in tune with the sound of the elevator ding, throws open her apartment door.

She whistles. "Look at you, Short King," she says, giving me an approving nod. I tried to tame my hair, but it's as unruly as ever. "Nice kicks," she adds, taking in my brown suede creepers. "How's our girl doing?"

"She tried to cancel."

"Not surprised."

"She said she had the plague."

Miriam lets out a big belly laugh. "I'll give her points for creativity. Let me know how it goes."

"I will," I promise.

When I get to Eloise's apartment, I can't help but laugh myself. The door is on the latch and there's a Post-it stuck to it with one word in block print: *HELP.*

I open the door quietly and hear voices drifting down the hall.

"This is a great lipliner." I recognize Sanvi's smooth, even tone. "Rachel's makeup line is legit."

"You look amazing!" That's Kate.

I close the door and turn to see Charleston scampering toward me, followed closely by Pip. "Hola chicos," I say, scooping Pip up in my arms. I carry him down the hall. The three women are in the bathroom—Eloise is perched on one of the stools from the breakfast bar while Sanvi circles around her and Kate leans in the doorframe. I can't see Eloise's face clearly, but I catch her eyes in the mirror for a moment, and she sends me a clear plea for help.

"Evening ladies," I say.

Sanvi looks up. "Agustín, hi! We're almost done." Hazelnut trots around her feet, anxious to be the center of attention.

"Oh, and we left a sample pack of our protein powders in the kitchen for you," Kate adds, her high ponytail swinging back and forth as she turns around. They're always trying to push various powders or supplements on me, and I haven't had the heart to tell them I don't work out. I keep fit—I like to run in Prospect Park on the weekends—but I'm not a gym bro.

"Okay, okay, I'm done," Eloise says, hopping down off the stool, still half hidden by the two other women.

"Just one last spritz," Sanvi singsongs, covering Eloise in a cloud of spray. Eloise coughs and swats the air. As Kate moves aside, and Sanvi packs up the makeup littered across the sink, Eloise steps out of the bathroom.

"Ta da!" Kate says, doing jazz hands. "Doesn't she look gorgeous? Sanvi's great. I suck at makeup. I never wear it, except when we're filming one of our workout videos, because this pasty skin does not love the camera . . ."

But Kate's voice fades as I feel an odd swooping sensation in my stomach, and my neck goes suddenly hot.

"How bad is it?" Eloise asks me quietly.

Her eyes are lined in black so they seem bigger than normal with a subtle gold sparkle on her lids. Her lips are painted a deep blushing pink, and the makeup accentuates her cheekbones, giving them just the right amount of color. Her curls are thick and lustrous, framing her face. She wears a midnight blue, knee length dress with tiny white dots like stars patterning it, along with a pair of dark blue espadrilles that gives her a little added height.

I can't stop staring. My heart is doing strange things inside my chest.

"Oh god," she says, taking my silence for a negative. "Is it bad? It's bad, right? Oh my god . . ."

"No," I say quickly before she talks herself into washing it off. "No, no, you . . . you look beautiful. I mean, you always look beautiful but tonight . . . you'll stop traffic."

Her cheeks turn a darker shade of pink. My own cheeks are feeling much warmer than usual.

"Are you sure?"

I nod. A lot. Lots of nodding here.

"I feel like an idiot," she admits, glancing down at her shoes. "What if I fall over?"

"I'll catch you." The words spill out before I can consider them. Eloise's eyes widen. My mouth goes dry.

"You guys look so cute together," Kate gushes, coming over to give me a hug.

"So cute," Sanvi echoes, kissing my cheek. We've told all the neighbors multiple times that we are not together, just friends, but they always seem to ignore us. "Do you need anything else?"

Eloise's throat bobs, and her jaw clenches, an indication that a panic attack might be coming on. I've gotten to know the signs.

"No, we're good, thanks so much for all your help," I say, putting Pip on the floor and ushering them down the hall. "I'll definitely check out those protein powders, okay, bye!"

I shut the door behind them and head back to the living room. Eloise is standing where I left her.

Her chest hitches, and she's shaking her head, tears filling her eyes as she struggles to breathe. She needs something sturdy, some way to feel grounded while she does her count five. Usually, a wall works best. But this party is on a rooftop and there won't be many walls there, and I want to do something to help, something physical, tangible.

I step forward and grab her hand.

"Count five," I say. I breathe in slowly as I count aloud. "One, two, three, four, five."

She grips my hand hard, her fingernails digging into my skin. I don't care. She can hold me as hard as she needs to. I keep her hand firmly in mine.

"Good," I say. "Now exhale."

I count again, exhaling with her, and she lets out a gasp as her breath comes back to her.

"One more?" I ask and she nods, blinking away her tears. I count in again, and she inhales with me. Her grip on my hand relaxes a fraction, then another. We breathe out together, as the Colonel pads over to lean against her thigh.

"Sorry," Eloise croaks.

"You have nothing to be sorry for. That was a lot of activity in your house."

"Oh fuck did I ruin the makeup? Sanvi worked so hard on it . . ."

Her hands flutter around her face, like she's scared to touch herself. I grab her wrists softly and put her arms by her sides.

"You're fine," I reassure her. "You're perfect."

She blinks, her eyes widening, and I realize that sounded like flirting.

It's been harder and harder over these past weeks to remind myself of the boundaries she set. That we have an expiration date. That I can't allow myself to become too accustomed to her presence. Because whenever I coax a laugh out of her, it feels like I've won the lottery. When I witness a moment of patience with one of the dogs (usually Charleston or Pip), my heart seems to throb straight out of my chest. There's something so fundamentally *good* about Eloise.

And now, as I look at her, the deep blue hue of her dress offsetting the cream-and-rose colors of her skin, I am overcome with the urge to pull her toward me. To tuck her into the crook of my shoulder. To make sure she knows she's safe.

Instead, I drop her wrists and give her the space I'm sure she wants. I have to respect her boundaries. She takes a step back, her blush reaching to her collarbone.

"Thanks," she mumbles. She touches her hair—her curls are very thick and shiny this evening—and takes a few tentative steps in her shoes. She doesn't fall over, which seems to give her some confidence. The Colonel mirrors her every movement. "Okay," she says, her voice sounding stronger. "Okay."

"Ready?" I ask.

Her phone pings. "The car is downstairs," she says. Then she looks around at the dogs. "You guys be good. Doggie cam is on, Miriam is on-call in case anything happens . . ."

"Nothing's going to happen," I reassure her. "It's only a couple of hours. They'll be fine."

She swallows hard. "I know."

And I know it's not the dogs she's really worried about.

"You're going to be fine too," I add.

She narrows her eyes at me. She hates my boundless positivity.

"You're not going to die," I amend. "And if you feel nervous, just squeeze my hand as hard as you can."

She bites her lip. "I don't want to hurt you."

I suppress my smile. "You're not going to hurt me." I offer her my arm. "Shall we?"

Her touch is featherlight against my skin, sending prickles over my arm. I try to suppress those too.

"Qué guapa!" Hector says as we walk out of the elevator. Over the course of traveling down nine floors, Eloise has gone from trying not to touch me, to clutching my forearm in a vice-like grip. A sleek black town car waits for us, courtesy of Diego Alvarez. Eloise told me he tried to get Rachel to use the cars and drivers his father provides him for all her travel in the city. She laughed in his face, asked if he'd ever been in midtown traffic at four PM on a Wednesday, and said no thanks, she'd stick to the subway.

I think I'm going to like Rachel very much. I've been dying to meet her, but I get the distinct impression Eloise has been keeping us apart on purpose.

I open the door for her, and she slides across the back seat. The car glides out into the traffic of Central Park West, the trees dappling the sidewalk in a patchwork of leafy of patterns in the warm, evening light of summer. There are joggers out for a run, moms pushing double strollers, men in suits shouting into their cellphones. I see a gay couple walking a pair of golden retrievers and tap Eloise on the shoulder.

"Perritos!" I say excitedly, as she cranes her head to get a look. It's become our thing. Whenever we go anywhere (which is admittedly not a lot, but I have coaxed her out to that wine bar where we first met, and we do go to the park), we always point out the dogs we see by saying, "Perrito." Sometimes we add descriptors: gordito, esponjoso, negro, feliz.

I feel proud that I'm slowly increasing her Spanish vocabulary. It's helping with Pip too, which I think is more important to Eloise than any words and phrases to use at the wedding.

As the car snakes through traffic and heads downtown, I notice Eloise's breathing starts to become a little ragged. She takes out her phone, then puts it away, then takes it out again.

"Is it hot in here?" she asks, fanning her face.

I angle the air conditioning vent, directing all the cold air toward her. When we finally pull up to the sleek building on Debrosses Street in Tribeca, Eloise is doing full on yoga breathing.

"Thanks," I say to the driver as I get out and offer her my hand. She wobbles as she steps onto the pavement, and I snake an arm around her waist to steady her. I somehow missed earlier that the back of her dress has a diamond-shaped cutout—my hand comes in contact with a swath of exposed skin, and suddenly I'm the one who can't breathe properly. I release her as soon as she's steady, my palm tingling where it touched her. I flex my fingers and shove my hand into my pocket.

There's a bouncer at the door with an earpiece and a clipboard. "Name?" he asks.

"Eloise Whitechapel and Agustín Martinez," I say.

He checks us off. "Take the elevator to the roof," he says, opening the glass doors and gesturing us toward a bank of elevators.

We press the button for the rooftop. Eloise is trembling all over, curls quivering, the pulse at her jaw fluttering.

"Take my hand," I say in a more commanding tone than I'd usually use with her. It works. She instinctively reaches for me, like she'd been waiting for me to ask, her palm the faintest bit damp with panic sweat, her grip like a vise. I don't care. I hold her hand like it's my own lifeline and the firmer I squeeze, the harder she squeezes back. And the harder she squeezes, the less she shakes.

The elevator doors open and we step out into the party.

23

Eloise

If it weren't for the strong, steady feel of Agustín's hand in mine, I think I'd collapse right now.

I squint in the light of the sun, glinting off One World Trade Center and shining right in my eyes. The lower Manhattan skyline greets us, the familiar shapes of the skyscrapers, the ribbon of the Hudson in the distance. The rooftop is decked out in ultimate style—flowers fill the space, perfuming the air with a sweet but not overpowering scent. Lilies and hydrangeas sit in large vases among wisps of baby's breath, towers of white and yellow roses bracket the couches and chairs set up in carefully crafted arrangements, and the floor is covered in shockingly realistic fake grass, to give the whole thing an air of being in a garden. There's a long table brimming with cheese platters and charcuterie boards, fancy looking canapés, and silver tiers of brightly colored macarons. Ornate lights are strung over it all, their tiny bulbs no match for the sun, but I bet they'll twinkle perfectly later.

I take all of this in in a vague kind of way, colors, and smells, and sounds washing over me because there are so. Many. People.

Then Agustín looks at me brightly and says, "It's not that crowded."

It's not? There are easily twenty people here.

He sees my expression and instantly pivots. "So, what first? Drinks or Rachel?"

I know he's been dying to meet Rachel. And she's been dying to meet him. And I have been determined to keep them apart for as long as possible.

One month into this whole plus-one arrangement and the sliver of sunlight Agustín brought into my world has only gotten bigger and brighter and frustratingly more potent. The stomach-clenching and mouth-watering that was already a huge distraction has now begun to include more annoying details, like thinking about what he's doing when he's not around, and lighting up whenever he comes over, and checking my phone a stupid number of times a day to see if he's reached out. It probably doesn't help that the Pack adores him. And so do my neighbors.

My life has suddenly started filling up with more people than ever before. Gretchen has taken to "just popping by" to say hi, Miriam is always coming over now to get more details about the wedding, Madame Boularès has sent a standing invitation for coffee on Saturday mornings, and Kate and Sanvi have been asking me to join them for their runs.

I don't run unless something is chasing me, thank you very much.

Mr. Bloom and I have taken to leaving each other small gifts outside the other's door. After the sopes, he left me a plate of lemon bars. And then I left him my battered copy of *Death on the Nile*, which I thought he'd enjoy, and he returned it with a copy of *Into Thin Air* by John Krakauer. Nonfiction isn't generally my thing, but I actually liked the book. Sometimes, we'll talk from down the hallway. But never for very long.

I like Mr. Bloom best of everyone on the ninth floor of the Archer.

Agustín is waiting for my response. I take a quick inventory of the guests and find my best friend. She's deep in conversation with a few of her influencer friends.

"Drinks," I say. All the drinks. Maybe if I have enough gin and tonics, I can make it through this evening without falling apart. I thought I was going to have another panic attack in the elevator, as the Wheel spun frantically between *I Will Be So Bad at This and Ruin Everything* and *AHHHHHH!*

But the feel of Agustín's warm rough hand around mine is surprisingly grounding. Like an electrode conductor, rooting me to the earth.

He leads me over to the bar, where a young man in a white button down and black vest is mixing drinks.

"What can I get you?" he asks. There's a large calligraphy list of specialty cocktails but my pulse is racing too fast and the letters blur and dance in my vision. Am I supposed to get a specialty cocktail? Is that what's expected? But I spent the whole car ride practicing my drink order!

I'll have a gin and tonic.

One gin and tonic, please.

Can I get a gin and tonic?

Over and over and over. All the iterations I could think of. And now it's showtime.

"Ginntonic," I blurt out, the words mushed together like I threw them in a blender. But the bartender just nods then looks to Agustín, who is of course deeply interested in the calligraphy special cocktails.

"What's in the Diego's Dream?" he asks.

I can't help rolling my eyes. Diego named a cocktail after himself? Barf.

"It's good. It's like an old fashioned. The Retro Rachel is more of a French 75."

Wait, Rachel has a fancy cocktail named after her too?

"I'll do the Diego one," Agustín says.

"Great choice." A voice from behind us makes me jump, and I nearly topple over in these stupid heels. Agustín holds my hand tighter, centering me, and turns us smoothly to come face to face with Diego Alvarez himself.

"The name is ridiculous though," he adds, rolling his eyes exactly the way I just did. "The event planner said it was 'all the rage,'" he uses air quotes, "to have these sorts of custom cocktails. Rachel was pissed when she saw the names but it was too late to change them. Hi." He extends his hand to Agustín. "I'm Diego Alvarez."

"Agustín Martinez," Agustín says, shaking Diego's hand warmly. "Mucho gusto."

Diego turns to me, smiling. "Eloise," he says. "I'm so glad you could make it. It's really great to see you."

He moves in for a hug, and I stiffen—thankfully he seems to remember I am not a hugger, so his arms fall to his sides, and he just nods. His eyes dart to my and Agustín's hands, still clasped together, and I release Agustín like a hot potato. Crap. Diego better not tell Rachel about that.

I can count on one hand the number of times I've hung out with Diego. I think the last time was four months ago, when he met me and Rachel at our favorite margarita spot, El Taco Loco. I mostly just shoved chips and salsa into my face then went home early.

There's a moment of pause, when the two men seem to be waiting for *me* to say something, which sorry, what, no, absolutely not. I shoot a panicked glance at Agustín, and he gets the hint.

"Felicidades," he says, and ohhhh yes, yes *yes*, thank god. They're speaking Spanish. I don't have to participate if they're speaking Spanish. They dive into a conversation where I understand absolutely nothing except CDMX (which sounds like Say-Day-Em-Ekeys and which I only recognize because I've heard Agustín say it so many times now). Then the bartender says, "Gin and tonic," and huzzah, I have a drink and absolutely no obligation to make small talk. I take a sip and let the tart, crisp flavor fill my mouth, hovering on the edge of the conversation and scanning the other people on the rooftop from a comfortable distance.

I feel extremely underdressed. Maybe Agustín was lying when he said I looked perfect. The memory sets my heart fluttering in my chest. He was obviously just being polite. The other women here are in glittery dresses with tiny straps or no straps at all, wearing the highest, pointiest heels imaginable. Rachel looks stunning, of course. She's wearing a midlength white pleated skirt with a beaded white crop top. Her hair is piled up on her crown and dotted with daisies and she's rocking a pair of Grecian style sandals that wrap up around her calves. Her makeup is flawless, as always. I'm sure she did it herself.

I was kind of glad Sanvi and Kate came over to help me with my own hair and makeup. I would feel even more out of place here if I'd come with my usual nighttime look, aka mascara and lip gloss.

Rachel offered to do it, of course, but I didn't want to be a bother. She has so much to organize. But she flat out told me she was doing my look for the wedding and threatened me upon pain of death to make sure I got a good night's sleep beforehand so she could have (and I quote) "a suitable canvas to work with."

I look back and forth between her and Diego. They do seem to fit as a couple. Diego is good-looking, I guess, if you like that angular-jawed, dark-haired, Disney prince in custom Brooks Brothers type thing. I like Agustín's look better. His shirt color almost matches my eyes. And I think his shoes are cool. He's not overly polished like the rest of the men here.

The two of them sip their fancy Diego-themed cocktails and chat in rapid fire Spanish, and I'm just starting to relax when Rachel shouts, "EL!"

Oh no. Here we go.

I brace myself for the coming onslaught of all caps level excitement.

"Eloise Madigan Whitechapel, look at YOU!" Rachel squeals, rushing over to scoop me up in a hug. "Oh my god, STUNNING. Magnificent. Exquisite. I DIE. Did Sanvi use the Recklessly Rachel lipliner kit I sent her?"

I nod.

"Ahhhh, that is going to sell out on the first day, I'm sure of it. Amor, doesn't Eloise look FABULOUS?"

"Fabulous," Diego echoes and it appears he, like me, has learned that when Rachel goes all caps, it's best to just roll with it.

"And YOU." Oh god. My stomach does a backflip and lodges somewhere at the back of my throat as Rachel turns her radiance on Agustín. I quickly chug the rest of my gin and tonic. "You must be Agustín."

"And you must be Rachel," Agustín says, shooting her a huge smile that's ninety percent dimples and makes my knees go weak. "We meet at last."

"We do!" She pulls him toward her with a quick "Sorry, I'm a hugger," and then releases him. "Ahhh, I've been dying to meet you, has Eloise told you I've been dying to meet you?"

"I've been dying to meet you too!" Agustín says. They both look at me, and I want to melt into the fancy fake-grass floor.

Surprisingly, Diego comes to my rescue. "Amor, why don't you go grab a spot for us to sit and hang out?"

Yes, go. Please go.

"Eloise and I will bring over more drinks."

What? No.

"Perfect!" Rachel says. "Agustín, come with me."

She links arms with him, and I gape in horror at the infuriatingly smug expressions on the faces of my best friend and my plus-one. The two of them look like little peas in a pod as they head off to a cluster of couches at the far corner of the rooftop.

And now I'm stuck with Diego. Alone. Ugh. My skin prickles and my pulse kicks up a notch. I wish I could hold Agustín's hand. Why did Diego send them away? What am I even supposed to say to him? *Hey, I really wish you weren't marrying my best friend and fucking up the delicate balance of my life? And also your wedding is massively inconvenient to me?* I sound like an asshole. Oh my god, I *am* an asshole. I'm a huge jerk, I can't believe I'm thinking all of this, and I'm thinking it right at his chiseled face, at his stupid fancy engagement party, what is wrong with me, why can't I—

"Sorry about that," Diego says quietly. "I thought maybe it would be easier to let Rachel get all her questions out one-on-one with him, so you wouldn't feel like you're under a microscope. She's been really excited to meet him." He glances over to where the two of them are chatting away enthusiastically. "Like, *really* excited."

He chuckles warmly, his gaze soft and glowing as he watches her. I feel a couple of realizations smack me in the face.

Diego is really in love with Rachel.

Diego was trying to do something nice for *me*.

The epiphanies wedge uncomfortably against my sternum.

"Do you want the same thing you were having?" Diego asks as the bartender takes his order.

I nod, then clear my throat. I should probably start using my words around him. "Yes," I say quietly. "Gin and tonic. Please."

He smiles. "Cool."

I glance back at Agustín and Rachel, wondering what they're talking about and hoping against hope it's not me.

But it's definitely me.

24
Agustín

"Eloise has been so cagey about you," Rachel says. "Did you really have to go to your second cousin's wife's birthday party two weeks ago?"

"What?" I say, chuckling and shaking my head. "No. I'm guessing you didn't really have a graduation barbecue last Saturday."

Rachel chokes on the last sip of her drink. "Graduation from what? It's July," she cackles, then glances over at where Eloise and Diego are getting the drinks. "That girl," she says, with a sigh that's completely infused with love.

"You have been friends for a long time, right?" I say.

"Since elementary school." Rachel scratches her ear. "We were both the odd ducks of our class. I was the kid in foster care and Eloise . . . did she tell you about her parents?"

"No," I say.

"That's for her to tell," Rachel says. "She's really private, as I'm sure you've figured out. And her uncle who raised her, Lenny . . . let's say he wasn't the most engaged guardian on the planet. That apartment was so quiet and so sad until she brought dogs into it."

I glance over to where Diego and Eloise are now walking toward us, drinks in hand. I can tell Eloise is focusing very hard on not falling over. Diego sets Rachel's drink down in front of her, kissing the top of her head and taking the seat beside her.

"Eloise was telling me that you taught her how to cook Mexican food," Diego says.

I glance at Eloise, impressed she talked to him about that. She's perched on the edge of the couch next to me, like she's ready to take flight at a moment's notice.

"Yeah," I reply. "We made sopes and aguachile. She did a great job."

"How cool," Rachel says. "I love sopes. And you're a writer, right? El said you're helping with her speech."

"A journalist, yes," I say. I feel a weird tug in my chest.

"What paper do you work for?" Diego asks. "Or are you like one of those independent journalists with a Substack?"

"I write a local column for *The Brooklyn Daily News*," I tell him. "Back home I used to write for *Reforma* and *El País* and some other publications."

Diego whistles. "Damn, that's impressive. You should be working for a bigger paper here, like the *Times*."

"I'm publishing an article in *The New Yorker*, actually," I say. Then I immediately curse myself. I don't want to talk about this. I haven't told Eloise about the article, much less about Ricardo and the interview. It's not like I've been keeping it a secret. She's just never asked.

She's staring at me, shocked.

"Holy shit," Rachel says. "That's amazing."

"Thank you," I say.

"What's the article about?" Diego asks.

"Um, El Rasca," I say.

Diego gives me a blank stare but Eloise and Rachel look at each other.

"That name sounds familiar," Rachel says. "Was he, like, an activist? Like an Al Sharpton kind of figure?"

"He was."

"Right. I remember him on NY1 when I was a kid, doing press outside courthouses and leading marches and stuff."

I give a terse nod. "He was also my grandfather."

I can feel Eloise's eyes boring into the side of my face.

"Wait, seriously?" Rachel says. "That's really cool."

It's a little more complicated than "cool," but I don't want to get into it here. Suddenly, I wonder if there's a way I could connect with Ricardo through Diego, without having to try and get the interview at the wedding. It's occurring to me that in order to talk to Ricardo, I'll have to abandon Eloise to find him and speak to him alone. And I don't want to do that. The interview was supposed to be the priority but now . . . I glance at Eloise, her lips parted, her expression undeniably impressed.

My priorities are shifting.

I turn back to the happy couple. "I hear your wedding is going to be quite a big event."

Rachel rolls her eyes, and Diego smooths back his hair, almost sheepishly. "Yeah, Dad doesn't do anything halfway," he says. "And I'm the only son and all that."

He looks at me with an expression like I'll understand, which I don't really, because being the only son means nothing in my family, where women are the dominant force. But I do get the sentiment in general.

"I heard that even people who work for Grupo Real will come," I say. "That's nice."

"I'm taking on a higher role next year," Diego says. "So I told Dad I wanted to invite the employees in my department. Make a good impression. Some people are coming in from the Buenos Aires offices, some from Miami, and some are coming from Beijing."

"I told him, how weird is it that people who work for you are coming to your wedding," Rachel says.

Diego chuckles. "And I told her, this is how it works. Business always intersects with pleasure. Dad liked the idea because he thinks of it as some kind of show of force. I'd rather see it as a way for the people who work with me to feel included. To have a personal connection to the company."

It's a smart move. But it doesn't sound like Diego knows Ricardo at all—it's just a coincidence that Ricardo happens to work in Diego's department, under Diego's management. If I were to pry about a certain employee, Diego would surely ask why, and that would get passed on to Rachel, who would tell Eloise. And even though Eloise made it clear that this situation is transactional, I don't want her hearing secondhand that I've got another reason for going to the wedding.

I have to tell her myself. I don't know why I haven't yet. It's just never seemed the right time to blurt out that I need to interview the uncle I never knew I had, from my grandfather's secret second family, who also happens to be a decade younger than me. Feels like some *Game of Thrones* shit right there.

We chat a bit more about wedding plans while Eloise sits beside me, quietly vibrating with tension and sipping her drink. But the party begins to fill up and soon, Diego and Rachel are pulled away to greet new guests.

I stand and offer my hand to Eloise. She takes it, looking excited.

"Can we leave now?" she asks.

"Not yet," I say. "We need to work on mingling."

She makes a horrified face, like I've just told her we're going to practice witchcraft. "No," she says.

"Yes," I say firmly. "I'll be with you the whole time. This will help you get accustomed to being around people. Look! You're doing such a good job already."

I gesture out to the milling crowds surrounding us. I see her jaw working furiously, and she swallows hard. I squeeze her hand to remind her that I'm not going anywhere, and she squeezes back. We walk forward together, cutting a little path through the guests. The sun is sinking toward the horizon, setting the city ablaze in a wash of scarlet and gold. Once we reach the far end of the party, we turn and walk back the way we came.

"This is mingling?" Eloise asks.

"This is mingling."

"So, we aren't talking to anyone?"

"Do you want to talk to someone?"

"No," she says quickly.

"Rachel said she and Diego are going to make a speech," I tell her. "We can go after that."

We make a few more circuits around the party. She's doing great. And I let her squeeze my hand as hard as she needs to. At one point, I can tell her flight reaction is kicking in because she's checking the camera on her phone to see how the dogs are doing. A glance tells me they're absolutely fine. Pip is exploring, coming in and out of frame, Charleston is licking the carpet, Hazel is bossing the Colonel around. A typical Friday evening. But I know she's going to pretend there's some disaster, and I want her to stay for the speech. I think it will be such good practice for her. And I feel like it will mean a lot to Rachel.

I catch sight of a darkened space, behind the elevators, at the back of the rooftop.

"Hey," I say, tugging her hand before she gets a chance to invent some urgent dog-related reason to go home. "Follow me."

We walk around the corner to where a huge fan is blowing air into the building, and pipes and hulking metal compartments form a sort of jungle gym of shapes and sounds. We can barely hear the party back here. The view stretches out over Tribeca and up toward midtown. Rich, warm light illuminates the buildings, winking off windows, and dousing the city in gold.

"Here," I say, leading her to a sturdy, jutting piece of concrete that connects to the bank of elevators. "Sit. I'll be right back."

"You're leaving me?" she squeaks.

"Just for a minute," I promise.

I hurry to the buffet table and quickly pile a plate high with cheese and charcuterie and fruit, grabbing a couple of macarons for good measure. I stop at the bar and ask the bartender if I can get a bottle of champagne, to which he shrugs and says, "Sure, man," reaching into a cooler and handing one over.

When I get back to Eloise, she's standing by the ledge of the roof, her eyes focused on the traffic below.

"Cheese!" I declare, and she shrieks and whirls around. "Sorry, sorry!" I cry.

She gives a breathy laugh but then her eyes light up at the sight of the food in my hands. I had a feeling her blood sugar might be a little low.

I sit on the concrete slab, and she comes over to sit beside me. "Thought we could both use some food," I say.

"Mm," Eloise says, shoving a whole piece of gouda into her mouth. She chews and exhales. "Mmm," she says again, swallowing. "Yeah, I was hungry."

She happily snacks on the food while I open the champagne.

"They gave you a whole bottle?" she asks, brushing some cracker crumbs from her lap.

"The bartender didn't seem to care," I say. "This party is a drop in the bucket for Diego's family." The cork pops, and we both jump, smiling at each other. "Salud." I take a swig and hand her the bottle. "To a successful mingle."

"Was it, though?" she says sadly, taking a drink. She passes the bottle back to me.

"Why do you always do that?" I ask.

"Do what?"

"Move your goals."

"I don't."

I cut her a look. "You are too hard on yourself."

"Ha."

"Why ha?"

"I'm way too easy on myself," she says softly.

I raise an eyebrow. "Do you really think that?"

"I mean . . . yeah. Look at me, Agustín."

I am looking at her. I'm always looking at her. The setting sun makes her skin glow golden against the rich blue fabric of her dress. Her curls cast intricate shadows along her jawline, and down the length of her neck. Her eyes are like green pools, endless in their depth.

Her breath hitches in her throat. "I'm not normal," she says.

"Normal is boring," I say. "Why would you want to be normal?"

"Because being normal makes the world an easier place to live in."

"Do you think *I'm* normal?" I ask.

"Obviously."

"I don't find the world to be an easy place to live in," I say.

"Yeah, but you can go to a party without having a panic attack."

"You are at a party right now," I point out. "Not having a panic attack."

She shoots me a sardonic glance. "We are literally sitting next to pipes and an industrial fan. Not out there being social."

"You're moving the goals again," I say. "When was the last time you said, 'I am proud of me'?"

She worries at her bottom lip and takes a long drink, then coughs. "You sound like my therapist."

I beam. She laughs.

"That wasn't meant to be a compliment."

I pluck a slice of cheddar from the plate, pop it in my mouth, chew thoughtfully, then swallow. "I am going to take it as one anyway."

25
Eloise

The light casts shadows across Agustín's face, highlighting his features.

His sharp cheekbones, his proud nose, the dent of his dimples. His eyes look onyx in this light. His dark eyebrows have a teasing curve to them, and his thick tousled hair falls across his high forehead playfully. I grip the neck of the champagne bottle tightly, prickles erupting over my thighs. Why does he have to be so beautiful?

I take another swig, the bubbles tickling my nose, then pass it to him. I don't want to argue when I'm know I'm right. That no amount of practice will ever make me normal. And the wedding will be so much bigger than this party. And I have to make a speech. And I have to leave my dogs for a week. And I've never been away from my apartment, or New York City, for that long. And—

I close my eyes and take a deep inhale, allowing the gin and the champagne swimming through my veins to pull me away from those feelings. It's nice and quiet back here—well, no, not quiet, but the giant fan helpfully drowns out the sounds of the party.

"You didn't tell me you were getting published in *The New Yorker*," I say, shredding a piece of prosciutto.

Agustín tenses ever so slightly. If I weren't so in tune to him, I might not have noticed. "You never asked," he says.

"Isn't that, like, really hard?" *The New Yorker* is the best of the best, in a city where being the best isn't easy.

He nods. "It's been my dream my whole life," he says softly. "Ever since I decided to become a journalist. It's a big part of why I wanted to come here. To live in this city."

"Wow," I say. "And it's happening?"

He looks at me, a frown creasing his face. "Yes. I think it is. The article is not quite finished yet."

"And it's about the Rasca guy who was your grandpa?" I ask. The name was vaguely familiar. I don't watch a lot of NY1. Or really much television at all.

He chuckles. "El Rasca. Rascacielos, that was his nickname. It means skyscraper in Spanish."

"So what's the article about?" I ask. Agustín seems weirdly reticent to talk about this, which is unusual since talking is like his favorite thing.

He sighs and takes a long drink. "My abuelo moved to New York City when I was five years old. My family all thought he was supporting us by working as a janitor. Turns out, he was keeping a lot of secrets from us. Not just that he was an activist in the Latino community here. But he also had a secret second family in New York."

I feel my jaw hanging open. "I'm sorry, he had a what?"

"A second family."

"Like . . . he married someone else? While he was still married to your grandmother?"

He nods.

"But . . . but . . . how? Isn't that illegal?"

"He pretended he was single. It's not like they were calling up Mexico to check. He took his new wife's last name after they got married. They had a son."

"Holy shit," I say. "Agustín, that's so fucked up."

He gives a sharp nod. "I agree."

"So then . . . is your article like a condemnation of him?"

Agustín slowly tears a piece of soppressata in half. "Yes," he admits. "*The New Yorker* is doing a series called *The Voices of the City*. They want to highlight important people in New York from the past twenty-five years. Obviously, I have a unique perspective on El Rasca." He chews the soppressata thoughtfully. "Yes, I want to condemn him. We were being evicted from our home when he was fighting for people he didn't even know. We had to move into this tiny apartment in a very bad neighborhood, and he wasn't there for us."

"Why did you have to move?" I ask.

"Corruption in the government," Agustín says with a defeated shrug. "It happens a lot in Mexico." He pauses, and when he speaks again, I can hear the echo of pain in his voice. "How can I *not* be angry at him? Am I supposed to make excuses for my abuelo not being there for his family? Family is everything, and yet he *lied* to us. It makes me so mad—he was my hero, and he let us down." His jaw clenches and his nostrils flare. "But he was also a real hero to people in this city. I've done the research, and I've seen the lives he affected, the positive change he made. He did so many things I agree with, things that I have tried to do with my own writing. To speak for the voiceless. Is doing good here meant to give him a free pass? I don't think so. He never even came to visit us after he left. He always said he couldn't afford to come back, but now I wonder if he just didn't want to."

He rakes a hand through his hair, and it flops back over his brow. "My sister Lupe is furious with me for putting our family's private life on display. Caro thinks Abuelo is no different than other men, and he should be called out for abandoning his family. It's unfortunately not that unusual, men moving to the US and having second families. It's just not something I ever thought my abuelo would do."

"What does your grandmother think?" I ask.

"I don't know," he says. "I haven't been able to ask her about it yet."

"Shouldn't you?" I ask timidly. I'm the last person to give familial advice, but it seems like her opinion should be the most important. She's the one who was betrayed at the fundamental level.

"I've tried," he admits with a sigh. "She doesn't have her own phone, and my mom and tías are not letting me speak to her directly. We are all very protective of Abuelita. I know they don't want to hurt her by bringing up the past, but still . . ."

Well, I guess I can't entirely blame them for that. How would you even start that conversation? *Hey Grandma, can we talk about the fact that your husband left you, married someone else, and had a baby, all while you were still married? Oh, and he also became an activist fighting for others' rights while you were back home getting evicted?* Talk about awkward.

"Anyway," Agustín says, leaning back on his elbows and looking up at the sky. The moon is a pale white crescent set amid a backdrop of deep blue. The first stars are just starting to peek out—the few that we can see in the city anyway. "Enough about my crazy family. Lupe will live, and she and Caro will find something new to argue about."

He smiles indulgently.

"Are you close with your sisters?"

He takes a drink of champagne. "Yes. Especially Caro. But I love Lupe too—even when she's being stubborn." There's a deep, burning passion behind his words, and it's impossible to doubt the truth of them.

I suddenly feel very empty and very, very small. I hold out my hand, and he passes the champagne to me.

"What about you?" he asks softly.

"What about me?" I know what he means though. He knows I know. He's mentioned his family a million times in the month and change we've known each other. I know them all—Lupe, Caro, his parents, his nieces. I think I've said Lenny's name twice.

Agustín waits. He always knows when to wait. He never pushes me.

"I don't have a family," I say. Agustín goes very still. "I have Rachel. And I used to have Lenny—my uncle, the one I inherited the apartment from. But he wasn't . . ." I pause and take another swallow of champagne. I don't ever *want* to talk about my childhood. But I feel, in this moment, that I should. I think Agustín has earned the right to know. "My parents died when I was two." My voice can barely be heard above the fan. "I don't remember them. No, I have one memory of my mom, like . . ." My throat tightens. "Like warm fabric against my cheek. Something soft. And her smell. I can't describe it but I remember it. But their faces or voices . . ."

A pigeon lands on the ledge and struts back and forth, looking at us with one judgmental eye.

I inhale a slow, deep breath. "They were taking a trip upstate, for my dad's work. I guess they thought they'd make a quick, child-free weekend out of it. They left me with Lenny. They were on their way back when the train derailed. Twenty-two people died. It was the biggest tragedy in Metro North history."

I can't look at him. I don't want to see the sympathy in his eyes.

"I'm so sorry, Eloise," he says.

"I don't remember it," I say, taking another sip of champagne and handing him the bottle. "The funeral, the papers, the lawsuit, nothing. All the families got a settlement. Money, that's what I got from losing the anchors of my entire tiny world. Like my parents' lives could be compensated by a dollar amount. It just sat in an account accruing interest. I never touched it until I started adopting dogs. My therapist says my anxiety stems partly from the trauma of losing them. PTSD. Abandonment issues. Whatever." I feel tears well up, and I blink them back quickly. "Both sets of my grandparents had died before I was born. My dad was an only child. Lenny, my mom's brother, became my guardian. And Lenny was . . ."

I hesitate. What *was* Lenny? He wasn't cruel or a disciplinarian or neglectful. But he wasn't a parent, that's for sure.

"Lenny was like a cardboard cutout," I say at last.

"Like a what?" Agustín's brow furrows.

I pick at the hem of my dress. "Lenny got up every day, and ate his Cheerios with sliced banana, went to work, came home, read the paper on Sundays in his armchair, and never, ever changed his routine. He provided me with food and shelter and sent me to school and signed permission slips. We never had deep conversations or talked about feelings or got to know each other in any meaningful way—I think the only activity we ever did together was watch reruns of *Alf*. Lenny and I both really liked *Alf*."

"That old TV show?"

I nod, and half smile, because it's such a depressing memory yet one of the only good ones I have of my uncle. "We circled each other like two ghosts haunting that apartment." The stupid tears come back, and one lands on my cheek. I brush it away impatiently. "I wonder if he was sad, when my mom died. I never saw Lenny sad. I never saw him happy either. He existed. His life was his work. His real home was his law office." A lump swells in my throat and another tear falls. "The apartment was so quiet when I was growing up. My world was so quiet."

I finally risk a glance at him. He's sitting up, leaning forward, those soulful eyes focused entirely on me. My skin tightens over my bones, and I brace myself for his pity.

"What about Rachel?" he asks.

All the air leaves me in a whoosh. It's the exact right thing to say. A smile breaks across my face like a sunrise.

"I met Rachel in elementary school," I say. "She was loud and funny and bold and didn't care what anyone else thought of her. I cared what everyone thought." I hiccup. "There was a boy who made fun of me every recess, called me a freak and stuff. He used to pull my hair too. He was really mean. Anyway, one day he said something about me having no parents and Rachel punched him in the nuts. She had to skip a week of recess after that, but she said it was worth it. And the kid never bullied me again."

Agustín chuckles and looks out over the skyline.

"My house was so loud," he muses, a gentle smile playing across his face. "And so full. There were always tías and primas visiting, or friends stopping by. My mom has a lot of friends. And of course, Lupe and Caro would get into fights. They were both very well-spoken. No, outspoken. Very outspoken."

I'm glad for the change of subject. Talking about my childhood leaves me feeling hollowed out and itchy.

"Not you?" I ask as the pigeon takes off.

"Nah, I'm a peacemaker. Like my dad."

This doesn't surprise me.

"Do you miss them?" I ask.

He nods. "A lot. But the US is where the opportunity is. It's where I can really grow. There are limits in Mexico. Not that I don't also love Mexico. But I always wanted more. And New York was this paradise in my mind, filled with people from all over the world, everybody working hard to make better futures for themselves. And there's so much to *do.*" His face lights up as he talks about the city. "So much to explore. It feels alive here, you know? Like the city is a living organism. I wanted to be part of that. Like my abuelo was."

His face puckers, and he looks down into the champagne bottle.

"This isn't how I thought my dream would go," he says. "It's very, very hard to get published in *The New Yorker*, especially nonfiction. Almost impossible, in fact. They just happened to be doing a series on prominent New York figures, and I just happened to hear about it through my boss, and I'd just happened to find out about my abuelo, pretty much the day I moved into my apartment back in January. It felt like a series of unlikely events, leading me to the cusp of the highlight of my career, but not in the way I'd planned. When I'd imagined my life in this city, I hadn't pictured so much complication."

"That's New York for you," I say.

He sighs. "It is very hurtful. That sense of betrayal. I am so angry with Abuelo, and I can't yell at him or demand answers." His mouth quirks up on one side. "Not being able to demand answers is especially hard for a journalist."

I think about that for a moment. "I can totally understand the feeling of betrayal, but . . . I don't think this makes your abuelo wholly *bad*, you know? I don't think anyone is really all bad or all good. Except maybe, like, Hitler. And Pedro Pascal."

"That is the spectrum?" he asks me wryly.

I smile. "I just think that if your abuelo knew that his story was your opportunity, to accomplish your dreams, I don't think he'd begrudge you exposing the less-than-cool stuff he did. And I also kind of agree with Caro—call him out. I wish there was more calling out of men in positions of power in general, to be honest. Maybe this is your way of yelling at him. So it might make you feel better, once the article is out there."

Agustín seems to be thinking very deeply about something. He taps the champagne bottle with his index finger, considering. "Listen, Eloise—"

"There you are!" Rachel's voice startles us as she comes around the corner. "Having a little private party, I see." She flops down beside me and grabs a piece of cheese from the plate. "Diego's work friends just arrived, so it's all big slaps on the back and work work work."

She mimes a talking mouth with one hand.

"But we're going to do a little speech," she says, standing and helping me up. "Ready, O Great and Glorious Maid of Honor?"

The Wheel jolts to life, spinning frantically as beads of sweat start to form on my hairline.

"What?" I splutter. "*I'm* not making a speech."

"No, oh my god, sorry, I just meant, I want you there," Rachel says, giving me a quick squeeze. "Then you can leave," she whispers in my ear.

And this is why we're best friends.

26

Eloise

Rachel: Eloise Madigan Whitechapel! I'm so sorry I've fallen off the face of the planet. This launch is killing me. But it's almost over! Just one week to go.

Me: It's going to be a smashing success! I'm really excited for you. Miss you though.

Rachel: Miss you tooooooo

Rachel: Oh my god, ALSO.

Rachel: Agustín is such a great guy!!!!

Me: Yeah, I know.

Rachel: He's really cute too 😉

Me: 😑

Rachel: Oh come on. Don't you think he's cute? I just mean objectively. As a human. A man-shaped human. He's a cute man-shaped human, right?

Me: This is a business arrangement. I picked his name from a list. I do not see him as a cute man-shaped human.

Rachel: What exactly do you think dating in this century is? It's all about picking names off lists.

Me: WE ARE NOT DATING.

Rachel: I know, I know, sorry. You looked gorgeous at the party btw. I can't believe I haven't seen you since then! Ahhh and the wedding is so soon! How is it August already? What are you doing for Labor Day weekend?

Me: I don't know. Agustín has a "plan" that he refuses to give details about because I might "freak out." So I'm freaking out.

Rachel: Fun, keep me posted. How's the speech coming along?

Me: It's not

Rachel: Well, that's not what Agustín says.

Me: Are you talking to him behind my back???

Rachel: No! I just thanked him for coming to the party and then asked how things were going.

Me: Goodbye

Me: I love you

Rachel: Mwwwwah!

27
Agustín

"We can't wait to see you, Tío Tín!" Sofia sings as she makes a tiny braid in Caro's hair.

The two of them smile at me from the screen.

"I can't wait to see you too," I say. "Just a few more weeks!"

I'm sitting on Eloise's couch with the Colonel while Eloise is on the floor, trimming Charleston's nails. She showed me the itinerary Rachel sent her for the events leading up to the wedding. Rachel reassured her that she only needs to attend the bachelorette party. Not sure how I can help prepare Eloise for that, having never been to a bachelorette myself. So I called Caro to ask, and she was getting a spa day from the Minions.

"Mom is going to make a huge lunch to celebrate you coming back for a visit," Caro says. I lick my lips. One thing I've really missed since moving to New York is my mother's cooking. "No, Vero, put the scissors down, you are not cutting my hair."

"You're no fun," I hear Vero grumble.

"You can paint my nails instead," Caro says. "What are you wearing to the wedding?" she asks me.

"A tuxedo," I say. After the engagement party, I got Diego's contact info, and he set me up with the company providing all the tuxes for his groomsmen. I never in my life thought I would have any reason to wear a tuxedo. It was a bit surreal going in for a fitting.

Caro whistles. "Minions, Tío Tín is gonna look sooooo handsome in a tux!"

I hear the twins fall to pieces offscreen, laughing hysterically at the image.

"What about Eloise?" she says, as Vero's forehead intrudes on the bottom of the screen.

"What about her?"

"Is she your girlfriend, Tío Tín?" Vero asks.

"No, she's my friend," I say, my stomach dipping as I glance at Eloise. We're speaking Spanish so it's not like she can understand what's being said, but still.

"Do we get to meet her?" Caro asks eagerly.

"No."

"Mom wants to meet her."

"Mom is going to be disappointed." This trip will be overwhelming enough for Eloise as it is. I don't need to toss my family into the mix.

"What's she wearing?"

"Who, Mom?" I ask.

Caro rolls her eyes. "No, you idiot, what's your not-girlfriend wearing?"

"What's with all the questions? You suddenly get a job with *Quién*?"

"I work in the fashion industry, dude. These are the details I live for."

I sigh and turn to Eloise, switching to English. "My sister wants to know what you're wearing to the wedding."

Eloise looks up from where she sits on the floor of her apartment, holding a pair of nail clippers and Charleston's front paw, a piece of clingwrap wrapped around her forehead with a smear of peanut butter on it. It's the best way to trim nails, she told me.

"A dress," she says.

"Un vestido," I say to Caro.

Caro huffs as Sofia finishes another tiny electric-blue-and-black braid. "You two are the worst. The worst! How am I meant to live vicariously when you're both so fashion-averse?"

"It's the cross you have to bear, I guess."

"Are you at her place right now? Show us the dogs!"

Suddenly, all four of my nieces' faces fill the screen. "Perritos! Perritos!" they chant.

Eloise looks up, smiling. She recognizes that word.

"Can I show them?" I ask her.

She nods. "Not me, though," she warns.

"No, I know." I switch the camera on my phone so the girls can see Hazelnut, shaking out her glossy coat. I scan to the rug where Pip is licking his butt, and they shriek with laughter. Then I show them the Colonel, lounging on the couch next to me.

Eloise goes back to trimming Charleston's nails as he greedily licks peanut butter off her forehead.

"Done," she pronounces him, with a scratch behind his ears.

I catch sight of the time.

"Shoot, I have to run," I say. "Besitos!"

"Besitos, Tío Tín!"

They blow me kisses, and I hang up the phone.

"Ready to go?" I say, standing.

"Ugh, what are we doing now?"

"You'll see."

"You know I hate surprises," Eloise says.

I grin. "Yes, but if I told you where we were going, you might say no."

"I feel like you're proving my point."

But she unwraps the clingwrap from around her head and tosses it in the trash in the kitchen, then slips into her boots. She's wearing an orange and yellow striped romper today, and she looks adorable. I try to squash the prickles in my stomach.

Ever since the engagement party, I've been slip-sliding into feelings that are going to land me smack in the pit of disappointment. Because I don't want to just be her friend anymore. I don't want to be her preparation coach or her plus-one. I want to be more.

And she doesn't, and I don't know what to do about that.

Nothing, I suppose. I do nothing. I shove these feelings in a jar and let them pickle and rot.

"You liked my plan for Labor Day," I point out as she refills the dogs' water bowl in the kitchen.

She cuts me a sour look. "Even *I* can handle a picnic in Riverside Park."

"The point was the surprise," I say. "You didn't know what was coming, and it wasn't as bad as you thought."

"Have you ever heard the expression 'nobody likes a know-it-all'?" she asks as she grabs her keys.

"I do not believe that is a real expression."

"It is. Look it up. Are we taking the train?" she asks, opening the door. "Oh, hold up."

She bends down and picks up an envelope with both of our names on it. "What's this?"

"No idea," I say.

Inside the envelope is some kind of invitation. It looks expensive, thick creamy stationary with elegant script and illustrations of flowers around the edges.

"You are cordially invited to an evening of camaraderie and celebration on the rooftop of The Archer at 7 PM, on Saturday the 15th of October," she reads aloud. "P.S. Bring the Pack." She looks at me. "That's the day before we leave for Mexico."

"Who's it from?" I ask.

"Doesn't say."

"Miriam?"

She raises an eyebrow. "Does this look like something Miriam would send?"

Not really.

"Rachel?"

"Maybe," she muses.

"Great, well, you can spiral about it on our walk," I say. "It will distract you from the surprise."

"Ugh," she groans again.

We step out into the warm evening air and head downtown. As September has slipped toward October, the humidity has eased and the days have begun to grow shorter. I'm excited for my first autumn in the city.

It's only a few blocks to where we're going, and I suggest we practice her speech. It's simple, short, and I told her we'll put it in a huge font in her Notes app so it will be accessible and easy to read.

"Rachel has been my best friend since kindergarten," Eloise recites as we wait to cross at 86th Street. The crosstown bus trundles past, leaving a gust of hot, diesel-scented air in its wake. "It's been a privilege to watch her grow into the amazing woman she is today. And seeing her with Diego, I know she's finally found her soulmate." She wrinkles her nose as the light changes, and we cross. "Do I really have to say that?"

She's been very resistant to the soulmate line. I've been trying to keep things simple.

"No, not if it bothers you so much," I say. A pair of tourists chattering in German walk past us, huge cameras slung around their necks. "What about: she's finally found the One?"

Eloise mimes gagging. "Forget it, I'll stick with soulmate."

"Why don't you like Diego?" I ask.

Her shoulders stiffen. "Diego's fine."

I raise an eyebrow. "That was not convincing."

Eloise runs a hand through her curls so that they bounce and sway in the breeze. Her teeth press into her bottom lip, and I feel a lurch in my chest as a wild image appears in my mind: stopping her right here on this street. Cupping my hand around her slender neck. Brushing my lips softly against hers.

"I do like him," she says quietly, and I'm jolted back to reality. We turn the corner onto 82nd Street, passing a brownstone with a huge Pride flag in the window. She goes back to practicing the speech, ending that conversation. "And seeing her with Diego, I know she's finally found her soulmate. Rachel, thanks for punching Brad Schifrin in the nuts for me back in elementary school."

"Hey, that wasn't in the speech," I say as she shoots me a grin. "Maybe no nut punching in front of this particular audience?"

"It's such a good story though," she says, laughing.

"You want to scandalize the abuelas?"

"Oh fine. Rachel and Diego, I wish you two all the happiness in the world. Congratulations." She mimes raising a glass. "And then I raise my glass."

She gives a little curtsy, and I applaud. "Perfecto," I say.

We enter the lobby of the nondescript building on 82nd and Broadway, nestled between a stationary store and a CVS, and take the elevator to the fifth floor. I lead Eloise down a hall to a door with a sign that reads **World Baile Dance Studio.**

Eloise stops short. "You've got to be kidding."

"What?" I ask innocently.

"You expect me to dance?" she hisses.

"There is going to be dancing at the wedding."

"Yes, and my butt is going to be firmly planted in a chair."

"Come on," I say, taking her elbow gently and opening the door. "This will be fun, I promise."

She grumbles, and shoots me dagger-eyes, and drags her feet. But! She comes with me. She steps inside the room. And I see no sign of an impending panic attack. I wish she could see the progress she's made over the course of the summer. She's nervous, yes, but she's doing it. She's not running away. She's not hyperventilating. She slips her hand into mine and squeezes hard. I think this is more to punish me, rather than for emotional support. And that, too, is progress.

"El!"

Eloise whirls around as Rachel descends on us, throwing her arms around both our necks and squeezing us together in a hug.

"Oof," Eloise says. "What are you doing here?"

Rachel releases us, beaming. "Isn't this fun? Agustín had the idea and of course I was like, Diego we HAVE to go with them."

Diego is close behind Rachel, and he greets us warmly. "Great idea, dude," he says to me.

"All right everyone, let's get this class started," a woman wearing tight black pants and low heels says, clapping her hands.

She puts us in pairs, Eloise and I facing each other, next to Diego and Rachel. There are only two other couples here for this class—a gay duo and an elderly man and woman.

"So we're going to start with a very basic salsa," the dance teacher says. "Men, put your left foot forward, ladies, right foot back."

As she explains the basic steps and we start to move, Eloise immediately uses the wrong foot and steps on me.

"Sorry!" she squeaks.

"You're fine," I reassure her.

"We pause on four and eight," the teacher says. Eloise's eyes are glued to the ground. "And . . . one, two, three, pause . . . and now the other way, five, six, seven. Good. Now remember it goes quick quick slow . . . and quick quick slow."

After a few more repetitions of this, Eloise actually begins to get the hang of it, though she keeps her eyes trained on her feet. Diego has clearly danced salsa before, and Rachel is a fast learner. The elderly couple are quite good as well.

"Very good," the teacher says. "Now, let's connect with each other. Salsa is not so formal, like ballroom." She seems to realize Diego and Rachel are the stars of the show, so she comes over and puts Rachel's arm on Diego's shoulder, his arm on her side, then links their other hands together lower down, by their waists. "This is more casual, more natural," she explains. "Now, everybody try."

My neck goes suddenly hot and my stomach tightens as I take a small step toward Eloise. We both reach for each other at the same moment and our arms clash awkwardly. The sweetest pink color blooms on her cheekbones.

"You go first," she mumbles.

My heart is beating uncomfortably hard in my chest. As soon as I put my hand on her waist, I feel her sharp intake of breath. Her lashes flutter and as she lifts her arm to rest it ever so gently on my shoulder, she raises her eyes to meet mine. I can feel the movement of her breath against my palm, beneath the soft fabric of her romper. Her green eyes are clear, and her lips tremble. For one second, it's like we're suspended in time.

The teacher claps her hands together, bringing me back down to earth.

"And . . . one, two, three . . ." She counts off the steps, but my brain is scrambled.

This time, it's me who steps on Eloise's foot. We grin at each other, our faces so close together. I catch a whiff of her citrusy scent as she tucks a curl behind her ear and takes my hand again. It feels like my mistake has given her courage. Her hand tightens around my shoulder, sending shivers across my skin.

"I can do this," she says. "Right foot back . . ."

And we dance. Slowly. Awkwardly.

Together.

28
Eloise

"I didn't know your building had a rooftop," Agustín says, fiddling with the collar of his shirt, and adjusting Pip in his arms.

"I didn't either," I admit as we take the elevator up to the roof of the Archer. The dogs are all on their leashes. Charleston sniffs at something on the carpet while Hazelnut whines at the doors impatiently.

"Seriously?"

"What, you think I'd *ask* someone about it? Plus, Lenny wasn't a rooftop kind of guy. I wonder if he knew about it either."

I don't know why we're wasting our time on this mystery event, when I have a whole host of more important things to do. Like freak out. A lot. I'm getting on a plane tomorrow. I'm leaving the Pack in Miriam's care. She says she can handle them, but what if she can't? What if something really bad happens when I'm away? What if Pip bites her? What if the Colonel has problems with his blood sugar? She already takes care of her two cats. What if she can't handle all the dogs? What if it's too much for her? What if it's too much for *them*?

Not to mention the whole host of issues I've been avoiding that are now staring me in the face. I've never flown internationally before. I have to meet like a thousand new people. I have to participate in activities. Rachel's getting *married*.

The Wheel starts to spin.

Rachel is getting married.

Everything is going to change. Who cares if Diego is actually kind of a nice guy? They'll do couple things and couples like to hang out with other couples. Case in point, I've seen a ton more of Diego and Rachel since Agustín came into my life. And guess what, the minute the wedding is over, Agustín is out of my life, because those are the rules. That's the agreement. The agreement *I* came up with.

Sweat starts to bead along my brow. I don't want Agustín to be out of my life. I think I kind of maybe want him to be in my life forever. And not as a friend. Definitely more than a friend. But oh my god, what if I told him that and he rejected me, because of course, I am not Girlfriend Material. I have never been Girlfriend Material. I can't even wait in line at Jamba Juice without having a panic attack. I was shoving cheese in my face next to an industrial fan at my best friend's engagement party. That's not party etiquette. I'm way too much work. He's probably really looking forward to this whole thing being over so he doesn't have to be my damn training wheels anymore, because really, I should—

Suddenly, a warm, strong hand slips into mine and squeezes. And just like that, my mind calms. My racing heart slows. The Wheel stops spinning. I look up into his eyes, and he flashes me that hot-chocolate smile, the one I've loved since the moment I first saw him.

The one I have no idea how I'm going to live without.

"Hey," he says.

"Hey."

That's it. He never overdoes it. Never says things like, "You're going to be okay" or "Don't freak out, Eloise" or "Why are you sweating so much?"

Just "Hey."

The elevator doors open, and Agustín and I gasp in unison.

The rooftop looks out over the park, and there are huge square pots with giant ferns and ficus and hydrangeas placed at various spots along the ledge. There's a long wooden table with chairs set up in the center of the space, and Édith Piaf is playing on a record player on a little folding table, plugged into an outlet near the ground with a speaker beside it. The long table is laden with vases of flowers, and fancy flatware, and silver ice buckets with wine, and smoke rises from a grill in one corner, where Miriam is cooking something that smells amazing, and Sanvi is cutting up some vegetables. Gretchen is sipping a glass of white wine and engaged in conversation with Kate.

"I've been taking those ashwagandha supplements every day, and I swear, it's really helping with my stress levels," Gretchen gushes.

"You'll be amazed what it can do for your stamina during workouts too," Kate says. "Check out our latest video, we just posted it last night . . ."

I see Madame Boularès and Mr. Bloom looking through a stack of records together. Mr. Bloom! I can't believe he's here.

"You do have a pretty good collection," he's saying. "But what about classical music?"

Over at the grill, Miriam is chatting with Sanvi.

"You're going to love my steak," she says. "The marinade is an old family recipe."

"I'm vegan," Sanvi says.

Miriam looks her up and down then shakes her head.

Suddenly, Gretchen catches sight of us.

"Eloise!" she shrieks. "You're here!"

She rushes over to give me a hug, and I let her, because Gretchen is a really good hugger. Kate is right behind her, saying hi to Agustín then giving the Colonel some ear scritches, as Sanvi hurries over to scoop up Hazelnut.

"What's going on?" Agustín asks, and I'm glad he did, because I'm dumbstruck.

"Well first of all," Miriam says, waving her set of tongs, "we thought you two deserved a proper send-off for your big trip tomorrow. And Eloise, honey, we figured you'd be spiraling, and we wanted to remind you that you're not alone. You've got the ninth floor community behind you, and those people at that wedding are gonna love you just as much as we do. Isn't that right?"

Kate and Gretchen nod eagerly, Sanvi smiles, Mr. Bloom bobs his head nervously as Charleston lumbers over to investigate his shoes, and Madame Boularès swirls her wine in her glass.

"But of course, they will love you," she says. "Unless they are idiots."

Tears spring to my eyes with surprising ferocity. It feels like there's a pebble stuck in my throat. Everyone is looking at me, but their gazes don't feel sharp, or biting, or uncomfortable. And Agustín's hand is so warm and strong in mine. Reminding me that I can take all the time I need to process this.

"Thank you," I say in a shaky voice. I blink away the tears and take a breath. "Thank you," I say again, my voice stronger. Mr. Bloom gives me a nervous smile. Miriam bustles back to the grill, Gretchen pours us wine, and Kate chatters excitedly about how much fun we're going to have in Mexico. I fear she might be overestimating my capacity for fun, but I go with it.

We let the dogs roam freely, except Pip, who sits comfortably in Agustín's arms. Sanvi starts to wax poetic about her and Kate's wedding, three years ago, and Miriam talks about her husband with wistful tears in her eyes. I switch to water after my first glass of wine, because the last thing I need tomorrow is a hangover. We all sit down to eat, and Miriam puts a platter of steaks and homemade sausages in the center of the table, alongside bowls of leafy greens and veggies (from Sanvi), pasta salad (from Gretchen), and potatoes au gratin (from Madame Boularès).

The food is delicious, and even more so because it came from so many people that I know. People I care about. I never could have imagined four months ago how much my life would change. That I wouldn't be actively avoiding my neighbors. That I would be comfortable sitting at a long table full of people, listening to them talk, and not feel a panic attack coming on. I hold Hazel on my lap and feed Charleston bits of sausage under the table and find I'm actually enjoying myself.

Once we've all eaten our fill, Miriam taps her fork on her glass and stands. "Now," she says, smiling widely. "It's time for the presents."

Huh? Agustín looks just as confused as I do. His face is so expressive, he's actually a great way to monitor if I'm overreacting to something.

"Oh, can we go first?" Kate says excitedly. Sanvi reaches down under her seat and pulls out two large pastel bags filled with cream-colored paper. She gets up and hands one to me and one to Agustín.

Inside, is the softest set of pale purple sweatpants and a matching sweatshirt, branded with the Herbal Pride logo. Agustín has a navy men's set. I also find a sleep mask, an inflatable neck pillow, and a bottle of Herbal Pride melatonin gummies.

"For the flight," Sanvi says warmly. "The melatonin will really help you relax."

"Seriously," Kate says. "I swear by them when I travel."

"Wow," I say, glancing at Agustín.

"Thanks," he says sincerely, running his hand over the velvety fabric of his new sweatpants. "These are great."

"We will go next," Madame Boularès says imperiously, and I realize "we" means her and Mr. Bloom when he slides a box across the table toward me. I open it and find a USB drive. "Zis is a compilation of soothing music. Some of it is from my own collection."

"And I recorded some songs for you," Mr. Bloom says quietly. "Mostly Bach. A little Brahms. And some Mozart."

I pick up the drive and grip it in my hand, my throat too swollen to speak. I give him a nod and he nods back.

"My turn!" Gretchen says. She looks at us excitedly. "So, mine doesn't come in a box or a bag. But! You two have officially been upgraded to first class on your flights."

"What?" I ask, wondering if I misheard her.

"Delta *loves* me," she says, primping her sleek bob. "I've got Platinum status. And Harrison has so many points from all his work travel. It was no problem. And you're going to die, first class is amaaaaazing."

I meet Agustín's gaze. "Have you flown first class before?" I murmur.

"No," he murmurs back. Good, we're in this together.

"And finally," Miriam says. "This last gift is from all of us. I know you're worried about leaving the dogs with me and the cats. Well, we are each going to look after one of them while you're gone. That way, they'll get the specialized attention I know you want them to have. Even though I could definitely handle them all myself," she adds.

I could be knocked over by a stiff breeze. "Who's taking who?"

Gretchen raises her hand. "Charleston. I'm used to diapers."

"Hazelnut," Sanvi says. "We are going to pamper her to death, and I can't wait."

Oh boy. Hazel is going to love that.

"The Colonel," Mr. Bloom wheezes. "I heard he likes classical music."

"I'll take care of his insulin shots," Miriam adds. "And I'm taking Pip, since he's the biggest handful of the bunch."

I don't know what to say. My head spins, my chest tightens, and I look into the faces of the people who have lived alongside me for years. Who I can now call friends.

"Thank you," I say. There's a flurry of activity as plates are cleared, glasses refilled, Madame Boularès changes the record, and Mr. Bloom gives the Colonel one final bit of sausage.

I glance at Agustín, sitting beside me, and know this would never have happened if he hadn't come into my life. If his name hadn't been on that plus-one list.

And in some way, if Rachel had never met Diego, I'd never have met Agustín. The threads that connect us, across boroughs, across countries, can weave a web we don't even know will ensnare us. Until it does.

The sun dips to kiss the treetops of Central Park and I reach out and take Agustín's hand in mine. Not because I'm anxious.

Just because.

29
Agustín

"Señoras y señores, bienvenidos a la Ciudad de Mexico. Ladies and gentlemen, welcome to Mexico City."

Eloise peels up one corner of her glittery, rainbow-patterned sleep mask and blinks at me. "We're here?" she croaks.

"We're here," I say.

This was the best flight of my life. I knew first class would be comfortable, but this was a whole other level. The leg room. The service. The free drinks and food. I think Gretchen has ruined flying coach for me for life.

And the sweatsuits Sanvi and Kate gave us are crazy comfortable. Even if Eloise and I do look a bit like that weird couple who wear matching outfits. Eloise had taken two of those melatonin gummies before we even got out of the cab at JFK. Then we had a Bloody Mary at the airport bar while she tried not to hyperventilate. I'm glad we were able to board the plane first, so she didn't have to wait in a long line. Once we got settled in our seats, I think the melatonin, vodka, and general anxiety over this trip just wore her out. She was basically unconscious for the whole five-hour flight. I didn't even have to use the backup plan I'd made in case of a major panic attack.

As the plane taxis toward our gate, I peer out the window and wait for my phone service to connect.

Ping. Ping, ping, ping.

Both our phones start to light up with notifications. We created a group thread last night before the party ended, with all the neighbors. What a special event. I wonder if Eloise realizes how she brought that whole floor together. How she created a community where there wasn't one before. She did that.

Everyone has sent photos with the dogs. Miriam's pic shows Pip in a standoff with Milhouse:

Adjustment period. They'll be besties soon, don't worry.

Mr. Bloom's shows a picture of the Colonel sleeping on his bed:

Is this allowed? He seems to really like the bed.

Gretchen sent a photo of Charleston licking Begonia's cheek, the little girl caught midlaugh. And Kate sent a photo of Hazelnut and Sanvi, wearing matching shades and wristbands:

Look at these ICONS.

I wonder when Sanvi got dog-sized gear, but then I realize they'd all been planning this nannying situation for a while.

Eloise lets out a long, slow breath. "They're okay," she murmurs.

"How many matching outfits do you think we're going to see Hazel and Sanvi in?"

Eloise groans. "Too many."

We grab our carry-on bags, deboard the plane—first! I've never deplaned first before!—and get to immigration before the lines get out of control. Eloise holds my hand the entire way, and I tell the guard she's my wife, so he lets us both go in the Mexican passport line. Glad she doesn't understand Spanish for that, but I think she'd appreciate the lie. I'm not about to let her go by herself in the Extranjeros line, which is far longer and slower than the Mexican line. We get our luggage at baggage claim and emerge out into the massive glorieta, a madness of cars honking and swerving around one another, swarms of people, and the shrill whistles of the airport employees directing traffic.

There's a driver with our names on a board waiting for us, standing in front of a huge black SUV.

"Hola," I say.

"Agustín?" he says.

"That's me," I reply in Spanish. "What's your name?"

"Enrique. Mr. Alvarez sends his greetings. Miss, please, let me take your bag," he says to Eloise in English. We slide into the cool, leather interior as Enrique loads our luggage into the trunk. The windows are tinted, and there are bottles of water, mints, and even a dock to charge our phones.

"This is nice," I say cheerfully.

"Mm," Eloise mutters. I wonder if she's even aware of her surroundings, or if there's a panic alarm blaring in her brain, whirling red and drowning everything else out. Enrique pulls forward, and we slowly make our way out of the airport traffic and onto the highway that leads into the city. We pass through a tunnel where advertisements for Liverpool, a big department store chain, give way to brightly painted street art, down a wide avenue lined with trees, and then the buildings begin to crowd around us, street vendors popping up beneath worn white tents, selling everything from tacos to clothes to bright orange bunches of cempasuchiles for Día de Muertos.

Eloise's leg is bouncing furiously the whole drive. And it's Mexico City, so the traffic is terrible. I mean, really terrible. I chat with Enrique as we creep slowly down Avenida Chapultepec, and he tells me he's only been working for Jorge Alvarez for about a year. He's surprised to learn my family lives in Colonia Napoles.

He tells me his sister lives there, and we find out she's only a couple of blocks away from Lupe's house. He's a lot less formal with me after that—he gives me his number and tells me if I ever need a driver while we're in the city, to text him. We circle the rotary at Insurgentes, before finally picking up speed for the last few blocks and arriving at our destination.

The Four Seasons.

The cream and gray stone building has Mexican and Canadian flags hung over its entrance. Narrow windows are fronted with beige awnings, and as Enrique pulls up to the glass front doors, two porters hurry out to greet us, one opening the door for Eloise as the other helps Enrique with our bags.

"Gracias," I say and shake Enrique's hand.

Eloise seems to be vibrating with nerves as she gets out of the car. One porter assures us our bags will be taken to our room, and the other brings us to the desk to check in with the concierge. She's a very polite young Mexican woman in a tailored blazer with a pin declaring her "Lupe."

"That's my sister's name," I say to her, and she smiles, her eyes sweeping curiously over my and Eloise's matching sweatsuits. We definitely don't look like the usual clientele.

"You are with the Alvarez party, correct?" she asks.

"Yup."

"Here's your room key, sir. If there's anything you need, don't hesitate to ask."

"Thanks," I say, then pause. "Wait, just the one room?"

"Yes."

I glance at Eloise, who is clenching her jaw so hard I think she might break her teeth. She's not paying attention to our exchange, just quietly freaking out as she takes in the opulent, bustling lobby.

I didn't realize we'd be sharing a room. I bet Eloise didn't either. I'm sure someone on Diego's end handled the reservations. Maybe they just assumed we were a couple.

"Is it possible to get two rooms?" I ask, though the thought of putting a full week at this hotel on my credit card makes my brain short circuit.

Lupe frowns. "I'm sorry sir, we are fully booked at this time."

"Okay, no problem, thank you," I say, because right now, I think the most important thing is to get Eloise someplace calm and quiet so she can acclimate. She's doing a great job, to be honest. I'm really impressed. But I think she's going to hit her breaking point soon, plus just travel exhaustion from the flight and the drive. And I'm sure she's missing the Pack.

The other porter is waiting for us. "Right this way," he says, leading us down a hallway of pale polished wood, lined with glass French doors. As he turns to the left toward a bank of elevators, Eloise inhales a quick gasp, and her eyes light up.

We're standing on the edge of an enormous courtyard, filled with plant life: abundant ferns, stout palms, elegant trees hung with pink blooms, and thick vines of ivy crawl up the arched windows that look down on us from all sides, spilling like a glossy green waterfall. There's a fountain in the center and a restaurant with white canvas awnings at the far side, tables filled with guests sipping cocktails or snacking on ceviche.

The elevator dings, and Eloise and I get in and head up to the seventh floor. When the porter opens the door to our room, our bags are already there. I thank him and we step inside.

30
Eloise

My knees lock.

Some part of my brain takes in the light, airy room, the patterned carpet, the little balcony overlooking all that green splendor down in the courtyard (my favorite part of this journey so far).

But the majority of my mind is now consumed by the fact that 1. Agustín appears to be sharing this room with me, and 2. I'm staring at a king-sized bed, complete with a dark wooden headboard, enormous fluffy pillows, and a pristine white comforter.

I look around like a second bed might be hiding under the marble topped table, or maybe in the closet.

No luck.

There's only one bed.

Agustín seems to have anticipated this. Maybe that's what he was talking to the woman at the front desk about.

My breathing picks up as the Wheel starts to spin.

"They booked us in the same room," he says, as if that weren't already obvious. "Apparently, the hotel is completely full."

Tears prick my eyes. I miss my home, and the Pack, and my own bed, and the sounds of Central Park West, and Hector at the front door, and Mr. Bloom playing Mozart. This is all too surreal. I feel so incredibly far away from the place where I'm me. I was hoping to be able to freak out for a second, have a nice little breakdown alone in my room before I had to pull myself together.

Agustín is looking around like maybe he too is hoping another bed will magically appear. "I can sleep on the floor."

"No," I say. "That's ridiculous. I'll sleep on the floor."

The carpet does seem very soft.

"Definitely no." Agustín shakes his head firmly. "You know what, I could just stay with my family."

My head whips around to meet his eyes. "You are *not* leaving me here."

Everyone else from Rachel's side is staying at this hotel. There is a zero percent chance I won't run into them at some point, and I need Agustín by my side.

"How about this," he says. "Lie down for a bit, or . . . or maybe run a bath! I'll go check back with the front desk. See if there's anything they can do."

Alone time is exactly what I need. And a bath sounds amazing. I take a deep breath and remind myself that I made it to Mexico City in one piece and the journey did not actually kill me. Am I still a little out of it from the melatonin? Probably. Was the Wheel spinning like crazy on the drive, in complete sensory overload? Yes. But I'm *here.* This is net positive.

"Okay," I say, nodding, like I can convince myself. "Okay."

He strips out of his sweatshirt, and the movement reveals a slice of smooth olive skin and a teasing dent at his left hip before his T-shirt settles down over his stomach. My heart gives a wild lurch as blood burns in my cheeks but Agustín just flashes his dimples.

"I'll be back," he says. Then he disappears out the door.

I take a minute to let the silence settle around me and soothe my racing pulse. I creep over the plush carpet and peer out the French doors of our room's little balcony. I like it up here. I can observe without being seen. The scent of flowers drifts up toward me, and the cheerful chatter of the guests in the restaurant mixes in the air. I take a big, calming breath. I may be shaky and fragile, but I'm not in full panic attack mode, and that's a win. I head back inside. There's a bottle of champagne in an ice bucket on the marble table next to a vase of flowers, along with a card.

Welcome, Eloise and Agustín! We're so excited to share this week with you. Enjoy the bubbles! Rachel & Diego

This is definitely not Rachel's handwriting (she writes in chicken scratch) nor do I believe it's Diego's. But it's a nice gesture. I leave the card and the bottle and head into the bathroom. There's a huge, wood-framed mirror, a marble sink, and a deep porcelain tub. I plug it and start to run the tap. A quick glance in the mirror tells me I do indeed look like I took two melatonin with a Bloody Mary chaser and then passed out on a plane for five hours. I head back to the room to unpack my bag. Then I grab my toiletries and brush, head to the bathroom, and find the tub has filled with hot water.

I strip out of my travel-worn sweatsuit and sink into the bath, leaving my phone on the little ledge beside me. Ohhhh yes. This is exactly what I needed.

My phone pings, and it's a text from Agustín, which causes a sudden jerk in my chest before I remember he can't see that I'm naked.

Agustín: I made this for the plane, just in case, but you didn't need it (yay!). Thought it might help calm you down.

It's a video file. I click on the link and gasp. He's pulled together pictures and short videos of the Pack from over the course of the whole summer and set it all to music. I burst into laughter as the theme song from *Alf* starts to blare over my phone's speaker then I watch, my throat tightening, as images of my dogs play out on the tiny screen. I sink back and lean my head against the cool porcelain.

There's Charleston in his diaper, licking peanut butter off a spoon. Hazel shooing the Colonel out of his own dog bed. Pip and Hazel, curled up and snoozing together. The Colonel doing one of his big stretches. Pip making a nest out of one of my favorite cardigans. Charleston in slo-mo jumping for a treat. The whole Pack out in Central Park, with me in a pair of denim shorts and a striped top giving Agustín some serious side eye.

I smile, remembering that day. We went for a long walk around the reservoir, and Agustín had to carry Charleston home at the end because he was so tuckered out.

There's a selfie of Agustín and Pip, and another of Agustín and the Colonel. There's a few that definitely came from Rachel, photos of Hazelnut licking her nose, and the two of us together with the Colonel snuggled between us on the couch. There are even some photos from the party last night, of Sanvi cuddling Hazel and Gretchen feeding Charleston a piece of sausage. Then an image of myself appears, and my brain screeches to a halt. I don't know who took it—maybe Kate, since she was sitting across from me. I'm at the table with Hazelnut on my lap, golden light spilling across my face, one hand curled around my glass. I'm looking slightly to the left of the camera, with Agustín sitting beside me, midlaugh. I can hear it through the image, that laugh he makes when something really hits his funny bone, big and echoing and full of joy. The kind of laugh that makes you want to laugh too.

I'm smiling contentedly. I look relaxed. I look . . . happy.

The video ends and white block letters appear on a black screen.

You've Got This, Eloise! No problem! Love, Agustín and the Pack.

My heart flips at that one little word: Love. But I know it's just a silly signoff and doesn't mean anything. Like Sincerely, or Best. I smile at the *Alf* reference. I'm surprised he remembered that.

I rewind back to the beginning of the video. One of the earlier pictures is of me feeding Pip chorizo, the day Agustín taught me how to cook sopes. When Pip finally started to relax around me. I didn't realize Agustín had taken it. And I can't help but notice the difference. There's a wariness to my eyes, a tightness in my shoulders, a defensiveness in my expression. I look like I'm bracing myself for something bad.

I fast forward to the end of the video. To that last image of myself, bathed in the sunset. Tears spring to my eyes again and fall without warning.

To see such a stark change in myself, there on a screen, staring me in the face . . .

My phone buzzes with a text and I shriek and almost drop it into the water. I lean over the edge of the tub and open my text thread.

Rachel: ARE YOU HERE YET???

I let out a breathy chuckle.

Me: Currently taking a bath in the ginormous tub.

Rachel sends a gif of people from *The Office* popping champagne, then a gif of Julia Roberts from *Pretty Woman* where she's in the bubble bath with headphones on.

Rachel: Isn't the hotel amazing?
Me: Yes.

I hesitate, my fingers hovering over the keyboard.

Me: They put me and Agustín in the same room.
Rachel: Oh shit, I bet the planner assumed you were a couple. Never fear! I'll take care of it. We have this dinner with some of Diego's family tonight (I am never going to keep all his cousins straight), but I'll see you tomorrow! Breakfast in the hotel at 9?
Me: Sounds good. Thanks, Rach.
Rachel: Hey guess what.

Me: What.
Rachel: YOU'RE IN MEXICO CITY!!!!!!

I chuckle and send back a gif of a cartoon cat waving a Mexican flag.

Me: Hey guess what.
Rachel: What.
Me: YOU'RE GETTING MARRIED!!!!!

The exclamation points don't feel as fake as I thought they would. *Rachel is getting married.* For the first time, I think the words without being overcome with dread.

Maybe I'm just jet lagged. Can one be jet lagged from only a five-hour flight with a two-hour time difference?

Rachel sends me a gif of Homer Simpson in a wedding dress, daintily walking down a flight of stairs. I laugh and put my phone aside. The bath has helped, I admit, but I one thousand percent need to not be naked when Agustín gets back to this room. My brain catches on that flash of skin I saw earlier, the flat plane of his stomach and the tempting dent at his hip. I press my thighs together as shivers erupt over my skin.

Get it together, Eloise. Between Agustín's charm and Rachel's force of personality, one of them has to be able to get us a second room. I cannot sleep in bed with Agustín tonight. Absolutely not. Even as jitters spiderwalk up my chest at the thought, and my mouth starts to water, and that sliver of sunlight inside me brightens.

I drain the tub and rinse myself off, then grab one of the fluffy white towels from the rack. My curls are damp, and I wipe steam from the mirror and stare at my reflection.

"You can do this," I say to myself, though what "this" is, I'm not entirely sure.

I peek out the door first, just to make sure the coast is clear. Then I scurry to the dresser, grab underwear and a bra, along with a pair of jeans, and a light knit sweater with a swirling pattern of lavender, peach, pink, and white.

I race back to the bathroom. My phone lights up on the sink and I see a text from Agustín.

Agustín: On my way!

I yank on my jeans, get tangled in the sweater, and pull myself together just in time to hear the door click open.

"Eloise?"

"Here," I squeak, then clear my throat and open the door.

"Hey," he says. "Cool sweater. So, no luck with the room—"

"Rachel said she'll talk to them," I say.

"Oh, good. I bet she can work it out. She is very good at not taking no for an answer." His hands are in his pockets and he shifts from foot to foot. Is Agustín nervous? It's such a bizarre concept that I dismiss the thought immediately. "Is it okay if I take a shower quickly?" he asks

"Oh!" I say. "Yeah, sorry, of course."

I shove my phone in my pocket and step out of the bathroom, almost colliding into him. The cotton material of his tee smells like fabric softener and Agustín, that smokey-leathery-cardamom scent I've become so familiar with over the past few months. An ache blooms in my chest, and I step to the left just as he does. We both step to the right, and then he laughs.

"After you," he says, gesturing toward the room. I skirt around him, cheeks aflame. When I hear the door close, and then the shower turns on, my whole body goes rigid with a big old NOPE.

I cannot be in this room with Agustín ohmygodtotallynaked just on the other side of that door. Nope, nope, NOPE.

I scurry out onto the balcony to clear my head and cool my skin, dewing with sweat from the bath and the anxiety.

We have to have separate rooms. I can't be exploding with shivers all week over Agustín when I have a whole Diego-sized family to meet at the wedding. Not to mention the fact that I am in a strange city where I don't speak the language (sadly I don't think *perrito* is going to be much help), miles and miles away from everything I know.

I feel the panic attack coming, the Wheel picking up speed. My scalp tightens, my skin goes clammy, and I grip the bars of the balcony and close my eyes. I try to focus on the sounds of the people below, the tinkling of the fountain, the tap of footsteps on tile. I focus on the breeze on my face and the scent that it brings, flowers and leaves and the faintest trace of window cleaner.

I inhale deeply. When I open my eyes, I'm still shaky and a little out of breath but I'm okay. I'm pulling at the seams, but I haven't fallen apart.

I refuse to turn around, though, until I know it's safe, and Agustín is fully clothed. Then I get an idea. I grab my phone and pull up the video he sent me. The theme song from *Alf* pulls an automatic chuckle from me, and I watch my dogs, the loves of my life, appear on the screen, in all their goofy, adorable, grumpy, snuggly glory. Tears fill my eyes again. I need to make sure Rachel uses waterproof mascara for the wedding.

"Eloise?"

Agustín's voice is so gentle, and I turn to see him dressed in dark jeans and a beige crew neck sweater, his dark hair falling around his face, wild and unruly, those deep brown eyes pinning me in place. My heart pulses out one longing throb before I blink and come back to myself. The message at the end of the video blares across my screen.

You've Got This, Eloise! No problem! Love, Agustín and the Pack

"I had an idea," Agustín says, his dimples flashing.

31
Agustín

We take the elevator down to the lobby, and as we're leaving, we see a group of gringas laughing hysterically, glittering in mini dresses and heels.

I recognize a couple of them from the engagement party—these must be the other bridesmaids.

"Girls, let's go get margaritas!" one of them says and the rest squeal.

Eloise shrinks to my side and stares at the floor, hoping not to be recognized.

"Do you know them?" I ask.

"Rachel's influencer friends," she mumbles. Once we're past them and outside, she breathes a sigh of relief. "I could definitely go for a margarita though."

"We are *not* getting margaritas," I say.

She pouts. "Why not?"

"They're not Mexican."

She crooks an eyebrow at me. "What are you talking about?"

"Well, no one knows the exact origin," I admit. "But they are very much a US thing. Not a Mexican thing. Except for gringas like you." I grin at her. "We have prepared all summer for this moment, and now, we are here. It is time to explore the places you have learned about! And time to eat. And drink a real Mexican drink."

"What's a real Mexican drink?"

"Mezcal." I sweep out a hand at the enormous avenue in front of us. "This is Paseo de la Reforma. Do you remember it?"

Eloise brightens. "Oh, this is where the jacarandas are!"

"Exacto," I say. "Unfortunately, they aren't blooming in October but look. They are planting the cempasúchiles, for Día de Muertos."

I point to where the brilliant blooms of yellow-orange flowers are filling the median that runs in the center of the huge street.

"You'll see this flower everywhere, on homes and in restaurants, and vendors selling them for the ofrendas in people's houses."

"Right. Like in *Coco*."

I sigh. "Yes, yes, like in *Coco*. Listo! How would you like to go to one of my favorite taquerias in all of CDMX?"

Her eyes light up. Food can always be counted on to help with her nerves, I think.

"Yes," she says emphatically. "But I don't want to do any talking, or ordering, or . . . or anything."

I smile and offer her my hand. "Of course not."

She takes it and we head off down Reforma. "This area is very loud and touristy, but we are going to go just over that way, where Roma Norte starts. Remember Colonia Roma? It's an area with lots of restaurants and bars. There has been a lot of controversy recently, because many ex-pats from the US are coming and renting apartments here, which drives out the locals. And they don't pay taxes in Mexico, so it's a very good deal for them, but a very bad deal for the city."

"That sounds really unfair," Eloise says.

"Yup." Once we cross over Avenida Chapultepec, the streets become smaller and quieter. Mexico City is a place of contrast—there are elegant buildings with Art Deco doors and windows next to squat, plain apartments made of drab concrete. There are buildings painted in pale yellow or cheerful pink, with colorful tiles proclaiming their street and address, alongside 7/11s and edifices covered in graffiti. And of course, hanging above every street are strands and strands of cables, forming dense knots and tangling up with each other as they connect the city's electricity and internet.

Eloise is definitely nervous at first, gripping my hand tightly, but once we enter the heart of Colonia Roma, I sense her relax a bit. We pass tiny, glass-fronted bookstores, cafés with tables spilling out onto the sidewalks, bars with graffitied doors that won't open until much later. There are clothing stores and jewelry stores and vendors under white or pink umbrellas on streetcorners, grilling meat for tacos with tubs of toppings laid out, onion and tomato and lettuce, salsas in all colors and spice levels, shredded piles of cheese, and bowls filled with crema. It makes my mouth water just passing them, and Eloise sniffs the air hopefully.

"No," I say with a chuckle. "Your stomach is not ready for street food."

When we pass a little jewelry store, lit from within by a warm golden light, Eloise stops short.

"Look!" she says, pointing. A pair of earrings shaped like two chihuahuas hangs on a stand in the window.

"Do you want to go inside?" I ask.

She hesitates, her fingers gripping mine. Then she takes a breath. "Yeah. I do."

We enter the shop to a light tinkling of bells. A woman in her twenties, wearing a pair of funky glasses and a black top with a parrot emblazoned on it, looks up from her phone.

"Hola, buenas tardes," she says, smiling at us. The shop is full of unique pieces that would fit right in in my neighborhood in Bushwick. There are thick ceramic bangles in a giraffe print, necklaces shaped like snakes, and earrings featuring all manner of animals, from black cats mid-stretch to smiling hedgehogs, to every breed of dog imaginable. I point out a ring in the shape of a black pug.

"Look, it's Charleston," I say to Eloise. She gasps.

"Oh my god," she says. "Can I try it on?"

"Of course," the woman says to her in English.

Twin pink spots appear on Eloise's cheeks but she slips the ring on and it fits her index finger perfectly. "I love it," she says quietly. "Oooh and that," she adds, picking up the giraffe bangle and slipping it onto her wrist. "This place is so cool."

"Let's look at those earrings," I say.

"You would like to see something else?" the woman asks.

"Yes, can we see those chihuahua earrings in the window?" I ask her in Spanish.

"Claro que si," she says, getting up from her stool. Eloise hovers behind me as she takes them out. "They're so cute, aren't they?" she says in English.

"Do you make all of this jewelry?" I ask her.

"I do," she says proudly.

"It's a great shop."

"Yeah, it is," Eloise says, and my heart fills with pride. Look at her, talking to a stranger. I think it helps that she's pretty much obsessed with everything in this store. She holds one of the chihuahuas up to her ear. "How does it look?"

"Great," I say.

"I love it," the woman says. "Chihuahuas are my favorite."

"She has four dogs at home," I tell the woman. "A chihuahua, a pug, a dachshund, and a German Shepherd."

"Wow," the woman says. "So many, that's like my dream."

Eloise blushes and mumbles something that might be "Thanks."

"Oh, let me show you this," the woman says. She leads us over to a glass case where there's a thin gold chain with an enameled dachshund pendant. "I don't have anything with German Shepherds," she says apologetically.

"What do you think?" I ask Eloise.

She nods.

"We'll take these," I say, laying all four items out on the counter. The woman chats to me in Spanish as she wraps the items. When I tell her we're here for the Alvarez wedding she gasps and says she read about it in *Quién*. Eloise hands over her credit card as the woman rings her up.

"Gracias," I say, as we head to the door.

Eloise clears her throat. "Gracias," she says.

"Buen día," the woman says with a little wave.

We step out into the street and Eloise exhales in a big whoosh. "That store was *so* cool!"

"I'm glad we stopped," I say.

She smiles up at me. "Me too."

I hold her pale green gaze. "You did great in there."

Her mouth twists wryly. "Yes, congratulations to me, I didn't have a panic attack while buying earrings."

"Yes," I say to her, without a trace of teasing in my voice. "You just went shopping in a completely new city. In a different country. You socialized with a stranger. And you got some very cool jewelry."

She considers that for a moment. "I tried to move the goalposts again, huh?"

"You did."

She purses her lips. "You know, you are very annoying when you're right."

I bat my eyelashes at her and she laughs. "Ready for tacos?" I ask.

Her expression brightens. "Yes."

I take her hand. I love how easily it happens now, this physical connection between us. It feels effortless, natural, like our hands were crafted specifically for each other. Eloise's palm fits snuggly in my own, her slender fingers twining through mine. I have to fight the urge to wrap my arm around her, tuck her into my shoulder, walk with her along this street as her boyfriend instead of . . . I don't even know what I am anymore. Her emotional support friend? It seems like we've grown into something else.

But I know that's just wishful thinking on my part. Eloise isn't mine and never will be.

I lead her through the little streets of Roma, toward one of my favorite spots and try to shake off the gloom that's taken over me. I wonder if Eloise can sense it. She keeps glancing sideways at me. I shoot her an extra big smile as we cross Calle Tonalá.

"Here we are," I say, sweeping my hand out at the small restaurant in front of us.

La Planta Madre is my own personal Mecca.

I really hope Eloise likes it.

32
Eloise

The restaurant has a bright red awning, with tables lining both sides of the sidewalk.

The chairs are painted in light colors, sea green and bubble gum pink and pale yellow. The ceiling is all exposed beams and there's a wooden bar tucked away in the back corner. The walls are covered in plants—shelves of ferns and spider plants and all different types of ivy that drip toward the tables below. A handful of them are full, people laughing and chatting, and sipping drinks or eating all sorts of delicious-looking food. The air is filled with the scent of meat and spices, and there's a large black dog, some kind of lab mix, following one of the waitresses around.

I instantly love this place.

"Tinito!" An elderly woman in a green top and a pair of beige slacks scoots around from behind the bar and comes bustling up to Agustín. "Cómo estás, corazón? No sabía que estabas en México!"

I have zero idea what she's saying but she kisses his cheek then embraces him warmly. Agustín says something back to her in Spanish then gestures to me.

"This is Dolores, she owns the restaurant," he says.

"Mucho gusto," Dolores says, smiling warmly. She's got a round wrinkled face, and her short dark hair is streaked with gray. She leans forward like she's going to kiss my cheek and oh god, I freeze, because I don't want to insult this woman but oh no, please, no touching. Agustín says something, and she pauses, frowns, then shrugs.

She gestures to the tables, says, "Esta es tu casa!" and gives him another hug.

"Gracias, Dolores. Oh, y dos mezcalitos, por favor."

"Espadín o Tobalá?"

"Un espadín para ella y un tobalá para mí, por favor."

"Bueno. Y para comer?"

"Un momento," he says. I understood that last part. Agustín turns to me. "She said we can sit wherever we want. Maybe there?" He points at a small table under the awning along the sidewalk. Its two chairs are side by side, facing out onto the street.

"Sure," I say, and he pulls out a pale green chair for me. "It seems like you know her really well."

He sits beside me, so close I can feel the heat of his body. "I used to come here all the time, first when I was in college and then after work. She saw me go from being this hopeful, dumb kid to a professional journalist."

"I don't believe that," I say quietly.

"That I'm a professional?" Agustín says, teasingly.

"That you were ever dumb," I say.

He laughs. "Thank you very much. But wasn't everyone a dumb kid at some time? Haven't we all made bad decisions or said stupid things?" His gaze softens as he looks at me. "It's okay to be dumb, I think. It's how we learn."

I feel itchy and sling my tote bag over the back of my chair, just for something to do. I keep getting distracted by how good he looks in that sweater. He's pushed up the sleeves and what is it about men's forearms? Why do I want to run my fingers over his, to feel every dent and groove of muscle? Our legs are almost touching under the table. If I moved half an inch, I could press my knee against his.

Agustín just keeps talking, because of course he does. "I remember the day I first got published in *El País*, she got the whole place drunk to celebrate. Dolores never had kids of her own—her life has been devoted to running this place. She works very hard. She built this restaurant brick by brick." He rubs his hands together. "So, what should we eat?"

My stomach suddenly roars to life. In all the walking and newness, I forgot how hungry I was. My appetite rears up with a vengeance. Agustín grabs a menu from a slot in the napkin holder and opens it. Various words jump out at me: **Tortas, En Verde, Paraempezar**. But my eyes are of course drawn immediately to the section titled **Tacos.**

I understand absolutely none of the descriptions and yet still I would shove all of them in my face right now.

"Okay," Agustín says to me. "I will say, let's get many things to share."

"Great."

"I will recommend the carmelita tacos—they are with shrimp—and the viajero orden. Those are with pig. Pig's leg and lomo is . . . loin? Pork loin?"

"Sold," I say.

"Those will be very big. Do you want to try one more kind?"

I give him a look. "I am here for tacos. All the tacos."

He chuckles. "Gringas y tacos," he mutters, shaking his head. "Bueno, let's take the flor de calabaza. Squash flower. Very Mexican, very delicious."

I rub my hands together and lick my lips as Agustín puts the menu back in its holder.

"This place is a bit unique, since they do not have the classic types of Mexican tacos," he says. "We will also have to get tacos al pastor and tacos campechanos."

"I could literally eat only tacos this whole trip and be happy. I will eat any taco you put in front of me," I say. He smiles at me warmly, his eyes crinkling.

"We will be eating more things than just tacos," he warns.

"Also great. Are we going to have sopes?"

He looks oddly touched. I wonder if the memory is as special for him as it is for me.

"Si," he says quietly. "Sopes y aguachile."

Suddenly, I wonder what would happen if I *did* press my knee against his. That's not the same as holding hands. A knee touch would mean something else. Would he want a knee touch?

Panic flips in my stomach as the Wheel spins and lands on *Rejection*. Heat floods through my body.

Of course he doesn't want a knee touch.

He only sees me as a friend. At best. Really, I'm just a big pile of issues, packaged together with a bunch of old dogs.

And what if I *did* touch his knee, and he pulled away? Oh god. I would die from the shame. I would melt into a toxic puddle of humiliation.

But what if I gave him a knee touch and he *responded*? What if he pushed back against my knee? What would I do then?

There's a faint rushing of blood in my ears as my gaze drops to his mouth.

"Mezcalitos," Dolores says, appearing out of nowhere with a tray with two very small glasses. I yank my eyes away from Agustín's face, grateful for the distraction. The glasses are almost like holders for votive candles: ridged and a bit larger than shot glasses. She puts them down in front of us, along with a plate of orange slices and some substance that looks like finely crushed salt but brown.

Agustín gives her our order, and they talk again for a moment in Spanish, while I examine my drink. It *is* a votive holder, I realize—there's a cross etched on the bottom. When Dolores leaves, Agustín turns to me.

"Ready for your first mezcal?" he says. "You will love it."

"We aren't doing shots, are we?"

He looks horrified. "No. Please do not shoot that. Mezcal is for sipping. First, we try it solo."

He takes a long inhale over his glass. I do the same.

"Whoa," I say. "It's very smoky."

He nods and sips. "Ahhh," he says, a look of satisfaction spreading across his face. "I missed this. Of course, you can get mezcal in New York but it's not the same. And Dolores has a great selection. Yours is an espadín—the most common type of agave used for mezcal. Great for beginners. Mine is a tobalá. More advanced." He winks at me.

I take a hesitant sip. It tastes even smokier than it smells, lingering on my tongue and sending a pleasant burn through my chest.

"Wow," I say.

"It's good, right?"

"Yeah." It's a very unique flavor. I take another sip and find that I really like it. It brings to mind campfires and sunsets. It almost feels like drinking the embers of a dying hearth. It's warm and woodsy, but with an herbal bite.

"Here, try it with some orange and Sal de Gusano." He dips the orange slice into the brown salty stuff, and I follow suit. We eat in tandem then sip.

"Oooh," I say. The smoky nature of the mezcal works wonderfully with the sweet flavor of the citrus and the savoriness of the salt. "What kind of salt is this?"

"Worm salt," he says, and I nearly choke on the orange.

"What?"

He laughs. "It is made with the larvae of a moth that lives inside the agave plant. Mezcal is made from agave, like tequila. They toast the larvae with chilies and then grind it all up with salt."

"Are you telling me I just ate ground up moth babies?" I cry.

He grins and nods, like this isn't horrifying news.

"No," I say, pushing the plate away from me. "I'll stick with the mezcal and the orange, but no moth baby salt, thank you."

"You know," he says, dipping another slice into the salt, "the moths would eat the heart of the agave if they could. So by removing them, there is more agave to turn into mezcal. Or tequila, for your *margaritas*."

He says the word in a very bad American accent that coaxes a laugh out of me. I lean back in my chair and take another tiny sip of mezcal. People pass by, chattering away in Spanish, and I let the language wash over me. It comes at me from all angles, and I find a real comfort in not having any idea what anyone is saying. I really like this neighborhood, with its narrow streets and cute restaurants and funky shops—Agustín wasn't lying about the sidewalks. Trees are everywhere and their roots punch up through the concrete, creating a dangerous walking experience. And the trees aren't planted in neat little rows, boxed in with iron fencing like in New York. No, here they're wild, and free, and have a very fuck-you attitude, which I respect. I got hit in the face by a low hanging palm on the way over.

Dolores returns with our food, and the black lab in tow. The dog pads up to me, and I rub his ears as his tongue lolls out happily. Dolores says something, and Agustín smiles and replies.

"She said he likes you," he tells me. "And I said all dogs love you."

I blush. "What's his name?" I ask quietly, not making eye contact with anyone but the dog. He leans his head on my knee.

"Cilantro," Dolores tells me.

I smile. A good name for a restaurant dog. "Qué buen perro," I murmur to him. He croons and pants up at me.

"Cilantro, ven aquí," Dolores says, setting down our food and patting her thigh. He leaps to attention and follows her back to the bar.

"Ready?" Agustín says.

"They're blue," I say, surprised. Some of the tortillas aren't the toasted beige color I'm used to.

"Si. Dolores makes tortillas with blue corn as well as yellow." Agustín points to the little tray set with small bowls of salsa. One is bright reddish orange, another dark almost brick red, and the last a creamy green. There's also a little a bowl of lime wedges. "I always suggest adding limón," he says, and I follow his instructions, squeezing a fresh spray of lime juice over one of the shrimp tacos. Then he points to the salsas. "Not hot, a little hot, very hot," he says, pointing at the green, brick red, and orangish one in turn. I spoon some of the salsa verde and the brick red salsa onto my taco.

"Am I allowed to eat now?" I ask wryly.

He's already taken a massive bite of his taco, moaning as his eyes roll back in his head. I dig in.

Oh, the explosion of joy that erupts in my mouth. How can food taste this good? The salsa gives off just the right amount of heat, and the crunch of lettuce contrasts with the firm juicy shrimp. I quickly devour the whole thing then turn my attention to the others.

The pork loin! The tender meat has been marinated in some kind of rich spicy sauce, then shredded. The sharp bite of red onion and the creamy slice of avocado create a panorama of flavors and textures. The squash blossom is really interesting, with an earthy heartiness, topped with more avocado plus strands of salty, shredded Oaxaca cheese.

When our plates are clean and our glasses empty, Agustín leans back in his chair. "Want to try a couple more?" he asks.

"Si," I say, and he chuckles. The light through the awning dusts his hair with patches of reddish gold. I can't help the way my eyes greedily trace the line of his arm as he raises a hand to signal Dolores. Maybe it's the food, or the mezcal, or the pleasant ambiance of the restaurant, but I'm feeling very relaxed. My knee still hovers a mere inch away from Agustín's. I watch him as he talks to

Dolores, the sharp curve of his jaw, the width of his cheekbones, the slope of his nose. He'd make a beautiful subject for painting.

I laugh at myself because I sound like an idiot. But I also kind of don't really care. Maybe it's okay to sound like an idiot sometimes. I'm just feeling however I feel.

It's almost like I have permission here, so far away from everything I've ever known. There are no ghosts haunting me, no routines to keep. I'm completely untethered and rather than scary, it's kind of . . . freeing.

"What?" Agustín asks as Dolores bustles away.

"Nothing," I say. My phone pings, and it's a text from Miriam on the Pack thread. She's sent a photo of Pip, peeing on one of the sparkly poufs while making direct eye contact with the camera.

Miriam: This motherfucker.

"Oh no," I gasp, as Agustín laughs.

"This does not surprise me," he says.

But the Wheels has started to spin, click-click-clicking in my chest until it lands on *They're Probably Mad at You*, because Miriam must be so, so mad at me. I should never have asked her to take Pip, he's terrorizing her cats and destroying her furniture, what was I thinking—

My phone pings again.

Miriam: But I love him. And so does Checkers!

Another photo appears of the two of them, orange tabby and black chihuahua, curled up together in that enormous circular chair by the window.

Suddenly, Gretchen chimes in with a pic of her own.

Gretchen: We took Charleston to the park today 😍

The photo shows Charleston in a stroller, tongue lolling out, Begonia holding up a fallen, orange-gold leaf for him to smell. The Wheel slows. No one is mad at me. And look at how happy

Charleston is. Agustín slings his arm around the back of my chair as he leans forward to get a better look. Several things happen at once.

His fingers brush against my back.

His hair flops into his eyes, sending a wave of his scent toward me.

His knee crosses that inch of space between us and presses into mine.

EEEEEEEEEEEP!

That's not a slice on the Wheel, and it's not a reaction I've felt before. The Wheel feels oddly distant in this moment, in fact. There's a faint ringing in my ears. I'm acutely aware of each unique beat of my heart.

Our knees are touching.

OUR KNEES ARE TOUCHING.

It's like my knee has sprouted a thousand new nerve endings, every one of them focused on that gentle pressure between us.

His face is so close to mine. My gaze skims over his mouth again, as it curves into a smile. My fingers ache to brush his hair back, to feel it, thick and sun-warmed, against my knuckles.

Dolores returns with more food and two bottles of beer. And while Agustín chats with her, and Cilantro gives my wrist a quick lick, we don't break apart. We stay knee-connected. Even as we eat. I try these thick oblong tortillas that Agustín tells me are called tlacoyos.

"Dolores makes them in house," he says. "They are stuffed with refried beans and topped with onion and lettuce and crema."

Everything tastes incredible. The air is cool, the beers are crisp, the food just the right amount of spicy. And the whole time, Agustín's knee is pressed against mine.

I wonder if he notices it the way I do.

33
Agustín

Holy shit, Eloise and I are touching.

And not in our usual holding-hands-for-emotional-support type of way. I'm desperately trying to act cool about this. When I put my arm over the back of her chair, I was certain it was going too far. That she would tense and pull away from me.

But she leaned *in*. And I swear I caught her looking at my mouth.

My heart pitter-patters in my chest like it's tap dancing. I refuse to move my knee, fearing to break this connection and lose it forever. Even as my left thigh has started to cramp. Too bad thigh. You stay right where you are. I'm not ruining this moment.

At any minute, the spell could break.

She sighs and leans back in her chair, taking her last sip of beer.

"I'm stuffed," she says.

"Me too."

"That was so good."

Her eyes are heavy, her mouth curving with contentment. I feel like she could be seconds away from her resting her head on my shoulder. I wish she would. I think she would fit perfectly in the crook of my arm. She rubs her stomach and grins at me sleepily. A shudder rips through me, my throat tightening.

"Shall we get the check?" I ask.

She nods. I signal to Dolores. After we've paid, we stand and stretch, then head back out onto the streets.

"Do you want to go back to the hotel?" I ask.

She checks her phone. "No," she says, and I imagine Rachel hasn't gotten back to her about the room.

I feel this internal battle waging inside me. We *should* get separate rooms. We *shouldn't* sleep in the same bed. I never want Eloise to be uncomfortable. But I can't stop the flashes in my mind. Waking up beside her. Her curls splayed out across her pillow. Her green eyes dewy in the morning light.

The echo of her knee against mine lingers.

"Want to go for a walk?" I ask. It's only five PM. "We could go to Parque México."

Her eyes light up. "Perritos!"

She slips her hand into mine and something about it feels different this time. More intentional, and less out of necessity. Or even habit. Hope buoys up inside me, bobbing just under my skin and dancing like light on water. I lead her off in the direction of the park. We wait to cross Insurgentes, as one of the large, bright red MetroBuses pulls up in the center of the avenue, where passengers wait to board on an elevated platform beneath a metal awning. We cross at the light and head down Avenida Sonora until we reach the edge of the park, where a line of trees greets us.

There's a man playing jazz on a guitar on one corner, a hat out in front of him, busking for tips. A small café with tables and wicker chairs set up under a pale green awning sends the delicious scent of fresh brewed coffee our way. I figure we could use some caffeine, so we stop in and I order at the counter. There are a few remaining pan dulce in a glass case next to the register, a sad looking oreja and a couple of deflated conchas. But tomorrow morning, this case will be filled to the brim with freshly baked pastries. Pan de muerto, rol de guayaba, garibaldi . . . my mouth starts watering at the thought, even though I just ate.

I order a latte for Eloise and an Americano for myself, and we cross the street and head into the park. The trees cast patches of shade over the paths, some dirt and gravel, others inlaid with curved patterns of brick that snake around playgrounds and weave between low hedges and wild blooms. I point out the Art Deco signs that say things like *Respect for trees, plants, and grass: is an unequivocal sign of culture.* We pass the enormous stone bust of Einstein, with a quote engraved on a plaque beneath it.

Si quieres vivir una vida feliz, átala a una meta, no a una persona o un objeto.

"What does that mean?" she asks.

"If you want to live a happy life, tie it . . . or maybe you would say attach it to a goal, not a person or an object."

We wander beneath elegant jacarandas and ancient ahuehuetes, with palms scattered among them, their spiky leaves punching up through the foliage, then pass the lake, where snowy white geese bob on the water, and arrive at the one place I know she'll love the most.

The amphitheater, the park's central feature, called Foro Lindberg. Supposedly, the famous aviator landed his plane here. It's fronted by a giant Art Deco sculpture called the Fuente de los Cántaros—a naked woman holding two water vessels. There are five enormous white columns at its back, and two pergolas lining each side, hung with bougainvillea, bursting with magenta flowers that cascade over the latticework and reach toward the ground in creeping fingers. In its vast center, a young girl wobbles on roller skates, a couple of teens zoom past on skateboards, and a dance troupe rehearses, women in sports bras doing handstands as shirtless men spot them. People sit on the low walls drinking coffees and chatting, while dogs roam freely.

Eloise and I take a seat beneath one of the pergolas, the sun filtering through a thatch of bougainvillea overhead, and watch. A roly poly pug, the color of a toasted marshmallow, races after a bright green tennis ball, only to have it scooped up by a much faster border collie. The collie's owner shouts at her, then apologizes profusely to the owner of the pug. An abuelita with a pair of chihuahuas sits in the shade of the pergola across from us, her two dogs growling at anyone who passes by. We can hear the faint strains of another street musician, playing just outside the park.

Eloise sips her coffee, her expression unreadable. I want to touch her knee with mine again. The wind teases her curls, and she tucks them impatiently behind her ear.

"This isn't as scary as I thought it would be," she says quietly. "Being in a new place. I've never been out of the country before." She sighs. "I don't know if I'm ready for the wedding, though. I like this." She sweeps her hand out. "Hanging out in a park. Watching dogs. With—" She coughs, and takes a sip of coffee, her cheekbones suddenly laced with pink. My heart trips in my chest, wondering if she was about to say what I thought she was going to say and then banishing the idea because it's only getting my hopes up.

I nudge her with my shoulder. "We can stay here as long as you want."

She nudges me back and shoots me a half-grin. "Okay."

We sit and sip and make up stories about the dogs and their owners.

"I bet that abuelita makes individual taquitos for those two chihuahuas every night for dinner."

"The border collie is in training for the dog Olympics."

"See that boxer? He's judging everyone. Especially the little girl on the roller skates."

"That golden retriever is named Fluffy McFlufferson, and he sleeps on a faux fur bed with his name emblazoned on it."

"The Xoloitzcuintli and the shih tzu over there are plotting the destruction of the world, like Pinky and the Brain."

She laughs. "That Xolo does look a lot like Pinky."

"No, no, he's the Brain," I say.

We finish our coffees as the sun begins to set.

"Any news from Rachel?" I ask.

She checks her phone. "No."

We both pretend to ignore the fact that this means we will have to share a bed. I feel the tension flicker between us. My fingers itch to take her hand.

"Want one more bite for the road?" I ask. "I know this great cocktail spot. But we need to take a car."

Eloise nods. "Sure."

We dump our coffee cups and head out of the park while I text Enrique and ask if he can come pick us up. He's too far away at the moment, in the suburbs of the city, so I just call an Uber. We head back to Colonia Roma, to a little bar called Las Brujas. It sits on the corner of a tiny square park called Parque Rio de Janeiro, a fountain in its center boasting a metal replica of Michealangelo's David. We get out of the car in front of a red brick building, with arched windows fronted with balconies crafted in intricate patterns of swirling metal, painted white.

"The architecture in this city is very cool," Eloise observes.

"It is. Many different styles all together. Lots of Art Deco. See that?"

I point to the top of the building where a pointed roof sits atop a tall turret, all brown shingles. "It's like a witch's hat," I say. "And those two windows below it are the eyes."

"Huh," Eloise says.

"They call the building La Casa de Las Brujas, the house of the witches. This bar is called Las Brujas—The Witches—and it's owned and operated by women," I say as we walk toward the varnished wooden doors, thrown wide open in the temperate evening.

"Well, I love that," Eloise says.

The interior is dimly lit, glowing orb-like lamps hanging over the sleek black bar, row upon row of liquor bottles illuminated in golden light behind it.

I ask the hostess if we can have a table, and she takes us to a spot in a dark corner in the back, tucked away from the bar. There are cushioned seats and a low table and as soon as we sit, I realize there is simply no way to keep any space between us. This nook was made for couples. Eloise's elbow bumps mine, and her thigh presses into me as she adjusts herself.

"Sorry," I say, as she says, "No it's fine," and we do this awkward dance back and forth before finally, I sling my arm around her to rest it along the back of the cushioned bench. It's the only way to be comfortable. She sits up primly, as much as the seat allows, but we're still touching. I feel her shiver, and it reverberates along the side of my torso. I flex my fingers, aching to pull her closer. To feel the curve of her shoulder beneath my hand. To brush the curls from her eyes. There's a candle on the table and its flickering light throws her features into sharp relief, her eyes like deep green pools.

I open the menu and show her the cocktail list.

"Every drink comes with a story," I explain. My voice sounds huskier than normal. "About a woman accused of witchcraft. Lots herbal influences. See, they call them potions."

Eloise's smile is brittle, her body thrumming with tension. I wonder if I should just call it a night—tell her she can take the room herself, and I'll meet her extra early. My family would be happy to have me home. I feel like I've crossed a line, that I've stepped through a doorway into a dimension I can't return from. Her faint citrusy scent fills my nose, her face so close to mine. I'm filled with the urge to tilt her chin up, to run my thumb over her lower lip.

She glances at me and her breath catches in her throat. "Do they have mezcal?" she squeaks.

I chuckle. "Si."

34
Eloise

I am freeeeeeeeaking out.

I wish I could text Rachel. But I also never ever want Rachel to know that I am currently tucked in a dark corner of a dimly lit bar, with one entire side of me touching one entire side of Agustín and ohmygodIamfreakingout.

My heart has sprouted a thousand wings, and they are fluttering and flapping in a way that feels like a panic attack except I can breathe. I can think.

I want to kiss him. So badly. I worry if I look at him too much, I'll just stare at his mouth. His arm behind me is a solid unyielding force against my back, and the candlelight plays across his face, his dimples like shadows in the night. I'm buzzing, humming, vibrating. I'm a thesaurus of feelings.

He orders us drinks, and I think maybe also French fries? I'm still pretty full from our feast earlier but I want something to do with my hands. And mouth. I need to distract myself from these urges but they're everywhere.

I'm aching to kiss him. I've never ached to kiss anyone before.

Rachel hasn't said anything about the room yet, and I don't want to bother her, but how am I supposed to sleep next to a man I want to kiss *this badly*? I keep clenching my jaw like I can physically swallow the desire. Like I can wrestle it into a box, because Agustín is not supposed to be anything more than my plus-one. He's just a date to a wedding so my best friend doesn't get cursed, so how did we get here?

Oh my god, what am I even thinking, it's not *we*. It's *me*. I'm the one here, with all the twisting, writhing thesaurus-feelings. He's probably wondering why I haven't moved a muscle since we sat down.

The truth is this has been one of the best days of my life. Despite the flight. And the newness. And the impending wedding. I've had so much *fun* today. Even away from the Pack and my apartment and New York. And I know it's because of him. Because I trust him.

Because I'm falling for him.

No. I have to reject that thought. Thank god, the waitress comes back with our drinks because I'm sure this silence is getting uncomfortable. He must notice it, right? Is it just me? Ugh, why can't this squirming coil in my stomach just knock it off?

As soon as the waitress leaves, I grab my drink—which is honestly incredibly cool, with smoke coming off it and a purple flower floating on top of hazy apricot-colored liquid—and take a ginormous gulp. Instantly, my mouth is full of the perfect combination of fruit, smoke, and citrus. I swallow and cough.

"Wow," I say, as the mezcal burns through my chest, relaxing me. I take another drink, less aggro and more savoring this time. "Wow," I say again.

"It's good, right?"

His face is so close to mine, his breath tickles my ear.

You can do this, Eloise. Turn your head and look at him. Don't make it weird.

I take a measured inhale, and one more fortifying sip of my drink.

I turn to him, and he's got his own tumbler in one hand, long, tan fingers curved around a glass of amber liquid with a desiccated orange slice nestled against a single large cube of ice. He's gazing at me from beneath those dark, expressive brows, his eyes utterly focused. When he looks at me like that, I feel like I'm the only thing that matters, the only thing that exists in his universe. It steals all the air from my lungs, making my throat catch. My heart pounds against my sternum. He's mere inches away from me.

The moment elongates, stretching out, thick and sweet, like molasses. My eyes dart to his mouth—I can't help myself. I feel a tremor run through me. His lips are slightly parted, almost as if in surprise. Slowly, like he doesn't want to scare me, he puts down his drink. Even more slowly, he lifts his hand to my face. The moment his palm touches my cheek, a flash of heat runs over my body, like he's lit a flame across my skin. His touch is achingly gentle. His thumb whispers over my cheekbone, and I feel something inside me begin to unravel. There's a pulsing throb between my legs and the air between us shimmers.

He tilts my head ever so slightly.

Yes.

I don't know if I whisper the word aloud or only think it in my mind. But Agustín knows. He's always been able to read me. He crosses the tiny space between us and brushes his lips against mine.

Electricity flickers. Stars explode. The heavens open.

His lips are soft and tender and I feel a give inside me as he kisses me. Gently. Serenely. But with an undercurrent of passion, like he's keeping himself in control. Like he doesn't want to scare me.

And I realize I am not scared.

He is saying yes too.

He is saying *Yes.*

I give a tiny cry and lean into him, my lips parting, my hand coming to cradle his face, to pull him closer. I finally—finally!—get to sink my fingers into his thick dark hair. It's coarser than I expected and tickles my knuckles. I am filled with sensations, discovering nerve endings I never knew I had. Every pore and particle of me opens for him like a flower to the sun.

Our kiss deepens. His mouth is so warm and rich. He tastes like whiskey and oranges.

I never want this moment to end. I want to curl up and live here forever.

When we finally break apart, we're both breathing heavily. He leans his forehead against mine, dimples flashing. I'm smiling too, a smile so big and wide, it's a wonder my cheeks don't crack. I don't want to lose contact with him. Every place he touches me is a tiny miracle. His forehead pressing against mine, my knee against his thigh, his arm around my back. Every touch is sacred. I reach up to grip the neck of his sweater, keeping him here, anchored to me. He rests his hand on mine, as if to say *I'm not going anywhere.*

My eyes dart to his mouth. I'm drunk on his kiss. I want more.

He chuckles hoarsely and sparkles burst between my legs and scatter across my thighs.

He kisses my temple and shifts to tuck me into the crook of his arm. His lips press into the crown of my head. My body is still humming, but in an entirely different way than it was just moments earlier. I settle in beside him as he picks up his drink. I pop a fry in my mouth and chew.

I am *comfortable.* This is the most comfortable position that has ever existed for anyone, ever. I'm sure of it. There is no cozier spot in the world than right here in the crook of Agustín Martinez's arm, in one of the coolest bars I've ever been to.

It suddenly occurs to me that we just had our first kiss in public. Which is wow, not even close to my style. I mean, I don't know what my style is besides being a little sweaty and always on the verge of a panic attack. But it feels like a bubble has surrounded us. Like a weight has been released. He wanted to kiss me too. I wonder if he's wanted to kiss me this whole time, the way I've wanted to kiss him.

I could ask but I don't want to break the mood with silly words that I wouldn't get right anyway. I want to surround myself in his scent, feel the scratchy material of his sweater against my cheek, sip my smoky apricot drink, munch some fries, and people watch. I want to absorb each and every detail of this most perfect of all nights.

The events for this week, the travel, even the wedding . . . it all feels so far away right now. Like this whole trip was really made for this moment.

For that kiss.

35

Agustín

I was right—Eloise does fit perfectly in the crook of my arm.

I feel like I'm floating, like my bones have become puffs of air. I can't feel the cushioned bench beneath me or the glass in my hand. Nothing except the spot where her head rests. Nothing but the ghost of her lips on mine.

I'm tumbling into an abyss. I'm falling without a safety net.

Eloise shifts against me, and I press my lips to the top of her head, breathing her in, feeling her curls, like silken tendrils, against my cheek.

All the tension of the day has dissolved, and even though the sun has long set, it feels like a sunrise has broken over us.

People filter in and out of the bar. We sip our drinks and don't speak. There's nothing to say—our words are the press of a hand, the curve of a finger, the stroke of a lock of hair. Her palm against my knee. My arm around her shoulders. The steady rise and fall of our chests.

Her phone suddenly lights up on the table. We both glance at it.

Rachel: So the hotel says they can have another room available but not for two more days. Is that okay?? Can you handle two days sharing with him?

I wait for her response, wondering if this will thread a line of tension between us. Instead, she turns her face up to me, her gaze glittering in the candlelight. She reaches up to brush her fingers against my jaw, her touch playing a nocturne over my skin. The smattering of golden freckles over her nose are like tiny stars. She is so beautiful. When she tilts her mouth toward mine, I gladly slant my lips over hers. She tastes smoky and sweet, her lips warm and soft. I feel a wild thrill run through me, that I get to be the one to hold her, to touch her so intimately, to experience the heady bliss of her kisses. I cup her face in my hand, my fingers stroking the length of her neck. She makes a tiny moan that sets my groin aching. I have to control myself. I need to go at her pace.

When she pulls away, she's smiling, her cheeks flushed, her eyes alight like green flames.

She picks up her phone.

Eloise: It's okay. Don't worry about it.

Rachel: You sure?

Eloise: Yup.

Three dots appear, then disappear, then appear again.

Rachel: Is everything okay???

Eloise: Yup.

Rachel sends a gif of Kim Kardashian poking her head out from behind a tree. Eloise laughs softly and I feel it reverberate in my sternum.

Eloise: See you at breakfast tomorrow.

Rachel: !!!

Rachel: OKAY!!!
Rachel: HAVE A GOOD NIGHT!
Rachel: YOU TOO AGUSTÍN!!

Eloise quickly flips her phone over and buries her face in my chest. Oh, the joy of being able to wrap my arms around her, hold her close to me. I can feel the angles of her scapula through her thin sweater.

"She's gonna be so annoying about this," Eloise moans, her voice muffled by my shirt. I laugh into her hair, memorizing the feel of her. I don't know what to say. I'm just so utterly, inescapably happy.

Eloise sits up, her face determined, and she opens her mouth—likely to come up with some adorably transparent lie to give Rachel tomorrow. Instead, she lets out a huge yawn.

"Let's get the check," I say. "It's been a long day."

"Mm," she says, then happily snuggles back against me. If I could live in this corner of Las Brujas forever, I would.

Eloise stays tucked under my arm the whole car ride back to the Four Seasons. We walk hand in hand to the elevators, grinning at each other like idiots while another couple going to the tenth floor chatters away in Spanish. When we get to our room, I open the door and switch on the light.

I don't think.

As soon as the door clicks shut behind us, I sweep Eloise into my arms and claim her mouth with mine. This kiss isn't like the others. It's urgent, passionate, almost desperate. Like something has been clawing its way out of both of us and has finally been set loose. I press her against the wall as her hands scrabble beneath my sweater, her fingernails raking over my back and sending shudders ripping through me. I sink one hand into her curls, tilting her head to kiss a line down her neck, then back to her eager mouth.

My cock is so hard, it presses almost painfully against my jeans. When Eloise arches her back, I feel it throb for her, pushing into her thigh. She gasps and jumps. We break apart and suddenly, she's laughing. Hysterically. Which is not necessarily the reaction one wants to their giant hard-on, but I think I know Eloise well enough by now to know this is not about me.

"I'm sorry," she gasps through fits of laughter. "Oh my god, I'm so sorry . . ." She clutches her side and gasps for air. Then she wraps her arms around my neck. "I'm just really tired," she says. "And punchy."

I tilt my head. "Punchy?"

"Like out of it. Loopy."

"Ah." I brush a curl from her eyes. "I see." She reaches up on her tiptoes and caresses my lips with hers. When I pull her close against the length of my body, my cock still straining against my jeans, she doesn't pull away. Or laugh, which is a good sign. But she breaks our kiss and for the first time, I see a familiar flutter of panic in her expression.

"I know you said you weren't looking for anything romantic when we first met," I say quietly. "I have been trying to respect that." She shivers as I press my palm against her lower back. "But I need to know. Have your feelings changed?"

A smile splits across her face, so wide it consumes her. "Yes," she says emphatically. "They have definitely, *definitely* changed."

Even though I had been guessing and hoping, hearing her confirm it out loud sends relief crashing through me. My heart thumps a painfully happy beat against my ribs.

"But," she adds, her voice growing timid, "is it okay if we just . . . go to sleep right now?"

"Of course," I say. "That is all I was planning to do."

She raises an eyebrow.

"What? I am not in a rush. I didn't think this was going to happen at all."

She swallows hard. "And your feelings for me. Um. Well. Did you . . . did you want this to happen?"

I tilt her chin up. "I have wanted it for a very," I plant a featherlight kiss on her neck, "very," I lay another one beneath her ear, "very long time."

She shivers in my arms, and I feel her pulse quicken as I nuzzle that tender spot beneath her jaw. "Me too," she whispers.

Something inside me roars in triumph. We disentangle ourselves, and she scurries into the bathroom, closing the door with a click. A second later, I hear the faucet turn on. I open the dresser and look at the clothes I brought, running a hand through my hair. I feel wide awake but exhausted at the same time. I usually sleep shirtless in just my boxer briefs. Absolutely no way that's going to happen tonight. I grab a fresh white tee and a pair of cotton gym shorts. I'm glad I have a moment to calm my body down.

When Eloise emerges from the bathroom, face scrubbed clean, still in her jeans and sweater, I trade places and give her a chance to change. When I glance at myself in the mirror, my eyes have a feverish look to them, my skin flushed. I brush my teeth and splash some water on my face.

Be cool, I think to my dick.

I listen at the door, making sure she's ready. I don't want to surprise her. I hesitate with my hand on the knob. A thousand questions flood my brain, about how to get into bed, which side to sleep on, whether I can pull her into me and cuddle her to sleep the way I want to or maybe she wants all the space she can get, and I should stick to my side of the bed.

I chuckle and rub the back of my neck. I sound like Eloise's Worry Wheel. I'll just go with the flow, like I always do. I open the door and step out into the room.

Eloise is tucked under the giant comforter, her head nestled on the plush pillow, sound asleep. Her breathing is slow and even, one hand curled beneath her chin, the other resting across her stomach. I smile softly. She looks so peaceful. I walk over to switch off the lamp on her nightstand. Then I turn off the other lights, slip beneath the covers and curl up on one side, sliding my arm over her stomach so my hand rests against hers.

36
Eloise

I wake up to the faint chirping of birds outside my window.

Before opening my eyes, I let my other senses kick in. I'm curled up on my side. There's a warm weight draped over my waist and a firm wall of muscle pressing into my back. I can smell leather and cardamom, mixed with the faint trace of flowers.

I peel my lids open. The room is bathed in soft morning light. We forgot to close the curtains last night. And the balcony door. The air is quite chilly, but I'm comfortable as a little clam, tucked against the heat of Agustín's body.

I feel a smile spread, slow and giddy, across my face as I look down at his arm secured firmly around me, his hand splayed out over the comforter. I can feel his even breaths as he sleeps, the cotton material of his tee rubbing against my own. I don't want to move. Ever. I want this bed to be my new home.

But I really have to pee.

Slowly, so as not to wake him, I ease out from under the covers, then grab my phone and the first clothes I can get my hands on (which turn out to be the travel sweatsuit from yesterday) and scurry into the bathroom. I immediately text Rachel. It's seven AM, but I don't care.

> Me: How soon can you meet me for breakfast or do I have to wait until 9?

Her reply is instantaneous.

> Rachel: I will be downstairs in THIRTY FUCKING SECONDS.

I slip into my white Birkenstocks and meet her at the hotel restaurant in the courtyard. She's seated in a corner table, beneath a canopy of white, the waiter pouring her water as she orders coffees for both of us.

"Eloise Madigan Whitechapel, what the actual fuck is going on?" she says.

Blood rushes to my cheeks. I blush so hard my ears burn, and the nape of my neck is on fire, and I feel the heat spread all the way down to my belly button.

Rachel gasps. "You kissed him."

I clap my hands over my face and nod. Rachel pulls them away, and I'm smiling so big, and tears are filling my eyes.

"El!" she squeals, so loud that the handful of other patrons look over at us. Then she tackles me in a hug, and we're both laughing. "Oh my god, tell me everything," she says, as the waiter arrives with our lattes.

And I do. I tell her about our day yesterday, and about the tacos, and the park, and the dimly lit corner where it all came to a head.

"Swoon!" Rachel says, leaning back in her chair. "This is incredible, El. He's such a great guy. Didn't I tell you he was a good-looking man-shaped human?"

I flush again. "You did."

She pokes me. "How long."

"Hm?"

"How long have you liked him? Because a lot of stuff is starting to make a lot of sense."

I grimace. "A while."

"Eeeeeep!" she squeals again. "Wait, did you sleep with him?"

My stomach does a backflip. "No! No. No, no, no. When we got back to the hotel, I . . . I accidentally laughed at his dick."

Rachel chokes on her sip of water. "What?"

"I didn't see it or anything," I explain quickly, flames scorching the sides of my face. "It was just . . . we were kissing some more and then he pressed me against the wall and I felt . . ." I cover my face in my hands again. "It just caught me by surprise. Oh, I probably made a fool out of myself. Or hurt his feelings. Who does that?"

"Hey," Rachel says softly. "It's fine. It's been a minute since you've been around a dick."

I meet her gaze, and we both burst into laughter.

"I'm sure he has a very nice one too," I muse.

Rachel waggles her eyebrows. "Oh girl, I bet he does." She glances behind me. "Speaking of nice dicks . . ."

I whirl around to see Agustín and Diego walking toward our table.

"Morning amor," Diego says, sliding into the seat next to Rachel and kissing her cheek. Agustín sits beside me. For a panicked second, I wonder if he's going to kiss my cheek too. But he just squeezes my hand under the table once then releases me.

"Diego was telling me you two have another family dinner this evening," Agustín says to Rachel.

"Oh yeah," Rachel says, huffing out the side of her mouth. "His dad's family this time. They rented out the entire restaurant. I really wish my Spanish were better."

"Your Spanish is great," Diego says. "And you know my family speaks English."

"Yeah, but only because *I'm* there. I don't want to be the gringa that forces everyone to speak a different language."

"Poco a poco," Diego says, taking her hand in his so he can kiss it. "My family adores you no matter what language you speak." Rachel smiles, looking mollified.

We order breakfast from the waiter. I'm hyper aware of Agustín next to me, the clean scent of his hoodie, one elbow propped up on the table.

"So what are you two up to today?" Diego asks us.

I look to Agustín, since obviously I have no idea. But looking at him sends all these wild flutters across my skin, my mouth watering, my stomach tightening. It suddenly occurs to me that I get to *keep kissing him*. This wasn't a one-time thing.

My pulse kicks up a notch.

"I thought we could go to the Museo Nacional de Antropología," Agustín says.

"Qué cool," Diego says. "That's a great museum, really spectacular," he says to me. "It's got so much history and artifacts from all the pre-Hispanic cultures of Mexico."

Rachel elbows him in the ribs. "How come you've never taken me there, babe?"

Diego smooths back his slick, dark hair. "Because we always have a packed schedule when we come."

She purses her lips. "Yeah, that's true." Her eyes brighten. "Hey, what if we all went to dinner this week! Just the four of us. Let's see, tomorrow is the bachelorette . . . oh, we have an evening free the day before the rehearsal dinner." I shoot her a warning look that says I will murder her if she mentions the words "double date." "We can go someplace cool. Agustín's choice. Sorry, amor, I'm sick of all your usual spots in Polanco."

"Sounds good to me," Diego says.

"Yay!" Rachel claps her hands together. "It's a date."

She winks at me, and I glower.

After breakfast, Agustín and I head back to our room to get ready for the day. I'm glad he showered already, so we don't have to do this weird dance of the bathroom. My pulse sprints as we walk side by side to the elevators, the Wheel click-click-clicking away.

What do we do now?

When do we start kissing again?

Does this mean we're, like, together? Does he want that? I know we talked about feelings and stuff last night but maybe he only meant that this was a casual thing. Casual feelings.

But I don't do casual feelings. He knows that right?

We wait by the elevator doors, and there's a faint ringing in my ears. They open, and we step inside the elevator. As soon as the doors close, Agustín pulls me into him, holding me tight.

"Hey," he murmurs into my hair.

All the tension drains out of me. My mind quiets. My pulse slows.

The Wheel click-click-clicks to a stop.

This is where I belong.

I don't have anything to be scared of.

I take a deep breath. It's ohhhh so very nice to be held like this. To feel like nothing exists outside the circle of his arms. I tilt my head up to him, and he smiles down at me. His lips brush softly over mine, sending zips of electricity over my skin.

By the time the elevator doors open, I'm calm. We hold hands and walk down the hall to our room. While I poke through the closet and debate what to wear, Agustín lounges in one of the chairs on the balcony. I think he's giving me space to get ready, and I appreciate that. For a moment, I run my fingers over the garment bag that contains the dress I'll wear to the wedding. I wonder if Agustín will like it. If he'll think I look pretty.

I'm suddenly very glad Rachel is doing my makeup.

I grab some clothes and scurry into the bathroom, turning on the shower and luxuriating in the amazing water pressure. When I get out, wiping steam from the mirror, I feel like I should pinch my cheeks to remind myself that this is real. I kissed a guy last night. And then again just now, in an elevator. And there is more kissing in my future.

And he's like the best person I've ever known. I've never felt this safe with someone before. Besides Rachel, obviously. But there's a deep sense of relief in knowing, all the way to my bones, that I can trust Agustín. That he will never let me down.

I dress in jeans and a green tank top. It seems to get hot during the day but cool in the mornings and evenings, so after I apply a tiny bit of mascara and lip gloss, I leave the bathroom to grab my favorite cardigan with the crotched flowers and slip my feet into my vintage boots.

Agustín is frowning at something on his phone when I get out on the balcony.

"Everything okay?" I ask.

He quickly puts his phone away. "Just work." He looks up at me and a sudden smile breaks across his face. "That's the outfit you were wearing the day we first met."

I look down at myself, and my skin prickles at the memory. "Oh, right." I have to smile now too. "I was terrified."

He chuckles and stands. "I thought I was doing something wrong."

"You? Never."

I see some flash of tension in his eyes, but then both our phones start to ping.

"The Pack," I say, grabbing my phone out of my pocket and watching the group thread light up. Hazelnut is clearly living her best life with Sanvi and Kate—today, she and Sanvi are wearing matching sequined jackets and aviators.

Kate: We put Hazelnut in one of our workout videos and guys . . . she's a STAR. A real natural.

There are updates from Miriam, and Gretchen, and then Madame Boularès uploads a video. It's in Mr. Bloom's apartment, I'm guessing—it's certainly not hers, with her husband's shrine and ornate furniture. Mr. Bloom stands in the center of a cramped but pleasant room that looks sort of like an eccentric professor's study, crammed bookshelves, sheet music everywhere, a squashy armchair by a window, a braided rug on the floor. He's playing his viola while the Colonel sits on the floor at his feet, gazing up at him, enraptured.

The Colonel does love Mozart.

Madame Boularès: He is very good.

I can't tell if she means the violist or the dog.

"She's in his apartment," Agustín says. "Do you think they're . . ."

He trails off and waggles his eyebrows at me.

"What?" I yelp. "No. No way." I pause and think about it for a minute. "Wait, do you?"

He shrugs. "Love has no boundaries. It transcends age or class or creed."

"I didn't know you were such a poet."

He points a finger at his chest. "Writer, remember?" I see that flicker of tension again, but then he clears his throat. "Anyway, today is for history. Are you ready to learn about some ancient cultures?"

"Yes," I say, slipping my arm through his. It's a beautiful sunny day, and the marigolds that line the center of Reforma burst with brilliant color.

"We can walk there, if you'd like," he says.

"I'm a New Yorker," I remind him. "I'd always rather walk."

He smiles ruefully. The sunlight catches on strands of his hair, errant locks twisting in the breeze. His charcoal gray hoodie contrasts with his white tee. I can't help the way my gaze keeps snagging on his chest. I feel like my stomach is filled with bubbles, rising and popping, making my steps buoyant. We walk down Reforma toward an enormous park.

"This is Bosque de Chapultepec," Agustín tells me, as cars whiz past us along the giant avenue. "It's like our Central Park." There are all sorts of trees, and I recognize more jacarandas, their elegant limbs reaching out across the sidewalk, as well as lots of palm trees. I wish I could see the jacarandas in full bloom, like in the pictures Agustín sent me all those months ago.

When we reach the museum, there are vendors outside selling trinkets and souvenirs beneath white tents. We walk up the broad steps to enter a huge courtyard with a giant fountain in its center—a massive stone column encircled on the ceiling by what looks almost like a wagon wheel, water pouring down from evenly spaced spouts around it. There are so many different wings, it makes my head spin. And it's not like the Met, with endless rooms filled with artwork—many of the exhibits are outside, artifacts presented as they might have been in their time.

I take lots of pictures to send over the group thread. It will be nice to give my neighbors some updates on our trip.

We have lunch in the museum café, which showcases cuisines from all the various cultures. Then we take a leisurely walk to the opposite end of the park, where a castle called Castillo de Chapultepec sits grandly—it's a museum now, but Agustín tells me it used to house presidents. We climb to the top of the tower and take in the views. While there are a few skyscrapers and a handful of taller apartment buildings, most buildings are quite short, only a few stories high. Agustín tells me that's because Mexico City has a lot of earthquakes.

"What would you like to do next?" he asks me.

I'm feeling pretty exhausted and overwhelmed, and talking about earthquakes made me unsettled. The Wheel starts to spin. I kind of just want to go lie down.

Can I tell Agustín this? Shouldn't I want to explore more?

What if I hurt his feelings? What if he is just doing that thing where a person pretends to let you decide the next activity, but secretly they want you to say, oh let's do whatever you want to do?

Beads of sweat prickle across my hairline. My fingers clench on the stone balustrade.

Suddenly, Agustín pulls me back against his chest. I don't know why, but something about this contact calms the Wheel. Like Agustín's heart is giving mine a hug.

"I want to lie down," I mumble, half hoping he doesn't hear me in case I'm saying the wrong thing.

"Perfect," he says, his breath tickling my ear. I feel a burst of tingles erupt in my stomach and suddenly, I'm not quite so tired anymore.

We walk back to the hotel and I kick off my boots and crawl on top of the comforter. Agustín lies beside me, taking both my hands in his and kissing my knuckles. It's such a tender gesture.

We lie there for a moment in silence, facing each other. I like just being with him in a way I never thought I could—with anyone. He doesn't demand that silence be filled. I think about dinner with Rachel and Diego later this week. It doesn't sound so awful. Certainly better than the wedding. But before that, I'll have to go to the bachelorette party. My pulse starts to race. I've kind of pushed that event to the side, what with all the kissing.

A bead of sweat trickles down my temple. I'll have to spend a full day with Rachel's friends. A full day doing whatever it is they've got planned—I was on the email thread for the party, but I didn't actually read the emails. No thank you.

"What are you worrying about?" he asks softly.

Of course he knows. Sometimes I wonder if he's psychic. "Bachelorette party," I croak.

"Hm." He's silent for a moment. "Can I ask what the biggest worry is?"

A thousand thoughts race through my mind, tangling together like socks in a dryer, spinning round and round.

"I say something stupid and everyone laughs and the shame is so great it haunts me forever," I admit.

"Okay," he says, nodding like that's not an insane thing to fear. "What else?"

"I'll have to do things I don't want to do. I don't like Rachel's friends. They're loud and . . . and I don't think they like me. But I can't embarrass Rachel. I have to be . . ." My throat tightens. Have to be what? Someone else who isn't me? Who likes going to parties and being social?

Agustín's thumb brushes across my temple, wiping the bead of sweat away. "Do you really think Rachel would ever be embarrassed because of you?"

His words catch me so completely off guard. I let out a surprised huff. "There's a first time for everything."

He chuckles. "Always moving the posts."

The truth is, it doesn't matter if Rachel's friends like me or if I like them—they will still be *there,* and I will still be *me,* and it will still be uncomfortable. People will talk to me whether I want them to or not. And this will only be a tiny fraction of the people at the wedding.

Before the Wheel can pick up steam, suddenly, Agustín leans forward and slants his mouth over mine. And I . . . just . . . melt. His body is warm, and his lips so gentle, and I feel myself shake loose, detach from the anxiety like releasing the string of a kite. I lean into the kiss, our tongues entwining, my palm pressing against his chest as his heart beats out a steady rhythm. I feel so anchored with him. So unafraid.

But then I wonder if he's thinking we should do more than just kiss right now, and then I wonder what *I'm* thinking about that. Like, yes, obviously, yes. But now? My shoulders tense.

His hands cup my face and our kiss slows.

Agustín presses his forehead against mine. "Quick nap?" he asks.

I exhale a long, jittery breath. He tucks me into the crook of his shoulder, and I wrap my arm around his waist. I wonder what all the contours of his body look like—I want to map them out, trace all his dents and curves, from his shoulders to his ribs to his thighs. Then heat floods my cheeks.

Agustín chuckles, and my head wobbles with the movement.

"I can feel you blushing," he murmurs.

I blush harder and then both of us are laughing.

"Stop distracting me while I'm trying to nap," I say sternly.

His lips press into my curls. "Duerme, querida," he whispers as my eyelids flutter closed.

37
Eloise

I am surrounded by penises.

Rachel's influencer friend, Mandy, rented some kind of party bus for the bachelorette party and now I'm sitting on a faux-velvet couch, with neon lights overhead, and phalluses staring at me from every direction. There are penis straws and penis balloons and an inflatable pickle at the back with a sign that says: *The Last Pickle She'll Ever Tickle.*

I wonder if I've accidentally landed in my own personal circle of hell. I got here early, of course, because I needed to find a seat before the twelve other women I don't really know descend on the scene. The van is parked outside the Four Seasons, and Agustín dropped me off a few minutes ago. He's heading out to spend the day with his family. I feel like he should have done that right away, but he said he was having so much fun showing me around the city.

"El!" Rachel's head pops through the open van door. She looks stunning in a vintage white satin minidress, her makeup flawless, a tiara on her head and a sash that says *Bride.*

"Hi." I'm sitting ramrod straight, awash in dicks.

Rachel catches sight of the pickle and rolls her eyes. "Oh my god, Mandy," she mutters, chuckling. "So, I know the itinerary is kind of a lot but—"

"Rachel!" I hear a squeal coming from outside and look through the tinted windows to see all twelve of Rachel's friends arriving en masse, all in cute dresses with short skirts and heels. I glance down at myself. I didn't know there was a dress code. I'm wearing acid wash jeans, my leather boots, and a sleeveless black mock turtleneck. Agustín told me I looked cool. I even wore my favorite gold hoops, and the giraffe print bangle from the shop in Roma. And I put on actual lipstick, not just gloss.

The Wheel starts to spin as the women descend on Rachel and begin to fill the bus. Some of them glance at me with quick smiles, but I see the confused frowns too as they wonder who the fuck I am. My hands are clammy and sweat gathers uncomfortably at the nape of my neck, as one of the girls plops down too close to me, laughing hysterically, her shoulder knocking into mine.

"Oh sorry," she says, then turns back to another girl who is popping open a bottle of champagne.

The Wheel jams on *This Interaction Will Haunt You Forever*. I can feel my face on fire, feel my tongue gluing itself to the roof of my mouth. The women just keep coming, streaming onto the bus, crowding around me, their voices loud, too loud. It's hot and stuffy and the neon lights are making my head hurt, and why must there be so many penises? The bus begins to feel smaller and smaller, so cramped that there's barely any space to move, and I'm smooshed between a woman in pink, drenched in perfume, and another in green, her hair constantly tickling my bare shoulder.

The air is too close. My chest constricts.

I can't breathe. I can't do this. I hate this.

I want to be a good friend but I don't belong here, everyone is talking over each other, and now my hairline is damp with sweat, and my lower back too, and it's so uncomfortable being like this. How am I meant to spend an entire day as a sweaty mess, I can't do it, but I have to, for Rachel, for Rachel, for Rachel. I ball my hands into fists and try to find air, try to think of Agustín, my anchor, my tether, but there's only shrieks of laughter, and now they're throwing penis balloons at each other and one hits me, and I don't know what to do. I don't want to touch the penis balloon. Then the driver climbs up into the driver's seat, and we're going to leave at any minute, and I'll be trapped, oh my god, I can't breathe, I can't breathe, I can't—

A cool hand closes around my wrist. Rachel's face swims in my vision.

"Come with me, El," she says softly.

I don't know how I stand and make it off that bus, except that I feel like a drowning swimmer who's finally seen the shore. Like my legs know if we can make it out there, we'll be okay.

I step off the bus, my body shaking. I press my forehead against the cold metal.

"Breathe in for five," Rachel says, and I do. My heart cramps and my lungs ache, but I force them to expand. "Breathe out five," Rachel says.

We do that a few more times until the panic attack finally passes.

"I'm so sorry," I croak.

"Don't you dare," Rachel says. "You have nothing to apologize for."

"But . . ." I gesture weakly toward the bus.

"I'm really touched that you tried," Rachel says gently. "You tried for me, and I get it. But El, this . . . this is not your thing. And that's okay." She takes out her phone.

"What are you doing?" I ask.

"Calling Agustín."

"What? No!" I yelp. "He's seeing his family today, I'm not interrupting that."

"Hey Agustín, Eloise isn't feeling up to the party bus . . . oh, great, see you soon."

She ends the call and smiles at me triumphantly. "Your boyfriend is amazing, you know that?"

I blanche. "He's not my . . ."

The words trail off. Rachel crooks an eyebrow.

"Yup," she says. "Boy. Friend. You, my sweet little darling dove, are in a relationship. There. I said it." She kisses my cheek. "He'll be here in two."

I groan. I don't want Agustín to change his plans because of me. I'm not a fucking toddler.

But I'm not getting back on that party bus.

And I can't deny that Rachel calling him my boyfriend felt . . . good.

"Hola!"

I turn and see Agustín jogging up to us. His thick dark hair falls into his eyes, and he's smiling a full dimple smile, like he didn't just see me fifteen minutes ago. The slice of sunshine inside me bursts with dazzling golden light. I instinctively reach out for him right as he takes my hand.

And just like that, I'm calm.

"Well, I gotta go get penised to death," Rachel says wryly. "You guys enjoy your day!" She climbs onto the bus and says, "Ready ladies?"

The ensuing shrieks and cackles make me flinch. I have made progress yes, but I'm not sure I'll ever be party bus ready. It's just not for me.

"So," Agustín says cheerfully. "What would you like to do today?"

"But . . ." I'm at a loss for words. "But you have to go see your family."

He shrugs. "I can see them another time."

Something inside me cracks. I may be too much of a nervous wreck to celebrate with Rachel, but I'm sure as shit not ruining Agustín's day too.

As the party bus lurches out into traffic, my determination hardens.

"No," I say. "You're not missing out on your family because of me."

"It's really fine," Agustín says, temporarily distracting me with his cardamom scent. "I like spending my time with you."

He wraps one arm around me, securing me close. He would do anything for me. I want to return the favor. And just like that, a lightbulb goes off. I can feel it, like in the cartoons, hovering right over my head and bathing me in a warm glow.

"I could come with you," I say. "To see your family." As soon as the words leave my mouth, I want to snatch them back. That's so rude! And he probably doesn't want his family meeting me yet. It's way too soon, and yeah, Rachel said he's my boyfriend, but *he* hasn't actually said it and—

"Really?" His whole face lights up, like this is the best idea he's ever heard.

"Just . . . I mean . . . if you think they wouldn't mind," I mumble.

"Mind? They'd love to meet you!" He whips out his phone. "Mamá! Hola." That's all I get before he chatters away in Spanish for a moment. He ends the call and beams at me. "They're so excited you're coming. And my mom is making her famous cochinita pibil. You will love it."

"Are you sure?" I ask nervously. "This isn't too weird or too soon or—"

"Too soon?" He sweeps me up in his arms and kisses me right there on the front steps of the Four Seasons. "No," he says tenderly, brushing a curl from my eyes. "It is not too soon."

I feel nerves start to wriggle in my chest as he texts Enrique to see if he's available to drive us, which he is. Once we're in the car, Agustín chatters away happily about all the people I'll meet. "I don't think all of my aunts are there, just Cristina, she and my mom are really close. And you'll meet Caro, of course, she's so excited you're coming. And Lupe." He purses his lips. I know he and Lupe have been on the outs over that article he's writing. "And the Minions!"

I laugh despite the wriggles. "I can't believe you call them that."

He grins, his left dimple popping. "They'll probably get sick of it once they're older, so I need to use it as much as I can now, while I'm the cool tío."

I nudge him with my elbow. "You'll always be the cool tío in my book."

He chuckles and slings his arm around my shoulders. Enrique takes us through the smaller streets, crossing the larger avenues where the big red busses collect passengers waiting on the platforms under metal awnings. We drive past a large rectangular building, all pristine blue glass, with some of kind of enormous abstract art installation out in front of it.

"That's the World Trade Center," Agustín says, and I can't help the shiver that runs through me at the name. The streets are lined with trees, and there are patches of construction, hidden behind plywood walls papered with advertisements and graffiti. The farther out we go, the more the streets feel residential, fewer apartment buildings and more houses. And everywhere there are pops of color, the bright bursts of orange marigolds celebrating the Day of the Dead. We pass grocery stores and pharmacies and little cafés, until we turn down a narrow street near a park, and Enrique pulls up to a two-story stone house, painted white with brick trim and a red tiled roof. There's a black gate that fronts a tiny patch of yard with a stone path leading up to the front door and a few scant bushes. Agustín presses a button on a buzzer next to the gate, and we wait.

I can hear a child laughing inside, and my pulse kicks up a notch. I grab Agustín's hand, then drop it. Should we be holding hands in front of his family? What do they know about me? I've said hello to Caro once or twice on FaceTime, but as far as I know, his family assumes we're just plus-ones. Transactional. It makes my stomach hurt thinking of how this all started. How terrified I was to let anyone into my life.

As if on cue, both our phones buzz with a notification in the group chat. Agustín glances down and smiles.

"The Colonel," he says, showing me his screen. Mr. Bloom has sent a picture of the Colonel in the park. He has his head in Madame Boularès's lap. She's reading a book and wearing her usual black ensemble but this time with a yellow kerchief around her neck. It's the first time I've ever seen her wear a color.

Agustín and I look at each other.

"Definitely something going on with them," he says, grinning.

The front door opens.

"Tinito!" A woman in her sixties, wearing a red sweater and slacks, bustles down the little path to open the gate, speaking rapid fire Spanish. Her thick dark hair is just like her son's, albeit with some strands of gray, and I see a dimple in her left cheek when she smiles up at him, opening the gate and enveloping him in her arms.

"Hola, Mamá," Agustín says, hugging her back. He gestures to me but before I have a chance to do or say anything, Agustín's mother sweeps me up in her arms. She's short, like me, and smells faintly of vanilla.

She gives me the longest, warmest hug and something inside me softens as she squeezes me, her embrace all encompassing, like she's speaking to me through it. As if she's saying, you are welcome here.

Agustín got hugs like this his whole life. I feel a pang of envy and also a pinch of sadness—for the little girl with the silent uncle, living among ghosts. I wonder if my mom would have hugged like this.

Unexpected tears prick my eyes, and I quickly blink them away.

"Martha," she says, pointing at herself.

"Eloise," I say, doing the same.

"Mucho gusto," she says. Then she grabs Agustín's hand and pulls him toward the house, chattering away in Spanish.

The interior is cool and dim, a foyer with a tiled floor, a weathered sideboard with a ceramic white lamp set against one wall. In front of me, the hall opens up into a comfortable sitting room, sturdy beige couches, a woven rug on the floor, and a squat leather armchair. Curtained windows look out onto a garden in the backyard. To my left, through an open doorway, I hear the laughter of children, the sizzle of food, and the scent of spices tickles my nose.

Agustín deposits the backpack he brought on the sideboard and glances at me. "Ready?" he asks.

I take a breath and nod.

38
Agustín

Here goes nothing.

Eloise definitely seems less nervous than I thought she would be, but she's only met my mom.

We step into the kitchen and immediately, we're surrounded.

"Tín!" Caro shrieks, looking up from the kitchen island where she's teaching Camila and Elena some kind of card game that will surely get her in trouble with Lupe. The girls hop down from their stools, abandoning the game to toddle over and throw their arms around my legs. Sofia is at the stove with Tía Cristina, and Vero is washing some vegetables in the sink.

"Did you bring us presents, Tío Tin?"

"Who's that?" Elena asks, looking shyly at Eloise.

"That's Tío Tin's girlfriend," Sofia says excitedly, coming over to stare up at Eloise. "Right, Abu?"

My mom tuts, as Vero abandons her vegetables and joins her sisters. "Everybody be nice to Tío Tin's friend, please," Mom says.

"Yes, Abu," the four girls chant in unison.

Eloise has plastered herself to the wooden frame of the doorway, her eyes wide, taking it all in. She can't understand anything anyone is saying, but I hope she likes the kitchen. The stout island is crafted from blue, white, and orange Talavera tiles, and there's a matching backsplash lining the walls, beneath cabinets painted a vibrant teal. There are several pots on the stove, and a blender standing nearby on the counter for the salsas. The arched windows look out onto the street, and I can hear a man selling camotes, the shrieking whistle of his cart piercing the air as it steams sweet potatoes off in the distance.

"Move, girls," Caro says, shooing them out of the way. "Eloise," she says in English, "it's so great to finally meet you!"

Then she scoops Eloise up into a hug as well. This is a lot of hugging for Eloise, and I can't quite get a read on how she's handling it. Then the Minions get in on it, shouting in rapid fire Spanish.

"I want a hug!"

"Tía Caro, it's *your* turn to move."

"I want to hug Tío Tin's girlfriend!"

They crowd around Eloise, whose eyes have gone wide with panic, and I leap into action. "Who wants presents?" I say.

There are shrieks of "Yes!" and "Me, me, me!" and I lead my nieces, like little ducklings, out into the front hall, where I stashed my backpack. I brought a jewelry making kit for Sofia, a journal for the ever-serious Vero, and some glittery markers and stuffed animals for the twins.

As the girls excitedly chatter about their gifts, I hear a familiar voice from behind me.

"You're back."

I turn to see Lupe standing in the hall, arms folded across her chest. Her thick black hair falls in a straight line down to her shoulders, and she's wearing a hunter green V-neck sweater with a pair of tapered slacks. Her mouth is pressed into a thin line, the small gold cross hanging around her neck catching the light.

"Hey, Lupe," I say.

"Mamá, look, Tío Tin gave me a jewelry kit so I can make my own necklaces and bracelets and—"

"That's wonderful, Sof. Why don't you all go show Abuelo your new toys? He's out in the garden," Lupe says.

The girls scurry down the hall and into the living room. I hear them shout for my father before the back door slams shut.

"It's good to see you," I say.

"What the fuck, Agustín?" Lupe demands. She only ever swears around me and Caro. "How could you embarrass our family with this stupid fucking article? You really want to be dragging our dirty laundry out in front of everyone? Here *and* in New York?"

"I didn't make Abuelo cheat," I point out.

"Well, you could have kept your mouth shut about it," she huffs.

"That's not my job."

"It's also not your job to humiliate your own family!"

"What do you want me to do, Lupe? This is my chance. To be published in—"

"Ugh, if I have to hear one more fucking word about your precious *New Yorker* and Ronan Farrow and changing the world, I'm going to lose it." Lupe takes a step toward me. She's always been the tallest of the three of us, and she sweeps her hair over one shoulder. "Now come here and give me a hug, you idiot."

I chuckle and embrace her. Like with all of Lupe's hugs, it's short, perfunctory, and she immediately goes back to chastising me.

"And who is this gringa, huh? Is she part of the whole plot to ruin our family?"

My stomach pinches with guilt. "There's no plot, Lupe!" I snap. "She's my girlfriend, okay?"

Lupe's mouth drops open. I hear Caro shout, "I knew it!" from the kitchen and realize I've left Eloise alone in there.

"Listen," I say to my older sister, "can we make a truce for today? No talking about the article. Please. I want to spend a nice afternoon with my family. I've missed you all."

"Fine, fine, whatever," she snaps back, pushing past me. "I want to meet this girl."

"If you'd FaceTime me like Caro does, you'd have met her already," I call after her.

Lupe whirls around, her eyes flashing. "You really want start with me, Tinito?"

I hold up my hands. "No, señora."

Her mouth curves up into a wry grin. "Very funny."

"Isn't that what they call you at church?"

"Don't mock the church, Tín. You could use more God in your life."

"I'm good," I say. I prefer my Sundays with coffee and dogs. Man, I miss the Pack.

We enter the kitchen, and I see Eloise standing at the stove as both my mom and tía explain to her about what they're making, talking over each other and correcting each other in a way that reminds me of me and Lupe. They've given her a wooden spoon, though I'm not sure what they expect her to do with it. And they're speaking Spanish, so all explanation is lost on Eloise. In one pan, tomatillos and serrano chiles and fat cloves of garlic are charring, while a small pot of water is simmering with dried ancho chiles.

". . . and this will be for the salsa verde," my mom is saying as my tía tuts at her to turn the tomatillos. "Not yet, Cristina," my mom says, shooing her away with the tongs.

Lupe strides right up to Eloise, who is looking pretty content, all things considered, as she watches the action on the stove. Caro starts quickly clearing up the illicit card game before Lupe sees.

"Don't think we won't talk about *that* later," Lupe says. Then she turns to Eloise. "Hello," she says in English. "I'm Lupe. Welcome to our home."

"Thank you for having me," Eloise says, her voice giving a little squeak on "having." It's so cute. And she looks so hot in that outfit. But then I banish those thoughts in case Lupe has started mind reading. I don't need another lecture about God.

Lupe does not go in for a hug, but instead gives Eloise a once over with her laser eyes. "So," she says. "You're my brother's girlfriend?"

I cringe as Eloise's eyes pop.

"Damn, don't embarrass her, Lupe," Caro says.

But then Eloise straightens her shoulders and swallows hard. "Yes," she says. "I am."

It feels like my whole heart does a huge backflip, lodging itself in my throat. *She is?* Of course I feel the same way, but I hadn't expected Eloise to confirm it in the middle of my family kitchen with Lupe acting like the Spanish Inquisition.

At that moment, Abuelita shuffles into the kitchen, leaning heavily on her cane.

"Tinito," she says in her wonderfully creaky voice, a big smile cracking across her wrinkled face. Everyone says I got my smile from Abuelita.

"Abuelita," I say, rushing over to embrace her. She smells like the same flowery perfume she's been using since I was a little kid. "How are you?"

"Good, good," she says, patting my hand. "Not dead yet. And who is this?"

Her sharp eyes land on Eloise, standing nervously with the wooden spoon still clutched in one hand. Abuelita only speaks Spanish—same goes for my parents—so Eloise doesn't understand her words.

I motion for her to come over, and she skitters around Lupe. "Eloise, this is my abuelita."

"Hi, um, hola," Eloise says.

"Come here," Abuelita says, gathering Eloise, spoon and all, into a hug. Then she pats Eloise's cheek. "So beautiful. And kind. I can tell that by your eyes. A perfect match for our Tinito."

My neck flushes, a little grateful Eloise can't understand her. "Okay, Abuelita."

"What? I can't say she is beautiful?" Abuelita smiles up at Eloise. Even as short as Eloise is, Abuelita is smaller. Her wispy white hair puffs out in a cloud around her face, and she wears her traditional knee-length navy skirt and a gray sweater, with a pink-patterned silk scarf tied around her neck. "Now, come with me, I am going to teach you how to make tortillas."

Caro is grinning as she helps Abuelita onto one of the stools, as Eloise follows dutifully behind, having no idea what she's getting into. Lupe looks skeptical, while my mom and tía go back to arguing over the salsas.

"Lupe, bring me a bowl and the flour. Caro, some water, please. Cristina, Martha, stop arguing in front of our guest and move those pots to make space for the comal. Tinito, go put on some music. Where is your father? We need music in this house. Eloise, you sit here with me. Yes, that's right."

Everyone springs to action at Abuelita's commands. I hurry through the small living room out the back door to find my father pulling up some weeds in the garden while the Minions play with their new toys at the long table on the flagstone patio, beneath the avocado tree.

"Papá," I say, and my father looks up from his work. He wipes his forehead with the back of his hand and smiles broadly.

"Hijo," he says, slowly getting to his feet and brushing his palms on his pants. "It's so good to have you home."

I give him a one-armed hug and look around at the garden. "The aguacates look good this year," I say.

"Yes," he says, "but I think there's a chipmunk eating the raspberries. Your mother says I should set a trap but . . ." He shakes his head. "We all have to eat, don't we? I think I'll just let the little creature have at them."

My dad has the softest heart of anyone I've ever known.

"Abuelita wants some music," I tell him. "She's making tortillas now."

"The girls were telling me about your friend," my father says, raising an eyebrow at me.

I shoot Sofia a look.

"What?" she says defiantly.

"Her name is Eloise," I say to my father, as we walk back into the house.

"Mm."

I run my hand through my hair nervously. "I really like her, Papá."

My dad just gives a small smile and a nod. Never a man of many words. I follow him over to the enormous cabinet where he keeps his record collection. "Do you think she likes boleros?" he asks.

"That might be a bit much. Why don't you just put on one of your jazz albums?"

"Davis or Coltrane?"

"Thelonius Monk," I say and my father nods again.

"Good choice," he says. I can hear light chatter coming from the kitchen and hope Eloise is doing all right in there. It sounds like mostly Spanish. I hope Caro and Lupe are keeping her included.

"So," Papá says as he pulls out an album: *Straight, No Chaser.* "How are things in New York?"

"Good," I say. Another glance at the kitchen. "It's nice Lupe is talking to me again."

My father sighs as he puts the record onto the old player. "She's always been the most stubborn of the three of you. More stubborn than Caro, and that's saying something."

"You aren't mad at me about the article?"

He shrugs. "Why should I be mad? You are simply telling the truth about your abuelo. If he wanted to be remembered better after death, he should have behaved better in life."

"You haven't let me talk to Abuelita."

My father holds up his hands. "I am not about to go to battle with your mother and tías. But you're here now. Go talk to her yourself."

He puts the needle down and the rich sounds of jazz piano fill the room.

"Come," he says to me. "I would like to meet Eloise."

We walk into the kitchen just as Caro and my mother laugh at something Tía Cristina is saying. But I only have eyes for Eloise. She's sitting at the counter with a bowl full of masa and Abuelita's orange tortilla press in front of her, expertly rolling out balls of dough and then pressing them. Then she hands them off to Abuelita, who is manning the comal, placing the flat circles on the hot surface until they puff and pop, browning just the right amount before she whisks them off the heat and piles them up on a nearby plate.

"Dude, your girlfriend is really good at making tortillas," Caro says to me in English, so Eloise can understand.

Eloise smiles at me. "Just like making sopes," she says. "But thinner."

She looks so content, here among my family. Not nervous. Not scared.

She fits here.

39
Eloise

I'm really surprised at how not overwhelmed I am, all things considered.

I've met so many people. I'm surrounded by newness. But there's something about Agustín's family that reflects the warmth I've come to know from Agustín himself over the past few months. I can see exactly why he is the way he is.

And honestly, I kind of love that I can't understand most of what they're saying. Caro has been translating for me here and there, but once Abuelita gave me my task, I'm happy to sit and press tortillas and let the sounds of Spanish wash over me in musical phrases. I don't need to understand the words to know that Martha and Cristina are always on the verge of an argument, that Lupe is a strict rule-follower, and that Caro likes to stir the pot.

It's freeing. There's no pressure for me to speak when I don't know the language. There's no fear of saying the wrong thing.

And even more than that, the love that permeates this kitchen is a palpable, living thing. It inhales joy and exhales laughter. Even Lupe, who is by far the most intimidating member of Agustín's family, isn't immune from its warmth.

As Agustín slides onto the stool next to me, his palm rests on my lower back for a brief second. That gentle touch says so much more than he knows—it says to me, *I am here. You are safe. You belong.* And I don't think I've ever really felt that way anywhere, outside of my own home with the Pack.

I wonder if I've been afraid of families. Like if I were to be around them, it would only prove that I've never been meant to be in one—that there is some fundamental flaw in me. And somehow, in the most unlikely of places, I've been proven wrong.

He introduces me to his father, José, a short man with a kindly, weathered face and black-rimmed glasses. As his aunt puts the charred tomatillos and chiles into a blender, his mom opens the stove in a cloud of steam and removes a baking sheet containing a misshapen form wrapped in banana leaves. It smells amazing.

"Cochinita pibil," Agustín whispers to me as his mom begins to unwrap it, to the delight of everyone in the kitchen. "Pork shoulder marinated in achiote paste, orange and lime, garlic, Mexican oregano, and other spices. It's been slow roasting for hours."

Abuelita says something approving, and Martha looks pleased. Caro and Lupe jump into action, grabbing plates and cutlery and heading out to the garden. I hear Lupe shooting orders to her kids at rapid speed. The sounds of jazz wind throughout it all, a comforting background melody. José takes over the meat, expertly moving it into a deep, ceramic dish. There's a smattering of activity as salsa is poured into bowls, avocados are sliced, and pickled onions are retrieved from the refrigerator. Abuelita lovingly wraps the mountain of tortillas we made in a white cloth, then places them in a wicker basket.

And through it all, Agustín sits beside me, his presence warming my side like the sun.

I can see him growing up here—well, not here, of course, but in a home like this, the place he lived in before his family got evicted. I can imagine that even in that tiny, cramped apartment where he spent his teen years, this same permeating love would have hung in every corner, painted every nook and cranny.

As Abuelita ushers us outside, I gasp in delight. The small backyard garden is ringed with a brick wall, one tree hung heavy with bright green avocados, a wild thatch of raspberry bushes, a carefully pruned hedge along one wall, ivy growing wild up another, a fig tree and a lemon tree and a spiky agave, along with various plants and bushes I can't name. There's a long table with chairs under the avocado tree, and Agustín's nieces are chattering away at one end, as Agustín pulls a chair out for me at the other.

I'm grateful for that. The kids are cute as buttons but they're a *lot*. José sits beside me, at the head of the table, and Agustín takes the chair on my other side. Abuelita is across from me. Martha and Cristina start to serve, shredding the decadent meat with forks and placing portions onto plates, passed around the table, while Lupe wrangles the kids down at the other end. The basket of tortillas is passed, along with all the bowls of toppings, and I happily make myself a taco and let the chatter wash over me.

I take a bite and moan, as the richness of the meat, the creamy avocado, and the sharp punch of pickled onions burst in my mouth. Agustín chuckles softly next to me.

"You like it?"

"It's orgasmic," I say and Caro snort-laughs so hard, I blush. I kind of forgot that his sisters can understand me even if his parents can't.

"It is," she agrees, shooting me a wink. "Our mom only makes it on special occasions. So I guess we should be thanking you, Tín." She brushes an electric blue curl from her eyes and grins at me. "Are you excited about the wedding?"

"Oh . . ." Honestly, I had forgotten about the wedding. It seems like another universe where I started this day on a party bus surrounded by penis balloons. But then I think about how happy Rachel has been this week, and even though Diego's family sounds a bit stuffy and over the top, Diego himself isn't like that at all.

He's a pretty nice guy, to be honest. And I can't deny he cares about Rachel as deeply as I do. "Yes," I say. I'm glad it doesn't feel like a lie anymore. I mean, am I excited about all the people? No. The speech? Hell no. But Rachel getting the happiness she deserves? Absolutely.

"Who are you wearing?" Caro asks.

"I don't know," I admit. "Rachel picked out my dress. I just went with it."

"Well, I'm going to need pics. Got it, Tín?"

Agustín shakes his head, smiling ruefully. Under the table, he takes my hand. "Yes, Caro, we will send you lots of pictures."

"On the family thread!" Lupe calls from the other end of the table. "We all want to see Tío Tín in a tuxedo."

She and Caro exchange wicked smiles and then Lupe translates what she said to the rest of the family. There's a lot of talk after that in which Agustín blushes quite a bit, and I get a few significant looks, and his dad seems very pleased about something, and everyone nods along with Abuelita when she speaks, and I'm really glad I don't understand because I just want to keep eating this delicious food, in this beautiful garden, with the man I'm falling in love with by my side, his hand in mine.

I only release it to help myself to more cochinita pibil.

40
Agustín

Once lunch is finished, the Minions go back to their toys, while Caro takes Eloise aside to chat, and my mom and tía head to the kitchen to clean up.

Abuelita has retired to the family room, sitting in the big leather armchair that Abuelo used to sit in—it's one of the very few things my family kept when we got evicted from our home.

She's alone. This is my chance to talk to her, to get some answers at last. As I start to walk over to her, suddenly Lupe grabs my arm.

"What are you doing?" she hisses.

I tug out of her grasp. "Lupe. You think I would ever do anything to hurt Abuelita? I just want to talk to her. And you can't stop me."

Her nostrils flare, and I can feel the sermon coming, when suddenly the twins start shrieking at each other in the garden, and I hear Caro call, "Elena, take that marker out of your nose!"

Lupe lets out a frustrated growl and rushes back to the garden. My pulse ticks up a notch as I approach Abuelita, pull up an ottoman, and sit beside her.

"It is so good to see you happy, Tinito," Abuelita says, smiling so that her whole face creases. "Eloise is very nice."

"She is," I agree.

"And you are happy in New York City?"

"I am. I'm very happy."

Abuelita nods. "Good."

I take a deep breath. "Abuelita, I wanted to talk to you about something."

"Hm," she says, pursing her lips and folding her hands over her stomach. "About Abuelo?" Her eyes flash, but with a kindly suspicion. I don't see any pain or anger in them.

I rub the back of my neck. Now that I'm finally able to talk to her, I don't quite know how to start. "Yeah. I just . . . don't understand." Unexpected tears prick the corners of my eyes. "How could he do that to you?" My throat tightens. "To us?"

Abuelita lets out a heavy sigh. "Oh Tín," she says. "Life isn't easy. Sometimes there is no right choice."

"But when—I mean, how long did you know? When did you find out? Why didn't you ever say anything? Why did he . . ." My voice trails off as my hand clenches into a fist.

Abuelita nestles deep into the chair, one hand toying with the knot of her silk scarf, her eyes growing distant. "I found out about his second wife when we were getting evicted. I called him and begged him to come home, to be with his family. I couldn't understand why he hadn't yet. He knew what was happening here. He was sending us money. But we needed *him*. I needed him." Her gaze turns sad. "That's when he told me the truth. About her. About their child. He said he had been so lonely. That he hadn't meant to betray me—but now, there were other people who relied on him too." She glanced at me with an almost rueful expression. "No right choices, you see?"

"But we were first," I blurt out.

"We were," she agrees.

The silence hangs between us with unspoken words. I guess it sounds pretty childish to say that makes us more important. But doesn't it?

"Your abuelo broke my heart clean in two that day," Abuelita says.

"Then why did you stay with him? Lie for him?"

She sighs, and I feel the weight of the years behind it. "Tinito, nobody is perfect. He made his choices, and I made mine. And you will make yours, and not all of those will be perfect either." My stomach wriggles with guilt as her words hit far too close to home. "I loved your abuelo. That's not something that can be turned off, like the switch of a lamp. We still needed him—needed the support he gave to us during those hard years. And I saw no reason to hurt our family further by sharing this secret." Her mouth hardens into a thin line. "But I told him: *do better*. Be a better man now than you have ever been."

I stare at her, my mouth falling open. "You said that?"

She nods. I slump back on the ottoman, putting the time frame together. Abuelo's first appearance in the papers, the first time El Rasca was seen defending the defenseless . . .

She cocks her head. "What is that look about?"

I tell her about El Rasca. I tell her about the article and all the research I've done. I tell her about all the things that Abuelo did for the Latino community in New York.

Abuelita's eyes grow wide. She presses her lips together, deep in thought. Then she smiles at me. "It seems like he took my words to heart. El Rasca." She chuckles. "He did better."

So Abuelita shamed him into becoming El Rasca. And I know that was a good thing, for many people. But I still can't shake my anger at his betrayal. At the lies we were fed.

Abuelita tuts. "I can read your face, clear as water," she says. She puts a hand on mine. "Don't put people on pedestals, Agustín. Those are meant for statues, cold and lifeless, not flesh and blood human beings. Our flaws are what make us real."

"How can you be so forgiving?" I ask her quietly.

"Oh, I'm not," she reassures me. "I was very angry, for a very long time. But I had a family here who needed me. What good would my anger do? Was the truth going to help put food on the table? I did not want anyone else to carry the burden except me." Her eyes go distant again. "And as time went on, I could not help but think about what life must have been like for him, so far away, alone. We were all together here. He had no connection to his family anymore. Or to his culture. He could not hear the whistle of the camoteros in the evenings or pick figs from our tree in the backyard for breakfast. He could no longer help our neighbors as he once did or gather them at our home for Nochebuena. How hard it must have been for someone with a heart such as his, a big caring heart, to be in that jungle of a city, all alone."

I absorb her words for a moment. And suddenly my thoughts flash to Eloise—how she was all alone when I met her, with her dogs as her only comfort. I've seen what it looks like for someone so bighearted but lonely to live in New York. I wonder if Abuelo felt a similar loneliness, intensified by being ripped away from all he knew. I try to imagine Eloise without her dogs and I can't. It's impossible—she would not survive.

Maybe it was similar with Abuelo and family. He needed something, some kind of deep human connection, in order to survive in the city. In order to be able to stay and support us.

"Ricardo—Abuelo's son—is going to the Alvarez wedding," I confess quietly. "That's how I met Eloise. I needed an invitation in order to interview him, or *The New Yorker* wouldn't publish my article." Shame trickles down the nape of my neck. "But I haven't told her that yet. I . . . I didn't know that I would fall in love with her when I first met her. And now . . . I don't know *how* to tell her. Not without hurting her. But if I pull the article, I lose all credibility. I lose the one shot I'll ever have at achieving my dream. And I think people deserve to know who Abuelo was. All of him. Not just the good parts."

Abuelita thinks for a minute. "Don't let the past ruin your future," she says. "And don't lose what's right in front of you. Maybe this is a different sort of story you're telling—not just about Abuelo but about yourself as well. You still have choices, Agustín. You still have a life to live. Don't waste it."

She's right. And Eloise deserves the truth.

But I don't know how she'll take it, and the very last thing I want to do is disrupt the harmony she seems to have found in Mexico City. She still needs to give that speech. And while she's happy here with my family—which brings me such deep abiding joy—I know that her anxiety isn't gone. It never will be. And she can't afford a single distraction right now.

So I'll wait. Once the wedding is over, and the speech has been given, and we're back at the hotel after the reception, I'll come clean and tell her everything. It's only a few more days—there's no harm in waiting just a few more days, right?

"Mama Rosita!" Elena scampers into the living room and throws herself into Abuelita's lap. "Quieres postre?"

And just like that, the moment is over. The rest of the girls come rushing inside at the very mention of dessert, clamoring for flan, while Lupe shushes them. Caro and Eloise come in last, and the moment my eyes land on Eloise, it's like everything clicks into place. I enter her orbit, and my whole center of gravity shifts.

Her hand reaches for mine in the same instant I reach for hers.

And as much as I love my family, suddenly, I can't wait to be alone with her.

"Get a room, you two," Caro teases us in English. Eloise's cheeks flame.

"Carolina, what are you saying to them?" Abuelita demands.

"Nothing Abuelita," Caro says, faking innocence.

After dessert, we say our goodbyes. The Minions don't want to let Eloise go—she's like the shiny new toy for them. Vero especially seems enamored by her. My mom gives her a big hug, and Eloise and Caro exchange numbers. Even Lupe seems won over.

"She's a good one, Tín," she tells me. "Quiet but you can tell she has a good heart." Then she levels me with a glare. "Don't screw it up."

So supportive.

We get into the sleek SUV, garnering impressed looks from Lupe and Tía Cristina, and my family crowds out onto the sidewalk to wave goodbye, the twins jumping up and down, Sofia smiling widely, Caro with her arm slung around Papá's shoulders.

As soon as they vanish from sight, Eloise slumps against me. I wrap my arms around her and chuckle into her hair.

"You were amazing," I murmur.

I feel her cheek press against my chest. "Really? I didn't do much. And no one could understand me except your sisters."

"Did you have a good time?" I ask, suddenly nervous.

She sits up. "Oh, yes," she says. "Your family is . . ." She swallows hard, and I see a flash of strong emotion in her eyes. "They're wonderful." Then she leans back into me. "But wow, the Minions are a lot."

I laugh. "What would you like to do now?"

"Can we go back to the park with the dogs?" she asks, hopefully.

I kiss her temple. "Of course we can."

I tell Enrique to take us to Parque México.

41
Eloise

Rachel: So . . . have you done it yet?
Me: I don't know what you're talking about.
Rachel: 👉👌
Me: How old are you???

"Are you two texting each other?" Agustín asks.

My head whips up as I hide my phone under the table.

"No," I say at the same moment Rachel says, "Yes."

I glare at her and she laughs.

"Sorry, we'll stop now," she says, putting her phone down next to her plate. She leans back in her chair and takes a final sip of her wine. "This place is incredible, Agustín. Thanks for taking us here."

I agree. It's a seafood restaurant in a quiet, less touristy neighborhood of the city, called San Miguel Chapultepec. Rachel and I are the only Americans in this place. And I just had possibly the most delicious branzino of my entire life. The food has been one of the best parts of this trip so far.

Second only to the kissing.

Over the past few days, the kissing has kind of gotten out of control. I can't seem to stop *wanting* it. All the time. At very inappropriate moments, like when we're buying snacks at Oxxo (the chain of convenience stores all over the city) or visiting Caro at the boutique she works at in Colonia Roma. And the more I kiss Agustín, the more I want . . . well, more. I shiver with nerves at the thought.

Of course, I trust Agustín implicitly. But there's trust and then there's being literally, physically naked in front of someone. Am I ready for that?

But if I'm not ready now, with him, then it feels like I may as well throw in the towel on sex forever.

". . . and tomorrow night is the rehearsal dinner," Rachel is saying. Agustín's hand rests lightly on my knee, and I thread my fingers through his as Rachel prattles on. "Apparently rehearsal dinners are not a 'thing' in Mexico but—"

"They aren't," Diego and Agustín say in unison, then laugh with each other.

"*But*," Rachel says again, firmly this time, "this wedding is a blend of two cultures and they are most definitely a thing in the US, and I am not about to miss out, thank you very much."

"Luckily, my mother loves throwing events almost as much as you do, amor," Diego says warmly.

She pecks his cheek. "Exactly." She glances at the time. "We should probably get going."

Diego pays the check, and we walk out of the restaurant where his black SUV and driver wait. Rachel gives me a huge hug, and I realize this is the last time I'll see her before the wedding. Tears spring to my eyes, and I hold her tight.

"He adores you," she whispers in my ear. "I've never seen someone so clearly head over heels. I couldn't have asked for a better man for you, my dearest darling friend."

Heat flames in my cheeks, and I cough out a "Love you" before she's embracing Agustín. I give Diego a brief, awkward hug, which he seems genuinely pleased about.

Agustín's hand slips into mine, and we start walking down the quiet, tree-lined street. I love this about us—how we always seem to be so in sync. We don't need words. My stomach dips as I wonder if that will apply to other parts of our relationship. I think about what Agustín's skin on my skin would feel like and my stomach gives a violent shudder as heat flares between my thighs.

My previous experiences with sex are all kind of vague and blurry in my mind. But the thought of intimacy with Agustín is crystal clear, images thrown into sharp relief, etched against the darkness of my imagination.

"You're very quiet," Agustín observes.

"Mm," I say, wondering if he can hear the nerves jangling behind the sound. I know there's no rush. I know that Agustín would wait a year if I asked him to.

But I don't want to wait a year.

And we have this giant bed. And no dogs around to ruin the moment.

My palms start to sweat as the Wheel spins. I'm glad we're walking. Movement is good. Keeps me from spiraling. Okay, keeps me from spiraling *too* hard. I'm certain he notices but he doesn't say anything or suggest we take an Uber. We just keep walking, back toward the Four Seasons. It's a long walk.

I try to force the Wheel to land on one of my happy slices, *Rachel* or *Dogs*, but *Rachel* just makes me think of her text at the end of dinner and *Dogs* makes me think about how they're not here to interrupt any potential romance this evening.

Instead, the Wheel lands firmly on *I Will Be So Bad at This and Ruin Everything*. Because how will I not be bad at this? I have next to no experience. I panic sweat at even the thought of intimacy. No one has seen me naked in years. I've never given much thought to my body. Is it . . . I don't know . . . good?

Will Agustín find me attractive?

What if I do the wrong thing? What if I accidentally laugh at his dick again?

I blink and realize we're waiting for the elevator at the hotel. A forty-minute walk, over in seconds. As soon as we step inside, Agustín gathers me in his arms.

"Will you please tell me what you're thinking?" he murmurs in my ear, sending spirals of want through my system. "Before I go insane?"

Hm. Apparently, my silence was noticeable.

"Are you okay?" he asks. "Are you worrying about the wedding? Or did I do something wrong? Did you not like the restaurant? Or . . ."

I silence him with a kiss, because I cannot have this incredible person thinking for one single second that *he* is the problem. He kisses me back eagerly. The elevator doors open, and we walk to our room.

When we get inside, the curtains to the balcony are open, letting in a bright slice of moonlight, falling in an almost too-perfect-to-be-true fashion directly onto the bed.

Our bed.

And when Agustín reaches for the light switch, I grab his hand to stop him.

"No," I whisper.

The door falls shut behind us. The darkness of the room makes the moonlight shine even brighter. Agustín goes very still as my fingertips trace over his chest, then his collarbone, exploring the tender dent at his throat before bringing his mouth to mine. This time, when I press my body against his and feel him grow hard, I don't laugh, and I don't pull away.

Our kiss deepens, becoming almost frantic. I simply cannot get enough of him. The room is so quiet, so tranquil. I can hear his heart beating. Or maybe that's my heart. It's hard to tell the difference.

His arms are locked around me like a cage, but it's not tight enough. Somehow, somewhere along my panic-spiral walk home, I've allowed a part of me to break free. A part of me that isn't constrained by anxiety. Because it's primal. It's natural.

And because I know I'm safe.

The moment I slip my fingers under the hem of his tee, Agustín freezes.

"El," he says, and my skin shivers. "Are . . . are you sure?"

I gaze up at him, his beautiful features half dipped in silver, his eyes dark with want.

"I'm sure," I whisper.

That's all it takes. In one swift movement, Agustín's shirt is on the floor, and I'm staring, awestruck, at the solid planes of his chest. He is more beautiful than I could have ever imagined. I reach out tentatively to touch him, the smoothness of his skin, the firm musculature beneath. My jaw tightens and my throat aches. How can this man be meant for me?

I blink back the tears that prick my eyes because the last thing I need is him misinterpreting me right now. I explore the dents at his hips, and he shudders with pleasure, a tiny gasp escaping his lips. I move my hands to his waist, then delicately touch each of his ribs, every curve its own miracle.

His fingers begin to slowly unbutton my blouse, one button at a time, agonizingly slow, and I know he's doing it on purpose, to make sure I feel safe. When he slips it off my shoulders, he lets out another gasp.

Slowly, he begins to explore me. He kisses the dip at my collarbone, his hands tracing the curve of my spine down to my lower back. His mouth travels down my sternum to the dent between my breasts. My pulse hammers between my thighs, a secondary heartbeat. There's a faint *click* and then my bra falls to the floor. I shiver at the sudden chill.

"Eloise," he murmurs against my skin. My nipples are hard and aching for him. I didn't know I was capable of these feelings. His lips brush the curve of my left breast, and I am awash in a pleasure that is so acute it's almost agony. I want him to keep touching me. I never want him to stop.

"Please," I whisper, and my voice cracks with urgency.

He cups me with one hand as he very softly takes me in his mouth. I let out a wild gasp as his tongue probes me, his teeth grazing my nipple and sending shockwaves across my skin. I twine my fingers in his thick dark hair, bringing him closer, arching my back, trying to show him without words that this is okay.

I want this.

I *need* this.

Suddenly, my back is pressed against the wall, as Agustín licks and sucks and teases me, first one breast, then the other, making me dizzy, the sensations almost too much to be borne, and yet still not enough. When he drops to his knees, I let out a faint sigh of displeasure at the loss of him, of his touch, of his mouth.

Then he unbuttons my short denim skirt and slides it down my thighs to puddle around my feet. I feel his hot mouth press ever so gently over my underwear, at the tender, throbbing spot between my thighs, and *ohmyfuckinggod* I think I might spontaneously combust. The heat of his mouth and the heat building inside me is creating a conflagration I didn't know the human body was capable of. I feel the flames licking over my skin, spreading out from that tight, pulsing bead in my center.

Agustín tugs at the hem of my underwear, and then those are on the ground with my skirt. The next thing I know, his tongue is on me, so gentle, probing me, encouraging me, caressing me. I can't breathe. I can't think. All I can do is hold on tight as he devours me, slow and steady, luxuriously. The crashing waves of sensation rise and fall and rise and fall, and I can feel the wetness gather, feel myself tighten as he moans against me, and just when I think I can't take anymore, that I really *will* burst into flames and burn this entire hotel down along with me, he reaches up and tweaks my nipple, and I shatter.

Stars burst in my vision as the final wave crests, arriving with a brutal force that knocks me breathless. Spirals of pleasure rocket me to the highest planes of bliss, above the stars, into the stratosphere, where nothing can touch me except him—his mouth, his hands, his skin, his scent. I hear a desperate wail fill the room and realize it's me. My body is shaking, my breath coming in sharp pants. The orgasm seems to last forever, a rippling, glittering thing, agonizing in its beauty.

I feel beautiful.

When I finally, at long last, return to earth, I'm breathing heavily, my skin dewed with sweat. Agustín gets to his feet, a smile touching those perfect lips. That perfect mouth. I shiver.

"I want more," I whisper.

He chuckles in my ear. "Me too."

42

Agustín

I sweep Eloise up in my arms, and she gasps with delight.

I remember the first time I held her like this, when I carried her to her bed when she was sick. How little did I know then that the trajectory of my life was about to change. I had no idea how deeply I would fall in love with her.

I gently lay her out across the plush white comforter on the bed. She is devastatingly beautiful, her skin shining like a pearl in the moonlight, her curls splayed out around her face. Her chest heaves, and my throat tightens as I watch her pert breasts rise and fall, her nipples dark little buds. My cock is painfully hard as I take her in. I can still taste her on my lips, still hear her wail as she came against my mouth, like no sound I have ever heard her make before.

I want to hear it again. And again. Every day for the rest of my life.

Something inside me has shifted, strengthened, like some great tree of change taking root. I know I will never want anyone the way I want Eloise.

I hastily unbutton my pants and strip out of my boxer briefs. As I stand before her in the semidarkness, I see her eyes pop.

"Wow," she mouths. I can't help the burst of pride, of excitement, at the word. She finds me beautiful too.

She reaches toward me and I comply, moving forward. The moment her small hand curves around me, I nearly come undone. She strokes me tenderly, almost curiously, her fingers light, her touch unbearably gentle. I feel heat surge through my cock as it stiffens even more, my blood pounding in my ears.

I fall forward onto the bed, framing myself over her with my forearms as her strokes become more confident. She's going to make me come, and I can't let that happen. Not until I have felt her myself. I bring her mouth to mine, temporarily distracting her. She kisses me urgently, without hesitation, claiming my mouth as much as I'm claiming hers. She meets me, kiss for kiss, with no fear.

My cock brushes against her wetness, and we both gasp. Then I lift my head to meet her eyes, darkened by the shadows of night.

"I want—" I begin but she cuts me off.

"Yes," she begs. God, that word on her lips sends a shudder of pleasure through me.

"I don't have anything," I admit. I had no idea this would be happening at all, so packing condoms never crossed my mind. "But I . . . well, I've been tested, and I haven't been with anyone in a while."

"Me too," she says shyly, then gives a breathy chuckle. "Longer than a while, really. And I have an IUD."

I kiss her again and her arms curve around me, her fingers making delicate patterns down my spine. The backs of my thighs tighten, as my cock probes her again. I dip my head to take one breast in my mouth, unable to stop myself. She cries out, more ready to use her voice now, and arches against me.

"Eloise," I murmur at her throat. "I love you."

Then I enter her—slowly, gently, cautiously. My eyes roll back in my head as she gasps. She is unbelievably wet, flowing around me everywhere, my cock slick in seconds. I have never felt such sensations before. It's like we were made for each other. I fit inside her perfectly, filling her up, and her tender muscles stroke me as I set a gentle rhythm, pulsing inside her, aching with every thrust. I dip my head to tease her nipple again, biting it gently and reveling in the small squeak she makes, the rush of wetness, the tightening of those ever-delicate muscles. I can feel her, already there, hovering on the edge. I feel in this moment that I know her body as well as I know my own. That her pleasure is my pleasure. And that once we fuse as one, there's no going back.

I pick up my pace, eager for that release, that connection, even as I want this moment to last forever.

"Oh," Eloise gasps as I nudge that secret spot deep in her center. Then, "Oh!" again, and I can't contain myself. I hitch one of her legs around my waist so I can angle myself deeper, one hand gripping the firm globe of her ass. "Fuck," she cries, and I feel her start to unravel, and I'm unraveling too.

I'm no longer being careful or delicate with her. And she doesn't need me to be.

"More," she moans, and I grunt as I thrust myself inside her primally, urgently, my whole body taut like a bowstring, chasing the high I know is coming. The tension builds, and just when I think I can't take it anymore, just when the sensations spiral inside me, tightening like a coil, growing more intense with every stroke, I hit just . . . right . . . *there.*

And we explode together.

I feel the orgasm take me like a tidal wave—an overwhelming force of ecstasy, a vessel of pure pleasure. For a moment it's almost like I cease to exist. There is nothing except this feeling of frenzied bliss anchored by the deepest connection I've ever experienced.

Eloise is the only thing keeping me grounded. The only thing keeping me whole. I feel as if I could explode into a thousand molecules and float off into the night sky.

When the tremors that rock my body finally subside, I slump onto the bed, trying not to crush her but also unable to move. She strokes my back gently, almost mindlessly, her body quivering beneath me. We're both breathing hard, our skin glistening with sweat. I kiss the curve of her neck, her breath hot on my shoulder.

"Wow," she says, out loud this time.

"Wow," I agree. I start to move off her, and she grabs me tight.

"Wait," she whispers. "Please."

I would give her anything she asked for. I'd lasso the moon if she wanted it.

"Okay," she says after a moment. "I think probably . . . I need to pee."

I chuckle. "Hold on." I shift out of her and grab a tissue from the nightstand, handing it to her. She scurries into the bathroom and closes the door as I use another tissue to clean myself up. My head is spinning, and I slump back onto the bed, my head sinking into the pillow. I smile up at the ceiling, allowing the surrounding aura of bliss to shimmer and stretch. I feel like I'm floating on a cloud.

I hear the bedroom door open, but I keep my gaze on the ceiling. I don't know how Eloise will react, now that the moment of passion is over. If she'll feel shy or vulnerable.

The next moment, she's curled up beside me, naked and warm. I wrap my arms around her and press my lips against her hair.

She tilts her gaze up at me, her eyes clear and wide. "Can we do that again?"

I let out a bellowing laugh that ripples through my body and then she's laughing too.

"We can," I say.

"Now?" She presses the length of herself against me.

I chuckle. "Just give me a couple minutes."

She grins and then rests her head against my shoulder. I trace patterns on her back lazily. "I've never felt like that before," she whispers into my skin.

"Me neither."

I feel her breath catch. "But you have more experience than me."

"Not like this." I tilt her chin up so I can look into those glass-green eyes again. "I love you, Eloise. I am in love with you."

I feel her blush beneath my fingertips.

"I love you too," she says.

We lie in silence for a moment, our heartbeats the only sound in the room. I feel an overwhelming sense of gratitude. And as I trace its origin, each step of the path that led me here, I realize it all started with Abuelo.

That doesn't mean I forgive him.

But it's a start.

"Agustín?" Eloise asks softly.

"Mm?"

"We only have plans for coffee with Caro tomorrow, right?"

"That's right."

"Do you think she'd mind if we canceled?"

I glance down at her, wishing I could see her expression. "Of course not. Is there something else you wanted to do?"

She wraps one leg around me, pressing herself against my thigh. Oh my god, she's still so wet. She glances up at me under a thick fringe of lashes and gives me a vixen's smile that just about makes my heart stop.

"This," she says, and pulls me back on top of her.

43
Agustín

The morning of the wedding dawns cool and clear, not a cloud in the sky.

I wake up with Eloise in my arms and allow my mind to spin out over the past day, where we did nothing except stay in bed, exploring each other in every way, and only stopping to order room service.

I feel a sense of impending release. Finally, tonight, I will tell her the truth.

She shifts and her curls tickle my cheek.

"Morning," she murmurs, nuzzling into my neck. I feel myself start to stiffen, her body warm and her bare legs soft as silk against mine. Even after all of yesterday's activities, I still can't get enough. I don't think I'll ever stop craving her.

"Good morning," I reply, kissing her forehead. "It's wedding day."

Her eyes fly open as tension freezes her limbs. "Right."

"You're okay," I remind her gently. "You've got this."

But I can pretty much feel the Wheel start to click away in her chest, her shoulders going stiff, her toes pressing hard into the tops of my feet.

"I've got this," she whispers to herself. "I've got this . . . I've got . . . What time is it?"

I glance at the clock on the nightstand. "Oh. It's almost ten."

"What?" Eloise yelps, sitting up and clutching the sheet to her chest.

"It's all right," I say, rubbing her back. "You've got time."

"I'm supposed to meet Rachel in her room at noon," she says, her breath hitching. "I need coffee. And a shower. And my dress. Where's my dress?"

"Your dress is in the garment bag in the closet," I remind her. "I will get coffee. You shower."

She whirls around and plants a kiss on my lips. "Thank you," she says. She scrambles out of the bed, rushes into the bathroom, and slams the door shut.

I throw on jeans and a sweatshirt and tuck my phone into my pocket, making my way down to the restaurant. I could call for room service, but I'd rather move my body. I'm feeling jittery too. I order at the bar and my phone buzzes as I wait.

My stomach sinks. Neil again.

Neil: Hey, Agustín, just checking in.

I sigh and rake a hand through my hair. How did the best thing that ever happened in my career somehow simultaneously become this weight around my neck?

Me: The wedding is at 4pm. I'll have the interview done today then write up my notes tomorrow and finish the draft asap.

Neil: Great! Looking forward to it.

I sigh again. I hate this. Maybe I should just tell Eloise now. Or maybe I should just abandon this whole project completely.

Neither of those options feel right, though, and both sit heavily in my stomach.

"Un americano y un latte," the bartender says, handing over two to-go cups.

"Gracias," I say and head back to the room.

Eloise is still in the shower, so I leave her cup on her nightstand and take my coffee out onto the balcony. I hear the water turn off, then a few minutes later, she comes out to join me, wrapped in a plush robe, her hair hidden in a towel twisted high on her head, coffee in hand.

"Rachel said I needed to be a clean canvas for her to work on. Is this clean?" She moves her head from side to side.

"Very," I say. "Never seen a cleaner canvas."

She purses her lips. "I feel like you're mocking me."

I grab her hand and pull her into my lap. "Never," I promise her. "But it doesn't matter to me what Rachel does to you. You're beautiful just like this."

"With a towel on my head?"

"Yes."

She narrows her eyes, then breaks into a pleased smile, leaning her forehead against mine. "I have a confession to make," she says quietly.

My breath catches in my chest, and my pulse starts to thrum. "Yes?"

She takes a deep, measured inhale. "I am so very grateful that I met you. And that you never gave up on me. You didn't let me push you away. And . . ." She puts her cup down on the table and takes my hand, twining my fingers through hers. "I'm grateful that you're here with me, on this really important day. I'm so lucky you're my plus-one. I honestly don't know how I could have done this without you."

I'm about to tell her I'm the lucky one when she holds up a finger. "I need to ask you one more favor," she says.

"Anything," I reply.

"I really don't want to have a panic attack at Rachel's wedding," Eloise says. "Even though she'll say it's fine and no one cares and she understands and all that. Will you promise to stay by my side the whole time? Will you promise to always be where I can see you? Especially for the speech. I . . . I need you."

My heart freezes in my chest. How can I keep this promise yet also find a time to talk to Ricardo alone? But Eloise is looking at me with such trust in those soft green eyes. She has put so much faith in me.

I'm nothing if not resourceful. I'll find a way to do both—get the interview *and* support Eloise.

I cup my hand around her cheek. "Of course," I say, pulling her in for a kiss.

"Thank you," she murmurs. From inside the room, her phone pings. "Oh, that's probably Rachel." She jumps off my lap and disappears through the French doors.

I sit outside with my coffee, guilt gnawing at my chest.

44
Eloise

"You are going to look so gorgeous," Rachel says as she attacks me with an eyeliner pencil. "Even if you ignored my instructions to get your beauty sleep." She cackles and I blush. "I forgive you though. A full on, day-long sex marathon? Yes, girl, get it!"

I wish I could hide my face in my hands but I'm too afraid to move lest I lose an eye. It feels like I've been sitting in this straight-back chair at the long table in the Presidential Suite at the Four Seasons for hours. I've had every conceivable instrument used to apply more powders and creams and shadows than I ever knew existed to my face and neck. Rachel looks gorgeous, her own makeup already done flawlessly, her thick dark hair falling in luscious waves down her back. Her brown skin is almost iridescent, smooth and shimmering against her silk robe with the word *Bride* emblazoned on the back.

Apparently, all the other bridesmaids are coming later, for a champagne toast, once I'm done. Rachel wanted this time to be just us. Also, she probably didn't want me anxiety-sweating my new face off before the wedding.

She puts the eyeliner down and grabs a tube of lipstick. "Final touch," she says. But as her hand moves toward me, I see it's shaking.

"Hey," I say. "You okay?"

"Yeah," she says breezily. I raise an eyebrow. She sinks onto one of the chairs beside me, in the warm glow of the modern ceramic lamps. "I'm really nervous," she admits. "So many people! I don't know most of them. But I'm also just like . . . so excited, El. I can't believe I get to spend the rest of my life with this man. That this incredible person chose me."

"Well, obviously," I say.

She chuckles. "And I chose him. Somehow, we found each other. I already had one person in my life, 'til death do us part.'" She bumps me with her shoulder, and I feel my cheeks warm. "Now I get two? It's unreal. I almost feel guilty. Like . . . do I deserve this much happiness?"

Her words strike an echoing chord within me. I have never, ever heard Rachel second guess herself and part of my brain simply can't compute it. But more importantly, I think I'm finally understanding that Rachel's love for Diego doesn't lessen her love for me. Just as my love for Agustín doesn't lessen my love for her. I've been so stressed and scared about losing her, as if a heart is only capable of a certain amount of love, and that love gets split when another person comes into the picture, into smaller and smaller pieces.

But that's not how it works at all. Our hearts aren't glass jars that measure love precisely. They're more like sponges that can absorb and grow and expand as more and more love comes into our lives. My heart is growing three sizes today. Or four. Or five. There's no limit. I can encompass so much more love than I thought I was capable of.

Tears spring to my eyes.

"El?" Rachel asks worriedly.

"I'm like the Grinch," I squeak.

Rachel looks confused. "O . . . kay?"

I laugh and sniffle and throw my arms around her. "*Of course* you deserve this much happiness," I say. "You deserve every good thing this world has to offer. And . . . I really like Diego. I'm glad I've gotten to know him better, and I'm sorry it took me so long. I guess I've been so scared I would lose you. That things would change. You know how I feel about change." I pull away to look her full in the face. "But I've changed a lot too, these past months."

"OH EL!" Rachel squeals, and then it's her turn to tackle me in a hug. "I love you so much, and that's one thing nothing and no one could ever change."

I squeeze her close before we release each other, tears in both our eyes.

"Sorry, I don't want to ruin your work," I say, trying to blink them away.

"Oh, don't worry, I gave you waterproof everything." She winks at me. "Now, pucker up." She holds up the lipstick, and I dutifully present my mouth. Once she's finished, she sits back and presses her fingers to her lips.

"What?" I ask warily.

She shakes her head and takes my hand, leading me away from the table covered with various blushes and tubes and eye-shadows and into the ginormous bathroom. "See for yourself."

My pulse kicks into a sprint as she positions me in front of the huge floor to ceiling mirror. "Oh!" I gasp, my hands flying to my cheeks. "Oh Rachel . . ."

"You like?" she asks.

The woman in the mirror is nothing like the furtive, skittish person I imagine myself to be. Her cheeks hold the perfect rosy glow, her eyes decorated in muted shades of gold and mauve, making their green color more vibrant than usual. Her eyes seem larger too, outlined subtly in kohl, framed with thick lashes. Her mouth forms a small O, lips painted a decadent red. Her curls are sleek and perfectly spiraled. One side is pinned up with a gold pin in the shape of a butterfly. A more elegant tribute to my favorite clips.

"It's me?" I say and Rachel laughs.

"It's you."

"I look so pretty."

She nudges me with her hip. "Yes, you silly goose. You're always pretty. I just highlighted that. Now, let's get you into your dress before the other bridesmaids get here."

My stomach flips. "Yes, please," I say quickly, rushing to grab the garment bag hanging on the bathroom door. I whirl around. "Do you think Agustín will—"

"Yes," Rachel says, laughing. "He's going to flip his shit when he sees how stunning you are. But," she reminds me, raising a finger, "he always thinks you're stunning. And so do I. You don't need the makeup, El." One side of her mouth quirks up into a grin. "But it sure is fun, right?"

I meet Agustín in the lobby at three thirty.

I spent the hour after leaving Rachel's suite practicing my speech over and over and over in our room. Agustín wasn't there, so he must have gone somewhere else to get ready. Or probably, he knew I would need a place to be alone.

As the elevator doors open, I take a deep breath and step forward. I'm wearing heels, but they're nude patent wedges—I'm not insane enough to try and balance on stilettos and thankfully Rachel knew that too when she chose these shoes. You can't see my feet anyway, with this huge, billowy skirt that cascades to the ground around me. I gather it up as I walk, very carefully, down the long hall toward the reception. The dress is gorgeous—even I, a nondress person, have to admit that. It's the color of burnished copper, with an asymmetrical neckline that leaves one shoulder exposed. And best of all: it has pockets. My phone, with my speech, is tucked away in its many satiny folds. A pair of simple diamond studs adorn my ears. They were my mom's, and I've never had an occasion to wear them. I am not a diamond studs type of girl. But it's nice, in this moment, to have them with me. Like maybe, every once in a while, I *am* a diamond studs type of girl.

My heart is a blur in my chest as the receptionist—Lupe, the same woman from the very first day we checked in—catches sight of me. I have never been someone who has garnered a second look in my life. But her eyes widen and she smiles broadly.

"You look beautiful," she says as I approach.

"Thanks," I squeak, then clear my throat. "Um, thank you. Have you seen the guy I . . . um, my boyfriend?"

A thrill runs through me being able to call him that.

She gestures to the front doors. "He is waiting outside."

I walk forward slowly, still clutching my skirts. God, I hope my palms don't start sweating. I don't want to ruin the satin. One of the porters opens the door for me, smiling. I step out into the warm, fresh October air as the now familiar sounds of the traffic on Reforma greet me. Agustín is standing with his back to me, chatting with Enrique. The moment Enrique catches sight of me, his eyes pop wide.

"Qué guapa!" he says.

Agustín turns and my breath catches in my throat.

Agustín in a tuxedo is a thing of utter beauty. It's been tailored to perfection, the jacket hugging his shoulders, his shoes polished to a high sheen, his bowtie perfectly straight. His dark hair is slicked back, but one errant lock curls at his temple, like his hair simply refuses to be tamed.

When he sees me, his lips part. His beautiful warm brown eyes grow wide. I stand before him, feeling elegant and awkward at the same time. His puts one hand to his chest.

"Amor," he says, and a thousand shivers run up my spine. "You take my breath away."

A smile cracks on my face. "You look like James Bond."

Agustín throws his head back and laughs. He snakes his arm around me and the air seems to shimmer. I feel it in my bones, in my veins, like light refracting off a crystal.

"Shall we?" he asks in a weird accent.

"What was that?"

"That was my Connery impression."

"Oof."

"Needs work?"

"Some serious heavy lifting."

He laughs again and offers me his arm. I take it as Enrique hurries to open the door for me. "So much dress," I groan. Agustín helps me with the skirt, and I somehow manage to climb into the back as he piles the dress in after me. He gets in on the other side and Enrique pulls out into traffic.

The wedding is in an area of the city called Centro Histórico. A lot of the buildings are large and square with orange or red brick façades and ornate molding. Tourists fill the streets, along with shops selling everything from shoes to clothes to electronics. We pull up to a huge, Baroque style building, red with gray sandstone details, pillars that shoot up above the flat roof in sharp points toward the sky. The windows on the first floor are rectangular while the second-floor windows are octagonal, which creates a cool effect. I see patches of graffiti on the walls as we park, so I guess nothing is immune from being tagged here. A set of enormous wooden doors, topped with more gray stone statues, is thrown open. There are men dressed in black with wires in their ears, security I'm guessing, who patrol the outside of the building. Other guests, women in gowns and men in tuxedoes, are waiting in a short line to enter, giving their names to another burly man in black with a clipboard who stands by the open door.

My heart seizes in my chest. This is it.

Agustín's hand slips into mine. "Ready?" he asks, as Enrique opens the car door for me.

"You'll stay by my side, right?"

He nods, and I think I see a flicker in his eyes but then it's gone. "I promise," he says, flashing his dimples.

He helps me and my giant skirt out of the car, and once I'm steady on my heels, we head to wait in the line. Agustín gives our names to the man with the clipboard, we step inside, and my jaw drops.

The interior is enormous: a huge courtyard, ringed with arches—two floors of arches that give the feeling of being transported to a different time. There's a tile fountain in the center. And everywhere, there are flowers. Cascades of lilies hang from the second-floor balustrades, white roses and peonies are overflowing in the fountain, freesia fills the air with a pleasant scent, and baby's breath adorns the rose-lily-peony centerpieces on the tables like little clouds. There's a dance floor already set up, made of sleek white tiles, four posts surrounding it ensconced in ivory petals. There are tables in every shape and size, long rectangles, neat squares, small circular tables, and at the far end, a special table on a dais in front of a veritable wall of flowers, for the bride and groom and family members. Rachel already assured me I wouldn't have to sit up there, and seeing it in person, I'm thoroughly relieved. I do not need eyes on me while I'm eating. But still, it's probably where I'll have to give my speech. My stomach clenches.

The ceiling is high and arched, glass and metal creating an airy outdoor vibe. Off to one side, there's a large staircase. The chapel. A lump forms in my throat.

Not every guest was invited to the wedding itself, Rachel told me, because the private chapel is quite small. I'm grateful for that now. Seeing this cavernous space, all the tables, the flowers, the guests filing up the stairs into the chapel, my mouth has gone completely dry and sweat pricks at my hairline. I grip Agustín's elbow tightly.

"I'll be right up close to the front," he promises. "Right where you can see me."

I can't speak. I just nod.

A woman dressed in black wearing a headset comes over to me. "Maid of honor?" she says in accented English.

Another nod.

"This way." She drags me away from Agustín to a small side room. Rachel and the other bridesmaids are already inside, drinking champagne. "El!" Rachel cries, coming over to hug me, her white skirts billowing out around her, her gauzy veil trailing down her back. She looks unbelievably gorgeous.

I flash back to that day in the fitting room of Atelier Unveiled—the day I first heard about the plus-one list. The day I didn't realize was about to change my life forever.

I clasp Rachel's hands in mine and try desperately to ignore the other women in the room, and the huge courtyard on the other side of this door, and the fact that I will have to give a speech later.

"Rachel," I croak. "I'm so happy for you."

And I am. I really am.

My throat swells up, and I see tears glitter in her eyes.

"We can't start crying yet," she teases, but her voice catches.

"No," I agree.

The woman in black mutters something into her headset. "It's time," she says.

The other girls squeal and give Rachel hugs. There are only five of us bridesmaids, and the only one whose name I know is Mandy. She smiles at me and I smile back—today, we're all on the same team. Rachel takes a deep breath as Mandy hands her the bouquet, a dream of lilies and peonies.

"Let's do this," Rachel says.

45
Eloise

I do not remember much of the ceremony.

I remember an organ playing. The chapel is smaller than I expected, which is nice. There's a huge golden altar, with winged angels, and a big painting of the Virgin of Guadalupe. It's all extremely Catholic and not Rachel. Definitely an Alvarez family decision.

But in the end, the room, the altar, the angels, don't matter. Rachel's face is lit up like the sun as she says her vows. Diego looks like he won the freaking lottery, which I appreciate and also totally agree with.

I stand by my best friend's side, like I'd promised I would. Even with sweat beading at the nape of my neck, and my knees quivering like Jell-O, and my pulse sprinting, I am there for her.

And through it all, Agustín's face shines through the crowd, right in the second row, like he promised. A beacon keeping me still. Keeping me calm.

"You may now kiss the bride," the priest says.

Diego dips her low, and we all cheer.

My best friend is married, at last.

46
Agustín

As soon as Rachel and Diego walk out of the chapel, to the great cheers of the waiting guests, I find Eloise.

She's trembling, and a bead of sweat trickles down her temple, but she's smiling too.

"Oh," she gasps when she sees me, flinging her arms around my neck. I think partly from relief and partly to steady herself. Her legs buckle, but I'm there to catch her.

"You did great," I whisper in her ear.

"Well, I didn't faint," she whispers back.

"Nope. No panic attack either."

"Success."

"Success. Champagne?"

"Oh dear god, yes."

We make our way out of the chapel and into the enormous courtyard. Waiters walk past with trays, and I grab two flutes and hand one to Eloise.

"Cheers," I say, and we clink glasses. Eloise gulps half her flute in one go.

"Okay," she says, exhaling. "Okay . . ." She glances over to where Diego and Rachel are chatting with some of the other guests. "Was it a nice ceremony? I kind of blacked out."

I chuckle at that. "It was fine. Not as long as I thought it would be."

She wrinkles her nose.

We stand on the outskirts of the crowd. Diego's mother, elegance personified in a shimmering, beaded designer gown, is entertaining a group of women her age, all dripping with diamonds. I catch sight of Nicolas and Eva chatting with Jorge Alvarez. I'll have to go say hello to them. Surreptitiously, I scan the room for Ricardo. I've basically memorized his face from the photo on Grupo Real's marketing team page.

"Should we go find our seats?" Eloise asks.

We peruse the tables until we find our names at a small circular one near the head table. "So many flowers," I say.

"Those are definitely Rachel's touch," Eloise says, flopping into the seat with her name in elegant script on a tiny card in front of it. A card with my name is next to hers. We sit and people-watch, sipping our drinks until our flutes are empty.

"Another round?" I ask.

"Yes. No. Yes, one more," she says, nodding so her curls quiver. "Then no more until the speech."

"Okay," I say, kissing her temple. "I'll be right back."

As I make my way toward one of the long bars set up along the side of the courtyard, I catch a glance into a neighboring hall where a full-scale candy store is being set up for later in the evening. It's a tradition at Mexican weddings to have a buffet table filled with jars of candy—but this is like nothing I've ever seen. Like something out of Willy Wonka. Clearly the Alvarez family spared no expense. I'm beginning to see why Eva could believe the rumor that Luis Miguel might be performing.

"Con permiso," a man says as he cuts in front of me, and my brain screeches to a halt.

It's him.

Ricardo is better looking in real life than in his photo—his smile less stiff, his movements fluid. He walks toward one of the long rectangular tables at the back and before I get a chance to follow him, I hear, "Agustín!" and then Eva bursts into my field of vision, kissing my cheeks. "Look at *you*," she says, nodding approvingly. "Where's your date?"

I'm very glad Eloise is not here to be dissected by her. Plus, Eva knows I needed this invite for an interview. "She's at our table," I say. "I'm getting us some drinks."

"How was the ceremony? The bride is muy guapa, and I heard her Spanish was pretty good for a gringa. Diego seems happy." Eva sniffs. "Come say hi to Nico!"

"I will," I say, forcing a smile. "Just a minute."

I extricate myself but when I look around, Ricardo has vanished. But then, there are so many people here. Five hundred people sounds like a lot, but it's a whole different thing seeing it in person. The space is simply enormous, with halls leading off to who knows where and waiters flowing in and out with trays of canapes. I get two more glasses of champagne and take the long way back to Eloise, passing the large table I'd seen Ricardo heading to. I catch sight of his place card.

I know where he's sitting.

When I return to Eloise, she's fidgeting nervously and scrolling her phone.

"Oh thank god, you're back," she says, and I feel an all too familiar pinch of guilt.

"Yeah, sorry, I ran into Eva Garcia."

"The woman who put you on the plus-one list?"

I grin. "The very same."

"Well, cheers to her," Eloise says, clinking her flute with mine.

The table begins to fill up with people, though ours is one of the smallest tables, which I'm sure was by design. Eloise actually jumps out of her chair when an elderly Black couple approaches.

"George! Mina!" she says, embracing them.

"Eloise, oh my lord, don't you look stunning," the woman says. Eloise introduces me to them—apparently, they were Rachel's foster parents when she was in high school. Even though Rachel was never adopted, Eloise told me that Mina and George have stayed in Rachel's life and are the closest thing she has to family, along with Eloise and Diego.

"Eloise used to come over to our house all the time on the weekends," the husband, George, explains to me. He smiles widely at her. "Look at you now. You and Rachel both."

We all turn to where Rachel is being helped onto the dais by Diego.

"Isn't she just the most beautiful bride?" Mina says, dabbing at her eyes. Eloise nods.

We all take our seats as the dinner service starts. To Eloise's delight, the appetizer is aguachile.

"A little more elevated than the one we made," I murmur to her as she takes a spoonful.

She shrugs. "I liked ours better."

I smile, my heart feeling tender. My phone buzzes in my pocket, and I glance at it under the table.

Neil: Any updates?

I put it back in my pocket without answering, my eyes darting to Ricardo's table. I can just see his profile through the sea of guests. I keep track of him all through dinner, waiting for the right moment. Just as the dessert plates are being cleared, the woman with the headset comes over to us. "Speeches in ten minutes," she says.

At the same moment, Ricardo stands and starts to make his way toward one of the many halls.

Shit. This is my chance.

I will be lightning fast—she's got George and Mina here so I feel slightly less guilty about leaving her alone.

"I'll be right back," I whisper in her ear. "Restroom."

"What? No, the speeches are in ten minutes," she hisses, grabbing my hand.

"I'll be back in two, I promise," I say, squeezing her palm and releasing her. I weave my way through the tables, walking as quickly as I can across the expansive courtyard and into the hall, lined with elegant sconces, my footsteps echoing off the stone walls. I wander down the hall, my heart jammed in my throat. Where did he go? I don't have much time. I turn left and nearly run straight into Ricardo as he's leaving the bathroom.

"Disculpa," he says to me.

I don't think—I grab his arm.

"Ricardo Cuevas?" I ask. He frowns and glances at my hand. I release him immediately.

"Yes?"

"My name is Agustín Martinez," I say in a rush. "El Rasca was my grandfather."

I can see the blood drain from Ricardo's face. As we look at each other, it's impossible not to notice the similarities. He has a dimple in his left cheek. Our hair has the same sheen, and his seems unruly as well. Our eyes are the same shape and color.

"No mames," he gasps.

"Can we talk for a minute?" I ask.

To my surprise, Ricardo looks . . . excited. "Yes," he says. "Absolutely. Wow."

We walk a bit farther down the hall. I glance at my phone—I need to get back to Eloise soon, before the speeches start. We find an alcove near a roped off staircase.

"I want to be up front with you," I tell him. "I'm writing an article for *The New Yorker* about El Rasca. My family only found out about everything at the start of this year."

Ricardo's eyes bulge. "Seriously?"

I nod. "I would really like to ask you some questions. And record this interview, if that's all right."

"Yeah, sure," he says. "Anything you need."

This is not quite the reaction I was expecting but I fumble quickly to activate my recording app.

"My mom only told me about your family after Dad died," Ricardo says. His Spanish is good but his accent is very gringo. He runs a hand through his hair, exactly the way I do. "It made a lot of things about my childhood make sense. I loved my mom, but . . . she was a very jealous woman. I loved my dad too. He was . . ." Ricardo takes a deep breath. "He was a very good father."

It's so strange to be talking to him after all this time spent tracking him down. He'd become this huge looming specter in my mind, like a monster hiding in a closet, but now that I'm talking to him, he's just a twenty-something kid.

"Mom had a lot of rules I didn't understand," he says.

"Like what?" I ask.

"We couldn't talk about Mexico. We couldn't visit. Dad was never allowed to talk about his home. And when you're a kid, especially growing up in the US, I wanted that connection. I wanted to feel like I was part of a bigger community. You know?"

I don't know, not really. I am one hundred percent Mexican.

He shakes his head. "I think once Mom laid down the law, that's when Dad really started getting into activism. Like if he wasn't allowed to visit his home, he was gonna help people here. That's what I always assumed."

"That wasn't it," I say. "Well, not all of it. He told my abuelita about you and your mom—he confessed everything to her. She told him to do better. Be a better person."

His eyes widen. "So she knew?"

I nod. "She never told us, though. We were going through a hard time. She didn't want to burden the family more."

"Fucking secrets, man," Ricardo says. "I think Dad only married Mom because she got pregnant with me. They both loved me—I don't know how much they loved each other. Enough, I guess. Whatever that means. I had a good childhood, don't get me wrong. Dad was all about education. About learning. And he really inspired me with the whole El Rasca persona. He was the real deal, I can tell you that. Lots of late nights out in the community. Lots of people coming over to our house."

I feel my throat go strangely tight. "I wish I could have known that version of him."

"I wish I could have known him longer. I was only ten when he had the heart attack." Ricardo hesitates. "Can I ask . . . what do you remember of him? What was he like in Mexico?"

What an odd way to phrase it. "I remember his beard," I say. "So scratchy when he would give me hugs. He loved to bring the neighborhood together and throw parties, especially on Nochebuena. And I remember his laugh. It was big and loud. Me and my sisters loved it. We always tried to make him laugh so we could hear it."

"You have two sisters, right?" he says eagerly.

"How did you know?"

"I did some digging on your family," he admits. "But I never had the courage to reach out. I figured you wouldn't want to hear from me."

I feel my head start to spin. All this time, Ricardo wanted to reach out to me.

"I'm not sure all of us would," I admit, thinking of Lupe.

Ricardo grimaces. "Fair."

"What made you want to work for Grupo Real?" I ask.

"Dad," he says. "Seeing him on the news, seeing the changes he made, it really inspired me to work in media. And then, of course, because Mexico was always so forbidden, it was the one place I've always wanted to go. So when I started looking for jobs, I knew I wanted to work for a Mexican company." He chuckles. "Then they sent me to Beijing for a year. I'm coming back though. I really like CDMX. I feel, I don't know, I guess closer to Dad here. Mom couldn't keep him from telling me everything. He said his favorite taqueria was—"

"El Huequito," I finish.

Ricardo's eyes brighten. "Yeah. First place I went after I landed here."

"The one in Centro?"

"Obviously. The original. Though I've gone to the one in Juárez too."

"Abuelo would approve."

We grin at each other.

"You're not what I thought you'd be like," I admit.

"What did you think I'd be like?"

"I don't know. More . . . resentful, I guess."

"Me?" Ricardo laughs. "Naw, man. I thought *you'd* hate *me*. I figured your whole family hated my existence. If they knew about me at all."

Something in me shifts, like the sun breaking through clouds. All this anger and resentment I've felt toward Abuelo, it seems so pointless, so silly now that I'm talking to Ricardo face to face. Abuelita was right. I've been searching for a reason, for the truth, for something to explain what happened in a way that I can easily categorize, put in a nice box with a neat label.

But the truth is, people are messy. People are complicated.

The truth is nobody is perfect. Not Abuelo. Not me. We're all just trying to do the best with whatever life throws at us.

The truth is my abuelo made his own decisions. And it's up to me to make mine.

"Hey," I say. "If you ever want to grab a beer, and talk more about—"

"I'd love that," Ricardo says eagerly. "I don't . . . my mom was an only child, and her parents died when I was little. I don't have any family."

"You do," I say, holding out my hand. He shakes it, beaming.

"Wow," he says. "This was really unexpected."

I laugh. "Not for me. I've been trying to get an interview with you for months."

"For real?"

I nod. "Can I use some of your quotes for my article?"

"Yeah, dude, sure thing," he says.

"Great, thanks," I say, hurrying to take out my phone and sending off a text to Neil.

Then I see the time.

Oh shit.

I've been gone a lot longer than two minutes.

47
Eloise

Where is he?

The best man is yammering away in Spanish as the crowd laughs and claps, while I quietly melt into a puddle of sweat and nerves, scanning the room for a sign of Agustín.

He promised. He *promised* me. So where *is* he?

The Wheel is a blur in my chest, my skin shrinking over my bones, my throat swollen. My pulse hammers in my ears.

Whereishewhereishewhereishe . . .

The clapping gets louder and the best man gives a silly bow then kisses Rachel's cheek and gives Diego a hug. The woman with the headset appears at my side.

"You're up," she says.

No. I cannot be up. I cannot go up there all alone, and say the words that are now blurring on my phone screen. I need my anchor. I need to know that I'm grounded.

Whereishewhereishewhereishe . . .

I walk on shaking legs up the short steps to the dais. Rachel is beaming, but I can see the worry in her eyes. She knows. She knows I'm losing it. I feel myself start to unravel at the seams. I feel my joints start to loosen and crack as I stare out at the sea of faces. Every pair of eyes is its own unique pinprick, pinching my skin, making me feel so exposed in a way no amount of satiny fabric could ever cover. My breath comes in shallow pants and sweat trickles down my spine. The microphone isn't at the right height, but the thought of somehow having to *adjust it myself* while everyone watches is just too much. There are too many eyes, too many murmurs, they're all looking at me, why can't everyone just look somewhere else for a minute?

My hand shakes so hard I'm worried I'll drop my phone. I catch Diego's parents exchange a look. I know that look. It says *What is wrong with her?* It says *Why is this weird girl here? She doesn't belong.* I don't belong. Not in this opulent room, or in this opulent dress, or with any of these people.

Where is my person? The one who reminds me I'm enough?

I glance at Rachel who is whispering something to Diego.

The silence has dragged on for so long it's humiliating. I can feel it, dripping down the nape of my neck, pooling around my shoulder blades, covering me like a cape. It's awful and uncomfortable, and I don't know how to break it.

I look down at my phone, at my stupid little speech I spent so much time practicing, and I can't even read it. It's a blur of letters, random shapes. I can't remember what I'm supposed to say.

Someone coughs. It's so loud in the silence.

"Congratulations," I squeak into the microphone.

It echoes with feedback.

And then I run.

I hide in the bathroom for what feels like hours.

I don't know how I'm supposed to go back out there. But I need to wait until the dancing starts, until everyone forgets. If anyone will ever forget that disaster. I probably cursed the wedding anyway, no plus-one needed. I'm sure Rachel will say it's fine but it's not.

And where was Agustín? This makes no sense. How could he have left me right before the speeches started?

I feel a tiny flame of anger ignite in my chest. This isn't fair. He *promised*.

I march out of the bathroom, buoyed by that flame, and into the courtyard, which is now thankfully much dimmer, the dance floor crowded with people, the speeches (hopefully) forgotten. Then I see Agustín, sitting alone at our table all the way on the other side of the room. He looks upset.

Determination hardens in me. I march over to him, and he sits up when he sees me. His phone sits on the table in front of him next to a small glass of mezcal.

"Oh, Eloise, I'm so sorry—"

"Where *were* you?" I cry, dropping into the seat beside him. "You promised me!"

"I know, I know, I didn't . . . I'm such an idiot. Something—came up."

"Something came up?" I croak, choking on a laugh. "What? What could possibly have come up? How could you just abandon me? You knew how scared I was."

"I know, Eloise, please believe me, I—"

Suddenly, his phone lights up with a text message.

Time seems to slow as I read the words printed on the little screen.

> Neil, THE NEW YORKER: Great job getting that interview with Ricardo! Get us the final draft as soon as you can. So glad you found a way to get an invite to that wedding!

For a moment, my brain rejects those words in that order. Because no. That's not . . . this doesn't make sense. It feels like the floor has dropped out from under me. I am weightless, suspended in time.

I look at Agustín and see guilt etched across his handsome features.

Things begin to fall into place.

"This is why you wanted to come to the wedding with me?" I ask. My voice is so quiet. I feel myself beginning to break apart for the second time this evening.

"No," he insists. "I mean . . . well, yes, I did need to talk to someone here. Ricardo is my abuelo's son—the son he had in New York. I tried everything I could to talk to him any other way but . . . and then I found out he was coming to this wedding and *The New Yorker* wouldn't publish my article unless I got a quote from him and—"

"You used me?" I say. The words hurt on their way out. "To get an interview for that article?"

"No," he says again, but we both hear the emptiness of the word.

I feel the pain coming—it's far away right now, like the sound of a train at the end of a long tunnel. It rumbles in my chest, getting closer.

"This was all an act," I say. "No wonder you kept pushing to be my plus-one. It was never about me."

"Eloise, please, let me explain—"

The pain rumbles closer as shame starts to burn inside me. "Explain?" I cry. "Explain what? You didn't care about helping me with my speech or teaching me about Mexico City. You just wanted to further your career. And you know what—I would have understood! You could have just told me the truth. But instead, you lied to me, and you abandoned me when I needed you the most. You made me trust you, and then you broke that trust."

I feel like such an idiot. Such a small, stupid thing.

Agustín leans forward. "I wanted to tell you the truth," he says, his voice radiating with intensity. "I've been wanting to tell you for so long, but . . . it never seemed like the right time, and I didn't want anything to distract you because I knew how nervous you were."

"Bullshit," I snap. "Don't use my anxiety as an excuse. You could have told me the truth at any point but you didn't. Instead, you lied and then bailed on me at the first opportunity."

"I'll cancel the article," he says grabbing his phone. "I'll tell Neil right now that I quit."

"Don't you dare," I hiss, leaping to my feet. "Don't you dare put that on me."

"I love you, Eloise," he says. His face is twisted in pain, his eyes blazing, but I can barely look at him anymore. "I'll do anything to make this right. Anything at all. Please. I can't lose you. Please, just tell me what to do."

I shake my head. The train is so loud now, the pain filling my limbs, roaring in my ears, snaking through my ribcage.

"I trusted you," I say, and my voice cracks. "And yet you never trusted me."

I knew this was too good to be true. I knew this kind of love was never meant for me, and I was stupid enough to allow myself to believe in it.

"This was only ever meant to be an arrangement. Transactional," I say, impressed with how steady my voice is. "That text makes it clear that's all it ever was for you anyway."

He opens his mouth but I silence him with a look.

"This is why I don't let people into my life," I say coldly. "Thank you for reminding me of that. I never want to see you again."

"Eloise, no, please, no," Agustín says, jumping to his feet and reaching for me. I shrink away from him.

"Don't you dare touch me," I say. The pain is fracturing into pieces inside me, shattering like a mirror, glass and jagged edges everywhere. I need to get out of here. "Find somewhere else to stay tonight," I warn him. "We're done."

Then I turn on my heel and storm out of the building.

48
Agustín

My world crumbles as I watch the woman I love run away from me.

I want to chase after her, to hold her close, to fall to my knees and beg her to forgive me.

How could I be so stupid? How could I have let this happen? I knew she didn't trust easily. I knew what a precious soul I'd found in her. I knew how goddamn lucky I was and now I've gone and fucked it all up. Possibly beyond repair.

My legs feel numb. The pain is waiting, just offstage, ready to emerge and drown me with its icy grip.

I need to get out of here. I need to get away from the glamour, from the shrieks of glee, from this wedding that brought me the greatest gift and yet now has caused me the most brutal agony.

It's time to take responsibility. I caused this. I have no one to blame but myself. I could have told her right away and I didn't. I chose this.

Now I have to live with that choice.

I take out my phone and text Caro.

Me: Can I stay at your place tonight?

Her response is instant.

Caro: Of course.

And then . . .

Caro: You fucked it all up, didn't you?

I wish I could laugh. But my face feels brittle, like a smile could shatter it.

Me: See you soon.

49
Eloise

I wake up the next morning feeling like utter shit.

My head throbs, and my eyes feel puffy and swollen. There was so much crying last night. My heart feels bruised and tender. My muscles are stiff. My ribs ache and my mouth tastes awful. I didn't bother to take my makeup off or brush my teeth. The dress is crumpled in a corner, the butterfly pin on the nightstand next to my phone.

I did manage to get one text to Rachel when I got back last night, telling her I was sorry about the speech and to have fun without me. Hopefully, she just thinks I left the wedding in shame.

My fractured heart throbs a painful beat. I roll onto my back and stare up at the ceiling.

I just want to go home. Home to where I'm safe. I want to go back into my cocoon, where nothing can hurt me anymore. I feel like such an idiot. A fool.

The tears well up again. My swollen eyes can't handle it anymore. The pain throbs at the raw edges of my heart.

A sudden pounding on my door sends a shockwave through me, launching me upright.

"Eloise Madigan Whitechapel, open this door right now, or I swear to god I will break it down!" Rachel's voice pierces through my fog of depression. I hurry to answer it, because her threats are real, and I don't want her causing any property damage.

The minute she sees my face, she gasps. "What happened?" she demands, sweeping inside the room and closing the door.

"Aren't you supposed to be at your post wedding brunch?" I mumble trying to avoid her eyes.

"No, no, don't you dare. Last night, I thought maybe you were just freaking out about your speech—which was fine, by the way." I cut her a glare. "Okay, obviously it didn't go as planned but whatever, who cares. Everyone got so drunk, and the party was such a blast, no one's ever going to remember anyway."

"I care," I insist.

"Well, I don't think that's what the problem is because I have been trying to reach both you and Agustín, and neither of you are talking to me, and that is not normal."

She glances around the room. "Where is he?"

My eyes fill with tears, and my throat clenches so tight it hurts. "I broke up with him," I say.

Rachel's face goes blank with shock. "What? Oh, El. Why?"

A fat tear trickles down my cheek. "He lied to me, Rach."

Rachel gathers me up in her arms. She squeezes me close and then leads me over to sit together on the edge of the bed. "Start from the beginning."

I tell her everything—the text, the interview, his lame excuses, how he broke his promise. "I knew it was all too good to be true," I say at the end, as Rachel hands me a tissue so I can blow my nose. "I feel so stupid. Of course he didn't really like me. Of course he just wanted to further his career. I never want to see him, ever again. I just want to go home, Rachel. I want things to go back to before. I wish I'd never met him."

"Hold up one second," Rachel says. "I definitely agree this was not Agustín's finest moment."

"Not his finest moment?" I yelp. "Rachel, he *lied* to me!"

"What would you have thought if he told you before the wedding?" she asks. "Would it have made you more or less anxious?"

My lips part, and I pause. "More," I admit.

"And he told you he tried to track this guy down before but there was no other way to talk to him except at the wedding?"

I shrug then give a reluctant nod. I don't want Rachel making good points when I just want to be angry and hurt.

"Do you believe him?" she presses.

I think about the pain in his expression last night, the urgency in his voice. I nod again.

Rachel's face has turned pensive. She absentmindedly tugs on a lock of her hair. "That's a pretty big deal, meeting a long-lost family member that he's been trying to find for almost a year. I'm not saying what he did was okay," Rachel says, holding up a hand before I can react. "His timing was absolutely abysmal. And I one thousand percent agree that he should have been honest with you, like, way, *way* before now. But . . . all things considered, I kind of get it."

My eyes flash wide in shock.

"He panicked," Rachel explains quickly. "You know a little something about panicking, don't you?"

I press my lips together. I don't want to see things from Agustín's side.

Rachel takes my hand gently in hers. "Eloise, look at you. Look how happy you've been—not just this week, but over the past few months. I've never seen you like this before, and I've known you my whole life. You're . . . fuller. Like you're finally letting yourself live a life in vibrant color. And honestly, it's been fucking magical to witness." She wipes a tear from my cheek. "My darling, beautiful friend—falling in love is hard. It comes with a lot of risks. Because people are flawed. We make mistakes. We aren't perfect. None of us are. I think you've tried so hard to live a life without risk. Without pain. Because of course, you suffered so much when you were so young." My chest squeezes. "But El . . . these last few months . . . you've finally been *living*. Really living, not just existing. Are you going to throw all that away? Do you really want to go back to how things were before?"

I think about the video Agustín made. I think about how I looked in June versus how I looked at that dinner on the rooftop. I think about everyone on the ninth floor of the Archer. I think about a kitchen with blue and orange tiles, and a wrinkled grandma letting me use her tortilla press, and a family that welcomed me with words I couldn't speak but could still understand.

I think about my life before I knew a hot chocolate smile. I think about the warmth of his arms, and the way his hand seems to fit perfectly in mine. I think about how grounded I feel when I'm with him—and how when he looks at me, it's like nothing else exists in his universe.

"Do you love him?" Rachel asks me. "Because one thing I can tell you, speaking from experience: love is always worth the risk."

My shattered heart rattles in my chest.

Just then, my phone buzzes. Rachel and I exchange a glance, and then I lunge across the bed to get it. It's not a text from Agustín though. It's from Miriam.

I open the thread and see a photo of everyone in her living room: Kate and Sanvi snuggled together with Hazelnut between them on that huge circular chair; Madame Boularès and Mr. Bloom together on the couch—he's got his arm around her, and the Colonel rests his head in Mr. Bloom's lap. Gretchen is beside them with Charleston in her arms, holding him like a big baby, her smile bright. Pip is on one of the sparkly poufs, baring his teeth. I see a cat tail peeking out on the floor behind him.

Miriam: We're having a movie marathon today! The Pack is missing you guys. Barks and woofs to Eloise and Agustín! Can't wait to have you both home!

More tears spring to my eyes and fall, silently, down my cheeks.

There is no home without Agustín. Going back to my old life isn't an option—and Rachel is right. I wasn't living. I was existing. And now I've felt the difference. I don't want to go back to that sad, silent person I used to be. I don't want to go back to a lonely life.

Maybe I need to start moving forward in this imperfect, messy world as an imperfect, messy person—and be okay with that. I look at each of my dogs, little pieces of my heart, and think about how overlooked they were, because they were old, or incontinent, or had an attitude. But to me, their flaws are what make them who they are. What make them more loveable, not less.

Maybe it's time to extend a fraction of the grace I give to them to myself.

I am no less deserving of love for being imperfect.

And neither is Agustín.

"I know he's made a mistake," Rachel says quietly, as if reading my thoughts. "I'm not denying that. But I've also seen the way he looks at you. The way he speaks to you—and speaks about you. I don't think he was putting on an act, El. Maybe this whole thing started because he needed that interview. But that wasn't the reason he stayed."

I meet her warm gaze. "I love him," I say.

Tears fill her eyes. "I know."

Panic seizes me. "Did I fuck this up?"

"No," Rachel says. "But we gotta find him."

I jump off the bed. "I bet he's with his family," I say, rushing over to the dresser and grabbing the first clothes I see. "Shit, I don't know where they live. Oh wait! Can you text Enrique, our driver? His number is in my phone. He took us to their house."

"On it," Rachel says, as I rush into the bathroom to change. I scramble into my jeans, realize I've grabbed a sweater with an embroidered pug emblazoned across it, and feel like that's a good sign—the Pack has my back. I grab my new chihuahua earrings for good measure, brush my teeth, and splash water on my face. By the time I'm ready, Rachel says he's almost here. We race down to the lobby just as Enrique pulls up in the SUV.

I throw open the back door.

"Do you want me to come with you?" Rachel asks. "I can skip the brunch."

I whirl around and put my hands on her shoulders. "No," I say firmly. "You were right. It's time for me to start living my life—risks and all. And you need to go be with your husband. You just got married, Rach!" I pull her in for a hug. "I'm so happy for you."

"I'm so happy for *you*," she says in my ear. "Okay, I'm going. But you better text me and let me know how it goes."

"Promise," I say, then I scramble into the back seat and shut the door behind me.

50
Agustín

"Tín, I say this with all the love in my heart—you're an idiot."

Lupe has her arms folded over her chest, leaning against the refrigerator, as I sit slumped over the kitchen island. Abuelita is on my right side, my mom on my left.

"Lupe," Mamá says. "There's no need to put lemon juice in his wounds."

"No, she's right," I say. My head aches, and my eyes are itchy. After spending the night at Caro's, we came home after breakfast. I needed time with my family.

I feel awful. Like everything hurts. I can't believe I fucked this up so badly. Except I also can. Because this is exactly what I was afraid of.

"Maybe Eloise just needs a little bit of time to process," Caro says. Abuelita pushes a mug of café de olla into my hands. For the first time in my life, the scent of coffee and cinnamon doesn't comfort me.

"Should I make something to eat?" my mom says. "Sandwiches? Chilaquiles? Oh, I could make those Turkish eggs you like."

"I'm not hungry," I say as my mother gets up and starts pulling things for sandwiches out of the fridge. Caro plops down on the empty stool as the sounds of *Amar y Querer* float in from the living room.

"Not sure this is a moment for José José, Papá!" Caro calls.

"It seems very on point actually," I say.

My father comes into the kitchen. "You need to get the sad out," he says. "Next, we listen to JuanGa. 'Hasta Que Te Conocí.'"

"Tinito," Abuelita says. "You made a choice. Now what are you going to do about it?"

"But I made the *wrong* choice, Abuelita," I say miserably. "I should have told her right away."

"Yeah, you should have," Lupe says. "What were you thinking, Tín?"

"Well, we can't all be as perfect as you, Lupe," I say.

My older sister's jaw drops, and she takes a deep inhale, the kind that says she's about to unleash a storm.

"Lupe." Mamá puts a package of deli meat on the counter with a loud thump. "Your brother is in pain. Have some compassion. His heart is broken."

It is. I always thought a broken heart was just an expression, but I can feel the fissure in my chest, the exact line where Eloise eviscerated me. And the worst part is, everything she said was true. I lied. I broke my promise. I let her down.

I could have—I *should* have—told her about the interview. It may have been why I wanted to be her plus-one at first but everything else, every single moment with her, every touch, every kiss . . . that was all genuine.

"A wrong choice, a right choice . . . that's life," Abuelita says as my mother starts assembling sandwiches with renewed fervor. "Now you fix it."

"How?" I say bleakly.

"You two were meant for each other," Mamá says as she slices a tomato. "I have never seen two people so well matched. Your souls recognized each other." She glances at my father with a tender look in her eye. Papá is already smiling at her privately.

"Yeah," Caro agrees. "I mean, I know I tease you a lot, dude, but it was clear the two of you were way into each other—even before you got here. I could sense that vibe through FaceTime."

Even Lupe looks like she agrees, as she fiddles with the gold cross around her neck.

"Thanks, guys," I say. "But none of this helps me get Eloise back."

Lupe smacks her hand down on the table. "Wallowing in your own shit isn't helping either," she snaps. "Sorry, Abuelita, Mamá," she adds with an apologetic grimace. "Come on. Let's go."

"Where?" I ask as she stalks over to grab her purse from the counter.

"I'm driving you back to the hotel so you can get on your knees, crawl over glass, and beg for her forgiveness," Lupe says. "I can't take this whining anymore. You screwed up, let's go fix it."

"But she won't talk to me," I insist.

Lupe rolls her eyes. "She doesn't need to talk. She just needs to listen."

She slings her purse over her shoulder just as the buzzer goes off at the front door. We all look at each other.

"Are we expecting company?" my father asks.

Mamá shakes her head.

"I'll get it," Lupe says huffily. We hear the door open, and muffled voices. Then two sets of footsteps coming down the hall. When Lupe appears in the doorway of the kitchen, she shoots me a significant look.

Behind her is Eloise.

Adrenaline floods my veins, so forceful it makes my head spin and my chest tingle. I shoot up from my chair as Abuelita presses her hands together.

"Tinito, look who's here," she says.

My eviscerated heart throbs out a longing beat. Eloise's eyes are red-rimmed and puffy, her curls wild and tangled. She's wearing the chihuahua earrings we bought that first day we walked around Roma. Her sweater has a pug stitched on it, and she looks so thoroughly Eloise that it makes my stomach ache.

She glances furtively at each member of my family, before focusing that clear green gaze directly at me.

"I love you," she says, and I hear Caro make a tiny gasp as a sudden rush of heat floods through me. "I love your endless optimism, even when it bothers me. I love the way your hair can't ever seem to make up its mind which way to go. I love your smile and the way you hold my hand. I love that you always give me space to be myself, and that you've never once made me feel like I wasn't enough. I love how you changed the way I see the world. I love how much you love my dogs. I love that you are never condescending, never impatient, never unkind.

"Before you came into my life, everything was the same for me. I thought that was a good thing. I thought if I never allowed anyone in, I could never be hurt. But mostly I thought—" She clenches her jaw, her eyes turning glassy. "I thought there was something broken inside me. That I wasn't made to be loved. And I guess I don't care if what made you stick around at first was some stupid interview. Because I would have succeeded in pushing you away otherwise. And when I look back at all those years before I knew you, it's like everything is in black and white." She shakes her head and a tear falls onto her cheek, glistening like a star. "I don't want to go back to that. I want to live a life in full color. You're my color. You're all the colors."

She shifts from foot to foot and brushes the tear away. "I'm not perfect," she says quietly. "Not even close. And I think you love me anyway. So it's like who am I to demand perfection from anyone else? I love you anyway. Perfectly imperfect."

I am struck dumb. This was maybe the last thing I expected. She just gave a whole speech. In front of people.

For me.

She loves me.

"What's happening?" Abuelita breaks the silence. "Lupe, what's she saying?"

"She's saying that she loves him, Abuelita," Lupe explains.

"Well of course she does," Abuelita scoffs. "Más claro, ni el agua." Not even water is as clear. She nudges me. "Agustín, don't just stand there!"

I stumble forward, and then Eloise takes a step and we crash into each other, right there in the middle of my family's kitchen. I press her mouth to mine as her fingers tangle in my hair. Caro whoops, Abuelita claps, and even Lupe is cheering. I release Eloise and press my forehead against hers.

"I'm so sorry," I murmur. "I promise to never keep anything from you, ever again."

"You better not," she says.

"I won't." It's the easiest promise I've ever made, one I know I'll keep forever. "That was a hell of a speech," I add.

She blushes, a delicate pink shading her cheekbones. "I didn't really plan it out very well."

I kiss her again, tenderly. "I love you," I say to her. "Perfectly imperfect."

From behind me, Abuelita gives a cluck of approval.

"I knew she was meant to be part of this family," she says with confidence.

EPILOGUE

Eloise

The doorbell rings, making the Colonel start to howl.

"I've got it," I call to Agustín, who's in the kitchen cooking up a storm with Ricardo.

I pass Hazelnut off to Caro, who's been listening attentively to one of Miriam's wild stories from her youth, and skirt past Lupe, deep in conversation about core-tightening exercises with Kate. Lupe managed to get a few days away from the Minions to be here in New York to celebrate New Year's Eve with us, which I know meant a lot to Agustín.

Charleston follows me eagerly down the hall as I hurry to open the door.

"Happy New Year, El!" Rachel squeals, enveloping me in a hug.

"We brought champagne," Diego says, holding out the bottle.

I hug him too. I've gotten a lot better about hugging in the two months since the wedding. But only with the people I know and love.

"Thanks," I say, taking it from him. "Come on in. You guys can leave your coats in the decompression room."

I slip into the kitchen, as I hear the other guests greet Rachel and Diego.

"It smells amazing in here," I say, interrupting a fervent conversation in Spanish between my boyfriend and his . . . uncle? I think they prefer to call each other cousins though. Way less weird.

"Gracias, amor," Agustín says, kissing my temple, his arm snaking around my waist.

"He knows how to make a mean pozole," Ricardo says. The similarities between the two men are striking, yet there are stark differences too. Lupe is finally coming around to accepting Ricardo into the Martinez family, and Agustín and Caro both welcomed him with open arms right away. So when Agustín suggested we throw a New Year's party (at my apartment of course, he wasn't about to force me out into the city on New Year's Eve, the worst of all nights in New York), and invite Ricardo, Caro, and Lupe, I happily agreed. And of course, I suggested we invite Rachel and Diego. And then Miriam got wind of the plan, so the ninth floor of the Archer got invited too.

"Gretchen says she's coming once she puts the kids to bed," I tell him. The doorbell rings again, and I hurry to open it. Mr. Bloom and Madame Boularès stand together, her arm linked through his. She's wearing a deep scarlet dress that matches the color of Mr. Bloom's tie.

"Welcome," I say, as Charleston bumps into Madame's leg and the Colonel pads down the hall to greet Mr. Bloom.

"Hello, old friend," Mr. Bloom says, scratching him behind his ears.

"Eloise Madigan Whitechapel!" Rachel shouts from the living room. I grimace, grab Charleston before he accidentally wanders off down the hall, and head into the living room, where she's seated on the couch between Caro and Miriam, looking at her phone. "When were you going to tell me about this?" she demands, holding up her screen to reveal the newly revamped website for Silver Snoot Rescue, complete with links to fresh new socials and another link to what I've called the Pawtastic Pantry.

"Oh, well, you were on your honeymoon and busy with stuff," I say.

"Are you legit incorporated now? Like a real rescue?"

I nod. Agustín helped me navigate all the paperwork and the talking to people and whatnot. And I can sell my specialty dog treats direct through the website, which is actually a lot easier and allows me to have more control over my business.

"I'm so stinking proud of you," Rachel says, as Hazel paws at her arm, demanding attention. Ricardo and Diego come out of the kitchen with drinks, while Sanvi and Kate greet Mr. Bloom and Madame Boularès, and Agustín joins us with a huge tray of appetizers. I perch on one of the stools in the breakfast nook, leaning against Agustín's side and sipping my champagne.

My house is so full. Conversation in English and Spanish washes over me, and there's laughter and good food, and music playing faintly beneath it all. Pip paws at Agustín's leg and he picks him up, as the little chihuahua happily licks his hand. Charleston prowls through the legs of the guests, successfully begging for treats, as Hazel gets fawned over by Sanvi and the Colonel pads over to rest his head against my knee. I stroke his soft fur and feel an overwhelming sense of contentment.

"How are you doing, honey?" Miriam says to Madame Boularès. "Isn't it around this time of year that your husband passed?"

"Oh, my husband is not dead," Madame says with a dismissive wave of her champagne flute.

If I had a record player, it would be screeching to a stop right now. Everyone in the room stares at her in shock, except Caro and Lupe, who don't know the whole backstory.

"What—what do you mean, he's not dead?" Kate stammers.

"He left me for a Pilates instructor," Madame Boularès says disdainfully. I notice that Mr. Bloom does not seem surprised by this information. Madame slips her hand through his arm. "It was easier for me to pretend as if he had died. I was holding onto something that I no longer wish to hold onto."

She glances at Mr. Bloom with a small smile, that he returns wholeheartedly. Sanvi presses her hand to her chest, her expression swoony.

"Oh my god," Kate mouths to her. Agustín and I exchange private smiles. Miriam's eyebrows have disappeared into her hair, then she chuckles and shakes her head.

"Happy Fucking New Year," she says, raising her glass, and everyone laughs.

Agustín's phone pings, and he checks it.

"Neil," he says, his voice tight with nerves.

I sit up, excited. "Is it . . ."

"Let's see," he says, opening his email.

> Agustín,
>
> I hope you enjoy this first look at your article, HECHO EN MÉXICO: The True Story of El Rasca. It will be featured in January's issue. It was a real joy to work with you, and everyone here at The New Yorker was truly impressed with the depth of your reporting and the caliber of your writing. We would love to speak more in the new year about working together again. But for now, enjoy the holidays. Congratulations!
>
> Best,
> Neil

Agustín clicks the link and there it is, the article with his name under it, all formatted and official with images: photos of Agustín now, and of his abuelo in Mexico and as El Rasca. Ricardo even allowed him to use some personal photographs from his own childhood. I feel a burst of pride in my chest.

"Guys!" I call and everyone in the room turns to us. Agustín holds up his phone.

"Is that it?" Caro squeals, coming over. She grabs the phone and starts to read aloud. "It was a cold day in early January when I got a phone call from my sister with a revelation that turned my world upside down. The man I had idolized since my childhood, my grandfather, was not the man I'd thought he was. The betrayal I felt then was brutally painful, a thousand shards of glass piercing a thousand memories. I was forced to rethink everything I had ever known about my life, my family, and the man I had so deeply admired. Little did I know then how much that one phone call would change the trajectory of my life. And how my search for answers—and, if I'm being honest, for revenge—would put me on a path I least expected . . ."

She raises her hand to high five him, and gives me a wink. "Trajectory changed a lot, I'd say."

"And for the better," Agustín murmurs in my ear, raising goosebumps over my skin.

"Felicidades," Diego says, raising his glass. Everyone cheers, and Agustín's phone gets passed around so people can see.

"So cool," Kate says.

"I love all the pictures!" Sanvi adds.

Pip nuzzles into the crook of Agustín's shoulder, and doesn't even growl when Agustín leans in to kiss me.

"So what's next, Mr. Big Shot Journalist?" I ask.

"I don't know," he says. "But whatever it is, I won't be working through it alone."

"No," I say, threading his fingers through mine. "You won't."

"A toast," Rachel says, standing up and raising her glass. "To Eloise and Agustín!"

Everyone cheers, and my cheeks go hot, but it isn't so bad, being stared at like this. Because I'm not alone anymore.

When I'm with Agustín, I'm home.

ACKNOWLEDGMENTS

This book was probably the most deeply personal story I've written, for many reasons—I, like Eloise, struggle with anxiety, live in New York City, and am a passionate advocate for senior dog adoption. And, like Eloise, I fell in love with an immigrant from Mexico City, a man who worked unbelievably hard to move to this country and achieve his dreams, a man I had the great fortune to marry this year, less than two weeks before the release of this book. It was quite a rare and exciting thing, writing about a wedding while planning my own. So it only feels right to start these acknowledgements by thanking my husband (eep!), Pep Funcia. Thank you for showing me what unconditional love is, for lighting up my world in vibrant colors, and for your boundless support. And thank you for reading countless drafts of this book and ensuring I got all the Spanish right. Gracias por todo, amor. Te amo para siempre.

As always, a million thanks to my editor, Jess Verdi, an endless font of wisdom, encouragement, and guidance. Without her keen eyes, unconditional trust, and ability to help me navigate the pitfalls of revision, this story simply would not be what it is today, and I am eternally grateful to have had her by my side throughout the whole process. And to the team at Alcove Press: Dulce Botello, Thai Fantauzzi Perez, Marcy Harris, Beata Garrett, Lindsey Staub, Haley Scull, and Julia Abbot, thank you for shepherding this book into the world, for all your support and for making the process seamless and joyful. And to my publicist, Jen Richards, thank you for your passion and determination to get this book in front of as many readers as possible.

To my agent, Charlie Olsen, who has been my anchor and my cheerleader for over a decade now, there aren't enough thanks in the world. I'm so lucky to have had your steadfast support over all these years—here's to the many more to come.

The "plus-one list" is actually based on a real list, something I learned about years ago while chatting with a then-stranger at a party. Fran Alamos, thank you for sharing your story with me and for giving me your blessing to take something real and weave it into my own, using it to bring Eloise and Agustín together.

To my friends who are like family—Caela Carter, Alison Imperato, Erica Henegen, Corey Ann Haydu, Jared Wilder, thank you all for your support over the years, for always celebrating the important moments and being there for me during the struggles. I couldn't do this work without you guys.

The ninth floor of the Archer was loosely based on my own experience in my apartment building, where neighbors went from strangers to friends. Thanks to Sarah (the Miriam of the building) and Jenny, Nick and Ezra, Mike and Blaine, Cindy, Marlon, Sway, and of course all the dogs—Donnatella, Scout, and Gretsky.

And speaking of dogs . . . I've been so fortunate to have known and loved so many dogs in my life. This book is dedicated in part to Pippin, my first senior rescue, but I would be remiss if I didn't honor the other dogs I have had the privilege to love, and who have passed: Benito, Gloria, Bibi, and Oscar. And the ones I still get to love every day: Sam, Matilda, Billie, and Mila.

To my Mexican friends, who are also like family—thank you all for welcoming this gringa with open arms, for always making me feel loved and included, and for sharing your beautiful, inspiring, unique city with me. Special shoutout to Esme Juárez, for being the most wonderful friend, for your humor and wit, for our monthly dinners, and for your endless patience with me as I navigate a new language. Tons of love and abrazos to Sué Leon, Cris de la Fuente, and Abril Mulato. And huge thanks to the friends whose names I pilfered for the Plus-One List itself: Rodrigo Sarmiento, Daniel Belmont, and Miguel Casco.

Y para mi familia mexicana, muchísmias gracias por su apoyo, su amor, y por hacerme sentir siempre parte de la familia. Especialmente Martha, mi suegra, Vero y Lalo, Sofia, Regina, y Jimena (las Minions!).

And thousands of thanks to my parents, to Ben, Leah, Otto, and Bea, and to my whole extended family for always showering me with so much love and support throughout all the ups and downs of this crazy career. Couldn't do it without you guys.

And to Faetra. I miss you every day.